Mildred Walker

The Quarry

Introduction by Ripley Hugo

University of Nebraska Press
Lincoln and London

© 1947 by Harcourt, Brace and Company, Inc. © renewed 1974 by Mildred Walker Schemm
Introduction © 1995 by the University of Nebraska Press
All rights reserved
Manufactured in the United States of America

☉ The paper in this book meets the minimum requirements of American National Standard for Information Sciences—Permanence of Paper for Printed Library Materials, ANSI Z39.48-1984.

First Bison Books printing: 1995
Most recent printing indicated by the last digit below:
10   9   8   7   6   5   4   3   2   1

Library of Congress Cataloging-in-Publication Data
Walker, Mildred, 1905–
The quarry: introduction to the Bison books edition by Ripley Hugo / Mildred Walker.
p.   cm.
Originally published: New York: Harcourt, Brace and Co., 1947.
ISBN 0-8032-9779-3 (pbk.: alk. paper)
1. Vermont—History—Civil War, 1861–1865—Fiction.   2. Quarries and quarrying—Vermont—History—19th century—Fiction.   3. Farm life—Vermont—History—19th century—Fiction.   I. Title.
PS3545.A524Q37   1996
813'.52—dc20
95-16578   CIP

Reprinted from the original 1947 edition by Harcourt, Brace and Company, Inc., New York.

FOR THE COWDENS

INTRODUCTION
Ripley Hugo

"Cutting the Pattern to Fit the Cloth"

Quarried from the Vermont hill country in the nineteenth century, soapstone was in widespread demand for its qualities. The smooth gray stone, which was soft enough to be hollowed into water pipes, can still be seen in the sinks, doorsteps, and front steps of old New England homes. Even a small piece held in the hand has a balanced weight, a durability, and a mysterious property that holds warmth long after the sun has left it.

I remembered that stone when I was rereading Mildred Walker's *The Quarry*. Not only because it is the stone in the novel's quarry—Walker's historical characters are like that surprising soapstone. They are given a solidity by the skillfully rendered details of their lives—are given surface, shape, and warmth. We are able to live the lives of her historical characters, and know their needs, despairs, and hopes to be contemporaneous with ours. They differ from us in their customs of speech, decorum, perhaps in their expectations of a worthwhile life, but not in their plight of being human.

The Vermont village in *The Quarry* is an earlier version of the one seen in Walker's *Southwest Corner*, also written in the forties and recently reprinted by the University of Nebraska Press. Both novels contain the same road and covered bridge, the same hill farm. Despite the different time periods, a reader of *The Quarry* will find that the historical Lyman Converse is beset by concerns just as compelling as those of the modern Marcia Elder in *The Southwest Corner*.

Walker has carefully, even tenaciously, worked out her characters' historical background for *The Quarry*. The American Heritage Center at the University of Wyoming holds the Mildred Walker Collection of her early manuscripts and, in the case of *The Quarry*, two handwritten notebooks containing extensive research into the period of the novel—1857 to 1914. Reading these notebooks, I saw how, as a novelist, Mildred Walker lived the period for herself. The small, unnumbered notebooks do not indicate which she recorded first and which second. Both notebooks describe conditions in the Civil War camps, specific Civil War battles, routes of the Underground Railway through New England, political ferments in the Vermont legislature on abolishing slavery in the South, and lists of authors who wrote on those subjects.

Just as meticulously recorded in both notebooks are details about Vermont soapstone and granite quarries, farming implements, horse-drawn vehicles, garden yields, and domestic rituals in both farm homes and village homes. And both include notes to herself about what the recorded fact could mean to one, sometimes several, of her characters as she thinks of how they would respond in the novel.

Walker calls the smaller of the two notebooks "The Quarry Wordbook." Her extensive handwritten notes begin with the year 1763, when a Vermont township is obliged to see to it that "all white and other pine . . . fit for masting our Royal Navy, be carefully preserved for that use." The next entry is the wording of a Vermont proclamation ordering that a soldier "drafted and accepted" during the Civil War be paid "$500 as a bounty to go himself or $500 to procure a substitute." Following that entry is a direction to the selectmen of a Vermont village: "That they be instructed to dispose of the apples in the graveyard & appropriate the avails of the same toward re-erecting fallen headstones and improving condition of grass in said yard." Next, a "Bibliography" lists Walt Whitman, Robert Lowell, Sidney Lanier, Ellen Glasgow, and others writing in or of the period covered by the novel. Then a note on education: "Webster's bluebacked speller, McGuffey Readers, selections of best Eng. and Am. lit."

By the sixth small page, Walker is describing what Lyman Converse, the protagonist, might say or think in living the events she has just recorded. In the novel Lyman *will* consider the history of timber cut from his family's land and his brother *will* want to send a substitute in his place instead of returning to the War—almost every historical fact that Walker records in her notes finds a place in the novel. Her knowledge of Yankee syntax, as well as psychology, leaps from her notes to her book. For instance, driving up to the hillfarm one day, Lyman remembers the admonition from his childhood copybook—"Quit Not A Certainty for Hope." Related to that is an entry in Walker's "Wordbook": "have Lyman slowly find that there was some awful lack in him that kept him from going out and making a place for himself."

Ezekial Williams is first mentioned in the "Wordbook" as the runaway slave boy, Easy, brought by the Underground Railway. In the novel he is hidden by the Converse family and stays on as a member of the household, becoming Lyman's lifelong friend. Again, much further along in the "Wordbook," interrupting her recording of historical facts, Walker comments on this friendship:

> Singing one of the bonds between Lyman and Easy. Lyman learns all the spirituals Easy knows. Lyman aware of certain things as he sings . . . the ease with which [Easy] held a long note; and something more, a feeling of music, a feeling of tears & laughter & exuberance that

The comment ends in mid-sentence.

Walker records the fact that Vermont declared for abolition as early as 1850. And in the opening chapter of the novel, Lyman explains to Easy (Lyman age nine, Easy eleven): "You don't need to be scared. Nobody will find you up here; they wouldn't turn you over if they did. Nobody can be a slave in Vermont." The stern belief in abolition in Vermont is made clear a few hours later in church by the congregation's visible dismay when Easy says he was not whipped by his master. The narrator describes the congregation's conclusion: "The meeting had been a little disappointing, not what you could call a real rousing Abolitionist meeting." In the "Wordbook," Walker also explores the attitudes of Vermonters toward southern blacks.

Statistics of the economic and social reasons for an exodus of young families to the opening West follow. "In year 1864," she quotes, "no less than 75,000 persons passed westward through Omaha." That these entries in the "Wordbook" bear upon Walker's sense of her protagonist Lyman Converse becomes clear in an entry that reads, "Lyman feels the exodus from Vt. It depresses him & at the same time imprisons."

"Research for Quarry" is Walker's title for the second notebook. It is a stenographic notebook, also handwritten, of forty-three pages, that begins with colloquial self-characterizations by Vermonters: "He stood out like a blackberry in a jar of milk," or "He don't know enough to pound sand in a rat hole." A few paragraphs later she quotes from an unidentified source: "What the Yankee was constantly trying to do was to arrive at maximum performance with minimum means. It was an economic dogma, expressed as 'cutting the pattern to fit the cloth.' " Pages following this quote concentrate on how the labor of wresting a living from a heavily wooded and hilly country in the late eighteenth and early nineteenth centuries shaped the Yankee—the caution to "make do with what you have!"

In the novel there are many scenes pointing to a quiet desperation or resolve with which Lyman Converse struggles. When these describe the way he sees his surroundings, they are often in poignant metaphor. At the end of Part III, he realizes a bitter consequence of what had seemed to him an inevitable marriage to Louisa: "Lyman went on up the stairs. His hand touched the white balusters as he went, breaking for a moment the pattern of bars that their shadow cast on the rug below." This imagery suggests what will become apparent to him: the meagerness of the pattern of his life.

The passage appears in the novel word for word as it was first written in her research notebook. The closeness of passages in the novel to comments in the notes suggests that Walker was pursuing her research at the same time as she was writing the novel. An early entry in "Research" reads: "have Willie an actress in the South—what has she been playing?" Notes that follow soon itemize the popular plays in the theaters, names of leading actors and actresses, the names of theaters where Willie might have performed, places the principles might gather afterwards, a typical restaurant menu in Charleston. In the novel Willie is the southern wife of Lyman's soldier brother who comes to live in the Converse household. Willie stands up to Orville Converse, the father of the household, when he speaks to her sternly. In the midst of recording facts about the Civil War and the theater in the notebook, Walker has reminded herself: "Have Willie address Orville as 'Sir'."

Many of Walker's observations about her characters transfer from research notebooks to novel as a character's remark or silent observation, as a conversation or description of scene, or as a motif that is steadily developed throughout. Walker's note to herself in "Research" will shape the last half of the novel: "As life in the village palls on [Lyman], Easy a life-saver—the only infusion of simple vitality in village."

Lyman's lifelong friendship with Easy is the center of the novel. The possibility of such a friendship, Walker said recently, was what first interested her in writing *The Quarry*. The contrasts in their parallel lives, steadily developed in the novel, strengthen their friendship year after year. Easy, brought into Vermont by the abolitionists, seizes the chance to make it his home, devotes himself to the life of the farm and quarry, and brings his new wife up the hill road with a sense of hope for their future. Lyman's hope burns less brightly. Still, throughout the novel Lyman's walk down the street will take him to the livery stable where he can take out his horse and buggy, drive through the covered bridge up the hill road to find the warmth of Easy's family, and, in Easy, find understanding.

The great anguish for Lyman Converse is his separation from his cousin Isabel, who went to live in Paris. Lyman faithfully sends her money from the quarry business, and this leads to a steady correspondence. His letters to Isabel on the operation of the quarry are based on letters the author found in her parents' house in Grafton, Vermont, location of a soapstone quarry. (The house had been bought by Walker's parents in 1903, completely furnished.)

Thirty years after the publication of *The Quarry*, when Walker had retired to the Vermont village, she contributed an article to the 1976 bicentennial edition of the *Grafton Gazette*. Titled "The Soft Gray Stone," it describes the success of the Goodrich quarry up Kidder Hill and its importance to Grafton's economy in the 1880s. Most of the article explains how the quarry is run and how it fared in the years that parallel Lyman Converse'e life in the novel:

In 1868, the Goodrich quarry was inherited by Sophia Goodrich, but because she was living in Paris, a cousin, Sidney Holmes, who lived in Grafton . . . represented her interests in all the dealings . . . for the munificent sum of $50 a year. Some of the correspondence spanning the years 1876–1896 has survived: Sophia's letters in a spidery handwriting on yellowed notepaper; and carefully made copies of Holmes' letters to her, many of them meticulously written on brown wrapping paper. They give, as nothing else could do, a vivid sense of the quarrying on Kidder Hill. (*Grafton Gazette,* Summer 1976, p. 8)

The 1976 article is a reminder of the correspondence between Lyman and Isabel in the 1947 novel. The original letters, quoted in the article, had suggested to Walker more than a business relationship.

Reading *The Quarry,* caught up in the lives of the characters, we respond again and again to the author's intense pursuit of the kind of people Vermonters were in the nineteenth century. How did they come to see their lives as villagers deep in the hill country? Once, about the time that she was writing the novel, in telling me of her grandfather who had left Grafton to settle his family in the midwest, she described him as having had ambition—unlike those who stayed. "Those who stayed must have had less *gumption,*" she said. (A very Yankee word!)

A reader of this novel lives in Lyman Converse's mind from the important event of his ninth year, rebels silently with him, questions his hesitancies with himself, and learns the responsibilities he feels he must assume. But the question steadily being put by the author is, What is he hoping for in his life? Up here, in the village of Painesville?

Early in the "Wordbook" she had written down advice from her writing professor; "Cowden—Oct. 25, 1945—'If you feel a scene hard enough, the words will hold that feeling.'" She has done that. *The Quarry* is one of Mildred Walker's tenderest novels of understanding a man's life, according him his anguish and his merit.

The Quarry

I

$500.00 REWARD

Run away from the owner on Saturday night, the 3rd. inst. from the neighborhood of Shelton, Va. my negro house boy, Ezekiel Williams, called Easy. Dark, reddish-brown skin, very lean, five feet two inches, eleven years old. He wore blue homespun breeches, gray shirt. Notify Shelton, Va. jail.

(Signed) Edwin Pennicook

Ashwood, Shelton, Va.
August 3, 1857

THE boy had kept himself awake by his will and nibbling at the apples he had brought up to bed with him. The moonlight helped. An August moon painted a white streak across the gray shingles of the woodshed roof and the wide painted boards of the bedroom floor. The curled oak leaf in the rug, that was really a bright green, stood out a kind of whitish gray. The white pitcher on the washstand looked more like a guinea hen than ever and its white porcelain breast shone in the light.

He had pretended to be asleep when his older brothers, Jonathan and Daniel, came up to the chamber above the kitchen. Jonathan was eighteen and Daniel fifteen. Lyman was nine, and a space as wide as the Connecticut River separated him from them.

He had heard the key turn in the kitchen lock downstairs and the window of his parents' bedroom raised gratingly till the little pegs at the side caught and held it in place. He had felt it must be long after midnight when he heard the steeple clock in the kitchen strike ten. He raised himself on one elbow and looked across the long ridges of his brothers' bodies under the quilt, John beside him and Dan next to John. They were already deep asleep. He had thought of telling them what he had discovered, but they had acted very grown-up lately and laughed with each other and told him "Indians" when he asked what they were talking about. Wouldn't they be surprised when they did find out and he told them he had known all the time!

Lyman pulled his pants over his nightshirt and climbed barefoot out onto the woodshed roof. He had done it often enough so that his toes found the right holes in the woodshed lattice easily. When he reached the ground, he stood still for a long moment that was filled with the smell of the phlox against the house and the mint against the shed. The tiger lilies looked dark by the picket fence, and the well sweep could have been a gibbet or a guillotine. The cat arched his back and ran across the grass to rub against his legs and opened his mouth in a soundless miaow as though he too knew the need for secrecy. The dog was shut in the kitchen because he had barked last night.

The road beyond the gate was like a tunnel, the woods grew up so tall and dark on either side. The night stillness wasn't still. There were rustlings, and the sound of quick small feet and drops of water on the leaves, though the sky was pricked all over with stars. Lyman wished now that he had told Dan and John. They would have come with him and he wouldn't have felt like this. He almost went back, then he straightened his shoulders. He was no baby. He would find out alone.

It was a quarter of a mile or more from the Converse farm to the quarry. Lyman's bare feet made a quick slapping sound on the cold hard mud of the dried ruts. But he stopped running at the quarry turn-in.

There was the foreman's shed. Lyman glanced quickly at it, trying to see if there were eyes peering at him from the dark windows. The moonlight struck full on them and made the wood between the small panes look like a white lattice made square instead of slantwise. Beyond the office, the uneven levels of the quarried rock stood out white and sharp. Watching the little house so hard, Lyman stumbled over something in the way and hurt his bare toe. He almost cried out, but his fear dulled the pain.

A block of soapstone had been left there in the way. Even in the dark it had a different feeling from other rock; it was smooth, not rough and hard like granite, less cold, just like the kitchen sink at home and the window sills and the front stoop. The feeling of the stone reassured him. Funny that a stone could feel almost soft and comforting! He set his foot flat on it until the smooth surface helped the hurt toe.

Lyman walked timidly around the little shed and came up to the window from the other side. He could just see above the bottom pane. The moonlight reached ahead of him into the corners of the small room. It hunted out the cot that was there in case a quarry worker was hurt. Samuel Green had died on that cot, Lyman remembered. The moonlight marked out the dark and light blocks of the quilt and the hump beneath it. It found a dark face on the pillow and the whites of two scared eyes staring back at the window and Lyman.

Lyman had never seen a Negro before except in the pictures in the copy of *Uncle Tom's Cabin* and on posters about runaway slaves hung in the village, posters advertising big rewards and threatening penalties if anybody didn't help the masters find them again. Folks in Painesville laughed. "Nobody in Vermont would ever help a master find a runaway slave. You could bet your bottom dollar on that," Obadiah Hall, the storekeeper, said.

Lyman stared curiously. The slave boy didn't look much older than he was himself. Lyman's own fear left him. He waggled three fingers at the boy through the window. The boy's eyes rolled away and back. Lyman whistled softly. The boy pulled his quilt up tighter.

Father had thought he was safe enough here, he guessed. Nobody would be going to the quarry on a Saturday night or Sunday, and anyway an agent might come through the village but he would never come way up on the hill. The door squeaked as he opened it. The boy had covered up his head.

"I won't hurt you," Lyman said softly, and the boy raised his head so that his eyes were on Lyman again. "You don't need to be scared. Nobody will find you up here; they wouldn't turn you over if they did. Nobody can be a slave in Vermont," Lyman told him.

"Wha' 'bout dem agents? Dey got houn' dawgs." The Negro boy's voice came in a hoarse whisper that was a scary thing to hear.

"There aren't any agents and there aren't any hounds around here. Our dog Shep is shut up in the kitchen at home."

"Dey aftah me wid houn's. Mah mammy an' me hide all day in de ribber, till a man he'p us git up heah."

"Where's your mother now?"

"She daid. She got cold an' took sick. De man at de train station say Ah better git out o' dere." Slowly tears filled the wide black-and-white eyes and ran down over the polished black cheeks. In the moonlight the streaks across the dark face were shiny.

Lyman couldn't think of anything to say at first. The boy's shoulders shook. He didn't make a sound, but the tears kept coming. Lyman wished he could go over and touch the boy, but he couldn't.

"You're safe now. Nobody would ever come way up on our hill if they did get to Painesville," Lyman said firmly. The boy wiped his sleeve across his face. The sleeve was ragged but the skin of his arm was so dark it was like no arm at all.

"How you come heah?" the Negro asked.

"I was getting in the cows when my father came up the road. I saw

3

him open the hogshead he had on the oxcart and somebody get out. I came down as close as I could, but Molly, our Jersey cow, has a bell and I didn't darst to get very near, but I thought he put a . . . someone in the quarry shed, so I came to see tonight when everybody else was asleep. Don't you tell my father I found you!"

The black boy shook his head.

"Look, why don't you come out a few minutes? It's bright as day in the moonlight."

The boy shook his head. "He tole me stay right heah."

"We won't go anywheres, just over on that wall. There's a stone wall there. Let's go and sit there. You must want to get out after being in that hogshead all the way from the village."

The boy shook his head again.

"Here, you want an apple? It's an asterkan and kinda sharp. Catch!" Lyman tossed the apple, but the slave boy missed it. It rolled under the cot. Lyman went over and got it. The boy took it. Hesitatingly he bit into it and his white teeth gleamed in the moonlight.

"Come on out!"

The boy got up from the cot. He was taller than Lyman, but thinner. There wasn't much to him but bones.

"You coming?" Lyman asked impatiently.

The boy followed slowly through the door. He looked at the wide chasm of the quarry that was white in the moonlight. Lyman saw his eyes roll fearfully.

"Aw, that's just where they get the soapstone. That's the quarry. I tell you you're safe."

The two boys sat on the stone wall, silent, munching their apples. The colored boy ate his so fast Lyman stopped eating his own.

"Do you want to finish this one? I only took a couple of bites out of it." He held it out, and a dark hand reached for it. "Didn't you have any supper?"

"Yuh pappy brung me sump'n', but Ah ain' eat much foh a lot of days," he whispered.

"I coulda brought you something more," Lyman began, then a dog barked halfway over the hill. The colored boy was off the wall and running for the wood before the sound was done.

"Hey, come back here! That was nothing but that old dog of the Davises'." The colored boy's fear made Lyman feel brave enough to shout.

Slowly the boy came. Once he was out of the wood, the moonlight struck full across his face like a blow. His lips were moving soundlessly. His eyes widened, his skin seemed less dark. Lyman watched

4

him. He had never seen such fear in a human being before. He had seen a yearling tremble from the feel of a halter, and felt the heartbeat of a rabbit he had caught in a trap. He had seen his mother press her lips together and close her eyes the time Daniel went swimming in the milldam and got back so late, but he had never seen a boy like himself cower and tremble at a sound. It made him feel ashamed.

"I tell you you don't ever need to be afraid again as long as you're in Vermont!" He heard the boy's breath close by him on the wall. There was a funny smell about the colored boy, sort of like the smell of the beets he dug up from the sand of the root cellar. "What's your name?" he asked.

"Ezekiel . . . yuh kin jus' call me Easy. Folks back home does."

"Where is your home, Easy?" Lyman had never thought of a runaway slave speaking of the South as his "home."

"Vahginya—'bout fifteen mile souf o' Richmond."

Lyman waited a few minutes before his next question. He asked it hesitatingly.

"Did your master . . . beat you?"

Easy shook his head. "Don' nobuddy beat Easy." Lyman felt misled. Wasn't that why the slaves were trying to get free? Hadn't he seen pictures of the lashes on the slaves' backs?

"Ef'n dey fin' me an' take me back dey beat me," Easy added, his face looking scared and ghostly.

"Why did you run away, then?"

"Mah mammy promise mah pappy she git me free. Dey wuz collud folk 'at got free 'at he'p us. Me 'n' Mammy wuz goin' to git us a little farm." The boy sniffed like any other boy, like Nat Burdick when the teacher struck him with a ferule. Lyman sat beside him on the wall, miserable and embarrassed.

"Tomorrow I'll show you where I have my cave," he offered. "I've got the whole jaw of a bear. It looks awful. And part of a gun that was used in the Revolutionary War."

Easy sniffed again and rubbed his arm across his face.

"Tomorrow, right after I get my chores done, I'll take you there. . . . How long you going to be here?"

"Ah reck'n Ah'm goin' stay right heah ef'n it's so safe."

Lyman looked doubtful. Maybe his father was going to keep the colored boy to help on the farm. He could do his, Lyman's, chores maybe, but the idea didn't seem likely.

They walked back through the wet grass across the road to the quarry shed. The little shack seemed warm after the night air.

"You won't be scared any more now, will you, Easy?" Easy shook his head, then he grinned. In the moonlight his teeth flashed white and his cheeks shone like the polished wood of the blanket chest. "How old are you, Easy?"

" 'Lev'n."

"I'm nine," Lyman said regretfully. "Here, you can have these if you want, I don't want them any more." He pulled out of his pocket a wishbone, carefully dried, one end broken a little, and an arrowhead. He held them out. "The wishbone is kind o' magic an' the arrowhead belonged to an Indian once. They'll keep you from getting scared."

Easy's brown hand reached across the streak of moonlight to take them. His fingers touched Lyman's. They gave him a start, they were so cold and quick. They closed on the treasures and withdrew again across the moonlight.

"Good night," Lyman said. He was running back home. He climbed up the lattice and through the window without waking his brothers. He crawled under the bedcovers without taking off his pants and lay there, his heart thumping against the quilt.

When Lyman came down the steep box stairs next morning and opened the door into the kitchen, his father was already reading the morning Scripture. His voice rose solemnly over the words. He never looked up or paused while Lyman slid into his place on the wall side of the table. Mother's lips curved ever so slightly into a smile, then she cast her eyes down at her plate to warn Lyman to do likewise. John and Dan were sitting, silent and proper, on the opposite side of the table.

Lyman was hungry. If he could just reach out a little way across the red tablecloth and help himself to the mush and crisp salt pork, or the pitcher of milk! His stomach felt lost inside his belt. Then he thought of Easy biting into the apple. He glanced quickly at the solemn faces of his parents. There was no sign of any excitement.

" 'Moreover the word of the Lord came unto me, saying' "—Father's voice had a fateful sound—" 'Behold, O Mount Seir, I am against thee, and I will stretch out my hand against thee, and I will make thee most desolate. I will lay thy cities waste, and thou shalt be desolate, and thou shalt know that I am the Lord.' " It sounded like a curse. Father paused. The silence held every eye on his face. He brought the open palm of his hand down on the printed page of the Bible.

"This is what will happen to the South if she persists in the iniquity of her ways!" Lyman held his breath, studying his father's scowling face.

Without another word Orville Converse closed the velvet cover of the Bible with a cushioned thud, pushed back his chair, and knelt. The wide blue-painted boards of the kitchen floor were cold under Lyman's knees. Lyman looked under the table at the warm huddle of his mother's hoop skirt and admired the overwhelming size of his oldest brother's shoes.

"Thou knowest, O Thou Lord in Heaven, the peculiar burden upon our minds this day. We thank thee that it is given to thy servant to be the servant also of Freedom, to help one soul out of bondage. Look upon this black-skinned fugitive with mercy, O Lord, and be with him as he continues his flight to freedom. Thou hast said, 'Vengeance is mine.' Oh, grant that for every lash upon the back of this innocent slave a lash may fall upon the back of him who called himself his master. A-men."

The only sound in the kitchen when the prayer was over was the roar of the water in the teakettle. Abigail Converse stood up and began to fill a plate for Lyman.

"Sit down, Abbie. Boys!" They sat again at the table. "I have something to tell you. Yesterday Deacon Bangert stopped in at the quarry office." Orville Converse glanced sternly from face to face. "As you do not know, Deacon Bangert has already helped many a fugitive slave to safety, harboring him in his own home. He is the principal agent of the Underground Railroad through here to Canada. As he had reason to think a man was in town from the South who might make trouble, he asked me to give refuge to a young slave boy. I brought the boy home with me and put him in the foreman's shed at the quarry."

Lyman watched his brothers' faces. Soundlessly he shaped the words "I've seen him!" John looked at him disbelievingly. Dan was watching his father.

"Orville, is he there now?" Abbie Converse's hand flew to the brooch at her collar.

"He is there now. I shall need to take him some breakfast. After service we shall drive to Malden, where a sympathizer will put him on the train for Canada at eight thirty-five tonight."

Excitement filled the calm kitchen, changing each object: the iron kettle with the steam charging from its spout, the face of the steeple clock. The very buttons that held the cupboard doors shut took on a secretive air.

His mother set a plate before Lyman, but now his appetite was gone.

"Can I take his breakfast to Eas— to the slave boy, Father?" Lyman asked.

"No, son. I must go myself and tell him the arrangements we have made for him. Eat up your pork rinds!"

When the Converse family drove down the hill into the village the late bell was tolling. As always, they let Abbie out and drove around back to the carriage sheds. Deacon Bangert was there waiting for them.

"Go along in, boys," Orville said sternly.

"I did see him, Dan, really I did," Lyman began in a quick excited whisper.

"Where?" John asked. Lyman had their interest for once, and he made the most of it. He brought out each statement separately, pausing for effect.

"At the quarry! When you two were asleep and snoring—at least you were, Dan. I climbed out the window and went over there."

"All alone?"

"Of course," he answered airily.

"What's he look like?" Dan and John had never seen a Negro either, except in pictures.

"Oh, just like the pictures in *Uncle Tom's Cabin*," Lyman said. "We better go on. Mother's waiting for us." He could see the boys didn't want to go. They wanted to ask more questions. Lyman took off his hat at the church steps and followed his mother down the aisle to their pew with a properly sober countenance. His eyes studied the yellow flowers on the red ingrain carpeting that ran narrowly down the aisle, but they held a gleam of satisfaction in them. Should he make the boys give him something before he told them any more, or should he just say "Indians" and not tell them anything?

"How old is he?" Dan leaned over to whisper to him when they were seated in their pew. Mother laid her hand in its black-lace mitt on Lyman's left hand, but he opened all ten fingers on his knees and then closed all but one. Abbie moved her hand to cover both of his. Lyman looked admiringly at his mother's wide gold wedding ring on her first finger, imprisoned under the black lace. He hooked one copper-toed boot under the long cricket and moved it closer so he could rest his feet on it. It was too high for Dan's and John's long legs and they usually pushed it away from them, but this morning they obligingly let it be and stretched their legs over it.

Father and Deacon Bangert came down the aisle together, separating at Father's pew. Father's face seemed more stern than usual, the back of Deacon Bangert's neck more interesting than ever before. "The principal agent on the Underground Railroad"—only it didn't mean underground, really. The runaway slaves were passed from place to place secretly. Lyman let his eyes rest on the parted hair of the Reverend Isaac Leland, but he was planning tunnels running underground from the quarry to the Connecticut River.

Before the benediction the Reverend Mr. Leland held up his hand. "Instead of the usual Sabbath school this afternoon we shall have a rare opportunity. There is in our midst—I can say it aloud because Vermont, at least, is a free state and all men who breathe Vermont air are free—there is in our midst a fugitive slave, as there have been many in the past, on his way north to Canada. Yesterday on these streets of ours, mingling among us, walked a wolf in sheep's clothing, an agent from the South, seeking a trace of this young slave. This agent, a fiend more savage than the savages of the South Seas who have never heard God's Holy Word, was discouraged in the pursuit of his mission." The faint shadow of a satirical smile flitted over the upper lip of the Reverend Mr. Leland, then disappeared under a sterner look.

"This afternoon at three o'clock I shall be able to present to this congregation, as the Reverend Henry Ward Beecher has often done to his congregation, this young African. You will be able to hear from his own lips the tale of his sufferings in bondage. Afterward a collection will be taken up to help him on his way. His mother, who fled with him, died of pneumonia at the stationmaster's home in Brattleboro. The boy is penniless and sore afflicted. Shall we not remember the words of our Master, who said, 'Inasmuch as ye have done it unto one of the least of these my brethren, ye have done it unto me'?"

The eyes of the three Converse boys met, then fell. Parson Leland was pronouncing the benediction now. He held his hand out over the heads of the congregation while he said it. His long bony fingers threw an angular shadow on the ceiling and made a bigger hand rest over their heads. Perhaps, Lyman thought uneasily, that was God's hand.

It was good to be out of church. Usually they had to eat lunch there and wait for the afternoon Sunday school. Lyman felt released from bondage himself riding up the hill at noon. The grasshoppers fiddled in the field just over the stone wall and the poison-ivy leaves on the wall were gray with dust. August heat made wet streaks on the horses' sides. The wagon creaked slowly up the hill and of their own accord the horses waited at each thank-you-ma'am.

"Is Deacon Bangert sure the agent from the South is gone?" Abbie asked quietly.

Orville Converse's smile was grim. "I guess he was glad enough to get out of Vermont—he got a free ride out. Whoa!" He drew the horse to a standstill opposite the turn-in for the quarry. "Daniel, you drive on home and I'll get the slave boy. Abbie, you better look up some old clothes. I'll bring him right to the house."

They were sitting at the table when Father came in with the Negro. The boys turned to look. The black boy looked blacker against the open doorway and the sun-braided green beyond. He was tall, and "thin as a poker," Abbie said later.

"Abbie, this boy's name is Ezekiel Williams. I calculate he's hungry."

Abbie pushed back her chair with a soft, hesitant rustle of her heavy silk skirt.

"Ezekiel, these are my sons, Jonathan and Daniel and Lyman!" The boys looked at him in embarrassment and their eyes moved away. Only Lyman smiled. He saw the wishbone slipped over the rope that held up the boy's ragged pants.

"Have him wash, Orville," Abbie said, frowning meaningly at her husband, wondering helplessly if he meant the boy to sit at the table with them.

"Ezekiel washed at the spring," Orville said. He seated himself at the head of the table. "Move over, Lyman. Ezekiel, you sit here."

Lyman shoved over on the bench. Ezekiel hesitated an instant, then sank down beside Lyman. Orville bowed his head.

"Lord God in Heaven, from whose bountiful hands cometh this ample provision for our physical needs, help us to share our portion with this stranger within our gates. A-men."

Lyman took a mouthful of the cold chicken. No cooking was ever done on the Sabbath on the Converse farm. He was aware of that smell he had noticed last night. Then he saw Dan pinch his nose in and look at John. Mother frowned.

"Help yourself, Ezekiel," Orville said.

"Folks call him Easy," Lyman said before he thought.

"What was that, Lyman?" his father asked.

"Tha's right. Mah mammy call me Easy an' Miss Lucy an' Marse Edwin, ev'ybody call me Easy." Lyman held his breath, but attention had moved from himself to Easy.

"Ezekiel"—Orville ignored the name Easy—"Deacon Bangert and the Reverend Leland felt it would be best for you not to proceed on your way until night. You can reach the Canadian border in the early morning hours and run less chance of trouble."

Ezekiel's face had a worried, mournful look. His eyes hung on Mr. Converse.

"We came back up the hill for the purpose of fetching you down to a meeting at the church. The members of the congregation will be glad to hear you speak. Just tell them about conditions on the plantation, the treatment by your master and . . ."

"Me tell 'em in de church?" Ezekiel's eyes sought Abbie Converse's tranquil face.

"Exactly, Ezekiel. They are your friends and the friends of freedom," Orville told him ponderously.

The boy's face was frightened. His mouth pinched together so that the full pink lips looked thinner. He laid down the piece of bread he had been eating.

"Eat your pie, now," Abbie said. Obediently, he picked up his fork and ate the generous piece of cold berry pie. It was the first time he had used a fork, but he had seen the folks up at the big house use them and he had polished them for his mammy.

"We'll need to start in ten minutes. Lyman, you help Ezekiel into the clothes Mother has for him," Orville said, looking at the big silver watch in his hand.

"Since he's going to stand up in the church, I put out your second-best pants for him, Daniel, and Lyman's blue shirt," Abbie murmured.

Easy pulled off his ragged shirt and pants. Lyman glanced quickly at him, standing in the patch of sun in front of the window. He measured Easy's shoulders and muscles mentally with his own. Easy was bigger all right. He could never wear his shirt. He didn't seem as naked in his brown skin as a white boy did, but he was dirty. Lyman looked over at the white pitcher and washbowl on the washstand.

"You better wash for church." Without looking at Easy he poured water into the bowl. "There's a towel and soap." Easy watched him, but made no move toward the washstand. Lyman felt funny. "You begin with your face and wash down and then at the end you can put your feet in. You better put one foot in at a time or the water sloshes over." He went out before Easy could say anything.

"He's taking a bath," Lyman announced importantly in the kitchen. "He'll hurry." There was an air of waiting. With her mitts and best Paisley shawl and bonnet on, Mother was quietly putting away the dishes. Daniel and John sat by the table. Orville was sitting with the Bible in his hands, but he wasn't reading. Lyman felt suddenly as though the Negro boy belonged to him.

"I thought he better," he added. "He kinda smelled. He's bigger than me, maybe he better have a shirt o' Dan's."

When Lyman went back up and handed in the shirt it seemed to him that Easy looked paler. He accepted the shirt without a word and put it on. Even Dan's shirt stretched tight across his chest. The yoke had shrunk and came too far up on his shoulders, but it would do.

Lyman looked at the washbowl of dirty water and emptied it in the slop jar. He did it without thinking, because Mother held it such a sin to leave dirty wash water. As it splashed into the hollow vessel, underneath the sound of the cataract of water, Lyman heard Easy say softly, "Tank yuh, Marse Lyman." Something about the way Ezekiel said it made Lyman realize that it was a strange thing to empty water for a slave boy.

"Oh, that's all right, Easy," he said condescendingly, feeling a lordly sense of superiority he had never felt before in his life. "Come on, they're waiting for us."

The meetinghouse was crowded when they entered. The congregation had been singing hymns to pass the time while they waited for the Converse family to return with their prize. Heads turned as far as was decorous to see them coming down the aisle—Orville Converse first with one hand on Easy's arm, then Abbie, then John and Dan, and Lyman last of all, still clothed in his new mantle of importance. Orville went on up to the pulpit and Deacon Bangert rose to meet him. Very gravely he held out his hand to Easy. The boy looked uncertain, then he took the offered hand. The Deacon seated him in the third of the carved walnut chairs upholstered in black haircloth. The sun coming in through the clear glass window struck out golden tints in Easy's brown skin and made the drops of perspiration on his forehead shine. The Reverend Mr. Leland offered prayer, but even the prayer was a waiting. He stepped forward in front of the pedestal that held the Bible.

"Friends in Christ, I know I speak to no brother or sister here whose heart is not bursting with joy at the sight of this black child escaped from slavery's yoke. We have heard from this pulpit the great Frederick Douglass. We have been stirred by the oratory of Wendell Phillips. But we have never before had in our midst to speak to us a slave escaped from bondage. These very walls must shrink back in horror at the sight of a human being who has been a slave. The soil of this state, the air above, the bricks of these walls, all have known and breathed and heard only free men. None of us, from the babe at the breast to the most venerable, know aught but freedom. 'Twould be a desecration indeed to bring this colored child into this place of freedom unless we could vouch with our lives for his freedom as he goes on his way, and that we will do!" The Reverend Mr. Leland's eyes burned under his black brows, his lower lip came up like a dam against his upper lip.

"A-men," Deacon Tompson called out in the manner of the Baptists down the street, and bonnets nodded vigorously and beards wagged.

The minister stepped back, and taking Easy by the hand, led him forward. The boy rolled his eyes from one side of the church to the other. He looked as shivery as a poplar in November. His head hung down.

"Don't cringe, my lad. You were born in fear. You know nothing else, but now there is nothing to fear."

"No, sah." After the thundering tones of the Reverend Mr. Leland the soft syllables of Ezekiel were no louder than the rustle of the birch trees in the cemetery behind the church. The congregation stared intently.

Easy shifted his weight and stood straighter, his head up, his shoulders back. The top button of Dan's old shirt popped off and rolled across the ingrain carpeting of the pulpit. The boy looked down unhappily, then the curve of a smile appeared. The shirt opened deeply at the neck, showing the black skin over his chest.

"Tell us about the trials and tribulations you have been through to get here. Tell us about your cruel master and the life of bondage you were forced to live," urged the minister. The room was so still that the sound of carriage wheels and horses' hoofs passing on the road outside came in clearly. For once, no one was sleepy at the afternoon service. Ezekiel shifted his weight to the other foot.

"Speak out, my boy. In God's sight there is only one race."

"Yes, sah," Ezekiel said softly.

Orville moved uneasily in the pew. Abbie looked down at the pattern of her mitts. John dug Dan's ribs with his elbow.

"Ezekiel came way up here from Virginia." The Reverend Mr. Leland was used to coaxing confession from the hesitant. "Did you work in the cotton fields there?" he asked.

The boy lifted his eyes and dropped them. "No, sah, I'se learnin' foh to be a houseboy up at de big house."

"Did your master beat you, Ezekiel?"

Ezekiel shook his head. "No, sah," he said softly. "Ain' none o' de house servants at Ashwood bin beaten."

The Reverend Mr. Leland frowned. Deacon Bangert's lips gathered the soft flesh of his cheeks to a shirred opening.

"What did your mother do?"

"She were Miss Cecilia's nursemaid."

"What did your father do?"

"Mah daddy were de head coachman." Ezekiel moved uneasily and rolled his eyes, dark and sad and less revealing than the clear blue and brown and gray eyes looking back at him. The minister shot out another question sternly.

"Did your father try to escape with you, Ezekiel?"

"No, sah, he were sole tuh Colonel Sears, las' year."

A murmur of sympathy, faintly tinged with satisfaction, ran over the audience. This was more the sort of thing they had expected.

13

"Why did your master sell him?" the Reverend Mr. Leland asked more gently.

Ezekiel stood straighter. His answer came a little louder. "Ah reck'n mah pappy brung a heap o' money, mo' money 'n any odder nigger on de place. Marse Edwin tole mah mammy he ve'y sorry he gotta sell him, but he gotta have dat money."

Blue and gray and brown eyes narrowed grimly. Mouths set.

"Mah mammy took on powerful bad," the boy offered. Indignation stiffened the taffeta and broadcloth and serge backs. Lyman Converse didn't need any pressure of his mother's hand, he sat so still.

"Why did you and your mother run away, Ezekiel?" the minister asked.

" 'Cause mah mammy say she wan' tuh take me tuh a place wheah Ah could call mah soul mah own 's' long 's' Ah live." The voice was not dramatic. Mrs. Bangert had to lean over to Mrs. Pringle to ask what the boy had said. The answer was not satisfactory to the rabid Abolitionists of the congregation, nor to the Reverend Mr. Leland, but it sank deeply into Lyman's mind, like a stone dropped in the well. He would never forget it.

"Your soul is God's, young man, you must never forget that. Whether you are slave or free man your soul is His."

"Yes, sah," assented Ezekiel, dropping his eyes with embarrassment and moving his toe closer to the big yellow flower woven in the carpet.

Deacon Elder and Deacon Bangert passed the collection plates on the long poles that reached to the middle of the pew's length. There was the pleasant sound of money jingling into the plates. They sang a hymn, and the meeting was over.

Some of the congregation crowded around the platform to speak to the slave boy, others talked together. The meeting had been a little disappointing, not what you could call a real rousing Abolitionist meeting. As Abner Perkins said, "The boy wa'n't a real good subject."

Orville Converse was anxious to get started. He and Dan would have a twelve-mile drive over the mountain to the next stop. He hurried his family out to the wagon. Lyman felt people stopping to watch as they drove right down through the main street with the colored boy in with them.

"Orville, I do think it would be better for the—for Ezekiel not to sit right up with the boys," Abbie remonstrated.

Orville drove ahead. "Why not, Abbie? Nobody would dare lay a hand on him while he's with us."

"You did real good, Easy," Lyman whispered.

Easy grinned. "D'yuh see me pop mah button off?"

Lyman felt confused. Easy had been so scared last night in the moonlight that it was a shameful thing to see and in church he could hardly lift his head, and now he grinned and talked about popping a button!

The wagon wheels thundered through the covered bridge and creaked up the hill in the green shade that was spotted with sun like the leaf of a wild adder's-tongue. The horses stopped to rest at the first thank-you-ma'am. Dan and John and Lyman and Easy sprang out over the side to walk up the hill to save the horses. It was like every other summer Sunday afternoon, and yet it was different because of the colored boy. Lyman watched for their shadows as he always did for his own wherever the sun lay clear enough across the road. Easy's shadow stretched longer than his, longer by a hand's breadth, and his hair was nubbly and his profile . . . But a beech tree wiped out the sun on the road.

The sun was down behind the hill when Lyman came up from milking the cows and he looked quickly to see if the horse was still tied to the hitching post. He wondered why they were so late starting. John was sitting on the wall at the side of the house and he gave a whistle when he saw Lyman, and pointed to the house. Lyman set his pails down carefully in the milkhouse and came back.

"Isn't Father going, John?"

John shrugged. "The boy doesn't want to go. Looks like Father's going to have to pack him in the hogshead and take him right along. I would. We don't want him here."

"That's what he said last night, John, that he guessed he'd stay right here," Lyman said.

"Well, he can't do that!"

Orville appeared in the doorway that led into the front hall. His face was flushed, and he had a look that brought both boys to their feet. Lyman started to move toward the milkhouse.

"John, show Ezekiel how to put the horse up. We won't need him." He went in and closed the door. Easy came across the grass of the front-door plot and the three boys walked over to the horse and buggy.

"Ah reck'n dat horse glad he ain' goin' any mo' tuhnight," Easy said in his soft, pleasant tone. "Ah reck'n he's jus' lahk me."

Inside the house in the square parlor Orville Converse faced his wife. In spite of his black beard and bushy eyebrows and the stern line of his mouth he looked as ill at ease as John or Dan or even Lyman could appear.

"But, Orville, we don't want a Negro here. I thought he was supposed to be fleeing to Canada!"

"He was, but he heard the Reverend say he was free in this state and he doesn't want to go any farther. He says he's not afraid here."

Through the window came the sound of boys' voices, their own boys' and another voice curiously soft and slurred.

"But, Orville, he would be the only colored person in Painesville!"

"I suggested that, but he said his mother and father were gone and he would be just as lonesome down South. We're Christians, Abbie. I guess we'll have to practice what we preach."

Abbie tilted her smooth brown head back impatiently. Her gray eyes were flint. "Orville Converse, I'm ashamed of you if you can't do something about a boy only two years older than Lyman. Just take him to the line and leave him. He has enough money from the collection to take him quite a piece. It's one thing to help a Negro on his way, but it's quite another to have him settle down and live with you!"

Orville rubbed his forefinger thoughtfully over his lip. "I just couldn't do that, Abbie. He's so sure he's safe here. If you could have seen him yesterday—he was scared of every sound. Today he isn't afraid at all. He trusts us, Abbie. I said he could stay."

"That'll make a fine muss, Orville Converse, mark my words!"

"Well, it doesn't have to, Abbie. Why should it? We might even get some good out of him."

2

BY 1862 Lyman had grown eight inches and moved into Dan's pants, but Easy was ahead of him—he was wearing John's. They had plenty between them. John and Daniel had both gone to war. Both had signed up first for three months, but they had signed again. You couldn't tell about the war now, the Secesh meant to fight for it. Lyman and Easy talked about it together.

"I wager I can get in if it lasts till next spring," Lyman said. "I'm fourteen, and near as tall now as Dan was."

"Dey might take me too," Easy said.

Lyman's mouth curled dubiously, then he switched it back into shape and looked away down over the young spruce trees and sapling maples to the spire of the church in the village, lest Easy be hurt.

"Ah betcha before dis war's ovah plenty collud folks goin' tuh be fightin', you watch, Lyman!" Easy's soft voice could be angry without losing its lazy drawl. "Ah betcha some o' de servants at Ashwood fightin' dis very minute. Dey's goin' to help deirselves get free."

Lyman chewed his spruce gum silently for a minute. "I should think they would." Then he added, "John sure don't like it much."

Both boys sat thinking of John, who had just gone back to join the army after a sick leave.

John on leave had been silent as a tombstone, not the way he used to be at all. Mornings at five-thirty when Orville Converse called his family John didn't stir. Lyman got out of bed and dressed quietly, looking over at John thinking he was still asleep, but he was lying there watching him. Lyman could see how yellow his skin was against the sheet, yellow as tansy blossoms.

"Aren't you going to get up, John?" he asked.

"I don't care if I never get up," John said, and his eyes moved wearily past Lyman and rested on the elm tree outside the window.

"John isn't getting up just yet," Lyman told his father, making it sound a little better than the way John had said it.

"Let him get rested up once, Orville," Abbie said gently, almost pleadingly.

"Seems like the army's knocked the stuffing right out of him."
Orville scowled as he said it.

" 'Tisn't that, Orville, it's dysentery has. Remember that time you
had the cramps so bad after haying? You took nearly a whole bottle
of my blackberry cordial before you got rid of it."

"But I got rid of it, and didn't go moping around for a month. John
doesn't have the dysentery now."

"Give him time, Orville. He's been through all those battles. We're
lucky to have him alive."

"We guess he has, he can't talk about any of 'em. Ephraim Davis and
Obadiah Hall were asking him about Fredricksburg. Ephraim's son
was killed there, and John didn't spark up at all. He just looked at
him in that kind of bloodless way and said, 'All I remember, Mr.
Davis, was seeing Amos with a blanket pinned over his shoulders to
keep off the rain before it started, and then I was busy trying to get
something to eat before I went to killing.'

" 'I guess you licked the rebels there, though!' Ephraim said, and
John shook his head and said, 'Night came and we stopped. That's all
I could tell you. And in the morning the rebs had cleared out.' I tell
you, Abbie, that's no way to talk, it don't sound good."

Abbie laid her finger fleetingly on her thin lips and glanced at
Lyman, and he saw she didn't want him to hear his father say anything against John.

All during his leave his mother was always urging John to go to
see Louisa Tucker. "John, I'll invite Louisa home with us after
church."

But on Sunday John said, "I'm not going to church, Mother."

The rest of the family drove down to the village in silence. After the
service when folks asked how John was, Abbie said, "He's been
through so much he's all tired out." But Orville brought out in his
firm voice that was so deep it could scare a fly off his hand, "He's
anxious to get back into it."

But Lyman was thinking of something else—of the time he and
Easy had come on Louisa and John by the springhouse. Easy and
he had been practicing Indian walking without making a sound, so
when they heard voices, stopping to hear who they belonged to was
part of the game.

"Dan's different," John was saying. "He likes the whole thing. He'll
get to be an officer before the war's over. He struck up an acquaintance
with a Southern girl down in Virginia and had a fine time."

"Oh, John, I don't see how he could!" Louisa said.

18

John shrugged. "Dan's that way. He's a good soldier, too, don't think he isn't."

"You are, too, John," Louisa said softly, and Lyman loved her for it.

"No, I'm not," John said, breaking pieces of bark off the butternut tree. "I never will be. I went down to see Abe Hopkins today to see if he'd go as a substitute for me. I've got some money, a little saved up, and I would work and make up the rest of the three hundred dollars. Maybe Father would give it to me. I'd be worth it to him."

Lyman saw Louisa's hand touch John's arm. "John, you wouldn't do that!" Louisa's voice sounded scared.

"Yes, I would, Louisa. You might as well know me. I'd stay right here if I could and help Father, and buy the Spring place on the hill and we could get married."

Lyman felt a chill through his knees where he knelt on the ground. He glanced over at Easy.

"I don't know as I'd marry a man who hired a substitute, John. If that man was killed, you'd feel you owed him your life; it would work on you."

"It might. I don't know. I guess I'd just feel grateful to him."

Lyman made a sign to Easy and began creeping up the side hill. Easy was coming. He could hear him breathing on the ground behind him.

Lyman felt the way he did when the funny light that comes after a bad thunderstorm shows up each spear of grass and the grooved lines of the shingles on the shed roof and the ants running up the bark on the tree. He had seen right into John's thoughts. He walked away carrying the strange knowledge of how John really felt about fighting. It was heavy on him, like the feeling of having told a lie. He wished Easy hadn't been with him to know it too.

But they had never mentioned what they had heard together until now.

"John went back, Easy, even if he didn't really want to!"

"Yessir, that's so!" Easy answered.

Lyman thought about John's letter that he had in his pocket this very minute. Mother was sending it to Louisa, as she always did any letter that came from John. And Louisa always told them when she got one and how John said he was. This wasn't much of a letter, just one side of a ruled sheet torn from a notebook. It read:

Dear Mother and Father,

It seems natural enough to be back in camp with the rain and heat and mosquitoes and wormy salt pork—more natural than being back

In Vermont with white sheets and good food and no bloodshed. In time a man ought to get so he don't want anything else but this. The boys sure liked the food you sent back with me, Mother, and the drawers and socks are fine. Love to all,

John

"He's glad to get back all right," Father declared when he read it, but Mother pressed her lips together and her hands lay still on her knitting.

Lyman and Easy cut off through the pasture that ran downhill. Quick as a thought Easy dropped behind the stone wall and cocked the stick he carried. Lyman ran zigzagging across an open space, snatching up a mullen stalk as he went, to use for a gun.

Easy yelled and Lyman yelled back, but Lyman's yell was thinner than Easy's, a piping note next to the half-wild cry Easy could make.

"I declare it scares me worse than a wildcat's," Abbie Converse often said.

"I got you. You're killed, you, Lyman!" bellowed Easy.

"I am not. I got you in the arm and spoiled your aim," Lyman yelled back, lying flat behind a low juniper. They played at war every day and argued between shots. Easy wanted to take turns being on the Union side and Lyman wouldn't have it.

"How could I be a Southerner?" Lyman asked indignantly. "I was born in Vermont. You were born a Southerner."

"Well, but they're fighting the war over the colored people," Easy retorted. His way of speaking was fast changing, giving place to Yankee ways of talking.

"Well, pretend you're not colored, Easy—pretend you're just a Southerner," Lyman insisted stubbornly.

Easy grew so solemn over that that he stopped playing altogether, standing there on the sun-swatched hillside like a shadow of himself. He shook his head.

"Can't never do that, Lyman. My mother tell me 'Never forget you is colored, Easy!'"

"Oh, well, we're too old to play, anyway," Lyman conceded, suddenly uncomfortable at Easy's solemn face.

The two boys came through the covered bridge at the bottom of the hill road into town. In town the road felt different to the soles of their feet. On the hill the packed mud was cool from the close-growing shade, but in town the road was warm and the soft dust came between their toes in spots.

The road led past the cheese factory with its rich smell, not quite sweet, not quite sour, and Thompson's Cashmere Mill. The boys stopped by the open window to watch the fast whirring of the big machines, but the smell of hot oil and wool came at them like an angry hornet and the wave of heat made Lyman swallow quickly. The faces of the workers were curiously white and shiny against the dark interior. Mr. Thompson wiped the sweat off his forehead onto his black-sleeved arm and waved to them.

The main street of Painesville was busy in the middle of the afternoon. Horses and buggies and wagons stood in front of the Converse & Holbrook Quarry office. The boys walked by slowly to see if Orville Converse sat there at his big desk, but they never ventured in unbidden. A new butter churn was being loaded into a wagon in front of the Abbott Churn Manufacturing Company.

As they went by Lyman gazed with awe at Judge Whitcomb sitting at his desk in his office. Easy rolled his eyes up to the big sign painted in black letters, outlined in gilt, over Hall & Peterboro's General Store; Dealers in Groceries, West India Goods, Salt, Fish, etc. " 'Member, Lyman, when you taught me to read that sign?" Easy asked with a grin.

"Yup, betcha still can't tell where the West Indies are!" Lyman took the responsibility of Easy's education very seriously.

The boys were too absorbed in their own talk to notice the glances people cast at them. Now after five years Easy was still the only Negro in the town, but folks no longer vied with each other in inviting him to their homes for dinner as they had done at first, nor gave their sons' outgrown clothes to him with such eagerness. The war was on now, they had other ways to vent their Abolitionist zeal. Easy had remained, an obligation and responsibility to Abbie Converse which she tried to bear patiently as her Christian duty.

Easy was a help, Abbie told her closest friends. "Gracious, yes! You ask him to do some chore once and he'll keep on doing it forevermore, and he's Lyman's shadow, you might say." "But to have him every meal, day in and out!" those friends chorused back sympathetically. Still, he was a symbol to the town of the South's wrongdoing, straight out of the slave advertisements that used to hang in front of the store.

The two boys stopped in the store to buy a stick of horehound candy and a box of salt codfish and two spools of thread. Then they went up the street to Louisa Tucker's house. It was a two-story-and-a-half brick house that stood at the top of the main street back of a picket fence. The brick chimney that faced its eastern end was built wider than most and had a bigger iron S to hold its brickwork. Iron S's were fastened to the long green shutters of the windows, and an iron door knocker marked the upper middle of the tall front door. Lyman thought it was a handsome house, in spite of Easy's saying he should see Ashwood. The single soapstone doorstep in front of the door seemed to Easy a poor substitute for the long stone steps that ran the length of the pillared porch he remembered. Lyman raised the door knocker and Louisa came to the door.

"Why, Lyman and Easy! Come in."

The hall was cool, and the white spindles of the straight stairs rose more coolly to a darkened hall above. The rag strip was warm under bare feet, but Lyman stepped off onto the painted boards that were smooth and cool.

"We had a letter from John, Louisa. Mother thought you'd like to read it. You can keep it and give it back to her at church on Sunday," Lyman said. "It isn't very long," he added quickly, because Louisa looked more pleased than he thought such a letter called for. Her face got pink, and a little place in her neck above her collar. Louisa had brown eyes and hair to match, gathered like his mother's in a net at the back.

"Oh, thank you, Lyman. Is he well? I haven't heard from him this week." He thought for an instant that she was going to say something more, but she didn't and he turned to go.

"Would you like some cookies and a glass of milk?" Louisa asked. Easy's eyes brightened and Lyman was about to say yes, and then instead he said, "No, thank you, Louisa, not today."

"Why didn't you want nothin'?" Easy asked as they went down the street.

"We're not kids any more, Easy, getting cookies everywhere we go."

"Oh," Easy said, nodding thoughtfully.

They stopped in front of Simon Marsh's stationery store and looked at the covers of the new ledgers in the window. Like scrambled eggs the covers were, only blue and red were scrambled in with the yellow. There were black leather-bound diaries with 1862 printed in gold on them, and marked down because the year was half-over. The back cover came over and slipped under a strap in front, or clasped with a metal fastener and had a key and lock. Lyman liked the secret look of the diaries. He wished he could buy one and write in it about Louisa Tucker with the color running up in her face. That must be why John wanted to marry her.

"Come on, we got to get home," Easy urged.

"Wait a minute, can't you?" Lyman was reading a handbill hung in the window.

22

CAVALRY AND BATTERY HORSES WANTED!

The subscriber will buy at the Cheshire Bridge House, Charlestown, New Hampshire, on Saturday, September 3, 1862. Horses to be 14½ hands high and upward, to weigh from nine to ten hundred and fifty pounds.

William Sabin

Aug. 29, 1862

"Look, Easy!"

Easy stepped closer to the window to read obediently whatever Lyman pointed out. "Advertisement . . ." he began slowly.

"Easy, you know what?" Lyman grabbed Easy's arm. "I'm going to sell my horse to the army!"

"Why for you goin' to sell the horse Mistah Converse give you?"

"They need them, don't you see? I can't go, so Ned can go!"

Easy shook his black woolly head. "You better ask him first."

"Ned's mine. I can do what I want with him. That's next Tuesday. Easy, after we do the chores you can disappear and ride Ned over to Charlestown."

Easy shook his head again. "Not me. I ain' goin' to get your horse sold."

"But, Easy, you can ride longer than I can without getting tired, you know you can, and I can keep Mother from asking where you are. We won't even sell Ned, we'll give him to the army!"

"Uh-uh," grunted Easy with a firm negative emphasis. "Mistah Converse ain' goin' like that one bit!"

"All right, then, I'll do it myself. If you had a brother that didn't want to fight for his country and you were too young to go, maybe you'd want to give your horse. I should think you'd want to do anything you could, Ezekiel Williams, when you think of all the United States is doing for you!"

Easy said nothing and looked glum. He could do that when he didn't agree with Lyman. He looked that way when the teacher made them sing the scale instead of songs.

"I've got to buy something. You can wait outside," Lyman said and went inside Mr. Marsh's store. He had decided to buy one of the diaries anyway, one with a lock. He felt a need to write about giving his horse to the army, since Easy was nobody to confide in.

He was gone a long time. Easy sat on the horseblock making a pattern of waves in the dust with his toes. Across the street in the parlor of the Pettingill house the Pettingill ladies looked out.

"There's that slave boy of Orville Converse's."

"Hannah, he isn't a slave any more!"

"What on earth the South ever wanted 'em for I can't see. I wouldn't want him around my house."

"It's a good joke on Orville Converse," Mr. Pettingill remarked with relish. "The boy wouldn't go and Orville had to keep him. He made a monkey out of Orville, but I'll be hog-swindled if he'd have made one out of me!"

The Reverend Mr. Isaac Leland, driving past in his buggy, called out to Easy. He looked on him almost with affection as the "slave whose body and soul we have freed from bondage." Ezekiel Williams was a baptized member of the Congregational Church of Painesville.

When Lyman came out his eyes shone as though they held sparks of mica stone.

"Easy, Jeb Holmes was in there, the one that had his leg cut off after Antietam. He was telling Mr. Marsh all about the battle and how he stuck two rebs with his bayonet, ran it through them before they could shoot. He says the rebs ain't such good shots after all, that our boys that have been hunting all their lives can outdo 'em any time. If you'd have heard him you'd want to give your horse, Easy! He says he'd just as soon give the other leg. I bet Dan's like that!"

The store door opened and Jeb Holmes limped out, one pant leg pinned up just below the hip.

"H'lo, boys."

"H'lo, Jeb," Lyman said, and Easy nodded his head. They watched with awe as he swung down the street under the elms. His crutches made a soft little thud on the road. He wore a battered campaign cap and the coat to his blue uniform over black trousers.

Lyman put the new diary in his pocket. He had had to buy the one with the flap, after all, the one with the lock cost too much. He felt as though the diary held all the secrets of his soul already, though nothing was written there. He didn't show his purchase to Easy. Easy wouldn't understand it, he felt. The diary marked a sudden difference between them, separating them, making Lyman feel superior.

Lyman lay in the sweet fern of the pasture, hidden from the sight of the barn by a big rock. His body ached rawly from his father's belt. He took care not to move. The crushed sweet fern was as good as an ointment. He buried his face against the ground.

"I hate him, I hate him, I hate him," he whispered into the roots of the ferns. In spite of the pain he kicked his toes into the dirt. Hot salty tears streaked his set face. "He's got no right to treat me like that. Ned was my own horse." And then the anger that he had whipped up in his mind failed him. Emptiness filled him. He would never ride Ned after the cows nor down the hill again. He could never curry him till his coat shone like the walnut table in the parlor.

"You'll never get another horse, young man, until you earn every cent of its cost and can pay for its keep," his father had told him in the barn.

"I don't want another horse," he had ground out between his teeth, and his father had swung the belt again because of the insolent look on his son's face.

Lyman buried his face again in the fern and went back over the whole trip to Charlestown. He had done one thing—he had ridden all night! He had gone through covered bridges that were so dark the noise of Ned's hoofs had almost scared him. When he rode through Pleasantville, a dog had barked and chased him and someone had banged a window up and looked out at him. Even now he could remember the way he had felt riding alone through the dark. He had told himself he was carrying dispatches to General McClellan. But when he rode up to the Cheshire Bridge House he was almost too tired to care what he was doing.

There were other horses there, standing in groups as the boys had stood when Dan and John volunteered. A man shouted and gave orders just like the officer from the Mexican War had done then. Some of the horses were rejected; they should have been too, they were nothing but tired old work horses. The appraiser had looked interested right away when he saw Ned. He looked at his teeth and felt his knees and slapped him on the flank. "Walk him up on the scales, boy."

Lyman had waited until the man told him how much he would bring. It would make his father feel better if he got a good price for him, he knew that. Then he thought again of John wanting to buy a substitute, of Jeb Holmes.

"I don't aim to sell him, sir. I'm *giving* him to the cavalry." He still felt proud thinking about it. The man had spat and then looked at him again.

"Hey, Major, here's a kid wants to give away his horse!" the man called out to another appraiser. And then the cavalry officer in blue with a sash around his waist and spurs on his boots came over to him. He put out his hand and shook Lyman's.

"Are you sure you want to give your horse away, my boy? What about your parents?" The kindness of his tone was harder on Lyman than the coarse brusqueness of the other men. He was afraid he wouldn't be able to answer him, his mouth drew down so badly.

"Yes, sir," he managed. "The horse is my own." What the man said then he hadn't heard. He went up to Ned and tangled his fingers in his mane and scratched him behind one ear. Then he started to walk away.

"Here!" The officer stopped him. He took out a piece of paper from a notebook and wrote on it. It was in his diary now. It read:

The Cavalry of the United States Army receives with gratitude Mr. Lyman Converse's gift of one part Morgan gelding.
(Signed), Major Wm. Huntley, U.S.A.

But the paper was worn and torn by now. It did no good. He wasn't proud any more of what he had done—he missed Ned too much to feel proud. He had slept most of the way back on the stage. He hadn't felt so bad until now. He wished he hadn't done it. No, not quite. He mustn't wish that, but he did, he did, he did. Tears, weak baby tears, started to come again, and he twisted his toes in the dirt. Did John feel like that after he'd joined up? After he went back again? He tried hard to think of Jeb Holmes with one leg gone. Did he really feel glad that he had given his leg? Maybe there were other times . . .

Lyman scrambled up stiffly and wiped his face with his sleeve. For one moment he had thought of telling his father why he had given his horse, about the way John felt, but he couldn't do that.

He stopped at the spring and washed his face in the cold water so no one could tell he had been crying. He leaned forward until his front hair trailed in the pool of the spring, his face dropping toward its reflection, eyes for mirrored eyes, a blurred impression of nose and mouth. His lips opened and his teeth showed in the mirror "Hello." He formed the word with his mouth and saw the mouth in the brown-green water move. He knelt there bending far over the spring, supporting himself by his hands, half-hypnotized by the nearness of his own reflection.

That was he, Lyman Converse—but who was Lyman Converse? What was he like? A disturbing sense of unreality held him, a deep sense of secrecy and mystery within himself—he, Lyman Webster Converse, no one else. There had never been anyone just like him before, there never would be again. A little breeze quivered over the pool and blurred the image the way the old frostbitten mirror in the parlor did. He tried grinning and the water jerked the grin into a grimace. While he looked a shadow slid across the water's surface. Someone was behind him in the woods. He froze, not wanting to look around, feeling the hairs on the back of his neck prickle. The shadow moved. Another head, darker than his, appeared beside his own. White teeth cut open the dusky image.

"Easy!" Lyman swung around. Easy was there behind him, laughing.

"I come to get you. Your pa acts kinda worried about you."

Lyman stood up, tossing the wet lock of his hair back over his head, and wiped the water that dripped down on his face. One hand bore the rough imprint of the granite rock that edged the spring, the other hand had rested on a block of soapstone and showed no mark.

"I'm coming," he said sulkily. "What were you trying to do, creeping up behind me?" It was as though Easy had somehow come too close to him, between himself and his own image. "Father still mad?"

"Oh, yes, he's still mad all right," Easy said.

3

OCTOBER 1863

LYMAN had gone for the mail on foot now for over a year. Orville Converse was not one to forget.

"Lyman, you go down and get the mail at noon," his father had said that next day after Lyman had come back from selling Ned. Lyman glanced up quickly, and his face flushed. His eyes darted to his mother, but there was no comfort there. She was spooning out the applesauce into separate dishes without looking up.

"Can I take Bess?"

"Why, no, you couldn't take Bess, Easy'll be using Bess to haul manure. If you don't have a horse I guess you'll have to walk, won't you?" It was the reasonableness of his father's tone that made it so cold. Lyman caught the inside of his upper lip between his teeth.

"I can walk," he said, and he had walked ever since.

It was two miles downhill and two miles back up. Lyman missed Ned all the way, every time he went. He tried to think he was a soldier in General Grant's army. McClellan was no longer his hero. General Grant was from the Middle West, but he thought like a New Englander, Deacon Bangert said. Lyman walked stiffly erect, setting down his bare feet as though they were in boots. He was fifteen, too old to play things, but no one would know. If Easy were along, he might guess, but then Easy would play too. The stone wall bordered the road on one side, on the other the timber came down to the bank.

Over that mountain and across a valley and another mountain range Dan and John were really fighting. He looked at the yellow-and-red painted hill and tried to see cannon smoke. Men were shooting from behind stone walls. Reuben Hall had got his head shot off as he was climbing over a wall, Dan had written home about it. Lyman glanced quickly along the stones wondering what it would be like to be shot at, or to see a man shot beside you, but the air was clear and only a chipmunk scrambled over the stones. The war was far away and he was here. The war would be over and done with before Father would let him go. There would never be another one, Reverend Leland promised God that last Sunday in his prayer. Lyman felt as he did when the folks drove off somewhere in the wagon and left him behind to do the chores.

28

In the last pitch of the hill the road sloped down steeply and Lyman broke into a run that took him all the way to the post office.

People were bunched around the office as usual. Mrs. Green was crying and Mrs. Davis was comforting her. There was always someone crying these days over mail or over not getting mail. The Reverend Mr. Leland and Dr. Tucker were reading the *Boston Post* together. There must have been a new battle, from all the excitement. Lyman made his way through the crowd like an eel. He had to stoop now to look through the opening. He came two tiers above the postmistress. All his life he had been measuring his height on the mailboxes in the post office.

He saw Dan's writing on the top letter the postmistress handed him. He sat on the railing outside the post office and examined the letter carefully, seeing Dan writing it by a campfire with soldiers all around. There was a big white envelope, stiffer than ordinary ones and with tall spidery writing on it addressed to Mr. Orville Converse, Esq., and postmarked Providence, R. I. The envelope was bordered in a heavy black band. He knew who that was from, Uncle Nathaniel Holbrook, Mother's brother in Providence.

As usual, he went through town to Louisa's house to ask if she had heard from John. It was getting so long now he hated to ask. He stood on the soapstone step in front of the door and lifted the door knocker. The house seemed so still he was about to go when the front door opened suddenly.

Louisa stood there against the dark of the front hall, her hair matching the dark stair railing and her face as white as the spindles.

"Yes, Lyman?" Then he noticed that her eyes were red and knew, uncomfortably, that she had been crying. He found his voice with difficulty and said what he had been saying for a month now.

"I wondered if you heard from John, because we didn't."

Louisa shook her head. "It's been four weeks now," she whispered, and he saw her eyes filling. Then she pushed the door closed and he stood alone on the step. He waited a moment, fearfully, to see if he could hear her crying, but no sound came from the house. It was almost worse to know there was weeping inside. He latched the little picket gate and went slowly down the sidewalk.

Father and Easy were sawing wood with a crosscut saw when he turned into the dooryard. Easy was stronger and bigger than Lyman still. Father told Easy he could start carrying in the wood to the shed now, and he came over to the house to read the mail. It was close to milking time. Lyman hadn't hurried up the hill, but he hadn't fooled any, either.

Abbie Converse sat on the bench on one side of the latticed stoop with the mail in her lap.

"No word from John, Orville," she said as he sat down on the opposite bench. "Maybe Louisa . . . Did you stop there, Lyman?"

Lyman nodded. "She hasn't heard for four weeks." He thought of saying Louisa was crying, but he didn't. Louisa had shut the door as though she didn't want anyone to see her.

Abbie's face was sad. "Oh, Orville, I'm worried."

Orville Converse scowled. "You've got to trust in the Lord, Abbie. You know John's fighting for the right. His life is in the Lord's hands."

"There's a letter from Dan, that's something to be thankful for," she said, and handed it to Orville. Lyman squatted just beyond the stoop, hoping he wouldn't be sent away. His mother was fingering the black-bordered envelope. Father was cutting open the letter from Dan with his knife.

Abbie caught her breath and her hand flew to her throat. "Orville, Nathaniel's gone—suddenly, in his office."

Orville rubbed his hand slowly over his beard just below his lip. "Nathaniel was a worldly man. I hope he made his peace with God before he was taken. He must have left Matilda and the girl well provided for."

Abbie's eyes filled with tears. "Oh, Orville, I haven't seen him for almost ten years!"

"He could have come to see you if he'd wanted. He had the money to go to Europe," Orville Converse said sternly, and then his tone softened. "This is no time to grieve for those that have lived their lives, Abbie. Think of Reuben Hall, killed at seventeen!"

"I know, Orville. Read Dan's letter." Lyman's curiosity was piqued. He had never known his Uncle Nathaniel had been in Europe.

Dear Mother and Father:

This letter will bring you some news that I hope will not disturb you too seriously. It should not if you recall that I have been twenty-one for three months past. In the carnage of war, when a man's life hangs often in the balance, it is good to find a refuge for the heart before it is too late. When I was in Virginia last winter I became much attracted to a beautiful and virtuous young lady, Miss Willie Delaney. On the twelfth of August Miss Delaney honored me with her hand in marriage.

Orville Converse's voice stopped a minute. Lyman did not dare look at him or at his mother. He could hear his mother breathing softly. Then Orville Converse went on:

30

Miss Delaney's father was killed in the Battle of Bull Run. Her mother has been dead for many years. I have persuaded her to go to you where she will be safe. I would like my son to be born where I was born and to grow up in the North.

Willie should arrive in Malden station on the train from Boston on November 10th. I am confident that you will make her feel welcome, and love her as I do. It will take time for her to learn to like the North.

You will be pleased to know that one thousand and thirty men of our brigade who had served two years and more have enlisted again for three years or until the war ends. I am among them. Thank you for the fruit cake and socks.

Your devoted son,
Lt. Daniel Converse

It seemed to Lyman that the only sound in the whole world was the sudden clatter of the wood that Easy dropped in the woodshed. Back across the grass of the dooryard he went, then another clatter as he dropped another armful.

"Why in tarnation would Dan marry a rebel?" Orville asked.

"She's going to have a child," Abbie murmured.

"Dan's an officer, just as John said he'd get to be," Lyman put in.

"That's so," Orville assented. "That's so." But even the pride in his tone did not lift the heaviness of his voice. "Lyman, it's time to milk." Lyman went without delay.

Sitting on the milk stool listening to the sound of the milk spurting into the tin pail, he could think over the letter. Dan married . . . her name was Willie. . . . That couldn't be her real name, it must be something Dan called her. November tenth. That was Wednesday, Thursday, Friday . . . three days from now. She was going to have a baby, a son, Dan said. It was going to be born here! She was beautiful, Dan liked only pretty girls. He used to say Louisa was too plain for him. Lyman thought again of Louisa standing in the hall; she was pretty, too. Dan's girl—no, Dan's wife would live here and have the spare room back of the parlor. She was a real rebel!

"Don't fall asleep at the job, Lyman," his father called into the barn as he went past. His profile was stern and dark. His hat brim came out as far as his sharp Converse nose and his heavy beard made his face seem longer.

Lyman moved his stool to the next cow, speculating on his father's anger, wondering how Dan had dared. When he was through milking he hunted up Easy. Abbie never wanted Easy to milk. "I know his color don't come off," she used to say, "but I don't like to see him handling the milk."

"Easy, you know what? Dan's married!"

"When'd he do that?" Easy held his load of wood easily on one hip

"August. He's sending his wife up here. She's coming Friday, Easy, and she's a rebel from Virginia."

"Comin' here?"

Lyman nodded. Easy's eyes were darker than his skin. They grew darker than ever. "She goin' to live here?"

"Sure!"

Easy moved across to the woodshed with his load. When he came back he said softly: "Southern folks is powerful dif'rent from Northern folks. I wonder if she goin' to like it here."

Willie Converse was pretty, prettier than Louisa Tucker—the prettiest woman Lyman had ever seen. When she stood at the top of the train steps he stared at her. Yellow curls bobbed under a green hat so tiny it was hardly a hat at all, and she wore a plaid dress. He felt his mother's fingers pressing his arm and looked up quickly at her face. It was paler than usual, and more stern.

"That must be her, Mother," he said excitedly. "In the plaid dress."

"I don't know, Lyman, I'm not sure."

Lyman felt a wave of disappointment. What if Dan's wife was the woman in black! No, he was sure that was Willie. He smiled at her. Orville Converse stood beside the conductor and watched the passengers get off the train. People pressed forward to meet most of them. The girl in the plaid dress stood holding her bag in her hands and looking over the station. There was no doubt. Orville Converse went up to her.

"Are you Mrs. Daniel Converse?" he asked.

"I am," she answered.

"I am Daniel's father."

"How do you do." She smiled gravely. Abbie saved the stiffness of the meeting.

"My dear, we're glad to see Daniel's wife." Abbie reached out both hands and took the girl's in hers.

"And this is Daniel's brother Lyman," Orville said, and Lyman muttered a "Pleased to meet you" and reddened. "Dan has told me about you," she said, and her voice was soft and gently slurred.

They had left Easy home because "just at first," Abbie had said, "it might seem queer to her."

"I guess she's seen colored people before," Orville declared. "We are fighting a war to free the slaves, and it won't mean much if we're ashamed to live what we fight for." Orville's voice had grown louder, as though he were making a public speech. But Easy hadn't been around when they left. Orville called and called him.

They took her to the carriage and Abbie and Willie sat in back and Father and Lyman in front. It was a long ride from Malden station to Painesville. Lyman's ears were flattened right back against his head trying to hear everything the women said. Father didn't say a word, either. Perhaps, Lyman thought, he was listening too.

"How long ago did you see Dan?" Mother asked.

"He put me on the train."

"Is he . . . does he look well? We haven't seen him but once since he left."

"Yes, he's very well. He had the dysentery, but he's well again. He sent his love to you," the girl answered.

"He's been in the war such a long time," Abbie said wistfully. "He was only nineteen when he went."

"I think you would find him much older. He has a mustache now."

"Well, think of it!" Abbie said wonderingly, trying to imagine Dan older-looking.

"Did you have any trouble coming up North?" Orville asked, looking straight ahead at the horses' heads.

"Oh, no, not as the wife of a Yankee captain."

"Captain!" Father and Lyman exclaimed together.

"Oh, yes, Dan's a captain."

"He must have shown your rebs—your soldiers a thing or two," Orville Converse said.

"Yes, I'm sure," the girl answered evenly. "Dan is brave."

They all rode silently the next mile or so. When they drove into town Abbie said: "This is Painesville. You'll get to know it well."

When they passed Louisa's house Lyman turned around. "That's where John's girl lives." He wanted her to see it, but she only glanced at it and nodded. "Dan told me about Louisa."

Beyond the covered bridge Lyman jumped out to walk up the quarry hill the way he always did, to save the horses. He lagged back so he was abreast of the back seat. He didn't dare to look directly at this strange new person who belonged to Dan, but he could look at her hands in their kid gloves. They were smaller than his mother's hands. His eyes traveled down the full gathers of the green plaid skirt. She had crossed her feet at the ankles, and one foot, turned toward the outside, showed its broken sole. A piece of cardboard had been fitted in to cover the big hole. It shocked him in so elegant a person, and he walked ahead a little.

"Dan said your home is up on the mountain, though he called it a hill," Willie said.

"Your home, too," Abbie insisted gently.

"Thank you," Lyman heard her say. He saw Easy move across the dooryard like a shadow when they drove into the yard and knew he had been watching for them.

"Here, Lyman!" Orville carried the small humpbacked trunk on his own shoulder. Abbie and her new daughter followed across the narrow box hall through the parlor to the parlor bedroom. Lyman felt that Willie must think it a pretty handsome room with the silk quilt and the feather bed plumped up so high, and the poppy pattern of the washbowl and pitcher.

"You must be tired," he heard his mother say.

"No, I'm not tired," she answered. "Call me Willie the way Dan does. He says it's a strange name up North, but I was christened that for my grandmother."

"Wasn't her name Wilhelmina?" Abbie suggested hopefully.

"No, just Willie."

Lyman ran outside to find Easy.

Abbie wanted to set the meal in the dining-room but Orville forbade it. "Let's start out from the beginning as we're going to keep on, Abbie." They had not yet exchanged one word about her. Abbie's soft brown eyes flew to Orville's sterner brown ones, carrying their anxiety. Abbie's eyes always carried on a gentler understanding with Orville's than their words had ever done. Orville had begun his courtship by glances years ago in the Congregational Church. But this time his eyes moved away from Abbie's to the table as he said, "Easy shall eat here as usual."

Abbie tied her best dimity apron over her black-silk dress in troubled silence. Easy was a good boy, far better at chores than any of her own boys, but she resented him. In a way, he was the reason Dan and John were away fighting, the reason John had come home acting so down in the mouth, the reason this stranger was in the other room now.

Obediently she set the table for five persons. Orville was a hard man, yet she admired that hardness as she loved the hardness of his body at night. She was shocked at her own thought.

"Lyman, call Dan's wife to supper."

Lyman washed his hands at the sink and combed his hair back without being told. He wished that he looked more like Dan. The passage through the dining-room across the hallway and through the haircloth splendor of the parlor was strange tonight. He stepped from braided rug to braided rug so that his feet would not clatter and knocked at the bedroom door.

"Yes." Her voice was different from anybody else's, a tiny bit like Easy's.

"Uh . . . supper's ready." He couldn't call her Willie.

"Oh." She opened the door. Her hair was down her back and she had taken off the dark plaid and put on something light.

"Supper's ready," he said again, feeling stupid.

"I'll be right out. I must have gone to sleep after all."

They were all sitting down when he came back to the kitchen.

"She's been asleep. She'll be here in a minute," he reported. They sat waiting, each busy with his own thinking.

"It gets dark early now," Abbie said. Orville went over to the shelf above the sink and took down a lamp. Lyman was glad for the kerosene lamp, it seemed to warm the uneasy air of the kitchen. Orville placed it in the wall bracket and the bottom of the lamp threw a round dark shadow on the table. They heard Willie coming across the dining-room floor. Lyman, looking at Easy, saw his eyes roll toward the door and back.

"I'm sorry I am late. I must have been more tired than I thought." She stood in the doorway, elegant and strange. When she moved her hand two wide gold bangles clinked against each other. Lyman wished his father would go and bring her in. He couldn't quite look at her.

"Sit right over here," Abbie said. Nobody rose. She wasn't coming. Now Lyman had to look at her. Her face was white.

"I don't sit down to eat with niggers," she said, so softly Lyman could hardly believe the words. She turned in the doorway and they heard her quick steps back through the house.

Orville bowed his head. "Our Father, Thou knowest all things and all men are alike in Thy sight, white and black. Root out all sinful pride and bring low those who set themselves up. Let the righteous cause of the Union triumph. Smite down our enemy quickly, O Lord, and let not bloodshed continue. Harken to the cry of innumerable Rachels weeping for their children, for they shall not be comforted until peace is come. A-men."

"Pass the bread, Lyman," his father said. Lyman passed it and glanced at Easy, but he was busy eating and his eyes were fixed on Orville's face.

"Miss Willie ain't to blame, ezactly, Mistah Converse," Easy said.

"Never mind, Easy, we are not sacrificing two sons to the cause of freedom to see that cause flouted under our own roof at our own board."

"Orville, please just let me fix her some supper on a tray. She needs to eat, you know."

"Now, Abbie, I'm not going to have you waiting on a young chit of a girl, either."

A terrible, stern silence crowded down on them and filled the kitchen more heavily than the grease from burning fat. It choked the throat in the same way. Lyman finished his supper, but there was no taste to anything he ate. He glanced at his father and knew the same thing was true for him. It was a relief to leave the table. He saw Easy follow his father outside, and he stayed inside to wipe dishes for his mother willingly.

"She's pretty, isn't she?" he said finally.

"Very pretty, Lyman, but I can't help but wish Daniel had waited, like John." He saw his mother was laying a tray, in spite of his father. The tray looked pretty, too. "Lyman, you just slip in with this," his mother said. Once again he made the trip into the parlor bedroom. This time he was bolder.

"Willie," he called softly. "Willie, it's Lyman."

She opened the door so swiftly he wasn't expecting it. Her room was dark and her face looked as though she had been crying.

"I really don't want anything to eat," she said.

Lyman set the tray down on the round marble-topped table. "Don't you want I should light the lamp?" he asked, and went to do it. When he was through, with the wick turned just right, Willie was eating. He sat down on the top of her trunk and watched her.

"I haven't had anything to eat since yesterday noon," she said, and she smiled at him. He wished his mother could see her now. He was trying to think of something to say when she spoke.

"I told Dan it would never work to have me come up here. It's just until the war's over, Dan says, and then we'll go away."

He wanted to ask where. He knew that his father expected one of the older boys to take the farm and the others to help run the quarry. He wanted to ask a lot of questions, but he held his tongue. Then he thought of something he had to ask.

"Didn't Dan tell you about Easy's being here?"

"No, we had so much more to talk about. I had no idea of coming here until Dan got his orders. You know how Dan is, I've never seen such a masterful man!" She smiled as though she were remembering something about Dan that pleased her.

Lyman carried the tray back to the kitchen, thinking about Dan. He never had really known him. Now his admiration for him rose. He would be a masterful man, too. Abbie was waiting in the kitchen. Her eyes swept the empty tray.

"She was awful hungry. She hadn't eaten since yesterday," Lyman said. "Dan never told her about Easy."

"Here, Lyman, take her a piece of fruit cake," Abbie said. "Quick, before your father comes."

The night rested uneasily on the brick house above the quarry. It rained a little after midnight and the wind that blew the lilac bushes against the woodshed lattice was cold.

"Orville," Abbie Converse said softly, "are you awake?" Though she knew well that he was from his turning in bed beside her.

"Yes, Abbie."

"D'you suppose the rain's coming in the parlor window?"

"The rain's in the east, Abbie. It couldn't come in there."

They lay still then, each thinking of the rain coming through the window of the parlor bedroom that did face east, where their new daughter-in-law lay.

"Orville," Abbie said after a long pause, "Easy's moved into the old smokehouse. He says he wants to."

"Well, I won't have it. That's nonsense!" The rumble of his voice reached through the ceiling to the parlor bedroom. It penetrated the wall of the room where Lyman lay with his head on his arm and thought about being a masterful man.

Only Easy slept soundly, in the old smokehouse. He had understood Miss Willie, she was the kind of folks he was used to. He would cook his own meals on the smokehouse stove. If Mistah Converse didn't let him, he could get a job somewheres else, maybe at the quarry, but they sure did need him here with both those boys off to war, he thought sleepily.

"If he wants to, maybe it would be just as well, Orville. It will take her time to get used to . . . to things up North, Dan said," Abbie urged gently. In the dark she brought her braids together around her neck and held them together at her throat for comfort.

"What put the idea in his head? Did you say something to him?"

"I didn't say a word, Orville. He came and asked me if he could take the cot on the porch out there. He and Lyman used to play there, you know."

"What did you tell him, Abbie?" His tone was accusing still.

"I said . . . yes, as far as I could see . . . if he wanted to."

"You should have sent him to me."

"We've got to be friends with Daniel's wife, Orville. Our ways are hard for her at first, I suppose."

Orville pushed his feet impatiently against the spooled foot of the bed so the cherry wood of the sides creaked.

"That's up to her. She'll have to take us as she finds us."

"But if Easy wants to, it might make it simpler, Orville."

"But why does he want to? Why should he?"

"He says he understands her, Orville."

"He's a fool," Orville said disgustedly, rubbing the place on his chest where his beard always tickled. "He's got to act like a white man if he wants to be treated like one."

But he hadn't said Easy couldn't stay there, Abbie told herself, and the relief she felt let her relax a little more into the feather bed. In gratitude she slipped one hand over till it lay curled like a dove against Orville's shoulder. "She's pretty, Orville, isn't she?" she asked, as Lyman had.

Orville grunted. "Where'd she get that name?"

"She was christened that, for her grandmother. It's a Southern name."

"Daniel never had good sense," Orville Converse said.

In the parlor bedroom Willie Delaney pulled the silk patchwork quilt up under her chin. There was little comfort in the cold silk that rustled stiffly under her hand. The rain blew against the sill and she could feel the curtains blowing in the dark. There was a faint smell of smoke in the rain that made her think of the wet smoky air blowing in the dressing-room of the theater at Richmond. This place was too alien, this house with one parlor and the windows all closed in it and the kitchen with Dan's mother bringing the hot food right from the stove. It might be cleaner than Mrs. Surratt's boardinghouse on H Street, but it was stifling.

"Be careful at first, Willie," Dan had said. He had seemed anxious just at the last at the station. But the nigger at the table had been too much. There were some things Dan couldn't expect her to do. If you were born impulsive, you couldn't change overnight. If she hadn't been impulsive, she would never have spoken to Dan in the first place. She had seen him during the very first act and his eyes had hardly left her all through the play. Afterward he had been at the stage door, leaning against the rickety wooden railing of the stairs.

"Hello, Yankee!" she had said as she went past him and got into the carriage. He had been there four nights in a row after that, and sent her flowers the night she played *East Lynne*. The fourth night he had been late, but he had come at the end of the third act. And in Washington he had come over to Mrs. Surratt's, too, and left a letter for her. That was the beginning.

"Father's a Yankee, of course, Willie. He'll seem stern at first, but you'll win him over," Dan had said. "Maybe you better not tell him about being an actress—I mean just at first. Mother will love you and Lyman will follow you around like a dog. It won't be long, lovely."

Willie clasped her arms around her shoulders under the coarse homespun sheets and the heavy quilt and heard the sound of Dan's voice as he called her "lovely." It mixed with the sound of the rain that came in over the sill onto Abbie's best braided rug. This narrow house was Dan's. She could try to live here until he came back, and she turned on her pillow and slept again.

4

ABBIE woke the next morning with a heavy feeling in her mind. She was not used to such a feeling. Her life had been virtuous and well ordered, at least until the black boy had come, and she felt resentment against Easy. Then she remembered that it wasn't Easy at all, it was Dan's wife, Willie. Willie was in the parlor bedroom. It was no longer an empty room where she could display her best walnut bedroom suite and fold her best silk quilt like a half-star on the foot of the bed or lay out her Sunday taffeta to air. It was occupied now by a girl who was a complete stranger and a Southerner and had put Orville into a state! The girl would be there goodness knew how long! Abbie sat up in bed and pulled her dressing-gown around her shoulders before getting up, but at that moment Orville threw back his side of the covers boldly and stood out in his nightshirt.

"You better call that girl, Abbie. She don't look to me like she was used to getting up very early of a morning. Better tell her to dress for church while she's about it." It was six o'clock of a Sunday morning.

Easy was not at breakfast.

"Sit down, Easy," Abbie had said when he came in from the barn and picked up the bowl of mush and milk that was set at his place. "Mr. Converse won't hear of your eating by yourself, and it'll just make a bad muss, Easy!"

"I'm fine, Missus Converse," Easy had said, carrying his bowl and a plate of salt pork toward the door. As he went out he gave her a wide smile that disconcerted her. Abbie's hands were still a minute as she looked after him, watching him cross the yard to the smokehouse. He acted sometimes as though he had no awe of Orville at all. It was queer when you knew Easy was really a slave—or he used to be.

Willie was on time for breakfast. Abbie was glad that she sat down so quietly. She said "Good morning" as demurely as Louisa might.

Orville ate his mush in a stern silence that rested heavily on the rest of them. When he had finished he turned to Willie, looking at her waterfall of blond curls, her blue eyes, and the coral brooch bordered by pearls.

"Willie, you might as well understand certain things. As Daniel's wife you are welcome here. But there are certain things that must be understood." Lyman wondered at his father's repeating himself, almost as though he weren't sure of what he was saying.

"What are those things?" Willie asked, and her voice had a strange distinctness.

"Well"—Orville Converse looked away from the intensity of her eyes to the shadow cast by the lamp—"we are a Northern household. We believe in certain fundamental truths." His voice was louder than it needed to be. Abbie's hands took refuge together in her lap. Willie's face was white now. Her eyes never left Orville's face.

"We believe," Mr. Converse went on, "that keeping slaves is wrong, an act against God. Easy fled from tyranny in the South. He found refuge here. For the last five years he has eaten at this board and been one of us. Now you come and he is forced to take his meals by himself."

"I never asked him to," Willie said. She sat so still, not moving her hands the way Mother or Louisa generally did, Lyman noticed. "I am quite willing to eat my meals in my own room and carry them in there myself. There are certain standards that seem important in the South."

"You think you are too good to eat with him!" Orville said accusingly.

Willie seemed to consider, pursing her lips, tilting her head. "It seems a queer thing to do," she said. "I told Dan it was a mistake for me to come up here. I didn't want to."

"No, Orville, Dan wanted her to be here!" Abbie cried out.

Orville Converse pushed back his plate as though to sweep nonessentials out of the way. "Lyman, go harness the horses. Abbie . . . Well, you might as well stay."

Lyman went out through the woodshed. Behind him he heard his father's voice. "Why did you marry Daniel?" The plank of the woodshed floor creaked loudly under Lyman's waiting foot and he stepped quickly down onto the dirt floor beyond.

"Did you have to marry him?" The tone of Orville's voice had an edge like a newly honed razor. Willie's voice was low, but it carried clearly out to the fall morning.

"No, Mr. Converse, I did not have to marry your son, and if he were here I think he would make you answer for such a question. In the South gentlemen do not insult ladies, but, as you say, this is a Northern household! I married Dan because I loved him. I wonder if you can understand such a feeling?"

Lyman fled now across to the barn. How did she dare? What would Father do?

"What's the matter with you?" Easy asked. He was already harnessing the horses.

"Nothing," Lyman said. "Say, Easy, Father's mad about your eating by yourself. You don't have to eat in the smokehouse."

"Oh, pshaw!" Easy said calmly, airing the latest Vermont expression he had picked up. "I like it by myself fine. I never did like eating in there, Mistah Converse takes his meals so awful solemn."

"My dear," Abbie whispered to Willie as they stood in the hall waiting for the carriage, "I was thankful for what you said about Daniel, that you . . . cared for him. I know everything will be all right. Mr. Converse just wanted to be sure, you know." Abbie's voice was tremulous.

But Willie stood coldly unresponsive to Abbie's sudden caress. "I was foolish to marry a Northerner," she said. "John warned me that it would be difficult."

"John? You knew our Jonathan too! You must tell Louisa that you've seen him. You'll meet her at church. She hasn't heard from him for over a month," Abbie said. "There they are, don't let's keep Mr. Converse waiting."

Lyman and Easy squeezed in in front with Orville. Abbie and Willie sat behind. They rode without speaking past the frost-touched wood-lot down the hill to the bridge. Other carriages were on their way to church. Bonneted heads bowed, gentlemen lifted hats, the bells in both churches clanged discordantly together.

It was a little hard, Abbie Converse thought, to have all of them craning their necks to see the Converse pew again as they had the first few times Easy was in church. She held her head high and smoothed her lace mitts over her hands. Willie wore long kid gloves with fancy stitching on them. The gloves wrinkled elegantly under a wide gold bracelet. Willie felt Abbie's glance and moved her hands in the smooth gloves.

Mr. Ephraim Whipple stopped by their pew and whispered noisily behind his hand to Orville Converse. He nodded in agreement and whispered to Abbie. Abbie leaned across Willie to speak to Lyman.

"Jim Bartholomew's joined the army. Mr. Whipple wants you to pump the organ." As she whispered Abbie pushed her knees sideways toward Willie, who did likewise. Both women held down their hoops. "Slide right out in front, Lyman."

Lyman felt embarrassed and important. He was taking the place of a man in the army. But the embarrassment made him redden and perspiration leaked out in his hands. He had never pumped the organ before. He walked back to the organ loft at the rear of the church, glancing uneasily at the gilded pipes rising above the shining oak. Mrs. Whipple and Mrs. Perkins and the Holmes girls and Philinda Bragg were watching him. His eyes moved swiftly to the back row to Mr. Kellogg and Asa Green and Jeb Holmes, who looked strong and able-bodied when you couldn't see his empty trouser leg, and Easy, of course. Easy had sung in the choir all year. Mr. Whipple led Lyman to the seat behind the organ and showed him how to take hold of the big handle.

"This way, Lyman, it ain't hard," he whispered to him.

Lyman laid his hand on it, trying it, feeling the smooth, worn wood under his hand. He heard the gentle swish of air filling the gilded pipes. Some of them were just for looks—only the big ones really did the business.

"Don't jerk it, just keep her going," Mr. Whipple whispered.

Lyman moved with it. When he swung the handle down, he could see only the back of the pipes; when he carried it up, he could get a quick glimpse of the church—too much to see all at once. There were Mother and Father and Willie . . . down again behind the curtain. Next time he would see who was sitting way over by the windows. The singing was beginning. Back here you could hear little wooden thumps the organ made that you didn't hear from the pews. The voices seemed to surround him. He could pick out Easy's voice from the others. "Praise God from Whom All Blessings Flow." Up and down, up and down . . . every time he could see over the backs of the congregation he saw people whispering, nudging each other. It made him feel that his own conduct in church was better than he had thought it. He saw people looking at Willie. He looked at Willie too, but all he could see was the waterfall of yellow curls under that little green hat and her sloping shoulders in the green plaid dress.

Once he forgot to push the handle and the music in the pipes faltered. He pumped strongly after that. During the sermon he could have gone to sleep back of the organ, but this morning he wasn't sleepy. He sat on his stool, moved out a little way where he could see. It was like looking through somebody's window to watch the backs of the people at church. He was more interested in the backs of his own family than in the others. Father never moved. Mother looked down in her lap a good deal. All of a sudden, Willie's head turned quickly, not the way a lady is supposed to do in church, and she was looking right at him. She smiled a tiny bit and turned around again. He felt hot all over. Didn't she know that everyone behind her could see her? The whole choir must have seen her. He moved back so he was half-hidden by the organ.

Willie Delaney Converse felt the hostile curiosity of the people around her. She knew it was hard for Dan's mother to have her here. Everyone asked with his eyes: "How did you get up here? How did you happen to marry a Northern soldier? You should leave him for a proper Northern girl. How did you dare?" Well, she had told Dan's father! She hadn't been careful at all, she was made that way. Dan's father couldn't hold a candle to her own father. She would like to see Orville Converse's face if she told him her own father was an actor who had come to Virginia from England!

Dan's mother acted half-afraid of her husband. She had kept telling her things about Dan this morning: "Dan liked wild strawberry jam best," "Dan always did the driving when he was home," "Dan never cared to go away from Painesville until he had to go to war," "I don't believe Dan would ever like a city."

What his mother was trying to say was very plain: "I know Dan better than you do," she was saying. "He belongs here on this hill, in this little village . . . don't you try to take him away."

But she didn't know Dan, neither did his father. No father and mother could know their son as well as the woman he loved could know him. Dan loved the city. He had been having the time of his life in Washington. He loved the theaters and the stores and the big buildings. He didn't look like a country boy any more. His brother John did, but not Dan. They'd never have him back here after the war! These little hills could no more hold him than . . . than the Confederate soldiers had been able to keep him a prisoner after Bull Run, she thought triumphantly while the Reverend Isaac Leland made his "fifthly."

"Did you have any trouble coming up North?" Dan's father had asked yesterday on the way from the station, curiosity lying heavy on every word.

"Oh, no," she had answered. "Not as the wife of a Yankee captain." Mr. Converse had winced at that. That was all she had told him. She could hardly tell Orville Converse that she knew theatrical people all the way to Philadelphia, that when the war was so hard on the theater in Richmond Wilkes Booth had persuaded her to go up to Washington. Edwin was playing there and Wilkes had an engagement. Wilkes had been a darling and found her a room at Mrs. Surratt's, where he was staying, when there were no rooms at all to be had in Washington.

She sat in the Converse pew and remembered her talk with Wilkes Booth. "But how can you marry a Northerner, Willie? How can you stand living in one of their damned towns? I know them, they're worse north of Boston, too—hard, narrow people with nasal voices and shop-keeping souls. They'll prate about John Brown as though he were a

44

saint until you gag." Wilkes couldn't say anything, even in conversation, without sounding as though he were on the stage. He moved his hands and shook back his dark hair as though he were acting Richard III. He would never be as good as his father or Edwin, people around the theater were always saying, but the South loved him.

They had had a glass of wine together at the hotel in Philadelphia where so many theater folk stayed. "We'll drink to the Confederacy," Wilkes had said. "I'm off tomorrow to take more quinine back," he had whispered. She had known then why Wilkes hadn't joined the army.

She stirred in the uncomfortable pew. If the war lasted very long, how could she stand it here? "You'll be safe there, Willie. I'll feel good about you there," Dan had said, but . . .

She felt someone's eyes upon her so strongly that she turned quickly, forgetting that she was sitting beside Abbie Converse in a pew in the Congregational Church of Painesville, Vermont. In that quick turn of her head she saw Lyman's face, clean and scrubbed above his Sunday collar, peering out around the organ. The sun coming from the window behind him showed the soft fuzz on his cheek. They had been Lyman's eyes she had felt. She turned back and fixed her gaze on the Reverend Isaac Leland. Lyman was like Dan, and yet he was different. She would be friends with Lyman.

Willie met Louisa after the service.

"How do you do," Louisa said gravely as Abbie introduced them. The girls' hands touched briefly over the back of the pew.

Louisa was a year or so younger than Willie, but she looked older, perhaps because her brown hair was brushed back from its white part into a net. Lyman stood beside them. They made a kind of island in the church. Other women looked their way, observing with veiled disapproval every velvet-edged ruffle on Willie's skirt, and her coral earrings. Mrs. Perkins's son was injured at Fredericksburg, and her eyes were hard as she looked at Willie. "I wouldn't want to be in Abbie Converse's shoes," she told her husband as they walked home from church.

"Willie knows Jonathan, Louisa," Abbie Converse said eagerly. Lyman felt Louisa move as though to brace herself.

"Yes, he had been sick but he was getting well again and about to leave for home. I haven't seen him since," Willie said, smiling.

"How did you come to know Northern soldiers?" Louisa asked.

Willie spread her gloved hands in a little gesture. Her shoulders shrugged ever so little. "I sang for some of the wounded ones. When they are wounded you forget whether they are Northern or Southern."

45

She didn't tell Louisa that she had sung on the stage in a public theater, that the soldiers had paid money to come and hear her.

"Oh, I see," Louisa said coolly. Then Mr. Converse brought the minister to meet Willie, and Louisa went on up the aisle. Lyman stood watching her. He wished she had said more, Willie couldn't see how nice Louisa really was, nor how pretty she could look.

"Perhaps the Lord has sent you to be in this flock so that you may see the error of the South, my dear. Perhaps you are called to be an interpreter of truth to the misguided South," the Reverend Mr. Leland pronounced in his preaching voice.

"I hardly think so," Willie Delaney Converse answered.

"Food for thought you gave us this morning, Reverend," Orville Converse said hurriedly.

"And a wonderful prayer," Abbie said in a low voice, shaking the Reverend Mr. Leland's hand, moving him up the aisle. Willie laid her fingers on Lyman's arm.

"Let's go on out to the carriage," she murmured.

Lyman felt her fingers through the stout material of his suit. His face flushed hotly. Easy had driven out of the carriage sheds. When he saw them he wound the reins around the whipstock and jumped down to help Willie in.

"I'll help her in," Lyman said crossly.

"Thank you," Willie Converse said, smiling on them both.

How could Easy be so anxious to help her after what she had said about eating with a—a "nigger"? Lyman wondered. He got in the front seat beside Easy, and after they had started up the street he asked Easy why he was so nice to Willie.

"Oh, pshaw," Easy whispered with a grin. "She's all right, Lyman. She's from down South, that's all."

5

NOVEMBER 1863

THE house was bigger the winter Dan's wife came to stay with them. Usually it drew inward to the two stoves—the one in the kitchen and the one in the sitting-room—and Abbie's bedroom and the back chamber above the kitchen where Lyman slept formed a chilly margin. The parlor was so cold other winters that Abbie used to set her mince-meat and fruit cake in there to keep. There was a stove in there, but they never used it except for company.

The parlor stove was a pretty one. Abbie had brought it with her when she came as a bride. It bore the name R. & J. Wainwright, Middlebury, Vermont, in raised letters and had a design of roses cast into the iron. Abbie had had some romantic and luxurious notion of setting it in the big bedroom she and Orville used. Of course she didn't mean to keep a fire all night, but it would be so nice to undress by. Orville couldn't understand having heat in a bedroom, and said it seemed a waste not to use it in the parlor. So they had bricked up the old parlor fireplace, the way folks were doing as soon as they could afford stoves, and set it there.

But this winter the parlor stove was always glowing in the daytime and gently warm all night from its banked fire. Easy made it his self-appointed task to keep fresh wood in the box Lyman had covered with wallpaper for Willie. Looking back, Abbie couldn't remember Willie's actually asking for a fire, yet she seemed to take for granted that there would be one, that they had always had a fire in there.

The first night Easy built a fire in the parlor stove was toward the end of November. Abbie had just finished setting her bread sponge. Orville was reading the war news in the kitchen in his stocking feet. It had turned bitter cold that night, and she was wondering where Daniel and Jonathan were sleeping, and whether she should offer Willie an outing-flannel gown to sleep in, when she heard the music. First the tinkling sound of the keys of the old square piano that hadn't been tuned in goodness knows how long, and then the voices: Willie's high as a bird's, and Lyman's, and . . . pity's sake, that was Easy singing with them! Abbie stood still listening. Orville put down his paper.

"It's a funny thing she'll sing with Easy when she won't eat **with** him." Abbie sniffed.

"Well, that sounds good!" Orville stooped down and fumbled for his Gladstone slippers behind the stove. Abbie had to help him, he never could find anything. "I guess I'll go in and hear them." Orville was partial to music, he had led the winter singing class year before last.

Abbie turned the kitchen lamp down low. The light from the parlor reached across the hall into the sitting-room, but the music came even farther. There was Orville's voice now, singing with them!

Abbie stood in the doorway of the parlor. "Well, Orville!" she said, but no one heard her. Willie had lighted the hand-painted lamp on the piano and brought in the one from her bedroom. The room was actually warmer than the kitchen, the fire was going so hard. Willie's curls were shaking with the movements of her head. Abbie would never forget the picture she made, Lyman on one side of her and Easy on the other. Abbie sang too.

Willie went from that song right into "Endearing young charms." Abbie saw Willie look up at Orville and smile. The girl was the flirty kind. That worried Abbie some, but she was glad Daniel had picked a pretty wife. Abbie had to admit that Willie wasn't lazy the way you might expect a Southern girl to be with having everything done for her by slaves. She had half a dozen petticoats all tucked for the baby already, with real fine stitches.

Abbie looked around her parlor as she hadn't done in years. In summer the shades were always drawn to keep the carpet from fading. In winter it had always been too cold before. It was a right pretty room, Abbie thought with pride, and she got up to wipe the dust off the glass bell jar that covered the wreath made of Orville's mother's hair—gray it was, with strands of black. Unconsciously Abbie's eyes were drawn back to Willie's hair that was as yellow as the glass hat that held toothpicks on the sideboard in the dining-room.

Easy's voice was almost too heavy, but Orville breathed more strength into his own. He had his arms raised now, directing the boys the way he used to lead the singing school. They made monstrous waving shadows on the walls, like the beating of a hawk's wings. Easy was grinning like a jack-o'-lantern.

Willie's hands idled over the keys after that one, then her waist seemed to stiffen, she threw her head and shoulders back, and struck into "Dixie."

Abbie held her breath. Orville's lips closed firmly. Easy and Willie sang together, though once Abbie thought Lyman was humming. He was watching Willie's face as though—well, almost as though he admired her!

Suddenly Orville's voice broke in like a noisy trumpet, singing "John Brown's body lies a-moldering in the grave." Abbie joined in defiantly, and Lyman. The noise in the square parlor was terrible to hear. Willie played the tune on the piano, but her lips were closed tight enough. Abbie felt the way she did before firecrackers went off. What would happen next?

Then Willie lifted her hands from the keys and turned around in her chair laughing. She pulled a white-lace handkerchief out of her full sleeve and waved it in the air. "Truce, truce!" And there was no explosion at all. Even Orville was laughing. It was the pleasantest thing a body could ever hope to hear.

"We can't tell who won out because we were all fighting," Orville said gallantly. Lyman went over and filled up the stove again, though it was already late.

"Wait, Lyman. We must go to bed now," Abbie said.

"That's fine. I undress out here," Willie said shamelessly. "And then I leave the door of the bedroom open or I'd freeze these cold nights."

Abbie waited for Orville to say something about such a waste, but he never said a word.

Willie did her sewing in the parlor afternoons, so Abbie got in the way of coming in, though she was always aware of the strangeness of sitting by a parlor stove when there was a good fire in the kitchen, and sitting there with a strange girl who was Daniel's wife.

One day Louisa came up the hill and Willie said, "Let me make some tea." She went out to the kitchen and brought back the teakettle and cups and saucers and the cake Abbie had planned for supper. "We might as well make the tea on this stove, don't you think, Mother?"

What could Abbie say but "Why, yes, I guess we might as well"?

Lyman came in from school just before sundown, his cheeks as red as a turkey's wattles from the cold. He stood in the parlor doorway a second.

"Want some more wood, Willie?"

"No, thank you, there's plenty yet. Come in and have some tea with us." And Lyman came, folding his long legs awkwardly on each side of the haircloth chair. Louisa looked at him and thought how much he looked like John, and Willie, looking, thought of Dan. Abbie wondered if she should give him sulphur and molasses, he looked so thin. There was consumption in Orville's side of the family.

Lyman studied his two sisters-in-law—or just as well as sisters-in-law, 'count of Louisa being promised—wondering at the difference between them. Louisa was pretty, too. Today the wild-rose color was in her cheeks.

"Oh, Lyman, I had a letter from John!" Louisa said, rocking forward in her chair so the high spindle back topped her head like a big black comb.

"Why, Louisa!" Abbie reproached her. "You didn't tell us!"

"No, I was just seeing how long I could keep from telling it, and then when Lyman came it didn't seem fair. He always comes way down to the village to bring me the letters you get."

Willie laughed. "Louisa, I didn't know you could be such a tease!"

"John says if they only keep still awhile now till he gets rested up he'll be all right. But it seems like there are rumors of moving on every day. He got my letter and he says something about you, Willie—here." Louisa took the letter out of her pocket and scanned a page before she began to read: "'And now you know Willie. She is a winner all right, and has good sense, just what Dan needs!'" Louisa looked toward Willie. "There, how's that for a compliment!"

Willie stood up and swept her a curtsy.

"There's more: 'I can't quite imagine her up on the hill, though, in our house.' That's all he says about you, Willie, then he goes on 'Some rebels were captured yesterday and brought in and they looked pretty down in the mouth and had no shoes. Maybe it won't last forever. I wish I were home this minute, cracking butternuts by the kitchen fire, and then I'd get dressed in clean clothes and come down to see you.'"

"That's about all," Louisa said, blushing as she folded the letter, and Lyman knew John must have signed his name with love. He went on thinking about it as he drank the tea that Willie passed him. What would you write a girl you were as good as married to? He would say: "I dream of the way your hair brushes back so dark and soft . . ." He studied Louisa. "The way your face is oval as a picture frame . . ."

"Lyman, whatever are you staring at?" Louisa asked, and Lyman blushed up to his hairline and knocked the silver spoon off on the floor.

"It's time to milk, I guess," he said as he got up and shambled out.

"My, Lyman seems big for fifteen," Abbie said. "Now, Willie, show Louisa how much you've got ready."

Louisa had guessed that Willie was expecting a baby, but no one had mentioned it to her before. The three women went into the parlor bedroom and Willie spread out part of the layette.

"See the featherstitching on those flannel shirts, Louisa! Willie made them from some flannel I had." Abbie showed off one daughter to the other and Louisa praised each garment, looking covertly at Willie to see how much she showed it.

"How old are you, Willie?" Louisa asked.

Willie laughed. "Twenty-one. How old are you?"

"Twenty. John's twenty-four," she volunteered with sudden transparency. "Did you teach school?" she asked Willie abruptly. Willie would never get used to the direct questions these Vermonters asked, yet somehow they weren't really rude.

"Gracious, no! I never could teach school. Whatever made you think of that?"

"Well, all the books you have." Louisa nodded toward the books that lay on the whatnot.

"Oh, those—those are just some plays I like to read."

Abbie thought she must remember to tell Orville about Willie's books. Orville set such store by book learning. But she never thought of it again until she was making Lyman's bed and found a paperbacked book under his pillow. The name on the front page was *East Lynne*. "Willie Delaney" was written in ink, and all through it there was writing in the same hand. Abbie wondered if it were good for Lyman to read plays.

Lyman seemed always to be in the parlor with Willie when he had finished his chores. Often Easy was there, sitting comfortably on one of Abbie's best rose-carved parlor chairs, watching Willie with his soft dark eyes or laughing or reaffirming what she said with "That's so, Miss Willie. That's just the way it was with us at Ashwood." Almost imperceptibly the firm sound of a *t* had crept into Easy's talk. He said "that's" instead of "tha's" now.

"Was it so very different from here down South, Willie?" Lyman asked one day.

"Oh, worlds different, Lyman. Of course, I've lived mostly in cities, in Charlestown or Richmond, but sometimes I've visited on plantations. My cousins live on plantations. Cousin Mary Lou Chestnut had the most beautiful place in the world." And Willie's hands fell on her sewing and she drew pictures of the South until Lyman could see everything.

"And the gentlemen don't try to rule the house, Lyman. They are brought up to enjoy their womenfolk and try to please them. Why, down South a gentleman would no more think of sitting when a lady came into the room than of saying his name was John Brown!"

"No, sir!" Easy emphasized.

"A gentleman always thinks of a lady's comfort first down South,"

Willie said softly, and Lyman learned manners listening to Willie.

"All Southern gentlemen shoot well," Willie said. "That's why your troops are having such a time of it." And Lyman would show new interest in going rabbit-hunting with his father's cumbersome old shotgun.

The front parlor became a wonderful place to Lyman. Always it held some fragrance of the toilet water Willie used. It came from Paris, Willie said. A gentleman had given it to her.

One evening Lyman sat with his legs sprawled out in front of him reading one of Willie's plays. "You haven't any book that isn't a play, have you, Willie?"

"No, I like plays best. If you could pull your legs in and sit like a gentleman and not scratch your head, I'll read parts with you. Here, read *Richard II*. I saw it in Washington on my way up here. Dan was there, too. You take the part of Richard II and the Duke of York and I'll take the rest."

Willie made fun of him at first. "No, Lyman, no! Read it this way. You should hear Edwin Booth say those lines!"

He began to see what she meant.

"Good! Richard is a dashing gentleman and a king, you know. Here, hold my shawl over your shoulder like this." Willie folded her Paisley so it made a cape. "Now!" He would be a dashing gentleman someday, Lyman vowed inwardly.

"Lyman, Willie!" Orville Converse called from the kitchen. "We're going to have a chapter and a prayer for our absent ones."

Willie folded the shawl and Lyman put back the Shakespeare and turned down the parlor lamp. Now it was second nature for him to step aside and let Willie go through the door first.

Easy came in from the shed, stamping snow off his feet. "Aunt Rhody sure pickin' her geese tonight. Yes, ma'm!" Easy said. "It's near two feet deep a'ready."

They all sat around the kitchen table and Orville Converse read from Isaiah. Once Willie lifted her hand and her gold bangles clinked. Once Abbie sighed, thinking of her boys. Underneath the sound of Orville's voice and the ticking of the clock they could hear the snow blowing against the window. Then they knelt in prayer, Willie and Easy and Abbie and Orville and Lyman.

"Thou seest into the blackness of each heart," Orville Converse prayed, mixing his metaphors freely, "and knowest the treachery and self-seeking that lurk in the shadows. Clean it out, we pray, purge us with fire and let there be no rotten timbers, even as Thou art purging the nation, forging a Union that will stand forever."

"Easy, wouldn't you like to sleep on the floor in the parlor tonight?" Willie asked when they were lighting their lamps for bed.

Lyman saw the shocked expression on his mother's face.

"No, thank you, Miss Willie, I'm snug as a bug out there. I got me that stove an' a feather bed." Easy grinned. "I guess I'm warmer 'n Lyman."

"Good night, Easy," Orville Converse said, and closed and barred the door.

Lyman slipped into bed between his cold sheets and drew his knees up to his chest so that his outing-flannel nightshirt completely covered his legs. He held both hands in the hollow of his thighs to warm them and shivered a little with the cold. He wished John or Dan were there beside him, he wished they were there to talk to, too. Easy might be warm out there with a stove, but he wondered if he weren't lonely. Easy must be lonely a lot of times, he thought suddenly. He was the only colored person in the whole county. Since Willie had been here, Easy seemed more like a servant, kind of Willie's houseboy. It wasn't anything Willie *meant* to do, it was just something in her voice when she spoke to him, something in her manner. They had all caught something of it from her, even his father. He thought of his father bolting the door tonight after Easy went out. How did that make Easy feel?

Lyman threw back the covers and stood out on the cold floor. Quickly he pulled on his clothes again, not minding that they had lost all their body warmth. Carrying his shoes in his hand, he tiptoed down the squeaking stairs into the kitchen. It didn't take him long to lace his boots and put on his jacket and cap. Quietly he slid the bolt and opened the door and went down the creaking planks through the woodshed that smelled faintly of the outhouse at the end of the passageway and more strongly of the damp ends of the wood piled against the lattice. It was still snowing, but it wasn't so cold out in it. Big flakes came against his face. He felt cleaner than he had upstairs in bed. Easy's tracks were already lost in the fresh snow. He ran across to the old brick smokehouse. There was a light in it.

"Easy!" he called. "Easy, it's me, Lyman."

Easy opened the door. He was all dressed, but Lyman could see that he had been lying on the bed. His books were there, schoolbooks. Easy was in the *Seventh Reader* now. He took to reading, but numbers were hard for him.

"What's the matter?" Easy asked.

"Nothing—lonesome, I guess. Thought I'd come and see you."

Easy grinned. "Sure. You hungry, too? I got some batter I can fry up."

53

"That'd taste good, Easy." Abbie expected her family to do their eating at mealtimes. "Say, it's comfortable in here."

"Sure is. I had my eye on this place a long time before ever Miss Willie came."

Lyman watched Easy greasing his griddle with a piece of salt-pork rind. Easy dropped a full spoon of batter on it and a good sizzling sound filled the little room. Lyman was studying about something. Why did Easy say that? Why was he trying to excuse Willie all the time?

"Like a hen chews with its teeth, you did!" Lyman brought out now, so long afterward that it seemed to hang in the smoky air unconnected with anything else.

"No, I did." Easy grinned. "Cross my heart and hope to die!" Easy didn't talk as Southern as Willie did, Lyman noticed. Then he forgot to notice anything but the gold-brown color of the hot cakes.

"Say, Easy, do you do this often, cook stuff at night?"

"Every time I get hungry I do." He turned the hot cakes out on a cracked and chipped plate and passed it to Lyman with a bent kitchen fork. "Help yourself to syrup." Easy ate his own with a knife. He had only one knife and one fork. They had both helped to make the syrup last spring from the maples in the sugar lot. Easy held the crock of syrup up high so the syrup fell in a long stream. "Same color as Miss Willie's hair," he said.

"Yup," Lyman answered thickly, surprised that Easy had thought about her hair too. "Say, this is great. It don't matter if it spatters or anything. Let me cook the next one."

They ate hot cakes until the batter was all used up. The last cake was no bigger than a dollar piece. Lyman threw it up in the air and they both tried to catch it in their open mouths. Lyman got it and Easy poured syrup in his mouth so it would land on the hot cake.

"Your stomach don't know the difference, boy," Easy chuckled.

Lyman lay crosswise on Easy's quilt. He was full and sleepy and warm. A delicious sense of bodily and mental comfort spread through him. Easy pushed another chunk of wood into the stove and shut the drafts. He turned down the wick of the lamp and blew it out.

"I gotta get me more oil tomorrow," he said. Then he lay beside Lyman.

"Easy, you know what I think?"

"Uh-uh."

"I think Willie was an actress." Lyman almost whispered the words.

"She don't ever live on a plantation like the Pennicooks an' be first-class white folks," Easy said in his soft melancholy voice.

"How can you tell that, Easy?"

"I just can tell. She don't treat me like she would if she were."

"You mean she'd treat you better?"

"Uh-uh. Meaner."

"Meaner?" Lyman was too sleepy to think it out. It was all mixed up. "You know those plays of hers I've been reading?"

"Uh-uh."

"Well, some of 'em have directions written in on the margin, and in the cast of *The Rivals* it has Willie Delaney opposite Lydia Languish. An' you know how she said she mostly lived in cities?"

"That's right."

"It don't make any difference. She's nice just the same!"

" 'Course she is. Dan got him a mighty fine wife."

The boys were still. Lyman felt better now that he had shared his secret.

"Easy!"

"Yeah."

"You won't ever tell?"

" 'Course not. What difference do it make whether Miss Willie's an actress or not?"

"Well, it don't."

"That's what I said."

Lyman fell asleep. Easy rolled him around lengthwise and lay down beside him so the quilt would cover both of them. Lyman flung one arm out across Easy's shoulder and they slept that way till morning.

6

MARCH 1864

THE annual spelling match was set for Valentine's Day, but it had
to be postponed to the next month because of the blizzard. Willie
had never seen so much snow. It fell silently for two solid days and
covered the stone walls and the pump and the hitching post. The lilac
bush under the snow looked like a small mountain and the verbena
bush was a little hill. The wind sprang up and blew the snow into
drifts, the windows frosted over and there was no seeing out. There
was no school. The whole family gathered in the kitchen. The little
parlor stove could not warm the parlor no matter how often it was
stoked, but Willie fled at last from the tight kitchen to her own room.

Abbie thought she was having a touch of morning sickness and
prescribed Dr. Rawson's Genuine Anti-bilious Pills that were good
for female complaints too, and brewed a strong cup of tea. Willie
drank a few swallows, enough to make her quite realistically sick,
and disappeared with Abbie's worried "I don't like to see you sick
when you're so far along, Willie. It isn't a good sign" in her ears.

But Willie knew her trouble was more than morning sickness; it
was homesickness. She was homesick for living among people, not
just one small family in a snowbound farmhouse. She wanted the
life of a city and the hubbub of the theater and young men to talk to
who made an art of talk instead of using it as a clumsy homemade
tool. She was sick to death of the food: boiled potatoes and fried salt
pork in milk gravy, baked beans for days on end, fried mush and
creamed codfish. Food was hard to get in the South with the blockade,
she knew that, but people knew how to cook what they had.

She wrote Dan humorously about it: "What I wouldn't give for
a dinner at the Willard with you! Let me tell you what I'd like, Dan:
clams on the half-shell, to begin with, and squab or partridge, and
then I think roast mutton and a plum pudding and some Dixie
Madeira, please. Did your family ever taste wine? Oh, Dan, when I see
what food you were brought up on it makes me long to show you in
your own house, *our* own house, what a fine table means in Virginia!"

Then she tore the letter into shreds and dropped it into the parlor
stove. Dan was living on worse food than this, in camp some place.

She mustn't whine. She wrapped the Paisley tightly around her and stood in front of the futile little stove, moving her fingers over the heat to take the stiffness out of them. She turned to warm her back, but her feet ached with the cold. The windows were opaque panels that admitted only a dreary light. At last she took refuge in the warmth of the feather bed and lay there fully dressed, crooning to herself and the new life within her:

"Baby, I wish we were back down South where we belong. I don't want you born in Vermont and I'll never let you live here. I'll never let your father live here. . . ." She reached up under one of the pillows and found the packet of Dan's letters, tied with a ribbon. Holding it helped some. She pulled the silk quilt closer and blocked out the sound of the wind blowing the snow against the walls of the house.

"Miss Willie?" Easy called in a low voice outside the door. "Miss Willie, are you asleep?"

"No, I'm not asleep. What is it, Easy? Did you go for the mail?"

"No, ma'am, Miss Willie, ain't no one can go for mail. All we done is feed the stock today. It's still driftin' bad." Willie heard the lid of the stove lifted and knew he was filling the stove again. "Miss Willie, Mistah Converse said to tell you it's time to practice the spelling."

"You tell Mr. Converse I don't care whether I ever learn to spell or not." Willie's voice was half-smothered in the pillows.

Easy was silent in the parlor. Then he said, "Yes, ma'am, but Mistah Converse sets a pow'ful store by spelling. Seems like you gotta know how to spell up North."

"Tell Mr. Converse that I'm not going to stay up North and I don't want to learn one more word."

"I knows how you feel," Easy said gently. "I feels the same way myself, but we gotta learn, Miss Willie, 'cause we're up North now."

"Bother!" Easy could hear a pillow hitting the floor. "That old man would make a good slave-driver, don't you think so, Easy?"

"Yes, ma'am. Mistah Converse'd do all right," Easy agreed, and his laugh was a warm sound in the cold parlor. "I'll tell him you be right out."

"I suppose so," Willie grumbled. "But I wouldn't do it for anyone but Daniel Converse."

The whole family was gathered in the kitchen. Four lamps illumined the dark-brown walls and gilded the gold picture on the door of the steeple clock. Abbie was knitting her interminable socks. Lyman sat against the wall making a cat's cradle with a piece of yarn beneath the edge of the table. Easy was waiting solemnly. Closest to the stove of anyone was Orville Converse with *Webster's Speller* open on his knee.

"Willie, you sit there by Abbie."

Abbie gave her an anxious glance. "I'm fine," Willie murmured, laying her hand on Abbie's sprigged merino skirt in a rare gesture of friendliness, almost of pity at her meekness. There was a hushed atmosphere in the kitchen as though of school or church.

"We'll begin with the fifth-form spelling and work on up," Orville announced formally to his family. "Ezekiel, appetite."

"A-p, ap, p-e-t, pet, appet, i-t-e, ite, appetite," Easy rattled glibly. Easy had improved in spelling.

"Lyman, niece!"

"N-i, ni, e-c-e, ece, niece." Lyman had difficulty cutting the word properly. It was sometimes an art.

"Abbie, Mississippi." Abbie spelled most swiftly of all, never pausing in her knitting.

Willie hated these spelling drills. They had spent many winter evenings this way. Willie had learned to read and write and add and subtract from a plantation governess on the plantation of one of her cousins. For the rest, she had learned most from her father's playbooks. Spelling was not stressed. She fastened and unfastened the catch on her bangle, waiting her turn. It was not easy to miss a word with Father Converse.

"Willie, interpolate."

Willie spelled rapidly as though she knew it. "I-n-t-e-r-p, interp, o-l-a-t-e, interpolate."

"Divide your word properly, Willie. There is less danger of missing. Now take it again."

"I-n, in, t-e-r, ter, inter, p-o-l, interpol, a-t-e, ate, interpolate." Now for five counts she was free again, and then there would finally be the chapter from the Bible and prayers and her own bed again. The clock crawled to nine.

"Willie, irresistible." Willie gave a weary sigh.

"I-r, ir, r-e-s, res, irres, i-s-t, ist, irresist, a-b-l-e, irresistable."

"Wrong." Orville Converse had a triumphant way of saying it. Willie's eyes flashed. She didn't heed Abbie's hand laid comfortingly on hers nor see Lyman's eyes on her.

"I-b-l-e then. I don't care which it is, ible, able, ible, able," she almost shouted at him.

Orville Converse looked at his daughter-in-law in pained amazement. "Why, Willie, I am only trying to help you make up for what has clearly been a weakness in your education."

"Mr. Converse, don't you worry any more about the weakness in my education. I imagine you have some in yours." Suddenly, unpredictably, Willie burst into tears, half hysterical-woman tears, half little-girl sobs. Then she rushed from the kitchen into her bedroom and flung herself again on her bed.

Orville Converse stroked his beard sheepishly. "Why, I never thought . . . What struck the girl?"

For once Abbie wasn't meek. "Orville Converse, that poor child's going to have a baby. Isn't that enough? Her mind's on something else than spelling words," she stormed, putting him completely to rout with the eternal mystery of maternity.

While Orville read the Scriptures that night Abbie went right on heating milk on the stove. She added a pinch of ginger and stirred it in spite of the noise the spoon made. She waited impatiently for the prayer to be over, and then took it in to Willie to drink.

"There, child, Mr. Converse understands," she told Willie, stroking her hair gently. "You just sleep late tomorrow if you feel like it."

And Willie, tucked in by Abbie's hands and warmed by the hot milk, thought for the first time since the cold weather began that Dan's home was a good place to be.

The spelling match was held in March. A thaw came the first of the month, and the roads were open. The schoolhouse was crowded back to the doors. Everyone was glad to get into town to discuss the latest war news and President Lincoln's second inauguration. Willie had talked of not going, but she made herself a new sack from an old skirt and trimmed it with little braided tabs that cunningly helped to disguise her condition. The sack was dark-gray over a fawn-colored skirt, and she wore a plume in her hat.

"There," she told herself in the mirror, "you look like one of Jeb Stuart's boys!" Willie was so glad for the excitement and the chance to see people again that she forgot the hostility she had felt in church. She waved to Louisa across the schoolroom and smiled back at Philinda Bragg's round staring gaze fixed on her hat and dress.

The Reverend Mr. Leland was to pronounce the words, and afterward the ladies of the Sanitary Commission would sell coffee and cakes to make money for their work with the soldiers. There was a whisper that Abe Marsh had a barrel of cider somewhere back of the school, hard cider, but that was only a whisper.

Willie looked wonderingly at the bare, smoke-stained walls of the schoolroom and thought of rooms lighted by crystal candelabra and papered in damask. She thought what a story she could make of these grown-up Vermonters whose idea of entertainment was a spelling match in a schoolhouse.

Two sides formed along the wall, with great laughing and joking. The men had to be drawn away from talking politics and the women from their visiting. Children lined up, too. Ten years old was the minimum age. Orville Converse was the head of one side, Dr. Tucker, Louisa's father, of the other. They took turns choosing. When Orville Converse chose his daughter-in-law on the fourth choice Willie gave him a little bow and the faint shadow of a smile. She was aware that everyone was looking at her as she took her place, but she forbore to pull her shawl more closely and instead walked proudly. This was not her first entrance on a stage. Willie didn't look as though the ride down the hill had hurt her any, Abbie thought.

Lyman hoped his father would choose him next so he could stand by Willie, but he chose one of the Ingram girls next and Louisa's father chose Lyman.

The Reverend Mr. Leland began with the words in the *Third Reader*. The spelling was rapid. "Hesitate—h-e-s, hes, i, hesi, t-a-t-e, tate, hesitate. Obscure—o-b, ob, s-c-u-r-e, scure, obscure"—on down to the *Fourth* and *Fifth* and *Sixth Readers*. Willie was still up. The ranks were thinning now.

"Enunciate"—"catastrophe" . . .

Lyman hoped his words would be hard. He was a good speller. Easy went down on "nymph." He shook his head and grinned. Someone laughed, and the whole room was laughing. In his embarrassment Easy stumbled over the foot of the school desk and fell against it. Lyman, standing tall against the wall, scowled. Why did people laugh at Easy more quickly than at a white person? Why did Easy take it so good-naturedly? Easy was no clown for people to laugh at, but when people laughed at him he changed and grinned back like a clown, or a "nigger." He, Lyman, resented it.

Abbie spelled without a trace of hesitation. Orville had admired her spelling in the days when he was "sparking" her. Once he and she had spelled out against each other and Abbie had won. The word Orville had gone down on was "phthisis" and she had consoled him afterward by telling him it was really a medical word.

There were seven on one side now and five on the other. The schoolroom was hot. Some of the small children were asleep in their mothers' arms. Fat Mrs. Peabody fanned herself with her husband's hat. Back of the schoolroom the sound of dishes clinking against each other told that food was being prepared. Over in one corner three men sat together. Obadiah Tuttle was drawing the map of Gettysburg on a slate he had found on a bench.

"Now this here's Cemetery Ridge and Pickett, he . . ."

"Tintinnabulation," the Reverend Mr. Leland gave Willie. Her cheeks were scarlet now. She had a way of spelling that drew attention to her, or perhaps it was the sound of her Southern accent against these others.

"Tintype," Lyman spelled. If it worked out so that he spelled just before Willie he would miss one just so she could spell it, he plotted to himself.

"Toupee." Louisa Tucker spelled swiftly.

The Reverend Mr. Leland finished with the *Ninth Speller* and took the dictionary. Now came the showdown. The spellers shifted from one foot to the other or stood more erectly against the wall. It didn't occur to anyone to ask for an intermission.

The Reverend Mr. Leland began with the *e*'s. The *z*'s were the last resort. Orville Converse was proud of his daughter-in-law. She had missed such words as "surprise" and "bouquet" when she first came. There was nothing like constant spelling drills!

Adam Sedgely went down on "ebullience" and Abbie spelled it. "Eschew" took gray-haired Benjamin Potter. As he went to his seat he said loudly that he thought the Reverend was trying to get him to sneeze. The schoolroom rocked with laughter. There had been so little laughter this winter that everyone was ready to laugh. Someone propped open the front door with a stick of wood and a fresh wave of cold blew over the hot room until the women shivered and covered their babies and it had to be shut again.

"Erysipelas" mowed down two from each side. It came to Lyman. He hesitated. "Erysipelas" was an old favorite, but he doubted if Willie could handle it, so he spelled it. Willie had "escutcheon." There was a little sighing sound of admiration when she spelled it correctly.

"What does it mean?" the small Potter boy whispered loudly to his father.

"Espionage" Louisa had. Louisa had asked Lyman how the President could be sure Willie wasn't a spy like that Rose Greenhow you read about.

"E-u, eu, c-h-a-r, car, euchar, i-s-t, ist, eucharist," Abbie spelled. She was watching Willie. Her face was too flushed, but then, she was standing right under the long stovepipe. Orville would think more of Willie after tonight. Abbie would write this all to Dan. His father had whipped Dan many a time for missing his spelling words.

The Reverend Isaac flipped over the pages of the dictionary rapidly. The spellers waited tensely to see where he would pause. Willie's turn was next. He pursed his lips, his piercing eyes under heavy brows fixed hers.

"Rebellion," he announced sternly.

A tiny sound no louder than the rustle of a taffeta skirt rose in the room. Abbie bit her lips. Willie had been wondering if she could stand up any longer. She had been going to miss this next word just in order to sit down. Now she lifted her head. Her eyes narrowed ever so little.

"R-e, re, b-e-l, bel, rebel, i-o-n, yun, rebellion," she spelled triumphantly.

Lyman caught his breath. Orville Converse's face was dark in a scowl. The little Potter boy tittered. Louisa shook her head. Willie's hand clutched at her shawl. "No, it's two *l*'s!"

"I am sorry, Mrs. Converse, I am afraid you were short one brigade. Wrong!" the Reverend Mr. Leland ruled. "Next."

Willie glared at him an instant and then started for her seat. Suddenly, the boards between the front of the room and the first bench rose up to meet her. The hot-iron smell of the stove and the odor of winter clothes long worn choked her. Pain twisted in her body. Abbie saw her face go white and went swiftly to her, but not before she sank down on the rising boards less gracefully than she had fainted on the boards of the Richmond theater.

Orville and Lyman lifted her up onto one of the benches with Abbie's arm to lean against.

"I'm sorry," she whispered softly. "I knew there were two *l*'s."

Orville Converse scowled. "You and I had better finish the spelling, Lyman. Abbie, you take Willie to Louisa's. Easy can drive you down."

The Reverend Mr. Leland resorted now to the *z*'s. Orville Converse won the match. Lyman went down on "zither," spelling it with a *y*. As soon as he could he slipped out of the schoolhouse and walked rapidly through the village to Louisa's. Someone in the schoolroom had whispered that Willie might have her baby before the night was over. Would she?

"Gosh all hemlock!" he muttered under his breath as he walked along. "Gosh all hemlock!"

Easy opened the kitchen door when he knocked. Lyman was suddenly embarrassed even with Easy. "I just came to see if Mother wanted anything." He felt he had to explain.

"Missus Converse sure wanted plenty a little while ago, all at the same time, but now there isn't nothin' to do but wait an' keep the fire goin' an' I'm doing that."

"Is she . . . Do you know how she is, Easy?"

"Yes, sir. She's goin' to have her baby born right here, Missus Converse says, but ain't nobody can tell how long it'll take."

And then both boys heard a moan. It made Lyman swallow

quickly. It came again. That was Willie! Lyman looked quickly at Easy and away again.

"It must hurt her to make her cry like that," he whispered, digging his fingernails into the flesh of his palms, wishing that he could put his fingers in his ears so he couldn't hear her.

"Guess it allus hurts to get 'em borned," Easy said. "White folks worse than colored. My mammy allus help 'em at the big house. She help borned 'em all and nursed three of 'em."

"Nursed 'em?"

"Sure."

Lyman tried not to look as he felt about such a thing. If women in the South were like Willie, how could they let a Negro woman nurse their babies? Quick steps sounded on the stairs and Abbie Converse came out to the kitchen looking flushed and hurried. They both looked up guiltily.

"Here, Easy, carry up this water for me. Lyman, run back over to the schoolhouse and tell your father to come here."

Lyman went quickly. The whole dark street had a waiting stillness about it. There was a knot of men outside the store and both lamps inside were lighted. He could see Ebenezer Gillette and Ezra Whitcomb. They were the kind who never went to spelling matches. He doubted if he would either when he grew up. Both contestants and spectators were eating pie and drinking coffee when Lyman went into the schoolhouse. He felt everyone's eyes on him almost as though he had war news.

His father drove silently up the street and left him to hitch the horse to the iron hitching post. Light streamed out of the upstairs window of Louisa's house onto the stone stoop and laid a bright white patch halfway down the front walk. Lyman sat down on the stoop in the half-cold March night, held there by the tremendous happenings inside the house, not wanting to go in but not wanting to leave. He was glad when Easy came around the side path of the house.

"You, Lyman?"

"Yeah. Is the baby born?"

"Not yet," Easy said. "She called for Daniel once."

Lyman wondered about Dan, somewhere down in Virginia. How would you feel if you had . . . begotten a child? That was what the Bible called it. Orville begat Jonathan and Daniel and Lyman, and Daniel begat . . . The cold spring air stirred Lyman strangely.

"I reckon Daniel feel mighty proud when he know he got him a child," Easy said.

"Gosh all hemlock, yes!" Lyman answered. "Have you ever thought how you'd feel, Easy?" he ventured shyly in the dark.

"Uh-huh." Easy nodded. "Someday I'm goin' to have to go back down South and get me a girl," Easy said. " 'Less I dye one brown with butternut juice."

Lyman hadn't thought about it, but there weren't any colored girls in Painesville of course. It must make Easy feel queer.

The light faded suddenly and the windows above them were dark.

"I guess it's over," Lyman said uncertainly.

"I don't hear no baby cry. I been listening for it," Easy said knowingly.

The door opened and the boys stepped quickly off the stoop.

"Father, is Willie . . . all right?"

"She'll be fine tomorrow. Daniel has a daughter," Orville Converse said proudly.

Abbie stayed with Willie that night in Louisa's house under the elms. Orville and the two boys drove up the hill to the farm. There was only the sound of the horses' hoofs and the wheels turning on the wet mud road.

"Wake up, boys!" Orville said when they were home, but neither boy had been asleep.

7

IT was the last week in May when Lyman and Easy drove the wagon over to Malden depot. The woods along the road were green and smelled sweet. The sudden white of a trillium or Solomon's seal caught the boys' eyes. May apples were all through the woods, and a jack-in-the-pulpit grew right out of the bank close to the road. The brook along one side of the road ran noisily. The air was so warm they had no need of coats, but they wore them. Lyman's best black boots felt stiff.

"Butterflies are thick as houseflies in here," Easy said, and it was the first time either of them had spoken for a mile.

"Funny they don't live longer," Lyman answered. The blinding bright yellow of a butterfly's wings was too bright today. That its life was so short was a satisfaction. He gathered up the reins and chirruped to the horses. They wanted to get there before Mother did. Dr. Tucker was driving Abbie over in the surrey and would bring Louisa and Father back with them. Lyman glanced back at the wagon swept out clean and lined with cedar boughs. It might have been decorated for a Fourth of July parade.

There were plenty of people at the Malden station. Some were waiting for the Boston papers, afraid yet eager for the latest news, some were there to meet their wounded that were drifting back from the Battle of the Wilderness. They stood anxiously, mouthing over the little they knew about the battle, about the losses. Some, like the Converse family, were waiting for their dead.

Thirteen boys from the little valley had died in the Battle of the Wilderness. Nobody knew yet how many were wounded. Lyman drove under the shade of a maple tree as near the station platform as he dared.

"Easy, you better stay near the horses' heads, the engine might scare 'em." Lyman assumed command today and Easy made no protest out of respect to the dead. Then Lyman saw his mother and Dr. Tucker and went to tie their horse up for them. Willie was home with the baby, Juliet. Abbie wore black and her face under her bonnet was pale and her eyes red.

"I'll be right over there," Lyman said, and went back to sit on the front seat of the wagon. Easy perched on a barrel on the platform close by.

"Sure seems good to see a lot of folks," Easy said to Lyman. "Folks don't bunch up much in Vermont."

Lyman only grunted. He didn't want to talk Now before the train came in he must make the fact that Jonathan was dead seem real. He didn't quite believe it. He hadn't cried a drop, and he wondered why. He kept thinking about John, his own brother, who hadn't wanted to go back after his leave—John, the tallest of the Converse boys, the one with the deep cleft in his chin and the scar where he cut his lip that time, the one who was promised to Louisa Tucker. Now, thinking back, it seemed to Lyman that John had never really teased him very much, hadn't teased him at all. Oh, the time about the snipe-hunting, but that was nothing. The time John had laughed at him when he got stung by hornets and his face swelled up. . . . Lyman sat still on the wagon seat, seeing John laughing. When John got started laughing he'd kind of snort as though he had hiccoughs. John was a private still. That was funny, when he had joined up with Dan and Dan was a captain in the cavalry now. John was infantry, he must have walked the whole time.

Lyman had read the letter so many times he knew it by heart. It was written in the hospital by a man named Walt Whitman. "Your Jonathan was shot through the lungs in the Battle of the Wilderness," the man wrote. He said he might linger on a week, that there wasn't any real hope for him, but he thought he was comfortable. Mr. Whitman said he would always remember "his bloodless, brown-skinned face with eyes full of determination. . . . He was delighted with a stick of horehound candy I gave him."

"That don't sound like John," Abbie had said, "but it's true he always did like horehound candy."

Father and Louisa had gone right away on the stage. Dr. Tucker hadn't wanted Louisa to go, and his mother and father had urged her not to. It was Willie who said, "She'll never forgive you if you don't let her go." Willie had given Father the address of a place to stay in Washington that wasn't as expensive as the hotels, which maybe wouldn't have a vacant room anyway, and she wrote a note to the woman who ran it, a Mrs. Surratt. Willie told Father where the hospital was and where to buy things for John, if he needed them. It was a good thing that she knew Washington so well.

They couldn't tell from Father's telegram whether he and Louisa reached there before John died or not. The telegram just said:

JOHN DIED LAST NIGHT. ARRIVE MALDEN WITH BODY FRIDAY. MEET TRAIN.

The hearse was spoken for when Lyman went to see Mr. Green about it, and he would be making trips all day. Then Lyman had suggested their own wagon. It didn't look as sad as Mr. Green's hearse anyway. He was glad their own horses were taking John's body up home.

There was the other thing that Lyman had to think about: enlisting. They needed more men. The selectmen of the town had had to raise the bounty to get soldiers. The army was taking Negroes and foreigners. He was seventeen now. Plenty of boys had gone in younger than that. General Grant's own son went through the Battle of Vicksburg at fourteen! Father didn't want him to go, but now that John was killed things were different. In the bright morning light Lyman's face was set. His brown eyes paled to the color of a shallow pool of water and had green flecks. Perhaps it was the thinness of his neck rising from too large a shirt collar that made him look so young. He measured five feet ten against the barn door.

Dr. Tucker was standing on the platform now, hands behind his back the way he stood by your bed when you were sick. Mother was there, too, talking to the minister's wife. Easy still sat on his barrel. His was the only dark face on the platform.

"The Vermont troops were the first to start the fighting in this battle!" the station agent was saying. "Grant mentioned 'em in his report. I've got the piece from the paper up at the house. Whitney's going to put it in the *Times.*"

A man standing near Lyman's wagon spat and wiped his white beard. "I guess the rebs know by this time 't the Vermonters hev got 'em all beat for fightin'."

And John was one of them! John was out in front with bullets coming right at him. Lyman's hands were cold on his knees. Was John glad he'd gone back? If John had got Abe Hopkins to go for him, he could be here now, starting to plant on the Spring place. He could be marrying Louisa and begetting a child, like Dan. Instead he was shot, in a strange faraway place called the Wilderness.

The train whistle sounded over the valley, long-drawn out and shrill and lonesome, as though it said the strange and awful words "the Wilderness" in this sunny place that had been cut out of the wilderness so long ago that nothing of the wildness remained. The talk subsided and a tense waiting fell upon the people there.

As the train pulled into the station Lyman jumped down over the wheel and went toward the tracks. He saw Louisa first, standing on the platform behind his father, and he looked away quickly and let his eyes travel along the little curtained windows of the train to the baggage car. Lyman and Dr. Tucker and Father and Easy helped the baggageman slide the long pine box into the wagon. Lyman gripped the corner of the coffin so hard his fingers ached, but he didn't really believe what he was doing. He felt Louisa standing there by Mother all the time, though he didn't look around.

"Gently there."

"Tilt your end a little!"

On top of the box was written in black crayon: "Pvt. Jonathan Ridgeway Converse, First Vermont Regiment, Painesville, Vermont."

"We didn't wait to have a plate engraved. We wanted to get right home," Father said. Mother was crying. Louisa laid a branch of the cedar on top of the long box. Then one of the ladies of the Christian Sanitary Commission brought a flag to lay on top. The flag was pretty against the green.

"All right, boys. You drive on ahead." Father's voice didn't sound quite natural.

"I'll ride with them," Louisa said softly.

"No, Louisa, you come with us." Her father led her over to the carriage.

"Did you get there before he died, Orville?" Mother almost whispered the question, but they could all hear it clear enough.

"No," Father said in a low voice. "He died the night before—our train was ten hours late. We met Mr. Whitman. He said John went to sleep like a tired boy."

Lyman's eyes met Louisa's. He hadn't meant to look at her. Her eyes were brown. They made him think of a squirrel he had trapped once, its eyes were like that, kind of bright and uneasy. Her mouth was closed together so the red edges were thin. That other time when she hadn't heard from John for a long time her face was sad, but not like this. Maybe she was sorry she hadn't married John before he went away.

Lyman climbed up in the wagon, glad for the long drive before they reached home. And when they got there he could go for the cows. Tomorrow would be the funeral. He had known where the Converse lot was in the older cemetery on the hill, but he had never thought of someone in their family being buried there, someone like John.

When they met a buggy or a wagon on the road the people in the other vehicle bowed gravely the way people did in church. Even Mr. Davis, who always joked, just nodded and looked at the coffin under the flag. Lyman felt proud when people passed. He almost wished he was the one killed and coming back up home under the flag.

He and Easy didn't talk much, nothing to show what went on in their minds.

Easy said, "John liked to farm best of all of you." And Lyman agreed.

"He always wanted to farm the Spring place," Lyman added.

The carriage with the folks in it passed them in Painesville. Mother and Father had left Louisa and Dr. Tucker at their house in the village.

"Take it slowly, boys," Father called out, but they were driving slowly anyway—it was just something to say. Lyman thought how sad their backs looked up ahead. Mother's head looked small in that black bonnet and Father's head was bowed a little. Lyman's throat ached, or maybe it was his head. He wished he could get out of the wagon and run a little way. How did John feel about dying? Anyway, you didn't feel when you were dead.

"Swing low, sweet chariot . . ." Easy began to sing. For an instant Lyman was shocked. He wondered uneasily if the folks could hear. They were past the last house in the village now and going through the covered bridge that led up the hill. Easy sang the words over and over until they seemed to run with the turning of the wheels. Maybe Easy was singing to Jonathan. The old wagon was the chariot.

". . . comin' for to carry me home," Easy sang.

Lyman let himself hum just under the sound of Easy's singing. He glanced quickly at Easy. His eyes were fixed on the road far ahead. What was he thinking? How did he feel about John?

"What you thinking, Easy?" he asked as Easy came to a pause in his song.

Easy shrugged and shook his head. "Ain't thinkin' nothin', just singin'. You can't think when you sing, can you?"

"Rock o' my soul in de bosom of Abraham, Rock o' my soul in de bo . . . som . . ." Easy moved his head slowly to the music. His face was mournful, empty of expression.

But you thought even when you sang, of course you did, at least he did—you couldn't help yourself. That was the trouble, you always had to be thinking, all the time. But maybe Easy was different, maybe he didn't have to think when he sang.

Easy repeated the same words so many times that Lyman sang finally along with him. That was almost all there was to the song, just that same line over and over again. The wheels rolled over the road as they sang. It did make the way seem shorter. The folks were way ahead now, they could sing out. After a while it didn't seem to matter that the song said so little.

"Jordan's mills a-grinding . . ." Easy sang out.

"Jordan's mills a-grinding," Lyman echoed. The two of them brought John home to music.

The day of the funeral was like a Sabbath, only it rested on Lyman with a heavier weight. After the cows were milked and breakfast was over he got into his best clothes and walked around the house waiting for the funeral service. Mother was busy in the kitchen and there were neighbors in to help. Willie was hanging up baby clothes on the line. Those were things that had to be done. A day like this was easier for women than men. He and his father were solemnly idle. Lyman walked over to the butternut tree and stood watching Willie.

Willie smiled. "Why, Lyman, you look so grown-up in that dark suit! You're as handsome as your brother Dan, I do believe." She went on past in her pink-calico dress that looked queer without the hoops in it. He was too embarrassed to say anything at first. He glanced anxiously toward the kitchen windows hoping his mother wouldn't look out. Then he followed Willie.

"Let me carry your basket, Willie," he said, though they were only a few steps from the woodshed.

Willie laughed. "Now that was worthy of a Southern gentleman! I must hurry and change my dress. Louisa will be here any moment."

"Louisa looks awfully sad," Lyman said.

"Yes, she does, but maybe it's just as well, Lyman. Louisa hardly knew John. I could tell from little things she said about him. I suppose the war changed him. I don't think she would have been happy with him, or he with her."

Lyman went upstairs to his own room. He had to stoop at the doorway now because of the gable. He was thinking about what Willie had said. It didn't make him feel any better about Louisa. She was sort of cheated any way you looked at it, if she'd lost John even before he was killed. "Changed," Willie said. That would hurt her if she knew it. Somehow he couldn't bear to have Louisa hurt.

Then his eyes found himself in the mirror. He leaned closer, rubbing his jaw with the side of his finger. The soft hair was a little stiffer. After all, he was almost seventeen. "You're as handsome as your brother Dan," Willie had said, only Dan was dark. He turned away, ashamed at losing his sadness on the day of John's funeral.

The lilac bushes were in full bloom along the stone wall of the cemetery. It was better outdoors under the sky than in the parlor at home. Lyman moved his toe carefully and turned the green grass-blades the other way. He read the epitaphs on the stones around him while the minister preached. The nearest was "To the memory of Abigail, beloved wife of Obadiah Weatherbee, who departed this life February 15th, 1784. Died in childbirth." Lyman looked at the weeping willow cut in the slate headstone. John's was going to be better than slate, his was granite. Lyman didn't see why they couldn't use soapstone from their own quarry, it was so much smoother than granite. Father said it wore away too easily, but only the corners wore away. He would have soapstone himself, anyway. Father had had Lyman copy off the inscription for the stonecutter. He had made another copy for Mother to keep in the family Bible. He did it in colored inks with clasped hands and a dove with laurel in its mouth and his finest penmanship. It read:

Jonathan Ridgeway Converse
April 4, 1839
April 28, 1864
Killed in the Slaveholders' Rebellion

Vengeance is mine, saith the Lord

Mother had wanted a different verse underneath, but Father said, "I want it just like that."

People were getting into their buggies outside the stone wall. Wheels flattened the new spring grass as they drove out toward the road leaving John behind. Some of the families who lived on the hill walked home, some lingered waiting to speak to the Converses. Lyman stood awkwardly near his father. When he remembered that Willie had said he looked grown-up he felt more comfortable.

"Brother Converse, it isn't as though he weren't a Christian," Ephraim Whipple said.

"No, I take great comfort in that," Orville Converse answered heavily.

Lyman walked on ahead. He tried to remember John praying or reading his Bible. He hadn't known him very well either, no better than Louisa had.

Lyman came up behind two women whose skirts filled the path.

"Louisa Tucker's only twenty-one. She's apt to marry just the same," Mrs. Davis said.

"You can't tell a thing about it, but she's the quiet kind. I wouldn't wonder a mite to see her die an old maid," Mrs. Bragg answered. "Anyone can see her heart's about broken."

Lyman climbed over the stone wall to get past them. He had a sudden terrible fear lest he meet Louisa.

Supper was a difficult meal. They all felt an empty place at the table, as though John had just gone away. They ate in the dining-room with all who were related either to the Holbrook or the Converse families. Louisa and her father ate with them, but Lyman took care not to look her way. He felt her sitting there across the table, two down from where he was, quiet and hardly eating anything. He heard his Aunt Jennie urge her to have a biscuit.

"Louisa, you could stand fleshening up!"

And he heard Louisa say, "No, thank you, I really don't care for any." Lyman admired her firmness with Aunt Jennie. He himself could never say no to her.

The men of the family talked about Grant and Meade and Lincoln, and like a sinister refrain the words "the Wilderness" crept in.

"The New York *Herald* says the Battle of the Wilderness was the costliest battle of the war," Cousin Amos Ridgeway said sternly.

"In the Vermont Brigade four out of five colonels and fifty line officers were killed or wounded," Dr. Tucker said. "I feared for John when I read the toll of casualties."

"Did you see the President, Cousin Orville?" Mary Baxter, who was born a Ridgeway, asked.

"No, but I guess I could if I'd waited around a little. They say he's just as common as any of us."

"I take three spoonfuls of sugar in my coffee, Abbie, don't you remember?" her brother-in-law said reproachfully. "I hear tell the Secesh are paying ten dollars a pound for sugar—when they can get it!" he added with satisfaction.

"Why didn't your brother's wife from Rhode Island come, Abbie?" Aunt Jennie asked.

"Matilda sent a telegram to say she couldn't," Abbie answered. "It's a long way from Providence."

"Do they still hold Nathaniel's stock in the quarry, Orville?" his brother asked.

"Oh, yes, Nathaniel always felt the quarry was a gilt-edged investment, and the business is growing."

Lyman ate his pie. He had only a faint memory of Uncle Nathaniel Holbrook coming on a visit with a little girl about his own age. This uncle was the only member of the family who had left Vermont and settled in the city. Lyman remembered Uncle Nate as an elegant person who wore a gold watch chain across his vest and smoked cigars.

"I expect it's crowded in Washington, Orville?" his brother from Brattleboro way asked.

"Yes, but they've got the Capitol dome finished, and it makes a handsome building of it."

"Did you stay in a hotel?" Henry's wife wanted to know. Even the funeral could not lessen their eagerness to hear about Orville's trip.

"No," Orville Converse said. "Daniel's wife sent us to a friend who keeps a boardinghouse, a Mrs. Surratt." His eyes moved across the table and met Willie's.

"It's a very modest place, but Mrs. Surratt is the soul of kindness," Willie said, wondering how her father-in-law had liked it there.

At last the funeral meats were eaten and the relatives drove off. They had plenty to talk of on the way home: about Daniel's wife, "almost too pretty, though Abbie did say she was a good hand to help," and "the baby takes more after Daniel." "Didn't that girl that was promised to John look poorly!" "That colored boy that hitched up the horse! If Orville don't have to pay him anything, how is that different from having a slave, Amos Ridgeway, tell me that?" his wife demanded on the way home.

Abbie folded her best black taffeta and laid it smoothly in the drawer of the tall chest. As she felt the stiff folds against her fingers the sadness that the day's busyness had kept in check possessed her. This was the drawer in which she used to hide maple-sugar cakes from Jonathan when he was just a little thing in dresses. He couldn't pull the heavy drawer open by himself. She twisted her fingers around the knob thinking of his fingers there. Tears she had kept back all day rolled down her face. Then she heard Orville. He stood in the bedroom doorway holding the big black family Bible.

"I've entered Jonathan's death, Abbie," he said, and the finality of his voice raised a fresh wave of anguish in her heart. Jonathan, her first child, part of her youth. Now she was forty-three and Jonathan was gone. She mustn't cry while Orville could see her.

Orville blew out the light. The familiar sound of his clothes as he laid them on the chair and pulled on his nightshirt comforted her a little. He raised the window to the first peg and wound his watch, and the rasping sounds seemed to be measuring off the short span of mortality.

"I learned a good deal about Daniel's wife, Abbie, from that boardinghouse keeper."

"It was fine that Willie knew some place where you could stay," Abbie answered. What did Orville mean? Something bad?

"She was an actress!" Orville announced sternly to the darkness.

Abbie caught her breath. "Are you sure, Orville?"

"Mrs. Surratt supposed I knew it. She said her son thought she was one of the best actresses in the South. An actor fellow brought her up from Richmond with him. She acted in a theater in Washington. That's where Daniel met her," Orville said with ominous emphasis.

"But I don't see how Daniel would meet a . . . an actress in the army," Abbie said faintly.

"I guess Daniel saw her act and then . . . made a point of meeting her. He was around Washington a good while in '61 and '62, you know."

"She don't act bold, Orville, or paint herself up or . . . or anything."

"I've doubted for a long time whether she's a confessing Christian, though."

"Oh, Orville, she will be, only don't hurry her," Abbie pleaded, fearful of the way Orville would go at it, of the sparks in Willie's eyes.

"I wish Daniel could have married a girl like Louisa," Orville said in a voice that was close to a groan.

"Poor Louisa," Abbie whispered. Orville lay in bed and the bed cords sagged in their familiar way. "Orville, don't say anything to Willie about . . . about being an actress or about the other, being a Christian, yet, please."

"She might have known I'd hear when she sent me to that boardinghouse. Most of 'em there were actor folk," Orville said.

They lay a long time in the dark, silently.

"Orville," Abbie asked timidly. "Orville, do you think Willie could be a bad influence on Lyman?"

"What can we do about it, Abbie? She's here till Daniel gets back home." They were still again, separate each in his own worries and sadness. "With the quarry taking all my time I've only kept this farm for Jonathan. I thought some day he could join it to the Spring place he always had his eye on. Dan and Lyman will have the quarry when we're gone," Orville said. And Abbie, feeling his sadness, moved against him and laid her hand on his shoulder, two human beings huddled together in the Wilderness.

8

LYMAN boarded the afternoon stage for Malden half a mile beyond the town. He was thankful that the one passenger, a stranger, was sitting beside the driver so he didn't have to talk to him.

It seemed to Lyman that he had never wanted anything before this—little childish wants, maybe—that it would be clear so they could have a picnic, or that the peddler would have a steel-bladed pocket-knife, things like that—but he had not wanted these things as he wanted this today. He had wanted Ned back after he had given him to the army, but that was a hopeless wanting that had spread an ache inside him like a stomachache. This was different, there was nothing hopeless about this. They had called for men again, hadn't they? "Not younger than twenty-one without the consent of parents." He had taken care of that. He took out of his pocket the note he had written last night in his best penmanship. He read it again and was pleased with it.

To Whom it may concern:
This is to certify that I am agreeable and willing for my son, Lyman Webster Converse, to enlist in the army.

> *Very truly yours,*
> *Orville Converse*

June 10, 1864

He thought about the uniform he would have, like Dan's. He had tried on Dan's cap with the green fir-tree insignia of Vermont on it. He had handled Dan's gun and felt the edge of the bayonet. Maybe Louisa would make him a housewife mending kit to carry as she had John, with his name embroidered on it. He had rolled John's blanket for him into a neat sausage and he knew just how to do it.

His name would go down in the town record and they would give him a bonus for enlisting, but he wouldn't take it. If he were killed, he'd have seen some fighting first, anyway. Maybe he could get into the Army of the Potomac with Meade and be with them when they took Richmond. He would see all the places Willie talked about.

Maybe he would be mentioned in a dispatch for bravery and Dan would read it. "Lyman Converse—why, that's my brother's name!" Dan would say. And when he saw Dan there wouldn't be any difference in their ages at all. On the way back, after he enlisted, he would stop and tell Louisa he was taking Jonathan's place, that he would kill a rebel to pay back—no, avenge was better—avenge his death.

He crossed his legs again and rested his chin on his hand, staring at the familiar road but not seeing it. He would probably take the train from Malden, since he was enlisting there. He had never been over the mountain, and suddenly that mountain seemed to hem him in. The train whistle would sound differently if he were on the train. Train whistles were for people staying home in the little villages along the way, they didn't matter to those who were going with the train. When he came back after the war he might only come to see the folks and then go away again. He would be too old for school by that time.

Easy would have to do his chores. After all those Negro soldiers were killed at Fort Pillow, folks had talked about recruiting more colored troops. Father had spoken to Easy about going, but Easy had said, "I don't guess I want to go down there an' fight 'em." Willie had smiled at him, but Father had been disappointed in Easy. He had been disappointed in Easy himself.

"Why not, Easy? You used to want to fight," Lyman said later in the woodshed.

Easy shrugged and went on out with a basket of chips. Sometimes he closed up so you couldn't get anything out of him. So Lyman hadn't told Easy about his own plans, either.

When the stage stopped at Malden, Lyman paid his fare and walked down the street as though he knew where he was going. He saw the flag and guessed that would mark the recruiting office as it did in Painesville. A sergeant with his right arm gone sprawled in a chair back of the table. A man leaning against the door spat and said:

"Good God, they're gettin' the babes from the cradle now!"

Lyman flushed uncomfortably and was angry at himself. He wanted to look completely at ease. Four soldiers were playing cards in the corner and Lyman felt them looking at him. He had never seen anyone playing cards before and he looked over at them and then away. They were laughing at something. Back of the table hung the same recruiting poster that hung in the store in Painesville. He knew it almost by heart and its familiarity encouraged him.

"Look out the boy ain't a girl dressed-up, Hank!" one of the players offered.

"What do you want, bub?" The sergeant with the one arm was civil enough.

"I came to enlist," Lyman said.

The soldier's jaws moved silently. He didn't look any older than Dan when you got close up. He didn't say anything for what seemed a long time. His silence increased Lyman's embarrassment.

"Where you from, sonny?"

"From Painesville. I have two brothers in the army, or I did have. John was killed in the Wilderness."

"So now you're just itching to go and get even with the rebs, are you?"

"I want to fight," Lyman said.

"Can you shoot a gun, sonny?" one of the men at the card table called out. Lyman blushed.

"Don't pay any attention to him," the sergeant said. "That feller couldn't kill a squirrel three feet away. What's your name?"

"Lyman Webster Converse."

"Age?" The sergeant's eyes were bright blue when they looked right at you.

"Sixteen. I've got a letter." He pulled the paper he had composed from his pocket. The sergeant read it carefully.

"Your father sure writes a pretty hand. So he don't mind your going, huh?"

"No, sir. He let my brother go when he was close to sixteen." Nineteen Dan had been, but that was only three years off. He felt more assured.

"Well, you fill out this here paper, then," the sergeant directed. He shoved an ink bottle toward him and handed him a pen.

Lyman wrote carefully in a firm hand, not bothering to shade any of the letters except the *C* in Converse. He hesitated and then put "quarryman worker" instead of "student." He had helped the men at the quarry summers. He handed the paper back.

The sergeant studied the paper. "Well, I'll tell ye, you're a slick young Yankee, sonny, but not quite slick enough for this old devil. Ye didn't write so fancy on this one, but any one-eyed fool could tell it was written by the same hand." He laid the letter and the form Lyman had filled out side by side and looked up at Lyman.

Lyman met his eye without flinching, but he could feel his face getting red again. "I write just like my father. I learned from him."

"I've got a first-class hunch your pa don't know ye're over here at all. Why'd ye come over here to Malden instead of signing up at Painesville?"

Lyman was silent a second. "I had to come over to Malden anyway, so I thought . . ."

"Uh-huh. Look, sonny, d'you want to lose an arm like I did?"

"Why, why, sure . . . if . . . I mean if I got it shot off in a battle."

The sergeant spat. "No you don't. You can't hug a girl so good with only one arm." One of the men in the corner guffawed.

"I ain't seen that stop you none, Hank."

The sergeant ignored the other. He lowered his voice. "Your ma's lost one boy, ain't that enough?"

"There's been plenty of families that've lost more," Lyman said. This sergeant with the blue eyes was going to keep him from going. "If I want to go, it's my own business," he said desperately, trying to make his voice sound rough like the voice of the man over at the card table. But he ended: "Please take me, sir. I'll go anyway. I'll run away and go!"

The sergeant spat. "Now don't get your dander up, sonny."

Just then four or five men came in with two soldiers. One of the men looked as old as Orville Converse.

"Pickin's poor, Sarge, but I got you a pretty husky mess this time. Two's goin' for substitutes, the rest of these bastards should've been in the army three years ago."

The sergeant stood up. His tone was brisk. "Nope, sonny. Mr. Lincoln don't want ye yet till you're done growing. You run along home to your ma and tell her Sergeant Daily's her friend. Here, take this pretty piece of writing along and keep it fer your memory book."

Lyman went down the street folding the piece of paper into a tiny square. He walked faster, wanting to get out of view of the houses. He turned down a side street and climbed a stone wall into a pasture. Then he threw himself on the ground and buried his face in his arms as he had that other time, after he gave his horse to the army and his father had thrashed him.

A grasshopper shot out of his way with a shrill sound of alarm and a chipmunk fled over the wall. The boy lay still so long the chipmunk came back, cocking his head to look at him. Then the boy's toes beat fiercely into the ground and the chipmunk scattered out of the way. After a while Lyman sat up and wiped his streaked face with his sleeve. He fished a paper fifty-cent bill out of his pocket. It was all he had. He couldn't get far on that. Maybe he could work a couple of days and earn enough money to get to Bennington. He'd say he was nineteen this time. Maybe he better go on to Albany. They weren't so damned—he brought the strange word out a little unsurely—so damned particular in cities.

It was time to milk the cows. Lyman took out the big silver watch that had been John's. It was past time, Easy'd be done by now. Louisa had the chain to John's watch, so Lyman wore the watch fastened to his galluses with a black string. He never looked at it without thinking that John had looked at its face on the battlefield. Its white enamel face with a pockmark between the four and five and the roman numerals seemed somehow eloquent. It was Lyman's proudest possession. Even now, the feel of it in his hand, the snap of the clasp as the cover sprung closed, comforted him. He slipped the watch back into the pocket of the pants John had once worn. Easy was too big for John's any more.

He was so hungry he had better spend his fifty cents for supper and start out even. Maybe he could chop some wood for a place to sleep tonight. Planning made him feel better. The storekeeper directed him to the house next to the mill and Lyman had asked if he could buy his supper there before he saw the sergeant and three other soldiers at the table just inside. There was nothing for it then but to go on in and sit down.

"Here's my friend Converse!" the sergeant called out. Lyman would have gone through the floor if he could have, but the wide boards were solid.

A burly middle-aged man came in and sat down at the table as Lyman took his place. "Well, Sarge, did you get any fish today?"

"One minnow and eight trout, one bloated," the sergeant answered. Lyman ate the beans on his plate with great concentration. "Threw the minnow an' the granddaddy back an' took the rest," the sergeant went on.

"Want some vinegar on your beans, sonny?" the soldier next to Lyman asked.

"No, thanks," Lyman answered. The beans were sour enough with his own anger. He would get out of here as fast as he could.

"Say, bub, there's a soldier here that's goin' to drive some horses over through Painesville. D'you want to earn a dollar ridin' with him?" the sergeant asked.

Lyman hesitated. "I'm not going that way."

"Oh, I think you can go round by way of Painesville this time, can't you? 'Tisn't every day you get a chance to ride a cavalry horse and earn a dollar to boot!" He started talking to the soldier next to him without waiting for Lyman to answer.

Lyman attacked his apple pie. The pie wasn't much like the kind he was used to, it had a soggy crust, but he was so hungry he ate it. He watched the sergeant eat his pie with his left hand and hated him, but he had a hopeless feeling that he was going to ride the horse to Painesville.

Lyman had never ridden a horse like this. Star was his name.

"He belonged to a feller that was killed, shot right off him an' the horse never scratched. In the battle of Coldwater it was," the soldier named Corporal Windham told him. "I rode him back up here to get some more horses for the cavalry. This little mare's all right too, but she's snaky. I don't know how she'll take to gunfire."

Ahead of them in the dark they could just make out the moving band of horses and the two soldiers that rode up front. There were thirty head, crowded close in the narrow road between the wooded hill and the steep bank to the brook below the road. Sometimes a break in the trees showed the horses' heads darker than the sky. Now and then a white marking on a horse made a sudden splotch of light in the dark or a shoe struck out a spark of fire against a stone in the road. When they broke into a run they sounded to Lyman like all the cavalry of the United States Army riding to a charge. Leaves brushed his head and he ducked to miss the lashing branch. No one could see him in the dark and he clung there, slipping one arm forward, knotting his fingers in the horse's mane the way he used to do with Ned. Perhaps the man who was killed at Coldwater was riding this way when he was shot.

Lyman's legs pressed harder and the easy surging strength under him swept him through the night. They rounded a sudden curve and his body leaned easily with the horse as though they were one. Night and the dark wind pushed past his ears and the stinging whip of the mane was against his teeth. He felt no fear, no ache from the day's disappointment, nothing but the pound of hard hoofs on the hard ground.

"Here, we're crowdin' 'em too much. Pull up!" the Corporal shouted. "You should see some of them Southern horses. God Almighty, them's horses!" the Corporal said when they were at a walk. "That's what gets me in a battle. I kin see any amount of men killed now and not turn a hair, but take a sweet piece of horseflesh screamin' an' kickin' on the ground an' it makes me sick in my stummick."

There was a light on the kitchen table when Lyman opened the door, but the flame was pale in the early dawn. He had walked up the hill. The soldiers were taking the horses two miles beyond Painesville, to the south.

"Sorry, sonny, we can't let you go any farther. Them's the sergeant's exact orders," the Corporal said when he begged to ride on with them. "I'd get mine if I let you past here."

Lyman wasn't tired, only his legs had a queer feeling as though he were still riding Star.

"Lyman!" His father had wakened or been lying awake waiting for him. There was anger in his voice. Lyman didn't care. He didn't feel the way he had before the ride.

"Yes, Father." There was no fear in his tone. Let his father thrash him, it wouldn't matter. It never would matter again.

His father came out in his nightshirt. Lyman noticed the sound of his father's feet on the bare floor, silenced when he crossed the braided rug by the kitchen table.

"Where in tarnation have you been?"

"I went to Malden to enlist in the army. I'm sixteen, going on seventeen. I've wanted to ever since John was killed, and before that."

"Well?"

"They wouldn't take me. They let me ride one of the army horses back." The kitchen was very still in the early morning shadows. Abbie appeared at the door.

"Oh, Lyman, I couldn't let you go . . . not all my boys." She hardly spoke above a whisper.

"Father, could I tell them here that you're willing for me to go? You'd go if you were my age. I would have run away to Bennington last night, only . . ." Orville's silence had fanned the little flame of hope.

"Orville!" Abbie pulled on her husband's arm.

"Wait till next year, Lyman," Orville said at last, more gently than was his way. "I'll not say a word against your going next year."

A year! A year was endless. He wanted to go now. He stood a moment looking at his father and mother, then he opened the door to the stairway and went up to bed.

9

APRIL 1865

EASY heard the news when he drove into town with a load of soapstone. He was working for wages at the quarry and helping at the Converse place in return for food and lodging. He stood two inches taller in his stocking feet than Orville Converse in his shoes and three inches taller than Lyman.

The stage-driver was yelling and all the passengers were waving their arms and screaming as though they had gone crazy. Folks spilled out of the houses along the main street. Women kissed each other and men clapped each other on the back, shook hands, and pressed nearer the stage-driver for news. He was hoarse from yelling it by the time Easy got there.

"The war's over! Lee's surrendered at Appomattox!"

Easy burst into the quarry office.

"Mistah Converse, sir, Dan'll be back soon now. It's over!"

Orville Converse removed his glasses and stared at Easy incredulously.

"Are you sure, Ezekiel?"

"Yes, sir! Look outside. Everybody's yellin' an' goin' crazy. There's the church bells an' school bells all ringing at the same time!"

Mr. Converse closed up his office and climbed up on the ox wagon to ride back home with Easy. A mile this side of the house he got off and walked, unable to stand that slow pace any longer. He picked little Juliet up in the dooryard, where she was digging with a spoon in the dirt.

"Abbie! Willie! Lyman! The war's over!" He stood in the doorway, his hair blown back, his face red from exertion, his nostrils dilated. "We ought to get Dan back soon now."

Lyman was plowing the south ten-acre piece when he saw Easy. "Good Lord!" he said under his breath, because Orville Converse's sons didn't swear aloud. Easy looked like a giant standing up on the stone wall, a great black man, as tall as the fruit trees on the other side.

"Whadya want?" he yelled, stopping the horses when he heard Easy call his name.

"The war's over. Hallelujah, praise the Lord!" Easy trumpeted back. He jumped from the wall and did a handspring right in the plowed dirt.

A sick sense of disappointment caught Lyman in the throat. It was all over, then. He'd been too late! Now he could never join, never know what it was like . . .

"Lyman, d'ya hear?"

"Yeah, I hear," Lyman called out, starting the horses again.

"Your father's going to have a prayer about it. You better come."

"I've got to finish this field. I'll pray while I'm plowing," Lyman called back with sudden boldness.

Easy stood again on the wall and then was gone back to his ox team and as the wagon creaked up home Lyman heard him singing with full voice "Go down, Moses!"

Lyman didn't pray. He drove the plow across the field till it was all plowed. The war was over and he had had nothing to do with it. "Damme, why didn't I run away that time?" he whispered to himself.

A few evenings later, Lyman stood in front of the kitchen mirror combing his hair with careful attention. He wore the dark suit he had worn to John's funeral and a white shirt and a black tie. He had shaved delicately upstairs, but he had a better light here for the finishing touches.

Abbie watched him anxiously. "Lyman, your father won't like your staying out late."

"I won't be very late," Lyman answered carelessly, lifting an errant hair to the left side of the part. He went in to show himself to Willie.

"Very handsome, Lyman!" Lyman bowed exaggeratedly. "No, this way." Willie brought her heels together and bowed with a masculine air in spite of her hoop skirt. "Oh, Lyman, do you know that Dan will be home next week? Where are you going all dressed-up?" Willie could skip from one thing to another with lightning speed.

"The singing class meets at Maudie Ingram's."

"Here, let me put toilet·water on your handkerchief. Easy going with you?"

"They need more men's voices." Lyman's tone was a little apologetic.

"Lyman, stop in just a moment and see Louisa, please." Abbie followed him outdoors.

"Oh, Mother, there's nothing to say. I can't just go and say 'How are you.'"

"Well, borrow a book then from Dr. Tucker, Lyman. She doesn't go any place or see anyone, just sits there in the house. People are talking about how bad she looks. Think of John, Lyman. He'd expect you to help her."

"If I'm not too late by the time I get there," Lyman muttered.

He was glad that Easy had gone on ahead—nice to arrive at Maudie Ingram's alone once. He wished he had the buggy, but Father always raised such a fuss if he asked for it too often. The fragrance of Willie's toilet water rose from his handkerchief, and his starched shirt scratched his skin pleasantly. If he went to Louisa's he was going to be late.

He quickened his steps past the cheese factory and the old cashmere mill that was boarded up now. There was a newly painted buggy out in front of the carriage works and Mr. Holmes was painting yellow lines along the shafts with his long paintbrush. It was a pippin. Someday he'd have a buggy like that. The village street looked gay enough of a Friday night, lights on in the houses and in the store. People were standing in front of Judge Gray's office talking politics. Queer sounds issued from the basement of the Congregational Church, where the band was practicing for the exercises to welcome the soldiers home.

Oh, shucks! He might as well go up and see Louisa and get it over with.

Lyman went up to the doorway of the brick house reluctantly and lifted the iron knocker. He hoped Dr. Tucker would come to the door. He hadn't seen Louisa except at church since Christmas. There was no light in the front parlor or the hall, but then it wasn't really dark yet at eight o'clock. The door opened. Louisa stood there. Her face was as pale as her collar and her eyes looked big. She gave a little gasp and both hands flew to her breast.

He found his voice slowly. "Louisa, I . . ."

She stepped back and leaned against the stair rail, breathing hard.

"Louisa, are you all right?" he asked fearfully.

"Yes, I'm all right. I thought for a moment that you were Jonathan. You look so like him in that suit," Louisa answered dully.

Lyman stood awkwardly. "I'm awful sorry, Louisa—I wish I could be John." He really wished he could run. Louisa still looked pale and she didn't say anything. "I just stopped in to see your father—that is, I wanted to borrow a book." He stepped inside the house and closed the door softly behind him.

"Father is in his study. Come with me."

He followed her down the hall, seeing how tiny her waist was in the gray dress. It was more slender than Willie's.

"Good evening, Dr. Tucker," he began politely.

"Oh, good evening, Lyman. We're glad to see you." Dr. Tucker put down the paper he was reading. "It's a wonderful thing to read about the cessation of hostilities, isn't it?"

"Yes, sir," Lyman agreed.

"Father, Lyman came to borrow a book to read."

"Well, that's fine, my boy. What will you have? Or would you like to look the books over for yourself? Your brother John was a great bookworm."

"John sure liked to read," Lyman said. What good did this do Louisa? Dr. Tucker was standing looking at the books on his shelves. Most of the books were bound in calfskin and looked dull.

"These are a bit dry, perhaps. Still, once you get your teeth into them, there's something to chew on, Lyman. None of your Maria Edgeworth pap that Louisa used to love to read." Lyman sensed that Dr. Tucker was trying to tease Louisa. He was just conscious of Louisa moving a little by the corner of the bookcase.

"That was a long time ago," Louisa said softly, not bridling at all.

"A year is a long time for all of us these days," her father said sadly. "Louisa, let Lyman look at those books in the upstairs hall. You better get a candle."

Louisa went ahead carrying the candle, shielding the flame with her hand. Lyman noticed how pink her hand looked held up that way. The nails were like little shells. He was taller than she was by a whole head.

"These are the books John used to read," she said softly.

Lyman was so afraid she might cry he couldn't look at her. His eyes and fingers moved along the shelves. He murmured the titles out loud: *"Moby Dick."*

"John didn't like that, but he liked this one." She pulled out *The Oregon Trail* and gave it to Lyman. "And this one. He read some of Longfellow aloud to me." She took the volume out of the bookcase and held it as though she couldn't let it go.

"I'd like to read *The Oregon Trail,* thank you," Lyman said hurriedly. He noticed that Louisa still carried the Longfellow book when she took him downstairs. He watched their shadows moving down the deep canyon of the stair well in the pale spring dark. What was there to say? Louisa blew out the candle.

"Thank you," he said again, standing in front of the door turning the knob.

"Are you as much like John as you look, Lyman?" Louisa asked, leaning toward him a little.

He laughed in his embarrassment. "I don't know. I never thought about it. Good night, Louisa."

He had a sense of relief at being out of Louisa's home. The cold April air cut clearly through his uncomfortable mood. For no reason he ran the short distance down the street to the Ingram house, not as a boy any more but in the long loose lope of a young man, nearly grown. He pulled the door pull harder than he needed. Maudie came to the door laughing and shaking her curls.

"We almost gave you up, Lyman! We're out in the kitchen because it's bigger." Lyman followed Maudie's laughter down the hall, his spirits lifting with every step. A dozen or so boys and girls were sitting on benches and chairs. Easy sat in Maudie's grandfather's Windsor armchair because he was so much the biggest of the boys. Ephraim Whipple had a tuning fork in hand. His face above his wide black-satin stock was red from his exertions.

They began with "When Johnny Comes Marching Home Again, Hurrah!" Lyman sang lustily with the tenors. Even as he sang he could pick out Easy's voice.

"Can you get down to help decorate the bandstand Wednesday night? The parade's Thursday," Thad Davis whispered to him.

"Sure, I guess. I hope Dan's home by then."

"The singing class will give three selections," Ephraim Whipple explained. "After the returned soldiers march up through town they will sit by the bandstand for the exercises. There will be a speech by our Senator and then we sing again. A salute to the dead will be fired and taps will be played. It will be the most grand and solemn occasion Painesville has ever seen," he finished impressively.

Lyman looked around figuring how many others had brothers coming back. The county had been one of the first to meet its quota.

"Now!" Ephraim rapped his tuning fork. They sounded the note obediently. "Tenting Tonight, Tenting Tonight, Tenting on the Old Camp Ground." They held the notes, tenors leaning toward tenors, basses toward basses. There were three times as many girls as boys, but Easy's voice made up for the weakness in numbers. They hummed the chorus, each face so like the next in expression because of the humming lips that it made them laugh. After the singing, and dough-nuts and milk, they moved down the village street in a body singing "Good Night, Ladies" as they went, not caring how many people they woke. The war was over and things were different.

"What time is it?"

"Near eleven."

"I ought to be getting back home," Lyman said, liking to be with the crowd.

"We have to see the young ladies home," Thad Davis remonstrated.

"Oh, yes, we'll do that first," Lyman said, touching Maudie Ingram's elbow, helping her across the ditch with a strange and delicious sense of daring. Willie would say he was gallant.

"See you afterward," Thad called out mysteriously as they separated at Stella Baker's house.

Maudie lingered on the bottom step by the lilac bush. Lyman wondered if she were waiting for him to kiss her. Thad Davis kissed girls, he said so himself. To gain time Lyman said, "Easy'll be waiting for me at the store."

"You're pretty good, Lyman, having a colored bodyguard." Maudie tittered.

"He's not my bodyguard," Lyman said, a little nettled.

"Here, I'll give you a flower for your buttonhole." Maudie broke off a little piece. "It's not really out yet, just buds."

"Smells nice, though." He moved nearer. Maudie was very close. The soft stuff of her hair touched his face, tickled a little.

"I'll give you a flower to wear in the parade Thursday," Maudie offered. "It'll be out full by then, I guess."

"Thanks" was all Lyman could think of to say. Now was the time. His arm moved a little at his side. He had never kissed a girl.

"I can't find one that's out really far enough."

"You can't tell whether it is or isn't in the dark."

"I can tell by the feel, though." She laughed.

His hand touched her waist now.

"Oh, Lyman!" she whispered.

Her waist was not as slender as Louisa's. He thought of Louisa's pale face tonight and drew his hand back. Maudie was fumbling at his lapel.

"Oh, it hasn't any buttonhole. Here, I'll pin it."

"Well, thanks, thanks a lot. See you Thursday. G'night." He felt she was disappointed, but he was glad to be on his way now.

He hurried up the street. All the houses were dark. The only light was in the store. Easy got up from the long front step.

"Where you been?" His voice seemed low and good after Maudie Ingram's.

"Oh, I was seeing Maudie Ingram home," he said importantly.

"That's what Thad Davis say. I didn't believe him though."

"Well, I couldn't let her go home alone," Lyman said. He wished now, unexpectedly, that he had kissed her. He wondered if he should say he had. "Where you going now? We oughta get started home," he said instead.

Easy laughed. "Thad and Ben an' Jeb say to meet 'em up back o' the church."

They walked up the street in the dark. Lyman had never loitered around the town at night as late as this. It gave him a wonderful feeling. After all, they were grown-up, old enough to be in the army. Old enough to be married even . . . and he had been afraid to kiss Maudie Ingram! Well, he wouldn't be again. He stepped out briskly, whistling boldly to the sleeping houses.

"What's Jeb want?" he broke off to ask.

Easy chuckled. "Thad say Jeb he wants us to have a smoke."

Nothing Lyman had ever done had been as good as this. The four of them lay on the cold ground back of the church, at their ease, smoking black cigars.

"These are the kind old Grant himself smokes," Jeb told them, taking a puff.

"Did you ever see Grant, Jeb?"

"Naw, I got this here before he come East," Jeb said, tapping his turned-up pant leg. "Most o' the men in my comp'ny chew. It's easier when you're shootin'. But back in camp a cigar's the thing. When one o' the boys got a cigar in his mouth we used to say, 'How're you, Ginral?' An' I guess it don't take more'n a cigar to make some of 'em."

Lyman drew in his breath. A strong wave of tobacco surged through him, threatening to carry his meal with it, but he ignored the heaving of his stomach and puffed again.

"Don't know what in hell you'd do in the army without tobacco," Jeb said. "God dammit, the stench of them wounds is so bad ye can't get away from 'em, seems like. An' the things ye see! I got sent out to bring in the wounded an' I'll tell ye . . ."

This was what Lyman had longed for. He had listened in the store to soldiers that were back. He had tried to get John to talk about the war, but John kept so mum. This was the real honest truth. He winced a little at the oaths, but he felt they were the way a soldier should talk.

"There wasn't a damn one o' them boys in my comp'ny that wouldn'ta got out if they could. Ain't worth it. How'd you like to go through the rest of yer life with one leg? Here, boys! Have a little drink." Lyman felt the cold bottle nudge his hand, but he passed it to Thad.

"Go ahead! It won't kill you," Jeb urged. Thad took a drink. Lyman admired his casualness. He heard Easy and Ben drink. Then the bottle was in his hands again. He lifted it to his lips and let just a little into his mouth, glad of the dark. He held it in his mouth before he swallowed, hoping he wouldn't choke and cough.

"Tell us some more, Jeb," Thad urged as the bottle passed around.

"Let's have another dose of that," Lyman said loudly. This time he took a good drink, liking the warm spot in his stomach.

"Well, the damnedest thing that ever happened to me . . ." Jeb began. "Who in hell's that?" he broke off as a horse and buggy rattled past on the road at top speed. They heard a man's voice yelling and they couldn't make out what he said.

"He's stopping at the store. Let's go!" The boys started off at a dead run, then they remembered Jeb.

"Gosh all fishhooks, we better wait for Jeb!" Lyman panted.

"You boys see what I mean?" Jeb hobbled up to them with Easy. "When you think of never runnin' again, 'tain't so fine, is it?"

"Sounds like a lot of people down there now," Thad said. A light blinked on in the house next to the store.

"Jehoshaphat, d'you suppose the rebs've started the war up again?" They burst into the store. A handful of men were there. The boys looked around from Obadiah Hall to Ephraim Whipple to Benjamin Holmes, questioningly. The men's faces were grave.

"Boys," Ephraim Whipple's voice sounded formal, then it seemed to choke and the sound made Lyman's eyes move away to the red calico on the top shelf. "Boys, the President was shot tonight in a theater in Washington."

"It just come over the telegraph 'bout two hours ago an' Ben Holmes brought the news from Malden," Obadiah told them.

"Is he dead?" Jeb asked. The man from Malden shook his head.

"He's unconscious. He can't live more'n a few hours "

"Who did it?" Lyman asked.

"The wire don't say. We'll hear tomorrow. Some damned Secesh slaveowner, you can bet your last dollar on that!"

"We ought to toll the church bells," one of the men suggested.

"Maybe you better wait till morning. Folks is happier sleeping without knowing such a thing," Ben objected.

"It's their President. The people have a right to know," Sam Perkins said solemnly. "Come on, John."

The two lamps in the store, one on the counter, the other in a bracket near the stove, threw queer shadows over the shelves. They showed the pads under one man's eyes, the wrinkles on Obadiah's forehead, the white hairs in another's beard, and the startled look of the boys' faces, white and black.

"Ain't nobody like Mistah Lincoln," Easy said suddenly, and the different timbre of his voice sounded strangely. His face looked solemn and his eyes rolled mournfully.

"That's right, boy," Ben Holmes said.

"We better go," Lyman said. "We better tell the folks."

They had walked and run through the covered bridge and past the second thank-you-ma'am on the hill road when the bells began to toll.

"They're ringing both churches," Easy said. The notes fell warningly on the valley, a pause between each sound as though the night held its breath, then the ominous clang again.

"Look at the lights coming on in all the houses."

"Everybody must be up by now."

They walked backward a ways to watch the lights, until Easy stumbled and almost fell. Lyman felt in his pocket and pulled out the dead cigar. He fingered it a moment, then he threw it off into the bushes.

"Whadya throw away?"

"Cigar. I didn't want any more of it."

"I'd have finished it," Easy said.

Easy was stout and no mistake, Lyman thought. He could eat a small trout raw, too. He had seen him do it once.

They lost sight of the lights in the village and the road was dark as a well. There were little rustlings and skitterings in the bushes, and Lyman was glad Easy was with him. The warmth in his stomach had disappeared and left in its place a queasy and uncertain feeling.

Easy was singing, something sad and cold-sounding.

"Hush up, Easy!"

Easy was still a moment. "My mother'll sure be glad to see Mistah Lincoln when he gets up to Heaven."

Lyman was startled. Now he saw the tall gaunt man with the stove-pipe hat walking into Heaven.

"I guess he was a great man," Lyman said weakly. He felt really sick now. "Easy, wait a minute, will you." He sat down against the stone wall that bordered the road. He felt too sick to go on but he didn't want to be left there alone either. If he just weren't so shivery and his head didn't ache like this. . . .

"D'you ever drink before, Easy?"

"Sure. Lotsa times. There's a man over at the quarry gives me a drink o' rum most any old time. Don't bother me none."

Lyman retched and was sick. When he walked on with Easy he felt weak and chilly, but his stomach was revenged.

"You better get some sleep 'fore you see Mistah Converse," Easy murmured softly as they came to the house. "It's most two o'clock."

There was a light in the kitchen, then Lyman saw his father standing out by the road, fully dressed.

"What kept you, Lyman?" his father called, and then as though that didn't matter, "What are the bells tolling for?"

"Oh, Father, the President was shot tonight in a theater in Washington," Lyman blurted out. "He can't live only a few hours. Ben Holmes brought the news from Malden. They got it over the telegraph."

"The President!" Orville repeated. "Abraham Lincoln! Go tell the others, Lyman. Easy, hitch up the horse."

As Lyman went across to the house he heard his father talking to himself. "That's what we have to expect from the South now that they're beaten. There'll be killings and riots for the next year."

"I didn't suppose the President would go to a theater," Abbie Converse said in a grieved voice when Lyman finished telling all he knew. She and Willie were in their night clothes.

"Who shot him, Lyman?" Willie asked. "I'm sorry," she added quickly.

"The telegram didn't say. He was shot in a theater at a play," he repeated.

"I wonder if it was Ford's or Grover's. I've seen him at a play. He often went," Willie said.

Abbie Converse stared at her daughter-in-law.

"You saw the President?" Abbie asked incredulously.

"Oh, yes, I've looked up from the stage at his box and seen him laugh. He doesn't look so homely when he laughs." Abbie was plainly shocked.

Lyman went over to the sink and took a dipper of water. It helped the taste in his mouth. He had smoked and drunk and almost kissed a girl and the President had been shot, all since he left here this evening. In the dim light he looked curiously at himself in the mirror over the sink. He was a little disappointed that his face showed no change.

"This is going to be a terrible thing for your father, Lyman," Abbie said anxiously as they heard the carriage go past the house. "You know how he felt about the President!"

Lyman was suddenly ashamed of the way he had spent this evening the President was killed. He went on upstairs and sat on the side of his bed. How did he himself feel about the President's death? He tried to bring him close to him, somebody he had known . . . Abraham Lincoln. He knew the pictures of him. The cartoons stuck in his mind best, the one in *Harper's Weekly* where he was so tall and thin he looked like a scarecrow. There was a picture of Lincoln on the fifty-cent greenbacks. He had one in his pocket now, but he hardly ever stopped to look at the picture on it. Lincoln was a big tall man, dark like Zadoch Grimes. Folks said he wasn't hard enough on the rebels. Now he was dying . . . at this very minute! Lyman wished he could feel worse, the way the men at the store tonight and his father felt. "The President," he said aloud . . . but he was so tired. He fell asleep across his bed with his clothes on.

IO

THE Converse place looked queer with black cloth draped across the front of the house and caught under the sash of the two end windows. The families from the farms beyond could see it, but there weren't so many farms on the hill any more, just two. The quarry workers saw it as they drove past, going the other way to Ledyard. But no matter: Orville Converse didn't put it up for people going by, he put it there for himself. He wore his black suit and cravat, and he had done no work since Friday night. There was part of the garden yet to go in and plenty of work to do, but Orville left the chores to Lyman and Easy. He walked a good bit Saturday, his hands behind him, his head bowed as though he studied the ground.

"The Sunday sermon ought to give him some relief," Abbie said to Lyman as they watched him climbing up the hill back of the house and walking slowly along the brow against the stone wall.

But Orville's face was set and stern as they came out of church. They were late driving back home because he waited for more news. The whole village seemed clothed in mourning, so many houses had black draped over their doorways.

When they reached home Orville said to Willie, "I'd like to have a talk with you."

"Of course, Father," Willie answered wonderingly. Orville followed her to her room and the door closed behind them.

Abbie and Lyman heard Orville's voice rising angrily and then an ominous silence. Abbie busied herself with setting the table for Sunday dinner. They were eating in the dining-room as though it were a funeral meal and the dead lay in the parlor. The door of the parlor opened.

"Take the child, and I'll give you money to take you back down South." Orville stood in the doorway and made no effort to lower his voice.

"I shall not go, Mr. Converse, before Dan comes and I shall never leave Dan. But you can be very sure that as soon as Dan comes we shall go at once."

Abbie dropped the knives and forks on the table and ran in to them.

"Orville Converse, what are you saying?"

Lyman started for the door, then he went back to stand by the window instead.

"Just what you heard me say, Abbie. No good can come of this marriage. Daniel's wife came up from Richmond in the company of that . . . that assassin! She knew him well. That place she sent me to stay was run by a Mrs. Surratt, and the paper says they've arrested her for helping in the plot, her and her son. I slept under her roof, Abbie, and ate at her table, thanks to this woman here!"

"But, Orville, you couldn't help it. You didn't know they were planning such a wicked thing. Willie didn't either. When she knew them maybe they seemed like decent respectable people."

"They were actors, Abbie. They just pretended to decency. How do we know but Willie . . ."

Then Lyman could stand it no longer.

"Father, you can't say a thing like that to Willie. I won't stand for it!" He stood in the doorway of the dining-room facing his father, his eyes flashing, his mouth tight. Bright color covered the high knobs of his cheekbones and made the hollows by his mouth seem more pale.

"Be still, Lyman. You don't know what you're talking about!"

"Yes, I do, Father. I'll leave this house too if Willie goes."

The narrow hall between the parlor and the dining-room was as close as a vault. Abbie looked at the gold pattern of the wallpaper, but she could not see it clearly, her eyes were so filled with tears. She could hear Orville breathing hard and wondered if it weren't bad for him to get so angry.

Suddenly Willie laughed, and the sound was so brittle it broke like mica scraped off a rock with your fingernail.

"What difference is there between acting a play on the stage, Father Converse, and acting it here in your own house? This would do for Act Three where the stern father sends the erring child from the door. As for my knowing Wilkes Booth, do you ask a person before you call him your friend to promise he'll never do anything wrong? You wouldn't ask your sons before you admit they're yours whether they'll be good and noble all their lives!

"All I know of Wilkes Booth is that he is a handsome young actor, a little violent, maybe, but talented and generous. He loved the South as you love your Vermont. I happen to know that he ran all sorts of risks smuggling quinine down South for the sick. When Richmond fell, perhaps he became unbalanced."

Orville Converse smote the doorframe such a blow with his fist that the whole wall shook. His face was a deep-red color and the little veins in his forehead were purple and knotted like a grapevine.

"Willie Delaney, don't name that murderer under this roof again. Abraham Lincoln's murdered! And you stand there and try to excuse him!" His voice was like a sob. With one hand he seized Lyman by the arm and Abbie with the other and led them across the threshold into the dining-room. Once inside the room, he let them go and tramped out of the house and down the road.

"He's going toward the quarry," Abbie whispered.

Lyman stood there uncertainly, humiliated that he had counted so little against his father's anger. "Shall I go after him?" he asked, hating his own indecision.

"No," Abbie said sadly. "He has to be alone. Oh, Lyman, why does the Lord do so? He should keep such things from happening! Oh, I don't mean that." She bit her lip to keep it from trembling.

Willie opened the door quietly. "I came to get Juliet's gruel," she said, as though she must explain her coming in. The baby's very name seemed to speak defiance. "Thank you, Lyman," she said in a low voice as she passed him. But when she came back through with the warm gruel she didn't speak, and Lyman sat with his eyes on his book, wanting to go to her but not going.

Willie stayed in her room at suppertime and Orville Converse ate his supper without a word. Abbie had put away the best silver and the white cloth and set supper in the kitchen as though it were any day. As heavy a pall of mourning rested on the house on the hill as John's death had brought. And that night Abbie could not reach out her hand to lay it against Orville's arm.

Orville was separated from them by his own dark anger. He never looked at Willie nor spoke any word to her. He spoke only once to Lyman.

"Lyman, I don't want you traipsing off down to town the rest of the week. You stay here and tend to your work if you have any notion of my sending you to college in the fall!"

One day followed another in a funeral procession. He went to the village for the newspaper but he brought it home and put it out of sight without letting anyone in the family read it. Easy heard the news from the men at the quarry and told it to Lyman in the smokehouse.

"They ain't got that Booth yet," he told Lyman one day. "But they're on his tracks."

Another day he said: "They've had the fun'ral in the Capitol an' Gen'l Grant sat right by the coffin. Now they're going to take him back West where he came from."

If Abbie wondered what was happening in Washington, loyalty to Orville kept her from asking. Lyman told Willie what Easy told him.

One day Easy brought home a newspaper and he and Lyman and Willie met in the barn loft to read it. That Willie knew the theater where Lincoln was shot made it seem as familiar as the Congregational Church. They read the reward of fifty thousand dollars offered for Booth.

"What was he like, Willie?" Lyman asked, half shocked, half fascinated to think that Willie knew him.

Willie tilted her head in that distracting way she had and looked out the hayloft door. "He isn't as tall as you are, Lyman, and he's very dark, with thick black hair and the blackest eyes you ever saw. I knew an actress—Henrietta Irving was her name—who was madly in love with him and used to talk about him all the time.

"He must have been mad to do a thing like that. And poor Mrs. Surratt. She's innocent enough, I know. I don't blame Father Converse for feeling the way he does, in a way, but he acts as though I . . ."

"I hate my father for it!" Lyman broke in.

Willie laid her finger on Lyman's lips. "Don't make any more trouble here than we have already. Dan will come, and we'll go away."

"Back down South, Miss Willie?" It was the first time Easy had spoken.

"I don't know. I hope so," Willie said. Then they heard Orville Converse calling and Lyman slipped out first, leaving Easy and Willie to come separately.

"When Daniel comes it will be different," Abbie comforted herself. "When Dan comes we'll go far away from here," Willie whispered to Juliet as she rocked her in the cradle that had been Dan's. "Next year I'll be going away to college," Lyman told himself. "I'll not be treated as a child any more." No one knew what Easy thought. He never appeared for meals, but he still did any errands he could find to do for Miss Willie and he carried the baby all over the farm.

One afternoon of the next week Lyman went down to Louisa's, ostensibly to return the book he had borrowed but in reality to get away from his own home. He dreaded the meals. He dreaded finding himself alone with anyone but Easy. The black cloth still draped the front of the house and the black mood filled the house inside.

Louisa sat out in the woodshed hemming a sheet. The wide lattice door was open and the spring sunshine was warm. She looked so peaceful there in her blue-and-brown sprigged dress with the white collar and the white muslin of the sheet billowing around her that he felt better at the mere sight of her.

"Hello, Louisa," he said, sitting down on a cricket that propped the lattice door open.

"Oh, Lyman, don't sit there. Come inside and take the rocker."

"I'm fine here," he said, and leaned back against the lattice, which swung so that he lost his balance and sprawled on the grass. He picked himself up and set the cricket right side up.

"Now you'll have to take this rocker," Louisa said, laughing.

"Well, what's going on here?" Dr. Tucker came out of the kitchen. "It's good to hear some laughter around here. How are you all up on the hill, Lyman?" he asked.

"Oh, we're fine," Lyman said.

"Has Willie heard when Dan will be back?" Louisa asked.

"No, Willie says she thinks we'll just see him someday walking in the gate. That's the way he used to turn up suddenly in Washington." Their separate strands of thought, as delicate as the lines of a spider's web spread across the grass, bound them to silence a moment.

"Well, we're going to have a great celebration Thursday!" Dr. Tucker broke the gossamer threads with his voice.

"Will they have it now that Lincoln's dead?" Lyman asked.

"Oh, yes. Life goes on. We've got to show these boys we're glad to see them back." Dr. Tucker glanced at Louisa as he spoke.

"Isn't it odd—the President and John," Louisa said in a hushed voice.

"The President and all those who died, Louisa," Dr. Tucker corrected quietly.

It was sad here too, Lyman thought, but it was only sad. No hate and suspicion were mixed up with it the way they were at home. He wondered suddenly what they would say if he should tell them about Willie—that she was an actress and knew the man who murdered Lincoln. He felt sure that Dr. Tucker would see how that could be, but Louisa—would she understand about Willie? His chair as he rocked made a regular thumping on an uneven board in the woodshed floor: "Would she, wouldn't she? Would she, wouldn't she?" He would try her out, but maybe Willie didn't want it known. Lyman jerked his chair off the uneven board and changed the rhythm of the thumping noise so it rocked out: "She would, she would, wouldn't she?"

"Do you think, Dr. Tucker, that the new President will be able to control the South?" Lyman asked a little importantly, but Dr. Tucker was silent so long he felt his question was somehow callow.

"No one man will control the South, Lyman, nor the North. Both sides will have to live with the ruin they have brought on themselves, and it may teach them something. I'm not sure."

"Ruin here, sir? You mean the South will have to live with it."

"I mean here too. Every little town in the North, like Painesville, in a different way, will suffer as much as the South. The victor often loses his own soul, you know."

The sun laid a lattice of shadow on the white sheet spread over Louisa's knee. Lyman was looking at it when Louisa noticed his glance and lifted the sheet a little. "It seems foolish to go on hemming sheets, but I bought the muslin and I hate to see something unfinished," she explained. Then tears filled her eyes and Lyman looked away uncomfortably.

As Lyman went up the hill, walking backward as he often did, he thought about what Dr. Tucker had said. Below him lay Painesville, white and red and green, the spires of the Congregational and Baptist churches rising higher than the three stories of the tavern or the old cashmere mill. The town wouldn't look any different to Dan when he came back. It was just as it had always been since he could remember. He stood still there in the road wondering how Dan would feel when he saw it. Dan hadn't been back once since he went away. If he himself had been away four years . . . Why couldn't he, Lyman, be one of those coming back and marching down the street and hearing the band play for them?

The peaceful town lying below the hills in the green trees looked too pleasant. Dr. Tucker was wrong, there was no sign of the war here. Vermont was too safely wrapped in these green hills to feel the war, just as he was. He turned around and walked swiftly the rest of the way, dreading the evening meal with Willie and his father not speaking a word.

He saw the blanket roll on the front step and a gray felt hat with a bedraggled plume in the band stuck on the end of a bayonet. It was a Confederate hat!

"Daniel!" Lyman burst into the kitchen.

Mother was crying. Crying, and Dan home! "Why, Mother?"

Abbie nodded her head. "He's home. He's in there with his wife. He's been wounded, Lyman, and in prison." Lyman didn't wait to hear any more.

"Dan!" he yelled.

He heard the parlor door open and Dan called back. They met just at the narrow front hall. Dan looked almost like a stranger.

"Well, hello there, Lyman. I'll be damned if you're not as tall as I am!" Lyman was shaking his hand and pounding him on the back, trying to get his voice under control.

"Gosh all hemlock, it's good to see you, Dan."

Dan had a full beard and he looked old to Lyman. He had a limp, his shoe turned up somehow—Lyman couldn't look now. Dan's face was white against his beard and his eyes looked darker than Lyman remembered.

"Here, Dan! Your daughter wants to come back to you," Willie said, holding out Juliet. "She began to wonder if she really had a father." Willie filled the strange moment with little talk, half to the baby, half to Dan. Dan's eyes brightened, or softened maybe. He limped a step toward Willie and took the baby.

"She's a good-looker, isn't she, Lyman? Just like her mother. You know what, Juliet? I brought you a hat. Took it right off one of Jeb Stuart's boys that your mother used to admire too much, an' I held onto it all through that goddam stinking prison. I beat a man for laying his filthy hands on it."

Lyman stood there hearing the swear words and the strange things Dan said. He had been in prison. He had beaten a man for touching a hat!

"Now listen, Dan. You've got a lady in your arms, a lady that's not used to soldiers, and if you don't talk pretty she won't have you," Willie bantered.

"Oh, yes, she will. This young lady is none of your strait-laced pantalette prune-faces. Not my daughter! Well, Lyman, can you chew tobacco yet? I kept expecting to see you turn up somewheres. I knew if it'd been me I'd have run away and joined up somehow."

"He tried to, Dan. He gave us a good scare," Willie put in. "But they wouldn't take him."

Dan laughed. Lyman was still testing out the laugh in his mind when Dan said limping over toward him and twisting his mouth up shrewdly: "Maybe you're just one smart Yankee, at that. You wouldn't want half your foot shot off. 'Tisn't pretty when you go swimming—but I wouldn't have missed the fun, sonny!"

"I wouldn't mind if I could have got in," Lyman muttered, hurt at the "sonny." "Does Father know you're here, Dan?" he asked in the next breath. He was sorry about Dan's foot.

"You mean has he welcomed home the conquering hero? Yep. He couldn't wait to tell me the wife of my bosom knew Wilkes Booth."

"Don't, please!" Willie pulled at his arm. "I'm going to miss Lyman when we go away. He's like you must have been, Dan. Look, she wants to get down. Carry her in on the bed, will you?"

Lyman lay awake a long time in the chamber above the kitchen where he and John and Dan used to sleep. John was dead and buried over on the hill where he could see the Spring place he had wanted—if he could stand up out of the grave, that is. And Dan was home, but he was not the same. He was sleeping downstairs under the best silk quilt with Willie, and the baby he had begot was there in the cradle. Dan's voice was deeper and his laugh was hard and he was thinner than old Smiley Painter who had consumption.

A May moon painted a white streak across the gray shingles of the woodshed roof and the wide painted boards of the bedroom floor. May moonlight didn't reach as far as the curled oak leaf in the rug, but it made the porcelain breast of the pitcher on the washstand shining white.

Lyman thought of the meal that should have been like Thanksgiving with Dan home but wasn't. Easy was there, Father brought him.

"Your wife don't care about eating with a 'nigger,' Dan, but I rather thought you've just given your last four years fighting so a white man could eat with one." Lyman didn't like the look in his father's face when he said that, and his father's words made him feel uncomfortable for Easy.

"Well, no, I wouldn't say that, Father," Dan said with a good friendly grin at Easy. "But, hell yes, I'll eat with him, cozy as you please. Willie can sit on the other side of me."

Lyman wondered that Father didn't say anything about the "hell." He just bowed his head and said a longer blessing than usual, asking the Lord "to help Thy servant to see the righteous path and turn not aside to evil."

Mother had cooked two chickens and made fresh apple pie and Dan was still eating when everyone else was through. That made Mother feel good, you could see.

"Well, Dan," Father said, "we were proud of the way you went up through the ranks to captain!" Father seemed like himself again, the way he was before Lincoln died or he ever heard of Wilkes Booth.

Dan shook his head and laughed. "You don't need to be. The man who was captain was killed and I was next to him there, that was all there was to it. I wish I could have seen John again," he added. "That jungle fighting in the Wilderness was the bloodiest mess you ever saw."

Father sat back in his chair and Mother left the dishes and came over to the table. Willie let Juliet sleep in her arms so she wouldn't miss anything, and Lyman and Easy sat at the table, too.

"The grand parade in Washington must have been a mighty spectacle," Father said.

Dan took another piece of pie from Mother. "I didn't stay for it. I skedaddled for home the first train I could get."

"Oh, Dan, that was too bad," Mother said. "After all you'd done you ought to have stayed to taste the fruits of victory."

"Fruits of victory, hell!" Dan said. "I'd rather have this apple pie." Somehow Lyman had known it was because of his limp. Dan wouldn't march in any parade if he had to limp.

"Daniel, tomorrow I want to take you over to see how we've increased the quarry business," Father said. "Your Uncle Nate always kept his share in the quarry, and his wife, your Aunt Matilda, has that third share. My two-thirds will go to you and Lyman some day."

"What happened to Uncle Nate?"

"That's right. That's since you went away," Father said.

"We heard about his death the day we got the letter telling us Willie was coming," Mother said, and a kind of wonder at the way things happened was in her voice.

"I always remember the time you took me to Providence to visit them, Mother, remember?" Dan said. "I must have been about five." And for a minute Dan wasn't strange. Mother smiled thinking of that time when she had held Dan securely by the hand. "I remember I thought they were certainly swells," Dan said, and the spell was broken.

"There's a growing market for soapstone, Dan. We've opened offices in Brattleboro and Burlington and a man in Nate's bank takes care of clients there. I want to see you work into the business."

Dan took another drink of coffee. The room waited.

"Thank you, Father, but I shan't be staying in Vermont. It seems that a grateful Government is ready to give its soldiers a nice piece of land out West to make up for the toes and legs and arms they lost. I thought Willie and I might try our luck. I didn't mean to bring this up the first night, but since you did—there you have it!"

Lyman lay in bed hearing the very sound of their voices again and Mother drawing in her breath. He hadn't dared look at Father, or at Willie carrying Juliet in to bed. The soft rustle of her skirts seemed to make a triumphant little sound. He looked at Dan. Dan's hair and beard were darker in the kerosene light. He wore his white shirt open at the neck and he had taken off his uniform as soon as he could. He was looking straight at Father, and Lyman remembered Willie's calling him a "masterful man" and he saw what she had meant.

After what seemed a long time, Father had said: "You better wait a little to decide, Dan. Pray over it. You'll be losing more than you gain if you go off out there to that heathen country. A man has to settle down sometime or he gets an appetite for a roving life."

"I've decided, Father, and I can make up my mind without praying. I've seen too many good men pray before a battle, and I've noticed it didn't always save 'em."

"If it's because of that actress wife you've taken unto yourself . . ." His father's voice had risen.

Dan's coffeecup came down on the saucer with the dull clank of heavy china. "Be careful what you say, Father. I didn't realize what I was asking when I sent Willie back here. I can't stand it myself any more."

Dan took a cigar out of his pocket. Lyman watched him bite off the end and light it, and the heavy aroma came back to them from the dining-room as he passed on through to the parlor with his slightly limping gait. For a shocked moment Lyman had waited for Father to say something, to go after Dan. No son of his had ever spoken to him before like that. Then he had known that there wasn't anything Father could say that would make Dan listen if he didn't want to, and the knowledge had made Lyman feel badly for his father.

Father and Mother and he and Easy had prayers that night without the others. Lyman hadn't listened to the prayer, and as soon as they rose from their knees he had come up here to bed.

If Dan and Willie went out West, he wasn't going to stay around here. He wondered if Dan would let him go along with them. He could be handy, there were a lot of things he could do. Maybe he could get into some Indian fighting. He thought he heard a sound outside his window and ran quickly across the streak of moonlight.

Dan was down there, under the apple tree. He was spreading a blanket on the ground, and the blanket made a swishing sound over the grass. Lyman pulled his pants on over his nightshirt and climbed out across the woodshed roof and down the lattice.

"Dan," he called softly.

Dan saw him and grunted. "Want half a bed?"

Lyman stretched out on the ground beside him.

"Feather beds don't fit my back so good, the ground feels more natural," Dan said. "I thought I'd suffocate in there. Here, move over and lie on a piece of this blanket. The ground's still damp."

It was a little cold, but Lyman liked being here beside Dan. The smell of Dan's pipe was strong and warm. He had a lot of things he wanted to say to Dan. He wanted to ask him what it was like in the midst of a battle, and about being captured. There were lots of things he wanted to know. He wanted to explain why he hadn't got into the army, he was afraid Dan didn't understand. There were things to say about John, things he couldn't say to anyone else. And he wanted to ask Dan if he could go West with him. He must make Dan see that he was grown-up now.

"Willie wants me to take Easy West with us, for a kind of servant. I don't know but that it's a good idea," Dan said. "It'd sure burn the old man up, wouldn't it? Easy'd probably end by getting him a squaw out West!" Dan laughed.

Lyman looked up through the starting leaves of the apple tree at the stars faint and cold in the sky.

"You couldn't do that, Dan. Easy's . . . he's different." Lyman's voice was stretched thin to cover his shocked feeling.

"The hell you couldn't, if you paid him a little something. Besides, he's crazy about the baby." Dan's tone was rough.

"Easy isn't like that, Dan. You've forgotten . . ." Lyman tried to explain. He held his arms tight to his body to keep from shivering. It was cold out here. He wanted to move closer to Dan the way they used to when it was cold upstairs but Dan might think he was just a kid. He wished Dan would lay his arm over him but Dan knocked out his pipe against the tree trunk and stretched his arms back of his head. Lyman was so cold his teeth chattered.

"Guess I'll go on in," he said finally. "It's cold for April, isn't it?"

"Not bad if you're used to it."

Lyman waited a few minutes longer, wanting Dan to say something else, trying to think of something to say himself, but it was no use.

"Well, good night, Dan." Lyman climbed back up over the roof feeling himself nothing but a child in his brother's eyes.

It was lonely back in the room by himself, worse than when John and Dan first went away. He had thought everything would be all right when Dan got back but now that he was here he couldn't seem to talk to him. He wished now that he had gone over to Easy's shack, he could always talk to Easy here.

PART TWO

I

OCTOBER 1865

WHEN he gave a written lesson, Professor Gilmore had a chance to look over his class as he didn't have when they were reciting. The quiet in the room was broken only by the sound of pencils on the long sheets of foolscap and once in a while the shuffling of a foot or the sound of some young man scratching his head to stimulate cerebration. Professor Gilmore was glad to have them busy and not to have to hear them recite back Spalding's English text.

He felt a little uneasy with these young-old men in the seats before him. They were very different from students of other years. They were older, most of them. Those with full beards or side tabs looked old enough to be teachers themselves. They had grown used to beards as soldiers, of course, and now it had become the style. Some of them had been in the thick of the war and grown used too to the idea of killing. It made him shudder to think of it. Sometimes he fancied their eyes had a hard look. They laughed with extraordinary abandon when anything tickled their fancy, and owned up to being unprepared with a discouraging lack of fear. Or they sat staring through him as though he didn't exist, which bothered him most of all.

Well, it was difficult, very difficult, for boys who had been soldiers to come back and be students again. He tried to appeal to these students in terms they would understand. Today when he had passed out the paper he had said:

"This is a battle, gentlemen. Engage in it to the utmost of your powers, and may the victory be yours!" But they had not responded visibly. Perhaps it would be just as well if they went on to business or out West . . . twenty-two, twenty-four, or twenty-five in some cases was old to learn English rhetoric.

"Finish your papers, gentlemen," Professor Gilmore said briskly, tapping on his desk with a penholder. Most of the students began to write more rapidly. One young man at the far side continued to sit idly staring back at him. There was something countrified in his appearance, and he was extremely youthful. Consulting his class roll, Professor Gilmore found the name: "Lyman Webster Converse." His grades so far had been irregular, good on the whole. Then he had him placed. He was the young upstart who had written in his composition on Wordsworth, "He seems to have lived in a part of England very like Vermont and his early life resembles my own. I like and understand his poetry because our minds seem very much alike. We feel the same way about life."

Professor Gilmore had been shocked at first at any freshman student's having the temerity to liken his own mind to Wordsworth's. It was preposterous when you thought about it. He lowered his glasses now to look over at the offender. The young man did have a serious face. It could do for the face of a poet. His hair brushed the top of his collar in back and his face was smooth. He must be aware of his looking at him, for a girlish color blushed out suddenly on his cheekbones and his ears reddened. He bent over his paper again.

When Lyman felt Gilly's eyes on him, he had been studying Chauncey Westcott III. Chauncey was a dashing young man with brown curly hair and brown beard and a twinkling eye. He should have been a junior, but being out during the war had disarranged his rating. Lyman had admired him since the first day. Already he tied his cravat as Chauncey did his, and he was cherishing the down on his upper lip. Chauncey had his own rooms, in town, and his own man to take care of them, which set him apart in the university.

Lyman walked out of the classroom behind Chauncey and his friend Ed Abbott.

"How'd you like Gillyflower's big battle?" Abbott laughed.

"Oh, I engaged in it to the uttermost," Chauncey mocked, so loudly that Lyman glanced back unhappily. When he saw Professor Gilmore just behind him within certain hearing distance, he turned quickly, reddening as though he himself had said the words. Professor Gilmore passed the loitering students with his head held stiffly. Chauncey and Abbott went into a new burst of laughter. Lyman admired their unconcern.

"Where you going?" Chauncey called out to a boy down the hall.

"Library," the boy answered.

"The library'll keep. Stop over at my rooms."

Lyman continued on his way to his room in University Hall, wishing Chauncey Westcott III would call out to him. He was slow at making friends. He knew a good many in his class to speak to and many of the sophomores were always coming up to haze them, but he didn't feel he belonged, even with the ones in his own class. He wanted to call them names and slap them on the back and be at ease with them, but how did you do those things? He had lived so long on the hill farm that he had acquired the habit of solitude, he told himself, and spent one lonesome Sunday afternoon composing a poem on solitude, but it was too mournful. He wasn't homesick. It wasn't that he wanted to be back on the farm, not with John and Dan both gone. It was just that he wanted to know these others and be one of them.

Sometimes he wondered if he were too serious in his application to his studies. Sam Andrews, his roommate, was serious too. Sam was taking the four-year course in three and going into the ministry at the end of it. He had had a call, and at night after their lights were out he talked about it to Lyman. In the dark Lyman envied him, but in the daylight he felt a little embarrassed with Sam.

Stub Hawkins down the hall was always dropping in his room and offering him pipe tobacco and some wine when he had it, but Stub was a fat young man who couldn't do Greek worth a tinker's dam and was always wanting Lyman to do it for him. There were Benny Bates and Will Barnes and the rest, but with all of them Lyman felt his separateness. He lost it a little in the free-for-all fights. The day they had a real one out in the hall and threw ashes from the piles in the corner he had a great time, but even when he was filling his bucket and throwing with the best of them he was watching the different ones, doing what they did, calling out the same things. And the day back of Manning Hall when they were playing baseball one of the fellows on his side had cheered him on. "Yeah, Converse!" someone had shouted from a window on the third floor as he ran, and he was a little ashamed of how he kept remembering that with pleasure.

When Dick Appleton had dumped his pail of slops from his window down on him yesterday morning, he had carried it off well, taking off his hat and bowing low in mock thanks, but he had hated Dick Appleton and would till he died. Everybody dumped his wash water from the window, and it often landed on the head of some luckless passer-by, but the feeling that Dick had lain for him persisted.

Once in a while when he went out to get a drink at the well back of Hope before going to bed he fell into talk with someone and lost himself in the talk. He must have stayed there by the well an hour last night talking with a chap who'd been in the war. Somehow they got on religion.

"If there is a God who cares anything about us, why would He let there be a war like that?" the fellow said.

"We'd just be puppets if we weren't free to get into a fight if we wanted to," Lyman answered, forming his ideas as he went along, but knowing he would have to think them all out by himself later. He liked to talk about abstruse questions. Sometimes he felt that talk was what he had come to college for.

"*Remember that the purpose of your going to the university is to acquire an education. Study diligently and make the most of your advantages,*" Orville Converse wrote his son. Lyman had written back:

Thanks to Mr. Pettingill's grounding I stand near the top of my Greek class. Rhetoric is not hard. Geometry is very difficult, and I spent two hours last night on one problem. The chemistry professor has told me some interesting facts about soapstone. I believe chemistry will be my chosen field of study. Do not worry, Father, I shall make the most of these advantages.

Today he got out the last letter from his mother. Abbie Converse wrote:

My dear Lyman:
The house is so lonely with you away and Dan and his wife gone. Your father is very silent and broods a great deal over Dan's headstrong ways. If only the Lord could have spared Jonathan! You must try to take his place in your father's heart. He is working very hard at the quarry office. They are waiting for snow to freight the largest volume of stone ever shipped out of the quarry.
Louisa was up one afternoon this week. She is very thin.
I want to remind you again to call on your Aunt Matilda and your cousin Isabel. She is one year younger than you, you remember. They will be offended if you don't call. We sent you to Brown instead of Dartmouth because you have relatives in Providence. I hope they will invite you for Thanksgiving so you will have a home-cooked meal.
Rhode Island is a damper climate than Vermont and I can't feel that it is as healthy. I hope you have put on your woolen underwear by now. Do not change to lighter before school ends in the spring. I am enclosing some powdered sulphur. Shake it in your shoes every two or three days and it will ward off colds.
I don't know what we would do without Easy. He is a great help.
      Your loving mother,
                              Abigail Converse

Lyman put a fresh shovelful of coal into their stove and stretched out on the bed, thinking about Dan. Mother would never call Willie by name again. Her name and Dan's and Juliet's were still in the family Bible, but they were not mentioned in front of his father. Dan and Willie hadn't written Lyman yet, but they had promised to. They must have taken almost the last boat of the season up the Missouri. He still wished he had gone with them instead of to college, but it had seemed too hard on his father and mother for him to go off too. Mr. Pettingill had urged college on him. "Believe me, my boy, it will make all the difference in the world in your future life!" he had said impressively. Sometimes, now that he was here, Lyman wondered what kind of a difference it would make.

But it wasn't any of these things that had decided whether he would go West or stay home, it was something Louisa had said that afternoon that Mother made him drive her up to the cemetery. He hadn't wanted to do it. He had been afraid Louisa would cry. But she had sat quietly beside him on the way up the hill and talked about his mother's health and the Baxters' leaving to take up land in Iowa and how they would have to go to Malden depot now to get any decent cashmere.

The only thing she had said about John was really about the cemetery. "I wish John were buried in the new cemetery instead of this old one up on the hill. He'll be the only soldier from our war buried here."

"That's right," he had agreed, thinking of it now for the first time. "The rest are soldiers from the Revolution and the War of 1812."

"Someday, like as not, the whole town will be moved down to the valley," Louisa said.

Then they came to the cemetery and Lyman planted the lilac bush Louisa wanted by John's grave, and he tried not to think about John's wanting the Spring place.

On the way down Louisa talked about Dan. "He's so different from John, so kind of bossy. You wouldn't want to go West with him, Lyman. You'd have to do just what he said."

He had kept thinking about that. Dan *was* bossy. Maybe he'd rather wait and go West by himself later on. Maybe Easy felt the same way. When Dan told Easy they'd take him along he said:

"No, Dan. I'd get scared of them Indians. I'm going to be a cutter at the quarry next week an' I don't guess I'll leave." Dan turned quite red in the face. "Miss Willie thought you'd be lonesome without Juliet here," he had said reproachfully.

"I'll sure miss Miss Juliet," Easy agreed. "But I guess I'll stay right here."

It was a good thing, because the folks needed him. He must write Easy a letter sometime.

The next Sunday after his mother's letter Lyman decided to call on his Holbrook cousins. Sunday was the right day for calls, and it was something to do, anyway. He dressed in his best clothes and tied the new tie he had bought in Providence carefully in the manner affected by Chauncey Westcott. The tie had cost a bit more than he liked to remember, but he had put it down in his accounts that he sent his father each month as "Book, classroom supplies, etc." The tie had tiny white embroidered flowers on a rich blue-satin ground. His hat was new, too. The hat he had come with was too wide in the brim.

It was pleasant walking on the streets of Providence of a Sunday afternoon marked clearly as "a college man."

His cousins lived in a handsome brick house, much more imposing than Louisa's. As he went up the box-bordered walk he noticed that the sills were of white marble instead of soapstone. The wide steps were marble too, and a heavy brass knob on the door shone like a gold cuff link. When he pulled the brass knob at the side of the door, it had such a strong spring that it seemed to leap out of his hand, and he could hear the sound of the bell reverberating through the house.

A middle-aged maid showed him into a long narrow parlor at the right side of the hall. She was the first maid in uniform he had ever seen. In Painesville folks had hired help who were part of the family. He watched her a little uncomfortably.

The room he entered was dimly lighted because the windows were hung with a double set of net curtains over the tasseled shades and made the outside world seem far removed. But even in that late Sunday-afternoon gloom he could make out a white statue on a pedestal back in the corner, the cool shining keys of an enormous piano, and the brass fender and white marble hearth and fireplace. The large pictures on the walls showed the size and heaviness of their gold frames to advantage, but the paintings themselves were part of the brown shadows of the room. Lyman was contemplating a tiered whatnot suspended in another corner of the room and draped with tasseled hangings when he heard the rustle of a skirt, and stood up quickly.

"Well, Lyman, how do you do. I am your Aunt Matilda. I had a note from your mother saying you were here at the college. It seems quite a way to send a boy from Vermont. We just got back from Newport or we would have sent a note around to you." Matilda Holbrook was a small dark woman dressed in gray silk. Her face was stern except for her eyes, which were as shining black as the jet bag fastened in her belt. She spoke so briskly Lyman could hardly do more than smile or nod.

"I don't know why Mina keeps the room so dark in here." She jerked the tasseled strings of the shades vigorously as she spoke and a little more light filtered into the room. Then she sat down across from him.

"Well, young man, how did you leave your family?"

"Mother and Father are very well, thank you, Aunt Matilda."

"Your father wrote us that your brother Jonathan was killed. Where is your second brother?"

"Dan has gone out West. He's married, you know."

"Married! Your father never told us that. One of those quick war marriages, I suppose. Where is the girl from?"

"Virginia," Lyman answered, feeling this was much like Professor Gilmore's recitation period.

"Virginia?" Aunt Matilda's voice was sharp with surprise. It pleased him. He heard footsteps crossing the hall as soft as cat's paws on the heavy carpet.

"Oh, Isabel, this is your cousin from Vermont, your Aunt Abigail's youngest boy, Lyman."

Lyman stood looking at his cousin while her mother introduced them. He thought first how thin Isabel was, and how homely. Her dark-green dress seemed to go from her neck to her ankles, and against it her face was colorless. She seemed to have no color in the cheeks, where girls usually were bright-pink, and there were freckles under her eyes and across her nose. Her hair was red, and she looked at him with great brown eyes.

"How do you do, Cousin Lyman."

"How do you do, Isabel." Her hand was in his and out again so fast he had only the impression of its small-boniness.

"I remember you the time we went to Vermont. You picked some raspberries, and I thought you were doing it for me and instead you popped them all in your mouth. You were a horrid boy!" Isabel's laugh made fun of him and herself at the same time.

"I don't remember that," Lyman said slowly, wishing he could think of something very bright to say. "That must have been Dan."

"No, I remember distinctly. You wore dresses," Isabel retorted. Her eyes crinkled with merriment and he noticed how her mouth twisted a little at one corner when she talked.

"I remember I thought you lived in the forest by the time we got up that hill. I never cared for Vermont," Aunt Matilda said, disposing of it.

"Father loved it," the girl said softly, and he could see that her father meant a great deal to her.

"Of course, he was born there." Aunt Matilda spoke as though that explained her husband's odd taste.

"Nathaniel thought the quarry had a great future, and it is turning out to be one of the best investments he made in his lifetime."

"When snow comes, we expect to get out the largest shipment we've ever taken from the hill," Lyman answered, feeling important.

"Well, I'm glad to hear it. Everything's booming since the war. I suppose you would like some tea. College boys are always hungry." As she spoke Aunt Matilda moved across the room and jerked the long bell pull by the door. Lyman had never seen such a device before, but he could hear the faint tinkle of a bell far away in the shadows of the house.

Sitting there having tea, he thought for a moment of tea in the parlor at home with Willie. He wished he could tell Aunt Matilda that he was used to having tea like this.

"Brandy in your tea, young man? Or don't your family believe in stimulants?"

"Thank you, I'd like it," he said.

"We had the most wonderful time at Newport this summer," Isabel was saying. "Have you ever been sailing?"

"Of course not, Isabel," said her mother. "Vermont doesn't own any body of water larger than a mill stream."

"We have a few rivers and lakes, and Lake Champlain took the British quite a while to cross," Lyman said.

"My dear boy, I didn't mean to insult your state." Aunt Matilda laughed. "But you see Isabel thinks in terms of the ocean."

Lyman was irritated that he had sounded angry. He didn't like his aunt at all.

"You'll have to come down to Newport and visit us some week end," Isabel said. "We know the president of the college and the dean and ever so many of the professors. I know Mother can get you leave."

He glanced at Aunt Matilda in time to catch her frowning at Isabel, so he answered coolly, "That would be pleasant, but I'm working rather hard."

"Whatever possessed your father to send you here to college, Lyman?"

"I think my parents preferred to have me in Providence where I had relatives than in Dartmouth where I had none."

"Oh, so we are to be responsible for you." She smiled, but Lyman did not like the way she said it.

The housekeeper spoke to his aunt, and she set down her teacup emphatically. "That umbrella-mender is here again, and I won't pay for that poor job he did. I'll speak to him!" She rustled indignantly out of the room. As soon as she had gone Isabel reached for the plate of cakes.

"Here, have two. They're such stingies." Lyman smiled and took two.

"I was so sorry about your brother," she said softly. "But it's more glorious to be killed in a battle than just to grow old and die in bed, isn't it? Do you know those lines?

> "'How sleep the brave who sink to rest
> By all their country's wishes blessed!'"

When she quoted the poetry her freckles seemed to grow paler or else more color came into her face and hid them. "Do you like poetry?"

"Oh, yes, I do," he answered, wondering whether he dared quote Wordsworth to her, but his aunt came back too quickly.

"I settled that individual!" she announced with satisfaction. "I gave him the umbrella rather than pay for such a poor job, and you could see he didn't want it!"

Lyman rose to take his leave. He was chagrined to see the little shower of cake crumbs that fell to the floor as he stood up. He felt his aunt watching them fall on the dark carpet.

"Must you go? You haven't told us how you like college or whom you know or anything!" Isabel cried out.

"Lyman has hardly been in attendance two months, Isabel," her mother reminded her.

"I like it," Lyman said. "I don't know many chaps yet, just a few in my class."

The maid brought his hat. "And his gloves, Mina. Did you have gloves, Lyman?" his aunt asked.

"No," Lyman said, blushing and feeling himself blush. "No, I didn't wear gloves today."

"You must come often. We're home every Wednesday afternoon," Isabel said. Out in the hall he could see what a deep-red color her hair was. She really wasn't homely at all.

"We'll have you for a family meal soon, Lyman," Aunt Matilda said.

That evening Lyman wrote in his old 1862 diary: "I found my cousin, Isabel Holbrook, a most unusual young lady. She is very fond of poetry and is interesting to talk to, though she is not really pretty except when she is talking or laughing. I am going to see her again on Wednesday."

On Monday he purchased some chamois gloves and recorded the item also under "etcetera." Then he crossed it out and set it down openly: "One pair gloves . . . $4.00." Why should his father not expect him to be properly dressed at the home of his relatives?

He pursued the poets more than before, and when Sam was gone and he had the room to himself he read aloud Wordsworth's lines:

She was a Phantom of delight
When first she gleamed upon my sight. . . .

They really didn't apply to Isabel. She wasn't exactly like a vision, and yet she made him think of poetry. He tried his hand at writing verse himself, but found his thought too constricted bv the words he could find that would rhyme.

Her tresses glow like copper bright,
Like fire plucked by Prometheus' hand.
Her glances burn with inner light
And of my heart make their demand.

If it be courage that they ask,
Or fame or wealth or power,
But let them name to me the task.
It cannot make my spirit cower.

He copied this last effort off on a stiff sheet of white paper in his finest hand and ornamented the margins with birds and garlands and Prometheus bearing a firebrand and slipped it into an envelope to mail. But he thought of his aunt picking the envelope up from that taboret in the hall and saying, "A letter from that young man with no gloves," and decided to carry it in his pocket until he saw Isabel on Wednesday.

But Wednesday something else happened.

He had been aware of the secret societies. He had seen the bejeweled pins on the lapels of sundry sophomores and upperclassmen. He had heard rumors of So-and-so "trotting" some freshmen and he had asked cautious questions, waiting to be "trotted" himself. Wednesday morning he sat in chapel and watched Howard Allison, who roomed across the hall from him, come in arm in arm with two upperclassmen and wearing a fraternity pin. Lyman felt the stir of excitement that ran through the student body, the nudges and significant glances. "They took Allison!"

Allison was a fine fellow, so were Hawkins and Bates and Will Barnes. He didn't wonder at their being chosen, but during chapel he studied them wondering why he too hadn't been approached. He looked at Sam and wondered if he felt as left out as he himself did. You had failed, really, if you didn't belong to a secret society, Homer Lang had said. You were an outsider and belonged to the Ouidens. There was a line drawn between the Ouidens and the secret societies and no one could ignore that line. All day he found himself meeting boys on the campus or in the corridors and looking not just at their faces or their eyes but hunting their lapels for one of the coveted Greek-letter pins, and then, finding it, he studied everything about them: the way they talked, walked, dressed. Homer Lang was pledged, and Jim Harper and Dick Appleton.

The Greek class was repugnant to him. The very words in the *Agamemnon* taunted him. The tragedy lost significance in the face of his own personal tragedy. He avoided noisy groups of students, fearing that he would not be wanted. He wished himself back on the hill above Painesville. How comfortable it was there! You didn't have to make an impression, everyone knew you. But at the same time all that the life in Painesville represented suffered because it hadn't made of him somebody whom the elect of the Greek-letter societies would recognize at once as desirable.

He sat in the library and watched the clock drag past the proper time to call at his Aunt Matilda's. Her black-jet eyes would sweep his lapel and find it bare. Isabel would see that he didn't belong. It wasn't just the lack of gloves that was wrong with him, it was something hidden and intangible. Dan would have been chosen at once. Dan was positive and certain. He was a leader. A doubt about himself stirred unhappily in his mind.

It was time for the evening meal and the library emptied itself, but Lyman stayed on, taking some pleasure in making himself more miserable. By seven o'clock he thought of himself as a recluse, preferring to live apart. He hunted out Thoreau on the library shelves because he had heard Thoreau had been something of a hermit. What he found there was so much to his present thinking that he took the book out of the library and back to his room. He copied out a long excerpt in his diary, which he decided now would be a commonplace book full of quotations rather than a diary of his own anguish.

"How alone must our life be lived! We dwell on the seashore and none between us and the sea," he copied out. "Parents and relations but entertain the youth; they cannot stand between him and his destiny. . . . This is the one bare side of every man. There is no fence; it is clear before him to the bounds of space."

But he found himself so hungry that even Thoreau could not feed him. It was too late for supper in the dining-hall, and he sauntered down the street to the town just as a steady drizzle began. He pulled his flat-crowned hat down a little and turned up the collar of his coat. He had meant to look on the world henceforth with a misanthropic attitude, but he felt suddenly cheerful. He had not felt his own independence so truly before. He was alone, with his destiny before him. Painesville was behind him, his parents could not stand between him and the world. John and Dan were separate from him. He, Lyman Webster Converse, was his own man. A whistle broke out of his lips and he walked to his own tune.

The lights from houses and places of business were yellow and warm. The people who passed him didn't know him and couldn't ask him what he was doing or where he was going. This was what Willie had meant about a city. No wonder she had missed it up on the hill. Thinking of Willie always made him feel a little more sure of himself. Willie had said he was handsome. He swung happily along the street until he found the oyster house he had heard Chauncey Westcott talking about in class one day.

The room was murky with smoke, and he had a confused but glorified image of a sawdust-covered floor, lamps with bright tin reflectors against the wall and hanging down from the ceiling, men and boys sitting at a long counter and at the bare deal tables. There was a fragrance of chops or steaks from the back that spoke loudly to his stomach, and the sour smell of beer blunted the sharp smell of fish. A large man in a leather apron stood back of the counter cracking open oysters. Lyman slid onto a high stool. He caught sight of himself in the mirror back of the bar and tipped his hat back so its angle was more rakish.

"Crackers?" the man next to him asked, proffering the wicker basket that was the common property of anyone at the bar.

"Thanks," Lyman answered, feeling himself warm toward such a friendly spirit.

"Dozen?" asked the man with the stained apron and bare hairy arms.

"Make it a dozen and a half," Lyman answered, wanting to enter into all of this as though he were used to it.

But he had never eaten a raw oyster before. He had never even seen one. He watched the man on his left spearing the gray flabby morsel, dipping it in a puddle of sauce, and swallowing it at a gulp. The process appalled and fascinated him. The oysterman slammed not one plate down before him but two. There were enough oysters for three men. Lyman looked at them, and then reached for the bottle of Tabasco sauce.

"Beer?"

"Yes, please," Lyman answered, and then wondered if the "please" sounded effeminate in this place. He had never tried beer before. He plunged his fork into the heart of the largest oyster on his plate, doused it with sauce, and popped it in his mouth. His tongue and throat contracted against the cold slippery texture. He swallowed and was surprised it was gone so easily. Two, gulp, three, gulp—he didn't really like them, but if he put enough sauce on them they weren't so bad. Why had he ordered an extra half-dozen? One was so big he had to bite into it. It was better to swallow them no matter what size. He took a swallow of beer from the heavy mug and washed the oyster down with the strong sour liquid. He didn't like the beer, and yet he did. He finished his mug and pushed it forward on the counter. The man back of the counter filled it.

Two men from the college took the recently vacated stools next to him.

"Say, you're class of '69, aren't you?" the youth next to him asked.

"Yes, I am."

"Thought you looked green. Think we ought to let a freshman drink beer, Seth?"

"If he buys us two beers to pay for it we might let him," the one addressed as Seth answered promptly.

Lyman paid, grinning. "Here's to you, son," one of them said, lifting his mug.

"He might go us a round of oysters too, don't you think, Seth?"

"By all means! What's your name, freshman?"

"Converse, Lyman Converse."

"Sounds like a banker. You can treat us a round."

"Feed the beggars," Lyman said to the bartender, laying a dollar down on the scrubbed maple counter, blushing at the laughter that rose along the bar but feeling he had had the best of that encounter.

"Hey, Gilbert, take care of this young cub, he's fresh," the man next to him called out to a sophomore across the room.

"Right you are!" A young man in a bowler came up to Lyman as he stood by the door.

"We want you at 18 Hope Hall tomorrow. There'll be some others of your class there. I don't know what freshmen are good for around here if not to entertain their superiors," he said with a grin.

The yellow leaves that littered the pavement shone in the light from the street lamps. The rain fell gently. Lyman took off his new hat and walked along bareheaded. All thought of the comfort of solitude was gone. He was happy in a strange new way. Lyman Webster Converse, Class of '69.

Not until he was in bed and heard those who had been out to their fraternities yelling and pounding their heels on the stairs according to custom as they came home did he lose his sense of belonging. He was not of the chosen. His earlier sense of pleasure faded.

2

"I HEAR that you sang some old slave songs the other night that made a great hit," Isabel said.

"How did you hear that?" Lyman asked, a little annoyed at her talking about him to someone else.

"Oh, I heard!" Isabel's eyes danced mischievously. Lyman's mouth tightened. He looked at her sitting primly on the sofa across the room.

"Who told you anything about me?"

"Oh, a little bird. Lyman, you look so funny when you're mad. You did the other day when Mother said that about Vermont not having any big body of water."

He tried to see himself in the shadowy mirror across the room. "I'm not mad," he murmured. "Only I do think . . ."

"I told you I heard you were good. Oliver Sears was here the other day and he said you sang for the sophomores when they hazed you. Where did you learn slave songs?"

"Oh, they were just some songs our . . ." There was a pause as imperceptible to the girl as the instant of growth in a leaf, but to Lyman it was an ugly gap in time. "Our colored man, Easy, is always singing them."

He heard her ask, "Was he a slave?" His conscience and his mind were facing each other. Well, what was Easy if he wasn't their man? Yes, but to Isabel it meant a Negro in a black coat and bow tie building the fire, bringing the teatray, answering the door.

"Yes, a runaway," Lyman answered. "He escaped to Vermont when he was eleven, just before the war."

"Did Uncle Orville buy him?" How wide her eyes grew when she asked a question! Her face changed every minute.

"No, not exactly. Father rescued him. You've heard of the Underground Railroad."

"How exciting!"

But he didn't want to be talking about Easy. How had they got started on this subject? Now while he had Isabel alone he wanted to say something that would make an impression on her.

"I wish I remembered more about Vermont. Father often spoke of it. We have some soapstone from the quarry in here. Father had it shipped way from there specially."

He followed her into the library to see the fireplace framed in soapstone. The library was dark in the late fall afternoon. Bookshelves lined one wall and most of the bindings were dark. A dark carpet covered the whole floor from wall to wall and swallowed up the sound of their footsteps but the soapstone frame of the mantel seemed to quiver out of the stolid gloom and give both light and life to the dark lifelessness of the room. It drew Lyman to it, and he laid his hand on it. It felt as familiar to his palm as the soapstone sink in the kitchen on the hill or the sill of his own window.

"Why, it's carved!"

"Yes, Father had an old Chinaman who was brought back by some sea captain do it. They make statues and art things out of soapstone in China, you know."

"What is it supposed to be?" Lyman bent nearer to it.

"The dragon of fire on one side, I think, and this side has the genie of water. See, it looks like a river flowing out of his hand. When I was a child I used to lie on the floor and watch the firelight on them till the dragon faces scared me."

He saw her on the rug as a little girl, slender as she was now and her red hair loose over her shoulders. It would glow in the firelight.

"I don't think I like it carved. Soapstone is pretty enough just plain," he said abruptly.

Isabel laughed at him. "Don't you think you're rather rude?"

Lyman reddened. "I'm sorry. I was just thinking about it so hard I said what I thought."

She laughed again. "I like you, Lyman."

The instant was warm and friendly. He wished he could tell her about not being pledged. In that moment he wanted her to know. Maybe Oliver Sears had already told her.

"Do you know a man by the name of Westcott, Chauncey Westcott III?" he asked.

"Oh, yes, do you know Chauncey? Isn't he wonderful! He enlisted as a private, you know, and was promoted to be a lieutenant after Bull Run."

"Yes," Lyman said, and then he added, "Dan enlisted as a private and came out a captain."

"He did!" Admiration and awe shaded her voice.

"I tried to enlist," Lyman blurted out. "I ran off to Malden, but they said I was too young. Father promised to give his consent the next year, but the war ended." Some inner compulsion forced the words out of him.

"I know. I wanted to go as a nurse, but that old curmudgeon of a Miss Barton wouldn't take any woman under twenty-five."

She understood. She had tried herself. Lyman looked at her adoringly. Some tight band that had bound his mind loosened and wasn't there any more.

"You're the only one who understands how I felt," he said, with wonder in his voice. She smiled at him with her eyes and her mouth. Color stole up under her pale skin. He couldn't take his eyes away, watching her face.

"Maybe you were kept out of the war to be something very special, Lyman, somebody great." Now her face was serious. "Mother says the country needs someone who can see more than two inches beyond his nose."

"Maybe," Lyman said, almost believing in that moment that he had been.

"Well, Isabel!" Aunt Matilda stood in the doorway of the library. She was bonneted and becaped just as she had come in from the street.

"Oh, Mother, Cousin Lyman dropped in to call. I was showing him the soapstone around the fireplace."

"So I see. How do you do, Lyman."

"Mother, can't Lyman stay for dinner with us?"

Aunt Matilda's bonnet strings made a silken sound as she drew them through her hands. To Lyman, her mouth seemed never going to open.

"I should be getting back. I have thirty lines of Greek to translate before bedtime," he murmured.

"Why, yes, Lyman. There will be just Isabel and myself." It was an invitation with the warmth thinned out of it. He wondered why Aunt Matilda didn't like him. If he had been pledged, perhaps . . . The warm security of the moment before was gone.

When the lamp was lighted in the library, the soapstone frame of the mantel turned silver. The carving had some white lines that looked, Lyman thought critically, like scratches. Isabel and he looked at daguerreotypes of Isabel's father and his own mother when they were children.

"Father left Vermont and came down to Rhode Island when he was eighteen," Isabel was saying. But Lyman hardly listened. He was watching her mouth when she talked and wishing Aunt Matilda hadn't come back so soon.

Dinner was an awesome meal to Lyman. The table seemed very

large for three people, since everything was passed and the wide spaces of the white linen cloth were bare.

"What are you training yourself for, Lyman?" Aunt Matilda asked. He had never seen a woman with earrings before. They were black and matched the brooch at her collar.

"I haven't entirely made up my mind, Aunt Matilda."

"I suppose Orville's sons will all go into the quarry."

"No," Lyman answered firmly, "I shan't."

"I wish we could go back to Vermont to visit, Mother. Couldn't we next summer?"

"Sometime, perhaps, not next summer, Isabel. Lyman, will you have some plum sauce?"

The freshman declamation class sat in a semicircle. Each student in turn stood before the class and delivered a speech on a subject of his own choosing. The best speech was given before the entire student body in chapel. It was a trial by ordeal.

The class was called on in alphabetical order. Sam Andrews had given his speech the preceding Wednesday on "Saul of Tarsus." Bates had followed with an oration on "Our Victorious Generals."

"Mr. Converse, I believe you are our victim for today," Professor Burdick said. He held a slip of paper closer to his eyes. "The subject on which you will enlighten us is 'The Postwar World'—certainly a pregnant title, underlaid with deep significance. I congratulate you, my boy, on your choice."

Lyman advanced on untrustworthy legs to the front of the room. He was very serious, and he compressed his lips to keep from showing it. He plunged his hands into his pockets to feel the crumpled paper in which the speech was written and withdrew them hurriedly, remembering that putting your hands in your pockets was poor form. To clasp them behind you was safer. Sam Andrews was smiling at him. Douglas Edwards made a quick gesture across his throat with one finger. John Blake was chewing something. Lyman looked above their heads at the blind bust of Cicero.

"Gentlemen"—his voice came out queerly in the silence of the room —"we are in a different world from that which surrounded the students of last year's declamation class, a postwar world. Whether we know it or not . . ." It was amazing that one sentence followed another out of his mouth. It was none of his doing. His voice grew louder and took on more authority. "The youth of today will not be satisfied with the world of the older generation which tries to think that the war has made no difference. The soldier comes back to find many changes. . . ." He thought of Dan talking about the two mills in Painesville closing and the number of people who had moved out West in spite of the war. "Why, the town's shrinking down to the size of a copper cent," Dan had said. "He sees his village or city or home more clearly after looking so long into the fiery heart of death," Lyman declared with fine fervor, proud of the figure of speech even as he said it. "He sees many evils and points them out to us: evils in government—it is not inspiring to the returning soldier to find Congress fighting the President and that unhappy President fighting back . . ." He was on page five now, only two more to go.

One lock of hair had fallen down on his forehead. His collar was damp along the back of his neck and perspiration ran in the little veins in the palms of his hands. He was all but through. His eyes viewed the class sternly. He stepped forward dramatically.

"Say it quietly, Lyman, when you want the most effect, almost whisper the lines," Willie had said when they read plays in front of the parlor stove. His voice sank.

"Unless the people of this country open their eyes and minds to the new world, we will be forced to say that Abraham Lincoln died at the right time and that he has been spared greater agony than death."

Lyman sat down carried away with his own eloquence.

"Well," Professor Burdick came back to the front of the room, "I would say that was delivered with a good deal of spirit. Yes, a good deal of spirit!"

"Lyman, it was the best one yet. You're sure to be asked to give it for the whole college," Sam said as they walked across the campus. Lyman's head still rang with the echoes of his own phrases.

"Oh no, Sam, wait till the rest give theirs. Mine is just some ideas I had." But he waited eagerly to hear Sam say again that no one could equal it.

"All right, wait and see, but I'll be very much surprised, Lyman, if it isn't the best one."

Lyman relaxed a little. "Well, it was a good subject," he said modestly. The subject that he had considered with suspicion yesterday today seemed inspired. He wished Isabel could have heard him. But if he gave it before the whole college she would surely hear about it.

He listened critically to the rest of the class giving their speeches at subsequent meetings, overly ready to see good in theirs that surpassed his, trying to remember his best sentences—that figure about the fiery heart of death, that was good. Perhaps he *would* go into politics. He took a volume of Daniel Webster's speeches from the library, and one of Emerson's. Sonorous periods rolled through his brain. He fell into argument easily. One day he argued fiercely with Stephen Hyde from Illinois about whether the United States would look for its leaders to New England in the future or to the Middle West.

"Look at the part New England played in bringing about the war," Lyman declared. "She saw that war had to come and led the other states into it." His eyes flashed.

"But they had to get a President from Illinois to carry the country through that war, you notice," Stephen crowed.

Lyman went back to the library and read more history so that he would have more answers. Poetry paled in interest for him. He had never known anything as exciting as this world of ideas he lived in now. Isabel liked to talk about ideas. He wondered if it would be too soon if he called again this Wednesday.

Professor Burdick discussed the four best essays of his class with a committee composed of the president, Professor Gilmore, and the head of the Greek department.

Professor Gilmore shook his head. "If Converse had been in the war I could understand it, but he wasn't. I asked him."

"An essay like that encourages restlessness and discontent. I shouldn't like to have him read it to the student body," the president said thoughtfully. "Point that young man out to me. We ought to keep an eye on him."

Only the Greek professor voted for it. "He's young, that's all. I like to see that spirit in the young. It would be a good essay for the students to hear."

In the end Silas Bates was asked to give his speech on "Our Victorious Generals." Lyman sat through the declamation with a pale face, his cheeks sucked in at the corners of his mouth. His eyes, dark and disappointed, studied the speaker. On Silas Bates's lapel blazed the pin of his secret society. But not *the* one he noticed with pleasure, not Chauncey Westcott's. Lyman felt sure his own essay was the best. It was better than this eulogy of the generals. He held his hand down behind the seat in front of him and cracked the joint of his thumb nervously, and when applause followed Bates's speech Lyman clapped loudly, but his curved palms made a hollow sound. When the assembly was over he went up to his room, taking two steps at a time as though he were pursued. He flung himself into a chair in front of Sam's chessmen. Sam was teaching him the game. Downstairs in the rhetoric class Professor Gilmore called the roll. He called Lyman Converse's name again and checked it "absent."

"What the hell's the use!" Lyman muttered, shoving a pawn so carelessly his hand knocked over the two knights in its way.

Dear Mother:
Aunt Matilda didn't invite me for Thanksgiving dinner. I think
they were invited out themselves. Isabel said something about it. But
I was not homesick and had a pleasant day here. We had a good meal
here at college, turkey and mince pie just as we would have had at
home, and there was a Thanksgiving service in the chapel. The presi-
dent gave a fine discourse. Our country has surely a great deal to be
thankful for on this Thanksgiving when we realize that last year at
this time our country was at war. One of the upperclassmen who was
in the first Rhode Island company to go told me that last Thanksgiving
they were in the woods in Virginia and all they had for dinner was
beans. His name is Chauncey Westcott III, and he was transferred to
Dan's company. He said all the men thought a great deal of Dan.
We have a whole week's vacation. It will give me a good opportunity
to prepare my work with extra care and do some reading.

Faithfully, your son,
Lyman Converse

P.S. Please remember me to Easy.

Lyman read over his letter with satisfaction. It was a very good
letter, considering that he had neither eaten at the college nor attended
the Thanksgiving service. He could hear his father reading it aloud
to his mother.

"There, mail it for me, will you, Sam?"

Lyman's roommate looked at him with concern. "You're sure you'll
be all right? You looked awful peaked."

"I'm fine. It's just this everlasting headache. I wish I could drink
without a headache every time."

"Maybe the Lord gives it to you to discourage you from drinking,
Lyman," Sam said seriously.

"I wouldn't be surprised, but it's a dirty trick," Lyman said, laying
his head carefully back on the pillow and pulling the blanket up over
his bare shoulder. The clothes he had peeled off half an hour ago in
broad daylight lay in a heap on the floor. In front of Sam, he felt like
a man of the world, as easy and devil-may-care as Chauncey Westcott.

"Well, I'll say you are sick. It's the truth," Sam said as he went out
to his own breakfast.

Lyman had lived for the last two weeks in another world than that
of ideas. It had begun on the day Chauncey Westcott had called to
him on his way out of class, asking him if he had a brother by any

chance, "a Captain Dan Converse in the First Vermont, a whale of a good fellow he was!"

When Lyman told him Dan had gone out West Chauncey slapped his thigh and said: "By God, that's like him. That's where I wish I were instead of puking around going to school again. So you're Dan's brother! All the men in his company would have followed him to hell and back. I guess we did. I'm on my way home now, come on home with me." Lyman had sauntered down the street with Chauncey Westcott and his friend Ed Abbott hardly believing his own luck.

Westcott's rooms were a revelation to Lyman. Brought up on rag rugs except for the flowered carpet in the parlor, he found the glowing Oriental rugs strangely rich under his feet. The rack of pipes seemed particularly opulent and masculine-looking, and in one corner of the study stood a piano. Lyman went over to it.

Chauncey had collapsed on the couch with his long legs in the air. "Try it, Converse. D'you play?"

"Just a little, by ear," he had answered, thinking of the evenings he had played a few tunes by ear while Willie urged him on. He felt his way through "Believe Me if All Those Endearing Young Charms."

"Here, for heaven's sake!" young Abbott cried out. "Give over, my boy!" But his smile as he said it was so merry that Lyman didn't feel chagrined. Abbott stretched his long coffee-colored trousers out under the piano and applied the toes of his boots to the pedals. His hands spread lightly over the keys.

When Lyman left Westcott's rooms a little after midnight, the music still sang in his head. He had been a little light-headed from the wine Chauncey had served, but more from the feeling of being one of these exciting fellows. He had actually sung a solo, another of Easy's old songs. "Swing Low, Sweet Chariot," the song Easy sang when they brought John's body back from Malden. They had urged him to sing another and then another and Abbott asked him to join a little singing club they had. It was wonderful how at home he had felt.

And then Thanksgiving! When Chauncey heard he was staying in Providence, he said of course he must spend the holiday with him. "Let Dan Converse's brother stay over there at the dormitory on Thanksgiving? Not on your life!" Chauncey had declared. "Why, if I'd known who you were . . ." He broke off. And Lyman had known he meant that he would have put him up for his fraternity.

Chauncey's family were in Washington and Chauncey invited some of the chaps from college, mostly his own fraternity brothers, which made it all the more exciting. He, Lyman, had been the only freshman.

Of course Abbott was there pounding on the piano every now and then and getting everyone to sing.

In spite of the dull throbbing in his head Lyman thought back on the wonderful dinner. They had had turkey and mince pie just as he had written in his letter, but not the way they had it at home—served by a servant in covered silver dishes, and wine with the meal, and more to drink afterward in the big parlor.

But thinking back, two things disturbed him. Norman Ballinger had said to him: "Chauncey's jealous of you because you're Isabel's cousin. He's been crazy about her all fall." And the other thing was the conversation about Easy. Ed had wanted to know where he had learned the slave songs and he had said from Easy. This time it seemed natural to call Easy "our colored man."

"Say, couldn't you get him down here, find him a job for a while?" Ed said excitedly. "I could use some of his songs in this musical thing I'm getting up."

"Well, he's really a . . . a sort of servant at home. I don't believe the family could spare him," he had said quickly. To these boys who were so used to servants there was nothing odd in mentioning a colored servant. What was the matter with him? He brushed off his uneasy feeling as though it were a film of dust. He wouldn't bring Easy into the conversation again.

He leaned out of bed until he could reach the pipe Chauncey had given him, and the jar of tobacco. He had tried it the other night for the first time. Chauncey said it was much better than cigars.

His head was still painful and the tobacco made the pain throb for a second, but the sensation of lying in bed in midmorning smoking a pipe was pleasant enough to counterbalance any other. He hoped Sam would come back and see him like this.

He punched his pillow into a bigger roll and lay there thinking about Isabel, trying to conjure up her red hair and lively face. She didn't wear her hair in curls the way most girls did, just straight around with a kind of roll in back. He thought of her long eyelashes over her brown eyes, but he couldn't really see her. It was easier to close his eyes and just think about her.

If he hired a cutter from the livery stable and drove over there, perhaps she could go out with him. He stepped out of bed too quickly and the ache in his head warned him to move more slowly. But by the time he had splashed cold water on himself and emptied the water out the window he felt better. He dressed with care, tying his tie a second time and brushing his hair into a shining crest above his high forehead.

"Not too bad, Converse," he said aloud to his image in the mirror. There was the awkward business of money. He was out for this month except for a little chicken feed, but surely he could charge it. Chauncey had charge accounts all over. That was the way a gentleman conducted his affairs. Pay them all up the first of the month when his money came from his father.

"I was afraid Aunt Matilda wouldn't let you come," Lyman said, thinking how different Isabel looked this time, all in gray and purple.

"Oh, Chauncey persuaded her. He was there calling when your note came and he said a good word for you. The Westcotts are old friends of the family," Isabel told him.

His heart warmed toward Chauncey and he was glad he had paid that boy to take over his note. When he had followed later with the rig Isabel had been ready.

"But I don't see why Chauncey would say a good word for me. I hear he's pretty fond of you himself."

"I'm going to a dance with him at Governor Sprague's next week. I suppose he felt generous. But he does like you, Lyman."

"Do you like him very much, Isabel?"

Isabel laughed. "Yes, of course I do, Lyman, very, very much."

He kept his eyes on the narrow white road for a long way.

"I hoped you could come to care for me, Isabel."

"Why, I do. I'm terribly fond of you, Lyman." He felt her looking right at him and met her clear brown gaze.

"But I mean more than that. I mean love," he said lamely. "In time, of course. I know it must seem soon to you to talk of love."

She was quiet now too. The runners slid over the snow more swiftly than their thoughts, but did not cut so deeply.

"But, Lyman, we're first cousins. We couldn't . . . shouldn't really love each other."

"Why shouldn't we? We can't help that."

"People don't fall in love with their first cousins."

"Isabel, could you love me if we weren't?"

"I don't know, Lyman. Maybe I could. Let's go home now, please, and not talk any more about it."

He was angry at leaving it like that. There were things he wanted to say, and she had closed the door. He had ignored the business of being cousins in his own mind. They both could. He glanced at her secretly, taking care to move his head only slightly. Her nose was red and all the color had gone from her face. When she was still, she was hardly pretty at all and he loved her more than ever before. Finally the rebellion within him was too much for silence.

"Isabel, I'll always love you, cousins or not cousins."

"Please, Lyman, I said don't talk any more now." Her hand in its knit mitten pressed his for an instant and was back in her muff. She glanced up at him and their eyes met.

"Could I kiss you once, Isabel?" he asked timidly.

The silence waited coldly and the runners made a squeaking noise on the snow. The silly little bells on the horse's harness jangled heedlessly.

"Yes," she said in an uncertain tone.

He put his arm awkwardly around her shoulders and drew her closer to him in the sleigh. Just as he kissed her they heard the bells on some approaching sleigh and Isabel pulled away quickly. But even that didn't matter. They drove all the way back to her home without a word.

When he went up the walk to the front door with her, he thought how short a time before he had come here for the first time.

"I didn't even know you three months ago."

"Nor I you," she said, and her brown eyes smiled under their lashes. "Thank you for the sleigh ride."

"Thank you for going," he said, bowing. He wished she had asked him to come in.

Lyman drove the cutter back to the livery stable and was glad only the stable boy was there. He used the last of his change for a tip and gave it to him with the free-and-easy manner he had seen in Chauncey.

"Just charge it to my bill," he told the boy. "Mr. Lyman Converse, Brown University."

"Yes, sir," the boy said, hesitating a little.

The walk back up to the college did him good. His spirits rose with every step as he dug his heels into the packed snow of the walks. Nothing was insuperable. He would go to Aunt Matilda and talk to her himself. He'd hunt up some famous couples in history who were first cousins and had married happily. There must be plenty. They would have to wait to marry till he was through college, then he would go into business here in Providence. Summers they would go back to Vermont. Isabel would love Vermont. He pushed the years ahead of him as though they were snow in front of his feet. The iron-gray light of the December afternoon was not gloomy for him. Isabel loved him or she wouldn't have let him kiss her. Had John loved Louisa this way? That question made him uncomfortable, and he wished he hadn't thought of John.

" 'Lo, Sammy!" He sailed his hat across their room and threw his muffler and gloves after it.

"Well, you look like a new man!" Sam's feet came down from the edge of his desk. His eyes were cobwebbed with study. "You have a package from home. I brought it over for you."

There was something reproachful about the brown unfrosted loaf of applesauce cake his mother had sent. It made him think of supper in the kitchen at home.

"Want a piece?" Lyman asked quickly, cutting into the cake with his jackknife. He passed the piece on the cover of his Greek book.

"Yes, I suppose so. I came all the way back from the dining-room with a pot of tea for you and found the room stinking with tobacco and you gone. You didn't pick up a thing. It took me half an hour to clean the place up so I could live in it."

Lyman filled his mouth with cake and grunted sympathetically.

"I don't mind that so much, but I hate to see a bright boy like you running after sports like Westcott and Abbott." Sam was very serious.

"I wasn't with Chauncey Westcott. I took my cousin out sleigh-riding," Lyman said. "I wish we had something to go with this cake." He cut another piece. "It's good, isn't it?"

Sam was not to be interrupted. "All I can say is that you've certainly changed since you came here. You're three years younger than I am, Lyman, so I can talk to you. If you'd ever been in a battle and seen men dying, you'd realize that you don't want to waste your life."

"But you see, Sam," Lyman answered thickly, his mouth full of cake, "I wasn't in battle. I missed the war altogether. Don't preach at me tonight. Tell me what Plato says in that stuff for tomorrow."

Sam sighed. After a few minutes he said, "I wrote out the substance of it for you, it's there in the book."

"Thank you, Sammy. You'll get your reward in Heaven!"

Sam always outlined his reading. Lyman had discovered that he could lay Sam's notes alongside the page and cover the assignment in a third of the time he could do it without them. Sometimes he didn't bother to read the original at all. Sam did it anyway, he might as well read his. Lyman added a fresh shovelful of coal to the fire and lighted his lamp.

He opened his copy of Plato's *Symposium* and spread out Sam's notes. "The Banquet treats of nature of love," Sam's notes read. This subject interested Lyman. He found the place and read for himself. "Try to explain to me then the nature of Love; Love is the love of something or nothing?" "Of something, certainly." The discussion of Socrates and Agathon seemed strangely pertinent and modern. He read intently.

"Is not Love, then, the love of that which is not within its reach, and which cannot hold in security, for the future, those things of which it obtains a present and transitory possession? Evidently. Love, therefore . . . desires that which is absent and beyond his reach. . . ." The words had an ominous sound.

"Plato's as crazy as a loon!" Lyman announced, shoving the book aside. He lay down on his side of the bed and pulled the quilt over his head to block out the light. "Sammy, I'm going to sleep now and I don't want you carousing with those sporting friends of yours!"

Sam studied the long hump under the quilt with perplexity and distaste.

3

"IT has come to my attention, Mr. Converse, that your work has fallen off since Christmas. I asked you to come here so that I could remind you of your obligation to those who have sent you here."

Lyman looked back at the president on the other side of the desk. The dignified face, framed in white hair and side whiskers, was too like his own father's to impress him greatly—a New England type of face with firm mouth and shrewd eyes. Lyman was not particularly interested in what Dr. Harcom had to say to him about his grades, and he sat there with a face that looked to the president both youthful and earnest and thought his own thoughts.

He, Lyman, had an obligation to himself too, not to miss out on any experience in college. How did he know what he would like, what was right for him, until he tried it? He wanted to show Isabel that he was no green cousin from the hills of Vermont but a young man who knew his way about. He already thought with pity of the young person who had come from Painesville in the fall. He had known nothing about fraternities or how to dress or to play high-low-jack or euchre or whist, or whether he could drink his share and hold it gracefully, or even how to smoke a pipe.

Dr. Harcom studied the young man in front of him. He had talked to many young men in his day. He prided himself on being able to tell dishonesty from honesty, conceit from deceit, to pick out fear, lack of assurance, ambition, courage, and all the staples of man's little store.

Lyman Converse seemed very young. His fairness was increased by the dark-green upholstery of the chair in which he sat. His eyes were certainly clear and honest and unafraid. Gilmore had told him about his writing in an essay that he and Wordsworth felt the same way about life. Dr. Harcom had a weakness for the poets. Perhaps this was a poet before him. There was nothing coarse about him, certainly. He must try to help him.

"Sometimes a young man with great talents and powers comes away from home for the first time and falls in with unwise companions and wastes his abilities—you might say that he sells his birthright for a mess of pottage," Dr. Harcom began gently. He had heard that Converse had got in with an older group, a more sporting set than the college liked to see.

Lyman's attention focused for an instant upon Dr. Harcom's words. If he meant Chauncey and Ed, he might as well save his breath to cool his broth. They were his friends. They had seen a little more of life than the average undergraduate. The faculty wanted schoolboys without any ideas of their own so they could tell them what to think and do.

"It is a pretty good idea, Mr. Converse, to seek out friends in your own year and let the common studies and experiences knit you together. I have always felt that the deepest friendships were formed within the class." The boy's eyes were clear, but they did not respond. His face was unrevealing, almost secretive. Dr. Harcom remembered something.

"I have learned that you are the nephew of the late-lamented Nathaniel Holbrook. I knew your uncle, Mr. Converse. He was a man of splendid integrity who prospered by his own labors. He gave to this institution because he appreciated the value of higher education."

"I don't remember him," Lyman said.

"But you know his wife and daughter." Dr. Harcom permitted himself to smile almost archly.

"Yes, sir," Lyman said, without any smile.

"Miss Isabel is a lovely young woman."

"Yes, sir," Lyman agreed.

Dr. Harcom sighed. Outside students were passing on the walk. The sound of their voices always refreshed him, there was never any weariness in them. There was a hesitant tap at the door. He had another appointment.

"Well, Mr. Converse, I feel sure that you won't disappoint these relatives of yours, and your parents, but that you will develop to the limit of your powers. From now on I want to hear only good reports of you." He held out his hand.

When Lyman had gone, Dr. Harcom glanced over the memorandum in front of him. Both the English rhetoric and the Greek professors had complained about his work: too many absences, indifference the last month or two. There was the memorandum from the livery stable about an overdue charge account. He had forgotten to take that up with him. A fine-looking young man. He hoped he would straighten out. Dr. Harcom rumpled the memorandum sheet into a ball and tossed it into the wastebasket. There were more cases needing disciplinary measures this year than in all the years he had been here.

The war, people said. Perhaps they blamed too much on the war, and yet after the tension of the last few years there was a reaction, he felt it himself.

"Come in," he called to the next boy, but he stood for a moment with his back to the room looking out the window. He could see Lyman Converse walking slowly across the campus. He watched him leap the four-rail fence.

"'Shades of the prison house descend upon the growing boy,'" he quoted, and the next appointee waiting in the room listened uncomprehendingly.

Lyman's spirit was not subdued by Dr. Harcom's admonishment, he had expected a more severe lecture. But he was angry because Isabel had not answered his last letter. He doubted if she had been allowed to receive it. The last three times that he had called on Isabel Aunt Matilda had sat in the parlor with them, working a peacock into a piece of tapestry. When he had left after half an hour of stilted talk Aunt Matilda had followed them out to the hall. She had been civil enough, but they couldn't say anything that mattered with her there.

Chauncey mentioned Isabel. He was always there. "That cousin of yours," he said when he spoke of her to him, accentuating the "cousin," Lyman thought.

But it was really Isabel's fault. If she cared about him she could find a way to see him. She could write to him, anyway. The last time he was there she had sat primly across the room, smiling at him now and then while Aunt Matilda kept asking him questions about the family. He should call today. He had a letter from Willie today and one from his mother. Aunt Matilda would love to know that Willie had been an actress. He tried to think how Dan would treat Aunt Matilda, and grew bolder thinking of Dan. Certainly Dan wouldn't stay away from Isabel just because of Aunt Matilda. He took his letters out of his pocket and read them as he turned his steps toward the Holbrooks'.

He read Willie's first. It had taken months to reach him.

Virginia City, Montana Territory,
February 4, 1866

Dear Lyman:

If I thought Painesville was too quiet last year I am being paid for it this year. Virginia City is never quiet a minute. We have a better house now, one that I can keep the dirt out of. Everything is very dear, because it has to come so far, I suppose. Juliet takes to the West and is talking now. Everybody here seems young. There are quite a few Virginians down here and we get together and cook Southern dishes and have a real old Southern time. We entertained Lotta Crabtree when she played here the other night in East Lynne. *Think of it! I know the play as well as I know my own name. After college you must pay us a visit. Dan is trying his luck gold mining.*

Your loving sister,

Willie

Painesville, Vt.
April 7, 1866

Dear Lyman:

Our syrup is going to be good this year. It is a lovely clear color and so sweet! The weather is just right. I kept thinking how you and John always loved the syrup poured on fresh snow. Your father is working too hard. Next year he says he will get somebody to do the syrup and busy himself only with the quarry. He was pleased to hear that you are progressing so well in your work, but he thinks Brown is a very expensive place. He is going to write Matilda to see if you could board with them next year more cheaply. They should invite you to stay without any charge even though my brother is gone.

Easy stopped in the other night and asked about you. Why don't you write him?

Affectionately, your mother,

Abigail Converse

P.S. You haven't mentioned your cousins lately. Please stop in to see them every week or so. It would please them.

Lyman thought grimly of Aunt Matilda when she had his father's letter. What would she say to Father? Did she suspect that he loved Isabel? Isabel wouldn't have told her. Could Dr. Harcom have talked to her? Anyway, this gave him an excuse for calling. His pace quickened and he stood on the white marble step pulling the polished knob before his impulse ran out.

The maid looked at him with distrust, it seemed to Lyman, even glancing at his feet to see if he were tracking in.

"Is Miss Holbrook home?"

The maid hesitated. "I'll see. Just you sit you down there." And she left him to wait on the sofa in the hall.

"Oh, Mina! Is he downstairs now?" Isabel's voice came down to him. He heard her running along the upper hall.

"Lyman!" She ran down the stairs and leaned over the polished rail.

The maid stood on the landing behind her. "Mina, will you give us tea in the library, please."

"You know what your mother said, miss."

"Oh yes, but you understand, Mina." The stern-faced woman seemed to soften visibly.

"Well, these spring days are risky without something warm in you," she murmured, trailing off down the hall.

"Lyman, I'm so sorry. Mother got the idea somehow that . . ." Her hand was in his and again he had the impression of quick, warm strength. He followed her dumbly through the parlor into the library. For a moment his mind did not take in what she had said. She stood against the mantel and the gray stone seemed to give her skin a glowing whiteness.

"She found one of the poems you sent me and was very angry and shocked. The one that began

" 'Her bones are beautiful as the bare branches of a winter tree;
I feel their strength through glowing flesh that clothes them in sweet
symmetry. . . .' "

Isabel closed her eyes as she said his clumsy, deep-felt lines. Her smooth head leaned against the mantel. Her lips moving with the words were so entirely adorable that he kissed them. His arms were around her.

"Isabel," he whispered.

"Oh, Lyman, we mustn't," she whispered back.

They heard the teacups clinking on the tray as Mina came down the hall, and sprang apart. Isabel sat down quickly in a chair by the fireplace and Lyman sat across from her, two proper silhouettes in the shy April light.

"Thank you, Mina. Tea will taste so good. Oh, Lyman, Chauncey was here last Sunday and he's going to invite you to Newport for the spring holidays. We planned it all out last Sunday while Mother and his mother were talking."

Lyman sat silent, shaken by the feeling of Isabel in his arms. How could she talk? He couldn't put his mind on what she was saying, his own blood beat in his ears so hard.

"Lyman," she said softly. Her hands clasped together and hid in a fold of her skirt. "Lyman!" She frowned a little. Her voice called to him imperiously across some vast space that lay between them.

"Yes," he answered and even the one syllable was hard to sound. He wanted to touch her again, not talk.

She tipped her head a little to the side. She had never done that before, not just that way. Then she sat back with her hands on the arms of the chair. She was looking straight at him. Her face was very sober. "But we mustn't love each other, Lyman, don't you see?"

"No, I don't." Now he could talk. "If you loved me, it's meant to be so. There's a girl in Painesville who loved my brother . . ." He saw Louisa coming down the stairs, carrying the candle and the book that John used to read from in her hand and her eyes so dark and wanting. If Isabel could see her she would understand what he meant.

"The one who was killed, Lyman?"

"Yes, John." What had he been going to say? Now it was gone from him. Instead there was Isabel's face waiting, not pretty like Louisa's but alive as no one else's was.

"Go on about her, Lyman. What was her name?"

"Her name is Louisa. Well, just that if you could see her you'd know what a terrible thing it is not to be able to love someone." That didn't explain what he meant at all. His words were childish and stupid.

"Maybe I do know," Isabel said in a very low voice, not looking at him. He went on trying to explain.

"You see, she loved him so, and now he's dead," he said.

After a minute she said slowly: "I see, Lyman, but if you love a person very much, someday you marry him, and we couldn't do that. Mother wouldn't . . ."

"Your mother doesn't matter. My father doesn't matter. Parents cannot stand between us and our destiny." His voice rose in its conviction. Thoreau had said it, but he, Lyman, knew it to be true.

"Is that so, young man!" His aunt came in upon them from the hall. He saw only the jet pupils of her eyes shimmering like the fringes of her dress, not the rest of her eyes nor her face.

"Mother, Lyman was just saying . . ."

"Be quiet, Isabel, and go up to your room. Lyman, I have seen some of the lines you have written and I have been on the verge of writing your father. Now I shall do so at once."

Then Lyman recovered quickly. "My father is writing you, Aunt Matilda. His letter is probably in the mail right now. He's writing to ask if I may board with you, as my bills have been too high." He saw the jet pupils dance with rage. "I know how you would like that, Aunt Matilda."

He was walking out now. He would never be back in this room, in this house. Hopelessness lay at the pit of his stomach and he had no care for what he said. Behind him came his aunt's voice, her words like hail bouncing off the woodshed roof. He looked up the stairs and saw Isabel's face between two spindles, looking down at him. She moved her head ever so little and her lips formed the words "I love you."

"I love you," he answered soundlessly.

"Isabel Holbrook, go up to your room." Her smooth red hair moved past the spindles. Her dress was dark, her hands were pink against the white wood. The fingers of one hand moved in the air as she waved to him.

"I shall have to ask you, Lyman, not to come here again, even if you are my husband's nephew. When I write your father . . ."

Lyman went out the door and down the white-marble steps seeing only Isabel's face, caring only about that. Not seeing her again was impossible. She loved him, she had said so. They were like two people in that play of Shakespeare's from which Willie had taken her baby's name. Aunt Matilda was old and unimportant. He had walked all the way to the pump behind Hope Hall before he began to worry about his father. He stood there drinking from the cup chained to the post. Would Father be angry because he loved Isabel? He had never objected to John's loving Louisa—just to Dan's marrying Willie, and that was different. He didn't care what his father thought, anyway.

"Say, you're as bad as a horse drooling over a watering trough." He turned quickly to see Pigott '67 waiting for a drink. Pigott was a fraternity man and an upperclassman. Lyman filled the drinking cup for him and handed it to him.

"Going my way?" Pigott nodded his head toward the red-brick building. Lyman walked beside him.

Five days went by. A letter came from his mother, but it made no mention of any letter from his aunt.

Your father would like to hear more about your church attendance. Why don't you write the subject of the minister's sermon and give the text sometimes? Your father feels the Reverend Leland has failed this last year. He preached the same sermon last Sunday that he preached a year ago.

Lyman felt relieved, but still uneasy. For three days he applied himself to his work and didn't go out of sight of the college buildings. He spent a good deal of his time finding new words with which to describe Isabel. She was like a willow blown by the wind, like a swallow darting. She was shadow and sunlight, and her hair was the autumn color on the hills. She should always lean her head against soapstone. He would build her a house someday far bigger than her father's house, and the doorframe would be soapstone and she would lean her head against it and wave to him when he went out the door.

A whole week passed, and then Chauncey Westcott took him home to his rooms.

"I've got a letter for you from the fair Isabel. First I told her I wouldn't be any Pandarus if you and she were playing Troilus and Cressida, but she promised me the contents would make me happy. Hey, Ed, play soft music." Lyman opened the letter while the two jibed at him. "Shut up," he muttered.

Dear Lyman:

After hours of begging, Mother has promised me faithfully that she will not write your father a word except to say that it will be impossible to have you live here, on the condition that I will forget you at once (as if I could) and not try to see you. I have promised—oh, Lyman, please understand, because I remember that Uncle Orville is very stern and he might take you out of college and stop your education, and I won't have that. You must go on and graduate and be somebody wonderful. If it were not for the cruel fate that separates us I would ignore both your father and my mother, but God made us as we are so I resign myself and think only of your good.

Your l—g cousin,

Isabel

Lyman folded the note and put it in his coat pocket.

"Ah, methinks the little lad likes not the contents of his missive, Ed," Chauncey said. "When unlucky in love always try your hand at cards, my boy—or a new love."

Today Lyman was not elated at being in Chauncey Westcott's rooms. He looked at his hand moodily. If he could not see Isabel nor write to her, he didn't care whether he stayed at Brown or not. Isabel might resign herself, but he never would. Let Aunt Matilda write his father, he might as well know now that his son meant to marry Isabel.

"Say, Converse, what I really brought you over here for wasn't to give you a letter from your coz, but to ask you to come to Newport with us during the vacation," Chauncey said. "The family'll all be away, but we'll open up part of the house and take Burwell, who does my rooms, and Abbott and you for servants. We ought to manage pretty well."

"Say, wait a minute!" Ed interrupted. "Converse, why can't you get that colored boy of yours that knows all those old slave songs to come along and help Burwell? Can he cook? Most of 'em can. And in between times I can get him to sing some of those songs. Now that's what I call an idea from a great mind!"

"For once, yes, Ed. That isn't a bad idea at all!" Chauncey agreed.

Lyman hitched uncomfortably in his chair. "Well, the only trouble is I don't believe the family can spare him. He isn't—he's more than a house servant, really. He works in the quarry."

"Oh well, if you can't get him down here, it's all right," Chauncey said. "Ed's too loony now about those songs. He thinks he's going to collect 'em and write music for 'em."

Ed ignored Chauncey. "There was a song some darkies used to sing at Andersonville. I thought maybe he'd know it. I can't get it out of my head."

"Andersonville! Were you there?" Lyman asked.

"Was I there? I left about fifty pounds of my good flesh there in that stinking hell."

"Did you know Wendell Hall from Painesville, Vermont?" Lyman might have been back home, following Jeb Holmes around listening to the talk about the war. "Wendell died there. His father had 'Murdered at Andersonville Prison' put on his headstone."

"And he wasn't telling a lie, either. You should have seen that Harry Wirtz."

"Don't get him started, Lyman. He raves when he gets going. I pity his children. They're going to fight the war all over with him. Now mine, I'll say, 'Children, it was one hell of a Sunday-school picnic!' "

"That's better than having to say you weren't in it," Lyman muttered, and found the old hurt in his mind just as sore as ever.

"I don't know. I wouldn't say that," Ed said quietly, flipping his cards with his fingernail. "How did we get on this subject?"

"By the way, Lyman, Pigott seems to think you're quite the boy. He's president of the Theta Delts, you know." Chauncey was busy lighting his pipe. Lyman was glad, for he might have seen the quick girlish flush Lyman could feel rising to his own face.

"Oh? I met him at the pump the other night," Lyman said, laying down a queen.

On the strength of what Chauncey had told him he drank too much and went home a little unsteadily after one. He had lost twenty dollars, but Chauncey told him to forget it. They'd settle up later. He might win it back by that time, and more too. He'd need more if he should be asked to join . . .

At the pump on his way home he stopped and splashed water on his face and head, stopping the rivulets that trickled down his neck with hasty dabbings of his handkerchief.

Sam had left a lamp burning for him. Good old Sam! It worried Sam to have him out late. He turned the wick up a little and set the lamp on his dresser. He perked up the corner of his bow tie, smoothed his hair over his temple, and raised one eyebrow at his own image. He saw himself with Chauncey and Ed Abbott, and perhaps Pigott, in Newport, sitting in a big parlor like Aunt Matilda's playing whist. Easy would bring in a tray with glasses on it. "Oh, Easy, Mr. Abbott would like you to sing for him." Pigott would be impressed. Lyman blew out the light.

But when he was in bed he lay awake a long time. He had said the family couldn't spare Easy. That was all there was to it. He had said he was more than a servant. That was the truth. None of the boys in college had servants except Chauncey, and Chauncey had come out of the war half-sick. He was as well off as most of them in his class. Think of the chaps who ate at the cheaper table in the dining-hall and those who did their own cooking in their rooms. Badgeley's room was never free from the stink of turnips. Still . . . it might impress Aunt Matilda, too. If Easy came a day or so before they went to Newport, he could manage to have Aunt Matilda see him. That would show her he was more than a country boy from a hill farm. He wondered if he could give a tea up here in his room. Chauncey had had one.

In the dark the bareness of the dormitory room was hidden, the washstand with its basin and pitcher, the wooden bucket by the door, the big chair that someone had cut all the spindles out of, the clothes hanging on nails against the wall. In the dark, with his head still light from the wine at Chauncey's, the difficulties of his plan seemed trifling.

4

Dear Easy,
I have thought of you so often all year and missed all the things we always did together, hunting and skating and fishing . . .

He crossed that out and took a fresh sheet of paper. He mustn't establish an atmosphere he wouldn't want to keep up here. But how could he get over to Easy that he wanted him to be a sort of personal servant without hurting his feelings? He began again.

Dear Easy,
I have a proposition I should like to put up to you. Could you come down to Providence for ten days if I paid you a salary? A friend of mine is opening his big house at Newport for the week of spring vacation and inviting a few of us to go with him. Mr. Westcott will have his man and I want to furnish someone to help, and of course I thought at once of you. You wouldn't have much to do. Most of the time you could enjoy Newport and see the ocean and join with us in some of our singing groups.
Of course Father would not hear of such a thing, but he need not know. After all, you are free to do as you like, and it would do you good to get a little change. I am enclosing some money for your fare. Let me know, so I can get lodgings for you. I would like you to come April 17.
It will be so good to see you,
Your friend,
Lyman Webster Converse

Lyman sold his second best suit and some books and sent Easy the proceeds. He would worry about paying him when the time came.

"Sam," he said offhandedly one evening, "my man Easy may be coming down to Providence to go to Newport with Chauncey and some others and me. I don't suppose he'll be here more than overnight, but we can have him slick up the room and do little things."

Sam stared. "Come off! Are you trying to tell me you have your own personal servant?"

"No, not a personal servant, but you see my family have this Negro and they want me to keep him here for a time for—well, reasons I won't go into."

Sam frowned. "You mean he's got interested in some white woman or something like that?"

"Sam! What a mind!" Lyman said, feeling uncomfortable.

A week later he received a note on quarry stationery.

Dear Lyman:
I shall arrive in Providence Friday at 10:30 A.M. Have not told your father or mother.

Yours truly,

Easy

The writing reproached him, it was so clear and well-formed. The very brevity of the note bothered him. He had a sickish feeling about ever proposing such a trip to Easy, and he poured himself a drink from the small bottle under his bed and smoked a pipeful to rid himself of the feeling. He dreaded Friday at ten-thirty worse than the day of an examination.

He reached the station before the train came in and stood well over to the side of the platform. He wanted to watch Easy get off without being seen.

Easy came out on the narrow porch at the rear of the train after all the other passengers. He was the only colored person among them, and head and shoulders taller than anyone else. He stood there bareheaded, his dark face shining with perspiration. Lyman had never noticed before how he held his head back as though to let the sky strike fairly down on it. His nose was too large, and flattened at the nostrils, but for a Negro he was good-looking. He had grown, of all things, a mustache like Dan's, Lyman noticed enviously.

The last white passenger climbed down the narrow little stairs from the train. Easy took it at one jump. He wore a dark coat and lighter tan-colored trousers. He carried a carpetbag Lyman recognized as the old one that used to hang in the woodshed filled with the extra spindles from his grandmother's spinning wheel. He looked unconfused by the bustle of a city railroad station. Lyman wished he had looked bewildered, so he could have come to his rescue and impressed him with his superior knowledge of the ways of stations and cities.

Lyman went up to him, acutely aware that he was four inches shorter than Easy. "Why, hello there, Easy." His voice took the color of his thoughts; it was pleasant, patronizing, and artificial. His eyes went to meet Easy's and took refuge on the collar of Easy's mended white shirt. He wore a cravat of John's. Then Lyman put out his hand and, feeling Easy's big and hard on his own, his eyes came swiftly to Easy's.

"Hello, Lyman," Easy said, grinning.

"Gosh, Easy, it's good to see you!" Unaccountably his voice was husky. Then the embarrassment rushed back over him as he realized why Easy was there. "Well, I don't suppose you've had your breakfast, have you?" He clutched at the straw of something to do.

"Yes, I got my breakfast early."

In his confusion, Lyman reached for Easy's carpetbag, but with his longer arm Easy secured it. They walked together down the busy street. Lyman had not thought this out. Did a gentleman and his man walk together down the street? There was no pattern of service in the part of Vermont Lyman knew. He would just have to do with Easy as he had always done. He saw what a mistake the whole idea had been. He must have been crazy—he had drunk too much that night.

"How are Mother and Father?" He plunged hurriedly into conversation.

"They're fine. Your mother worries herself about Dan'l and Miss Willie being way off out West. Your father don't talk much about them."

"Are you there a lot, Easy?"

"I get over every day, but I'm working pretty hard at the quarry. I guess we're gettin' out more soapstone 'n the whole United States put together."

"They—I mean the folks—don't know you're coming here?"

"Nope. I jus' told Mr. Perkins I had to be gone awhile."

Lyman had found a temporary room for Easy with a colored family by the name of Green. Green was a waiter in one of the eating places and Lyman hoped his example would teach Easy.

Lyman introduced them. Easy was very dignified and quite silent. His great dark shining eyes seemed too bright to Lyman, made of some soft stuff like celluloid that registered every shade and tone of voice too quickly.

Mr. Green was deeply respectful, calling Lyman "the young gentleman" and "sir."

"Well, then, Easy, I have a class until three, and then if you'll be at my room . . . Mr. Green will tell you how to get there—and oh, if there's any little thing you can do to tidy it up . . . it's usually in a mess . . ." His voice trailed off inconclusively.

Easy stood in the low doorway looking at him. "I'll do that, Lyman," he said gravely.

Lyman walked rapidly across the campus and up the path to the door of University Hall. He ran his finger under his collar to cool his hot neck and smoothed back his hair.

What was wrong about it, anyway? Why did he feel so uncomfortable? Easy liked doing things for his mother and father and Willie. He did things around the house at home. This was a change for him, that was all. Well, then! But his mind was not taken in. He knew what was wrong. It was just that he was asking Easy to act as "his man" not because he needed anything done for him but to puff himself up in Chauncey Westcott's eyes, to show off. That was what made him feel so uncomfortable when he met Easy's eyes. But he couldn't back out now. He would have to go through with it because he had told Chauncey . . . Maybe he could make it up to Easy sometime. He picked up his books for Greek class. At the door he came back, and taking some clothes from the pegs on the wall, dropped them on a chair. He tossed his hat over onto the table. Easy would have something to do when he arrived, he told himself in apology. Then he ran down the stairs to his class.

Lyman dreaded going back to the room after class. He waited in the main hall for Sam. "Easy came all right," he told him. "I asked him to come up to the room and pick the place up a little."

Sam stared at him, then grinned. "I never thought there was anything to picking up the place, King Croesus. If he had dropped in in the winter, now, he could have kept the stove full. You must be crazy, Lyman."

Even simple, good-natured Sam irritated him today. Lyman wished he had asked Ed or Chauncey to come back with him. They would have known how to treat a manservant. The boys laughing and talking on the stair above him looked so carefree that he envied them.

When he pushed open the door, Easy sat on the chair by the window. He must have watched him coming all the way across the campus, Lyman realized uncomfortably.

"Well, Easy!" he said. He was grateful that Easy stood up as they came in the room. Had he used to at home? He was so uncomfortably conscious of every little thing Easy did here.

"Sam, this is Easy I was telling you about. Easy, this is Mr. Andrews."

"How do you do, Easy," Sam said. "I've got to meet Stub Hawkins, Lyman. See you at suppertime." He nodded to both of them and banged the door behind him. Lyman was left again with Easy. He had hung up all the clothes, he noticed. The old cigar stub that had been in the tray over there was gone.

"You've got a nice place to live, Lyman," Easy said.

"Yes, it's a pretty good dump. I'd like to have rooms in town, though, so much more freedom. Maybe you could come down and keep them for me. You'd have a great time in Providence." There, that would give Easy the idea. He had been looking out the window as he talked. Now his eyes came back to Easy. He wished Easy would stop watching him.

"We do a lot of singing here, Easy. I've sung some of your songs and Ed Abbott is crazy about them. That's one of the reasons I wanted you to come down here, because of course I can't begin to sing 'em the way you do." Now he felt better. He hurried on before the uncomfortable feeling came back.

"You'll like Mr. Westcott and Mr. Abbott. They're gentlemen, Easy. Chaun—Mr. Westcott's the one who's invited me down to his family place at Newport. He'll have his man and we'll just batch it, sort of. I thought you could help him." Lyman had been playing with the charm on his watch chain as he talked. That too was a little thing he had bought himself this year. Most of the Brown men wore them, upperclassmen at least. As he looked up he caught Easy's shining dark eyes. Was Easy grinning? He couldn't be sure. He stood up restlessly.

"You're sure my father won't think of your coming here?"

"You can't ever tell about Mr. Converse, but I don't think he would think of that!" And the way Easy said it seemed to Lyman to place his father above thinking of such an idea.

Lyman sat back in the chair with the spindles gone and stretched his legs out on the couch. "Bring me one of those cigars over there, will you, Easy?" He must begin somewhere while he was alone with him. Easy was farther from the shelf than Lyman was, but he brought them, leaving Lyman to light his cigar for himself. Lyman was glad of something to busy himself with. He felt uncomfortable at not offering Easy one as he would at home. He listened to any footsteps passing his door with dread lest someone come in. It struck him suddenly that Easy must be the first Negro ever in this room. He seemed big in it. It used to be so comfortable with Easy at home. He was the one person he could talk to about anything, but now he had to hunt for something to talk about.

"How's Louisa?" He asked, not because he wanted to know but because it was a safe question.

"She kind o' keep to herself. Her father ain't been too pert lately. Your mother say Louisa was helping over at the schoolhouse."

Lyman could see her in the schoolroom, standing up in front of the room holding a book in her hands. Her face would be pale, likely, none of that wild-rose pink in her cheeks. She seemed so many years older than Isabel. Against her dark coloring Isabel seemed all golden, golden freckles and gold lights in her eyes and her hair.

"Does she like it? Louisa, I mean?"

Easy shrugged. "I s'pose she wishes John was back and they could get married."

"I guess she does."

"But there's four girls in Painesville's lost their sweethearts. She ain't the only one."

"That so? Who are the others?"

He and Easy might have been right back in Painesville, walking down the hill road into town talking about things. He mustn't go on this way.

"I been thinking I might go back to Virginia."

That Easy could think of going back down South shocked him. "Why, Easy, you wouldn't go back after all these years?"

"I don't know, I kinda thought I would."

"But, Easy, you wouldn't like it down there any more. The South is beaten and everyone's poor."

"You kinda like where you were born, Lyman. I never did like cold weather so much."

Lyman studied Easy's dark face that told so little of what he was thinking. It seemed like disloyalty that all the time over in the old smokehouse Easy could have been thinking about the South, planning to go back.

Ned Bowers popped his head through the doorway, glanced in amazement at Easy, and withdrew with a muttered, "Excuse me!"

"Well, I've got to stop in at the library, Easy, to bone up on some Greek for tomorrow. You go along with me and I'll start you out so you can find your way back to the Greens'. Uh . . . here's some money to get yourself around."

"I got money, Lyman. You keep it. Your father says it's mighty costly here at the university."

Lyman slipped his hand back into his pocket gratefully and yet uncomfortably. He hoped they wouldn't meet many fellows. Now he began to wonder if it was against the rules to bring a colored person up in the dormitory. Easy didn't look enough like a servant, he thought critically. Lyman felt thin and short beside him. At the corner he paused.

"Well, so long, Easy. You see the sights and I'll come and get you tonight. We'll go over to Mr. Westcott's rooms. They'll want to hear you sing."

To walk along unimpeded by any responsibility was a relief. He ran up the steps into the library.

At Chauncey's things were better. Chauncey knew how to handle such a situation. His tone of voice was just the right mingling of friendliness and superiority. Ed asked Easy about singing right away. He and Easy drifted over to the piano. Soon Ed was feeling out that tune, the same tune he was always playing when he sat idly at the piano.

Easy shook his head. "They sing different songs in South Carolina 'n Virginia, I reckon." His eyes shone. He leaned on the piano listening. Ed repeated the plaintive little tune over and over.

"My Lord, I'd have died in that hole of a prison without those niggers singing. They'd go by sometimes all chained together and carrying picks over their shoulders and sing. I'd decide I better try to keep alive a little longer. There was one about 'Nobody knows the trouble . . .'"

Easy's face quickened. He leaned both arms on the piano and began to sing in a low voice:

"Nobody knows de trouble I've seen . . . nobody knows but Jesus."

Ed struck a chord now and then, shaking his head a little as he tried to get it, his face intent in its listening.

Over on the sofa Lyman tried to talk to Chauncey about the week at Newport.

"How will we go, Chaunce? I mean with Easy?"

"Oh, Easy can go tomorrow evening with Burwell. We can go down in the morning," Chauncey said lazily. "Say, he's quite a husky, isn't he?"

"Yes, he is. You should see him tote a barrel of flour on his shoulder all the way up the hill!" he boasted.

"Listen to him sing!"

Easy's big voice surged through the room, his words half-lost in his slurred way of speaking them.

"Sing 'Go Down, Moses,' Easy," Lyman said in a proprietary voice. Easy began it without a second's hesitation, closing his eyes as he sang it, his head moving with the tune.

"Tell ole Pharaoh, let ma people go."

Lyman filled his pipe from Chauncey's tobacco jar. Was he trying to keep Easy from going ahead—getting him to come down here so he could show him off as a servant? Easy didn't have to come if he didn't want to. Lyman came back to the sofa and sat smoking his pipe and frowning across the room. The song Easy sang bothered him.

"Easy, you remember those cousins Mother's always talking about?" Lyman began the next afternoon as they walked up the street.

"Your mother's brother's folks, the one who owns part of the quarry?"

"Yes, only Uncle Nate's dead. Well, my cousin Isabel and her mother live here." He didn't know quite how to go on. "I—Easy, I'm in love with Isabel . . . Miss Isabel." He stopped. He had never thought of telling anyone.

Easy's face broke into a grin. "That mus' be why you seem so different, Lyman. Is she prettier 'n Miss Willie?"

"She's different, Easy." They walked up College Hill in silence.

"Well, loving her ain't bad, is it, Lyman?"

"Yes, Easy, it is, or at least Aunt Matilda makes Isabel think it's bad. We're cousins, you see, and Isabel thinks people who are cousins can't marry. I don't believe it, do you?" Lyman was unconscious that he was asking Easy's advice just as he used to.

Easy scratched his head. "Why for can't they?"

"Oh, I don't know. Your children might turn out crazy, I guess," he said uncomfortably. "But I'm going to marry her, and I think part of the way Aunt Matilda feels is because she thinks I'm just a country boy from Vermont and not good enough for the Holbrooks in Providence. I kind of thought if she should see you—I mean see that we have ideas about living . . . Look, we'll go past their house and you'll see what I mean," he ended in embarrassment.

Easy was looking down the street. He seemed to be thinking over what Lyman had said, at least he made no comment. As they came to the brick posts and iron fence of the Holbrooks', Matilda Holbrook and Isabel were coming down the walk from the house. Lyman had no time to think what to do. He hadn't meant to meet them like this, but they had seen him, there was no avoiding them.

"Why, Lyman!" Isabel cried out, dropping her parasol with a quick movement that was like a salute. Aunt Matilda stared at him. Lyman stepped up to her quickly.

"Aunt Matilda, I've been wanting to thank you for not writing my father—I mean about the verses I sent Isabel. You couldn't have or he would have been angry. I presume I was hasty and a little rude the other day. I want to beg your pardon." He had not known he was going to say any such thing to his aunt. He stopped, aghast at himself.

Aunt Matilda stood still in the path looking at him. Her eyes moved to Easy, who stood at ease looking at them all.

"Oh, Aunt Matilda, this is Ezekiel, who—our man, you know, at home. He came down to go to Newport with Chauncey and Ed Abbott and myself. Chauncey is taking Burwell and Easy here to cook for us." He stopped in confusion again.

Easy ducked his head in a quick bow. "How d'you do, ma'am, miss."

Aunt Matilda's eyes rested momentàrily on Easy and moved back to Lyman.

"Lyman, I think your parents must be out of their minds allowing a young schoolboy like you to go down to Newport for a week's carousing, let alone having a servant! Unless Abigail and Orville have changed very radically they know nothing about this! I doubt their ever keeping a colored servant!"

"Mother, Lyman has told me about Easy. He was a slave and Uncle Orville rescued him before the war and kept him for a servant."

Lyman winced at Isabel's words. He was angry now. He had hoped so much from the impression Easy would make on Aunt Matilda, and it had worked quite the other way. He reached for his dignity as though it were a hat that had slipped off his head.

"I see you are determined to believe only evil of me, Aunt Matilda," he said stiffly, "but you will find you are mistaken. Come, Easy." He felt himself crossing the vast distance of two feet between them and his aunt, Easy a little behind him. "Good-bye, Isabel," he said as he faced her.

"Good-bye, Lyman." Isabel held out her hand and he took it and felt her quick pressure that said so much more than her words. "And I'm glad that I've met you, Easy," she said, smiling at him.

Now they were walking down the street. The ladies were going in the other direction. Lyman tried to see if he could pick out the sound of Isabel's feet. He was burning inside with disgust with himself and the sorry mess he had made of everything. He couldn't say anything to Easy. He watched the shadows they threw along the pavement, Easy's longer than his, as it always was on the road at home. They came at last to the pump back of Hope. No one was there, for a wonder. Lyman leaned over the curbing and felt the coolness of the water far below reach up to his hot face. When he stood back Easy lowered the bucket and handed Lyman a cupful.

"Easy, I'm sorry," Lyman said abruptly. "You must hate me for getting you down here and trying to act as though—well, you know." He was looking at the water bucket, following the rusted hoops with his eye.

"Why, that's all right, Lyman. Don't you worry none. You jus' wanted to put on kind o' for your aunt," Easy said softly.

Lyman drank from the cup. The water was as kind as Easy's words.

He looked at him and Easy grinned cheerfully, as though it were nothing.

"Why don't you go back home, Easy? I don't blame you if you never want to see me again."

"I thought we was goin' to Newport?"

"Well, we were, but . . ."

"Well, we might as well do what we set out to do," Easy said like any Yankee.

Newport wasn't all Lyman had dreamed, and it was more. There was a look of the main street of Painesville about it, but there were more white clapboarded houses and taller, with more elaborate fans over the doors and some with fluted pillars, pretty enough for meeting-houses. The elms were larger and bowed their leafless branches more deeply over the streets in the old part. And there were the amazing big porched hotels not yet open for the season, and close-shuttered shops in the market part.

"You must come down in summer and see what it's like at the height of the season," Chauncey said. Lyman smiled, but he knew he would be haying in the summer or working in the quarry.

The Westcotts' house was bigger than any of the houses in Paines-ville, with a wide porch on three sides and a view of the ocean so that you felt the porch was the deck of a great sailing vessel. The furniture in the house was encased in white covers and the candelabra and sconces were covered with bags. The house smelled damp at first, but Burwell and Easy laid fires in the big living-room and dining-room and two of the upstairs bedrooms and the dampness was soon gone. Burwell was an old Irishman who had been with the Westcotts a long time, a bent old fellow, but Lyman noticed uncomfortably that he ordered Easy about loudly enough and soon had him in a white coat for serving.

They stayed up till two or three or later in the morning and slept till noon and had lobster and clams and oysters and terrapin and Chauncey Westcott I's wines to drink with them. Lyman learned what champagne was and the difference between Madeira and apricot brandy. Some day he would drink with Dan and Dan would be surprised at his knowledge. He learned songs with many verses, verses he would never dare sing at home, and kissed a village girl who came up with three others one night to dance to the music Ed and Easy made, Easy picking at a banjo with clever but unaccustomed fingers. But the girls meant nothing to them. They were just girls they drove home together and serenaded more for the joy of waking the town in the dead of night than to please the girls. They had more sport by themselves playing cards in front of the fire or tramping miles along the coast while Chauncey told the old sea captains' stories he had learned as a child.

Lyman had never dreamed of play like this, or that men could play. Sometimes he forgot to play himself in watching the others. Chauncey was twenty-six and Ed was twenty-seven. Pigott was there, too, Pigott was twenty. They were the ages of men at home who had families to support and were farmers of some experience and sat at the end of their own pews in church. He wondered what Easy thought of all this. They could talk about it back home.

But the play was easily spoiled for Lyman by little things. There was the day they spent on the shore and baked clams in the sand. It had been one of their best days. When they came home, Pigott took off his boots in the kitchen and tossed them over to Easy.

"Clean these up for me, Easy, so I can wear them tomorrow," he said.

Lyman caught Easy's eye as he went through the kitchen with them.

"Want yours cleaned, too, Mistah Converse?" Easy said to Lyman.

"No, thanks, Easy." Lyman had gone upstairs remembering how he and Easy had often cleaned their boots together in the woodshed. The day was spoiled a little.

But he got to know Pigott. Pigott looked as ordinary as Sam Andrews in the morning in a nightshirt, with his hair standing straight up. And Pigott broached the subject of his society to Lyman. "You'll like it. We have the best bunch in the university. You didn't give us a chance to know you in the fall when school began, Converse," he said by way of explanation. "We thought at first you were just an old sobersides from the hills."

He and Lyman had this talk at the end of the long parlor. Chauncey and Ed and two boys who lived in Pawtucket and had come down for the day were playing high-low-jack under the light of the big brass lamp whose yellow globe resembled a full moon. Lyman felt a pleasant glow as he listened to Pigott and thought of no longer being an outsider. Now he too could stamp and bang up the stairs after a fraternity meeting and roar down the hall oblivious of the miserable wretches who belonged to no fraternities and lay stupidly sleeping. He would be a fraternity brother of Chauncey Westcott's, who was in Dan's company. He had proved something.

"Oh, here you are!" Pigott cried out, looking up as Easy came in carrying a tray of glasses. Easy looked blacker in his white coat with a black bow at his stiff white collar. His manner was perfect, as though he had been serving young gentlemen all year instead of driving an ox sled of soapstone blocks down a steep Vermont hill to the mill. This was the way Lyman had seen it in his mind's eye, and yet as he took his glass and murmured, "Thanks, Easy," the pleasant glow ebbed, leaving him dissatisfied. He sipped from his glass and waited for Pigott to say more. But Pigott had said all he meant to and moved over to try his luck at cards.

Lyman stepped through the French doors onto the long wooden porch. The night was different from an April night in Vermont. The cold air had salt on its breath, and a dark wind came up from the sea below the bluff. Lyman let himself over the railing and set out down the walk, unhappy in a vague, causeless sort of way. It was funny, too, after what Pigott had just said. He tried to keep his mind on that. Now that the fellows knew him, of course they wanted him in their fraternity. Or was it because of Chauncey, after all? his mind insisted. And Chauncey had only taken him up in the first place because of Dan and later because he was Isabel's cousin.

He walked beyond the summer places to an open stretch that might have been the pasture at home except that he could feel the sea down below, and hear it. The wind blew his hair back and felt good on his face. He wished suddenly that he were back home.

When he lay down on the ground he put his arms under his head and his fingers pulled at the dead winter grass. The sky was too cloudy for stars and it was cold lying on the ground, but for a few minutes he didn't stir. He wouldn't think, he wouldn't go back over the days of this week here. He tried to still his mind with the thought that when he got back home he could make up to Easy for all this.

But his mind was stubborn and not to be driven. Well, then, think about it! It was easier to face it here alone in the dark. He saw himself meeting Easy at the station and he went back over all they had said. Easy had understood that he wanted to show off. He hadn't thought about it at the time, but now it seemed strange that Easy should have understood so well.

Lyman thought of Easy putting him to bed the other night when he had drunk himself into a silly stupor. Chauncey had called Easy to do it. Ed and Pigott and Chauncey had all drunk too much, but they had held their liquor. Perhaps they had laughed at him. He felt a wave of nausea at the thought. "Youngster, you drank too much last night!" Ed had said to him the next morning.

He had been sick after he woke up, but no one had known that but Easy. He had lost at cards again last night to Pigott. He had to pay Pigott up and he had stooped to asking Easy if he had any money.

Easy had forty dollars in a bag inside his belt and gave him what he needed without a word. Lyman wondered what Pigott would think if he knew he had borrowed from Easy.

His stubborn mind could not stand the squirming of his soul. To get away from his thoughts he started back.

"By God, you're a fool, Converse!" he said aloud, and it helped his self-respect. Tomorrow he would say he had to go back to school, any excuse would do. He would put Easy on the train in Providence, then he would go back up to the university and put in the two days left of the holiday in work. No more reading Sam's notes, he would read every word for himself. He liked the stuff when he had time. The picture of himself forswearing every amusement, working studiously, pleased him. He would bring up his work and Gillyflower would look at him approvingly. He felt exhilarated as he made his plans. His new resolutions were like the dose of sulphur and molasses his mother used to give him in the spring.

5

LYMAN walked soberly back to the college after seeing Easy off on the train.

"I'm afraid you didn't have a very good time, Easy," he had said.

"Sure, I had a good time, Lyman. I never did see Providence nor Newport nor a gentlemen's college before. I seen 'em now," Easy had answered.

"When do you think you'll go back to Virginia, Easy?" He didn't like to think of Easy being gone when he got home.

"Maybe in May, after I put the garden in."

"And you don't think you'll be coming back to Vermont, Easy?"

Easy had shaken his head. "Reckon not, Lyman, not if things is right down there."

The noisy, dirty train puffed into the station and Easy grabbed his carpetbag. Lyman held out his hand.

"Good-bye, Easy. Thanks."

"Good-bye, Lyman. I guess maybe I had a better time than you did," he had answered with a grin.

Lyman had watched the train out of the station. Easy stood on the back platform and waved to him, his face matching the darkness of the train's interior. Easy's going was a relief—not from home, he didn't want Easy leaving Vermont, but—his going from here was a relief. Lyman felt like himself again, not somebody acting a part. He could do what he wanted without thinking of anyone else. Ever since Thanksgiving he had had Easy on his mind. Or he had worried about the impression he was making on Chauncey and Ed Abbott and Pigott. His mind felt stiff, like his neck when he kept it turned too long in one direction. Now he could move it any way he chose. Chauncey and Abbott weren't what he wanted, nor their life. They were the war generation, like Dan. They were older. Pigott wasn't, but Pigott didn't interest him any more. He just hung around with Chauncey and aped everything he did. That he himself had been guilty of the same thing a short time before didn't occur to him at this moment.

"I left a lot of work to make up before college begins, and the family need Easy back," he had told Chauncey. "I've had a great time here, it was certainly fine of you to ask me . . . but I think I better leave

Friday." Chauncey and Ed and Pigott had been a little cool, he thought. Maybe he imagined it. Maybe the week had grown long to all of them. Anyway, he didn't care.

"Old Sobersides!" Pigott said, clapping him on the shoulder.

"Not the other night, boy, when Easy had to put you to bed!" Chauncey said.

If Pigott didn't pledge him after all, it didn't seem so important now. If Chauncey thought him just a kid, there were others at college. Sam wasn't such a bad sort and Stub Hawkins . . . He picked up a stick and held it tight against the rails of an iron fence, liking the racket it made. He had thought of doing it every time he went by this fence but he hadn't until now. He felt enormously free and independent.

The six buildings of the college had the deserted air of vacation but it wasn't depressing to him today. There were a few signs of life and as Lyman went into University Hall a smell of boiling cabbage met his nose. He felt he had been away a long time. The worn treads of the stairs looked familiar. The ashes usually spilling over the cans at the corners of the hall had been emptied and many of the doors of the rooms were closed, but the place looked good to him. He had never liked it half so well before, not even in the fall when he first arrived. In sheer high spirits he kicked the bucket that stood outside the door of Number 19 where the famous John Hay had lived. He was glad that he had come back early. There were a lot of things he wanted to do, he thought with a sudden stir of anticipation. He might even drop over and have a talk with the chemistry professor; he had wanted to but he'd just never got around to it. He turned the knob of Number 21, gave the door a kick with his boot, and carried in his bag.

Orville Converse stood in front of the window, going through his son's table drawer. Lyman stopped in the doorway. His astonished glance went past his father to his own trunk that stood open on the floor, half-full of his belongings.

"Hello, Father!" he said.

His father studied him a long scornful moment before he spoke. "I've come to take you home. Get your duds together."

Lyman's head whirled with a dozen half-thoughts. He couldn't help noticing how out of place his father looked here in this room, and he hoped fervently that none of the boys could hear him.

"But, Father, the final term begins Monday. I have to finish the year or I'll lose all my credits."

"What you've done so far is no credit to you or me either. Look at these!" His father thrust his hand into the table drawer and brought out a handful of unpaid bills that he had kept from month to month:

three from the livery stable, one from the tailor's, one for the cane he had bought. Lyman knew them all without looking at them. His father's face was dark with anger. His brows met in a long black line below the lines on his forehead. "You wrote that you were staying to get ahead in your work and I find you were down at Newport with some wealthy young wasters. You got Easy down there to wait on them and you."

So he knew everything. Aunt Matilda had written him, then. Lyman raised one eyebrow in the way he had practiced so carefully in front of the mirror, tightened his lips so they would show nothing, and let his eyes follow the length of the lazy cord that dangled above the bed. He wondered whether his father had seen how cleverly it opened the door without your having to get out of bed.

"Lyman, are you listening to me?"

Lyman moved his eyes back to his father.

"I don't think you understand, Father."

The elder Converse swayed in indignation so that the skirt of his best black coat swayed too. He brought his fist down on Lyman's desk, scattering the pens onto the floor.

"I understand perfectly. I've seen your Aunt Matilda and heard how you made love to your cousin against her wishes." His father's voice made the truth into an ugly, sneaking, perverted thing. Lyman's face went white.

"I love Isabel," he said doggedly, his lips drawing down against his will so he could hardly make the words. "There was nothing wrong about it."

"You've disgraced your mother and father in front of our relations. You've lied and run up debts and gotten drunk." His father whirled around and picked up an almost empty bottle of peach brandy Lyman had hidden in his closet. He hadn't liked it very much and had drunk only a little of it. His father threw the bottle across the room, where it smashed into glassy fragments against the wall and the brandy made a wet stain on the pitted plaster. Lyman found himself trembling and he held onto the corner of the dresser to keep from showing it. Outside on the middle campus he could hear someone playing catch. He wondered who it was.

"Oh, go to hell!" a strong young voice yelled happily farther down the hall. The swearing acted like a match to his father's anger.

"If I had known how you were going to behave and waste my money, I would have seen you dead before I'd have let you come off down here. You get your things together as fast as you can. We're taking the train back today."

"The last train has gone for today. I put Easy on it," Lyman said.

"I'll find some train. You'll not stay in this town another night." Orville Converse began throwing everything he could find into the trunk. Only once he stopped to ask: "Are these books paid for? Or did you write for money and use it for foolishness?"

"They are paid for, Father," Lyman answered, and took the first good breath since he had entered the room. He had stopped trembling now. But he didn't want to leave college. It had taken him all this time to know what he wanted here. "Father, let me finish out the term. I'll show you what I can do."

"You've shown me enough," said Orville Converse bitterly. "No son of mine is going to make a fool of me twice."

On the tiresome train home, through the several changes, Orville Converse maintained a complete and heavy silence. Lyman slept as much as he could, often hiding behind his closed eyelids when he wasn't asleep. They got off the train in the morning at Malden depot and went to the livery stable for their own horse and buggy.

"Well, Lyman, you home for a holiday?" Mr. White, the owner of the stable in Malden, asked him.

"He's come home to stay," Orville Converse answered for him, in such a tone that Mr. White puckered his lips in surprise.

"Well, that's good. Too many young men are goin' away these days. Seems like since the war they all want to get out an' see how far they can go from home."

Lyman got into the buggy angrily. His father didn't need to tell everyone all about him. The feeling of independence he had had when he came back from Newport was gone. The indifference he had managed to maintain on the train withered into self-pity. He felt like a child dragged to the woodshed by his father to be whipped. He knew now how Dan had felt toward Father and why he had left home.

"Do you want some breakfast?" his father asked. They had not stopped for any supper the night before.

"No, sir," Lyman answered sullenly.

There was some snow still in the woods. Lyman could see little patches from the road, and the leaves were still tight-curled buds. It must have been a late spring. At college he had lost sight of the changes of the season.

"Lyman!" his father began sternly.

Lyman waited.

"Answer me!"

"Yes, sir," Lyman mumbled.

156

"You ought to be disowned. You've wasted your substance in riotous and profligate living and I'm ashamed to call you my son."

Lyman kept his eyes on the cold pale-green of the woods. He was growing used to his father's anger.

"But there ought to be some good in you." Orville Converse's tone was almost sorrowful instead of angry. The change bothered Lyman. "I've been studying all the way home and I've prayed to the Lord while you sat there sleeping."

He hadn't been sleeping all the time. He had been thinking about Isabel some of the time.

"And I have decided to give you one more chance. You have never shown much of a leaning toward the farm like Jonathan did. You and your brother Daniel are different from Jonathan." For just a moment Lyman felt sorry for his father for losing John. He felt as though he weren't his father's son or John's brother, but someone else looking on.

"I'm going to give you the chance I gave Daniel. You always wrote a neat hand, and you can go into the quarry office and write letters and learn to keep the books. In time, if you show yourself to be capable and worthy, I will take you into the business. It's an opportunity most young men would give their right hand for!"

Lyman didn't answer at once. He was still someone else, someone who felt sorry for his father. He had to get back into himself.

"You can think it over and let me know by the time we get to the spring. I want to know before we get home to your mother. She's almost beat out with crying over you and your sins."

"And if I don't stay?" Lyman asked.

"After you've paid your debts I'll give you just one hundred dollars and you can go where you like."

Lyman knew this road by heart. It was a long way to the spring on the hill. He had plenty of time. He didn't need to think about it right away. Instead he was remembering the trip over this road to meet Willie and the trip to bring John's body back. Easy had sung most of the way, the slave songs Ed was trying to write music for. He wondered whether Easy was back yet. He dreaded being home alone with just his mother and father.

It was raining when they drove through Painesville. His father stopped in the covered bridge and put on the boot before they came into town, but Lyman held it down on his side so he could see things. There was the post office and Hall and Peterboro's General Store. "Groceries, West India Goods, Salt, Fish, etc." he read through the slanting veil of rain. Abbot Churn Company, Thompson's Cashmere Mill, boarded up now. There was the quarry office. Lyman looked at it curiously, at its double door with glass panes in the upper part, the soapstone step up to the door. There was one wide front window with a table just in front on the inside with samples of the soapstone on it. Across the glass of the front window bright gold letters formed an arc.

CONVERSE & HOLBROOK SOAPSTONE CO.

Quarry at Painesville   Mill at Malden Depot

Est. 1814

"I'll stop here a moment. You hold the horse," his father said. The buggy tilted to one side as he stepped out. Lyman watched his father take a big brass key from his pocket and fit it into the lock. He heard the sound of the door as it shut. Had his father stopped here just to give him a chance to sit and look at the name in gold letters? The only time he knew of that he had sat and looked at his own name printed in big letters was on the gravestone in the cemetery. It wasn't so pretty cut into granite, it looked too sharp-edged.

His father came back out and stood on the doorstep in the rain, the key in his hand. He looked at his watch. Lyman took out John's watch. It read 7:35. His father was frowning, then the frown cleared.

"Good morning, Oliver," his father called out as Oliver Weatherbee came past the buggy under a big black umbrella. Oliver was the book-keeper.

"I had to stop a minute in the store, Mr. Converse. I'm sorry to be late," he said apologetically, closing his umbrella.

"Close to ten minutes, it looks like, Oliver. I've got to go up home first. I'll be back down at ten."

"Yes, sir. Did you have a pleasant trip, Mr. Converse?" Oliver asked as he opened the door with his own key.

"I went for duty, Oliver, not pleasure." The buggy leaned toward the road as he got in, and then steadied again. Orville took the whip out and snapped it in the air without touching his horse, but the effect was the same. The horse sprang forward toward the quarry road.

"Oliver Weatherbee isn't very punctual," Orville said, pulling up the boot. "It's a mighty good thing to check up on him."

"Would you keep him if I . . ."

"Yes. The business is growing. We need two men in the office. It has a great future." His voice forgot to be angry for a moment.

They clattered through the covered bridge that led up the quarry road. They passed the third curve. The stone wall was tumbled down in one place, Lyman noticed. If he *were* interested in the quarry he wouldn't want to be in the office down in the village but up here on the hill.

158

But he wouldn't work in the office, there where his father would always be checking up on him. No, he'd clear out. He could work at something until he got enough money to go West. Willie wanted him to come. All the young men were getting out these days, as Mr. White had said. Plenty of excitement out West. He could mine for gold, too. If he struck it rich, he'd go back to Providence and give them money for a new college building. He wondered if Isabel would get his letters now if he wrote to her.

One more curve before the spring. Orville flourished his whip. The horse sprang ahead with such a leap that their heads jerked ludicrously.

"What horse is this, Father?" Lyman asked.

Orville Converse rubbed the back of his neck as though the jerk had put a crick in it. "It's a young horse I traded for. He's only a four-year-old and the man used him for a saddle horse. I broke him to the buggy myself. Your mother won't ride behind him yet." Lyman remembered that his father prided himself on his skill at breaking horses.

As they rounded the last curve before the spring all Lyman could see of it was a space in the alders that grew along the bank and a muddy place in the road. But when they came abreast of it he saw the two large flat rocks that edged the pool, one granite, one soapstone.

Orville Converse pulled in on the reins. "Well?"

Lyman swallowed. It hurt him to hurt his father, after all. He wished he were more like Daniel, more like granite than soapstone, he thought unhappily, his eyes still on the spring. "I'm not going to stay, Father. I wouldn't like it, so there's no use starting. I'm sorry."

Orville lifted the whip. This time he let the young horse feel it and Lyman wondered if they would make the turn into their own driveway. His father's face had grown the color of red brick.

"Very well," he said when he had pulled the horse to a walk. "You've lost your chance at an education and now you throw away your chance at a good job. You'll never amount to anything, neither you nor your brother. Your debts came to eighty-seven dollars and forty-three cents and I wouldn't be surprised to find you've left some more behind you. Before you go you'll work at the quarry office at six-fifty a week until you earn enough to pay every last cent. I pay Oliver seven. You might as well go see your mother. I'll put the horse up."

He drove rapidly away as though he didn't want to be there himself.

PART THREE

I

LYMAN'S pen moved across the sheet of paper with the smooth sound of a clean pen point. His face was as intent as though he were trying to find a rhyme.

You may be sure, Aunt Matilda, that the business of the quarry will be carried on exactly as it was under my father's hand. It was not my desire to assume this position, but Mother feels that it would be my father's wish, and from a talk which I had with him the week before his untimely death, I am convinced of it myself.

You doubtless remember only too well some of my indiscreet and foolish actions in the near past, but I hope to redeem them. My father's friend and legal advisor, Judge Whitcomb, will help me in many ways. As you say, you have a considerable share in the quarry, and that share, I assure you, I shall make it my sacred duty to care for, not only because I am in honor bound to do so, but also because of my deep love for Isabel.

He paused over what he had written. It didn't sound like something he had composed; it was as though his father had pronounced these sentences and he had only transcribed them. He turned the sheet of paper over and blotted it against the black-velvet desk top, then he turned it back and wrote a sentence that was entirely his own, free from any tincture of his father's diction:

Please ask Isabel if she has seen Sam Andrews, my roommate. He is studying theology, and I am sure you would approve of him. He was quite homesick and Isabel said she would be so kind as to ask him to call sometime.

My mother wishes me to send her compliments to you.

> *I remain,*
> *Your respectful and obedient servant,*
> *Lyman Converse*

He had already written Sam and enclosed a note for Isabel. He could trust Sam. If Isabel invited him for tea, it would be an easy matter for him to give the note to her. He could have sent a note to Chauncey for Isabel, but he didn't want to ask a favor of Chauncey. Last month he had sent Chauncey the money he had lost to him at Newport, with a note saying he had just remembered. It embarrassed him to think of it, and he caught one ankle around a spooled leg of the big cherry desk.

"Here, Oliver, drop this in the afternoon mail and then you can go. There's nothing urgent."

Oliver pursed his lips, stuck his pen behind one ear, and tipped back in his chair. "It's early for stopping time, Lyman. Your father always kept me working right up to six o'clock."

There were drawbacks to having a man work for you who was your senior by ten years and who called you by your first name.

"Judge Whitcomb may drop by, Oliver, and I have some matters to discuss with him of a confidential nature. The stage will be in from Woodstock at four-thirty. Be sure the letter gets on it," Lyman said firmly.

"Well, I'll go, but it makes me uneasy to think of what Mr. Converse would say." The disapproval he felt showed plainly in Oliver's face.

When he had gone Lyman relaxed. All day he had to assume an assurance he did not feel. Before Oliver he had to appear industrious, and he was not naturally so. He shucked farther down in his father's barrel-backed chair and made a rest for his head with his long thin fingers. His eyes drifted out the window to the tall elms that lined the main street of Painesville. When he had come to this office in April the trees had been bare of leaves. He had sat at his desk and written letters and copied off orders and watched brown buds swell out along the branches, turn into reddish-green blossoms, become pale-green pendants, and fall before the green saw-toothed leaves covered the trees. He had never watched anything so closely before.

Hate and disgust and rebellion had limned those branches, swelled with the buds and grown with the leaves, but he had kept his anger to himself. His father had been fair enough. Orville Converse wasn't the sort to give a second chance and his son wouldn't ask for one; he had seen the hard justice of his father's decision. He had meant to stay here until the debt was paid, but then he would be through fast enough with this business and this office and Painesville. Midsummer was to have seen him on his way. And now the leaves on the elms were turning yellow and those on the maples red and he was still here.

His father had kept him close to the office while he himself made the daily trip to the quarry and over the hill to the mill. Lyman would have preferred it the other way, but he did what he was told. His father had wasted few words with him. Lyman gathered some knowledge from the letters his father dictated. He learned that the soapstone was of the finest quality, that the vein his father quarried was a rich one—nothing like the gold Dan was after out West, but a money-making thing. He could see for himself how the business was growing. They had to take on seven more men in July, making a total of thirty-five at the quarry without counting the number of men at the mill, and his father had recently employed a salesman in Boston to handle orders. There was a great demand for soapstone stoves, wash-tubs, and bathtubs as well as griddles and warming stones and the like. One order had come in for an oval soapstone bathtub adorned with iron claw feet. He had thought of Isabel in a bathtub like that, her skin so white against the smooth gray stone, but he had blushed at his own thinking.

Three drivers had been hired and fired during May. Nobody could drive oxen like Easy, his father had said. "If you hadn't got him down to Providence and given him a taste of the city, like as not he'd been here yet. What on earth he wanted to go back down South for I can't see!" his father had stormed. And Lyman had looked out the window and thought with scorn how little his father understood either his sons or Easy. But he missed Easy too. He had left the first week in June.

Riding up the hill from the office in the village at night his father sometimes talked to Lyman as though he were talking to himself.

"Vermont is changing," his father had said one time. "Railroads are going to open up all that Western country, and we can't compete with the West in grain, or dairy products either, if they can get 'em to the markets cheap enough. The future of Vermont is bound to be in industry and business. No other part of the country has such marble and granite and soapstone. The Lord put it right here at our doorstep so it would be here when we needed it." His father's nostrils dilated and his lips showed pink above his beard and his eyes gleamed like Dan's when he talked. Then he would touch the horse with the whip and pull the reins up tight and let him go as he wanted to make the business go.

Lyman had listened to him and wondered why he wasn't excited in the same way, and he worried a little—not too much—that he wasn't. He was interested in himself, not Vermont. Perhaps he could have been drawn along and absorbed in the army if he had got in, but he hadn't, and he wondered, looking out that window at the signs of June showing timidly along the street, if he would ever find something

162

to be really excited about—certainly not the business of developing Vermont's industries or making money.

Only the thought of Isabel really excited him, and that let him into a daydream that he could always summon at will by a single thought. It began: "If Isabel were not my cousin . . ." He was sure Isabel loved him, but she would do nothing about it. It wasn't Aunt Matilda, it was Isabel herself, slender and straight and firm standing against the soapstone mantel with her face pale and clear as moonlight, who set herself against him. In the dream she always went away with him. Sometimes they were in Vermont together, climbing to the top of the hill above the quarry and drinking from the spring. They went berrying together one time and he could see her mouth stained blue with berries as plain as though the dream were real. Sometimes they were living in Providence and he was working at something—what was never very clear—and coming home to Isabel's house in the evening, a winter evening. Isabel always let him in herself and brushed the snow off his shoulders and the velvet collar of the overcoat he had gone into debt to buy, and kissed him standing tiptoe to reach his mouth. This daydream was with him sometimes at night and he woke in the room above the kitchen and thought she lay beside him. But even when he woke to find himself clutching the feather pillow and sank into the flatness of reality, he never doubted that someday the dream would be reality.

There was another dream and it too began with a single thought that opened the door into it like a key fitting a lock: If his father had not brought him home from school . . . if he had not played the fool and brought down his father's rage, if he were still there now— and always he moved in this dream with a bejeweled pin on his lapel and was chosen to give an oration at the Junior Exhibition. Isabel and Aunt Matilda were always present and came up afterward to congratulate him. He went on through all four years in his dream, and sometimes he was playing baseball on the middle campus while someone from the window of Hope Hall called out, "Go it, Converse!" Sometimes he leaned on the curb at the well and talked with a young man named Pigott or ate oysters and drank beer at Pete's, and always he graduated with honors at commencement while his mother and father looked on.

Time passed swiftly between these two daydreams, and the leaves came out on all the branches of the maples and elms up and down the street and he hardly minded his present life.

He was dreaming the afternoon in July when John Perkins, who was foreman at the quarry, came into the office and told him about his father, found dead just below the spring with his coat caught in the spokes of the wheel and the buggy smashed to a fare-thee-well astride the stone wall. Lyman was ashamed still that he had felt no grief then, only an incapacity to believe what Perkins stood telling him.

"It's that horse. I never did think he should put him between the shafts of a carriage, but you know how your father was, Lyman, always so headstrong, and he did like a spirited horse."

"Yes, I know," Lyman agreed soberly, and even then his mind smiled that he should be standing here hearing his father spoken of as headstrong, but he kept his face properly mournful. He felt grief later and it was a relief to him, and in September he felt more than grief, he felt lonely for him here in the office. His father had loved the business and liked this office. He didn't. He hated it, but he couldn't walk out and leave it, because his father had cared so much about it. He couldn't leave it to Oliver Weatherbee. Oliver meant well enough, but he was a prig and a fool who would go on the rest of his life doing what Orville Converse had told him to do when he was alive, no matter how times changed.

It was funny what a little thing made him feel badly about his father. When Mr. Adams, who did an undertaking business along with his feed business, brought him the coat his father had been wearing when he was killed, Lyman put his hand in the pocket and found a handful of little blue pasteboards advertising the quarry.

His father had asked him to write out the advertisement to be printed on them. He had written it in a fair hand with some little scrolls around the capitals and the important words in bigger letters to make them stand out. His father had been pleased with them. It was the only time Lyman could remember his saying anything faintly resembling praise. He had said, "That's just the ticket, Lyman, confident and firm without boasting!" Lyman remembered that now with some comfort, but all he had done really was to compile a list of all the things soapstone was used for. It read:

HOLBROOK & CONVERSE
M'f'turers and Dealers in Every Description of
SOAPSTONE WORK
Painesville, Vermont

Soapstone in Blocks and Slabs, Soapstone Stoves, Fireplaces, Stove Linings, Sinks, Wash and Bathing Tubs, Griddles, Register and Funnel Stones
All descriptions of Soapstone Work Constantly on Hand and Fur-

nished to Order at Short Notice. All Stone Sold by us is Taken from the Holbrook & Converse Quarry, Painesville, Vt.

Please Examine Stone and Specimens of Work before Purchasing Elsewhere.

There was a pile of the little blue pasteboards on the desk beside him and he reached over and fingered one. Then he sailed it across the office, noticing that it landed in one of Oliver Weatherbee's large lank overshoes. His momentary satisfaction changed to discontent with his still being here.

"Quite an opportunity for a young man, Lyman," Mr. Peterboro at the store told him. "You'll have to grow to fit your pa's britches!" Jeb Holmes chaffed him. Jeb himself seemed to have given up all thought of other occupation than the one of professional army veteran. "What about Daniel? I supposed he'd come back and run the quarry," Mr. Perkins said, frowning a little.

Lyman glanced over at the shelf where the box labeled Personal Correspondence stood. Dan's letter was there, but he knew it by heart without looking at it. Dan had written Mother too, but it seemed hypocritical to Lyman after his own letter from Dan—the last paragraph, particularly.

The old man came a cropper trying to break a horse just as he did with his sons, this one anyway. Too bad it killed him. Thanks for offering me the management of the quarry. I don't believe even a gold mine would get me back to Vermont, let alone a vein of soapstone. You cut your eyeteeth on it and welcome. It may suit you. Willie and I will be content with our shares and some steady dividends. Love to Mother. She has lived so long with the old man she ought to feel a little relief now, but she will mourn for him instead. Willie and Juliet send their love,

Dan

The letter had made him feel the way he had that night that Dan came home. But Dan was wrong—the quarry didn't suit him. It hadn't in the beginning and it didn't now after a whole summer of trying to carry on just because it was here and it belonged to them, to them and Isabel's family. His mother expected him to go on with it. Judge Whitcomb told him it was the right thing to do. Dr. Tucker had urged it on him, too.

"It's as good as anything, Lyman, until you find yourself."

But how could you find yourself sitting in an office figuring out how much profit you could make on finished soapstone if the slab cost . . . Why did Dr. Tucker think he was lost? How had he guessed?

Lyman unlocked the padlock on the box marked Personal Correspondence and dropped in Aunt Matilda's letter full of indignant remonstrances against his being entrusted with the running of the quarry. He was pleased with his answer. Then he snapped the lock and returned the key to his pocket.

The other file boxes were unlocked, each painted tan to match the woodwork of the office, each equipped with a hinged lid, and on each were painted the years: 1854–56, 1856–58 . . . 1866–68, 1868–70, to 1880. Lyman glanced around at them, ranged along the high shelves. Would those beyond '66 be filled with letters and bills and contracts all in his hand? He would be thirty-two and middle-aged in 1880. He couldn't think any farther than that.

The stage rattled past the office window and Lyman was glad there was a message to Isabel on it. Then he settled down to check the new orders. He must talk to Stiles at the mill tomorrow and see what they had in stock.

Stiles didn't take him seriously yet, but Perkins told him that he was a chip off the old block when he sent up word to have the men work overtime to fill a special order. Lyman had been pleased because he knew it was a compliment on Perkins's tongue, but at the same time he had known it wasn't so. He was no more like his father than soapstone was like granite.

As soon as Judge Whitcomb had gone, Lyman tidied up the big desk that seemed still to belong to his father and locked the door of the office. In the late afternoon light the gold letters on the front window were dull. He walked briskly up to the livery stable, feeling as he had when a class let out at Brown. He drove Scout, the same horse that had run away with his father. Abbie had wanted him to shoot the animal, but he hadn't done it. He was a fine horse, a chestnut with white on his forehead, mostly Morgan and sired by a cavalry horse. Lyman had gone out to shoot him, but he had brought him back instead and put him in the barn. His mother must have seen him come back with the horse, but she had said nothing, only she averted her eyes when he drove away each morning. Lyman felt he had to drive the horse—why, he could not have explained even to himself. Sometimes he lingered for a game of checkers in the feed room of the livery stable, or a game of high-low-jack. He had a reputation at the livery stable and he had taught the regular players a variation on the game brought back from Brown.

But tonight he didn't linger at the stable, though why he should

hurry home he didn't know. Abbie would be waiting for him, de-
terminedly cheerful above the deep sadness that had spread like a
sickness through her blood, making her pale and thin and hollow-
eyed. Dan should see her, Lyman thought sometimes.

They would eat in the kitchen and tell each other the sparse happenings of the day. He would try to remember talk last winter at
college when you were never through, your thoughts came so fast, and
laughter rounded the talk like wind in a sail. Here they were done
with a subject so soon, and there was never any laughter. Louisa was
good about going up to see Abbie. She did her a lot of good.

"How happy she could have made poor John," Abbie would say
after one of Louisa's visits.

The hill road had the steepest pitch of any around Painesville. The
horse climbed steadily. Lyman sat back in his father's buggy and
lighted his pipe. Each day on this road he checked the show of color:
a branch of yellow leaves there, one scarlet patch against that fir tree,
and yellow leaves already scattered on the road.

"Come on, Scout!" He gathered the reins in a little. Scout trotted
on the nearly level stretch to the watering trough, stopping there as
his natural right and then lingering on, just fooling, letting the water
run through his mouth and over the bit without drinking. Lyman
pulled him away.

It was lighter up here on the hill than down in the village, but he
was too late tonight to meet any of the men on their way home from
the quarry. He took out John's watch to check the time. Scout trotted
on the curve to the spring, his ears pricked forward as though he saw
someone ahead. Lyman stared up the road in the twilight.

Two figures were ahead of him, walking: a tall man and a slight
woman who came no higher than the man's shoulder. The man carried
two bags and the woman had a bundle on her back. They walked on
either side of the road in the wheel tracks, dark against the light sky.
The man must have heard the horse; he turned to look.

Lyman stood up in the buggy and let out a great yell and the horse
laid back his ears at the sound.

"Easy!" Lyman wound the reins around the whipstock and jumped
out of the buggy. The tall man ahead set down his two bags and came
toward him. The woman stood still in the road.

"Easy, you old scoundrel you!" Lyman grabbed Easy's hand in both
of his. "You came back!" Gladness flowed through him, gladness pure
and simple.

"I came back, Lyman. Things don't look so good down there. Maybe
I been away too long. So I came back to Painesville."

167

They stood there together. Lyman forgot the horse that wasn't to be trusted and Easy forgot the woman with him. Then Lyman was aware of her.

"You—you got married, Easy!"

Easy's teeth flashed white in the dusk. "I didn't want no white girl colored up with butternut juice, Lyman, so I married a girl down South. Come meet her."

Lyman walked with him, looking curiously at the woman. Her skin was the color of butternut juice just the same, not so dark as Easy's. Shyness wrapped her head and shoulders like a shawl. Her dark bright eyes watched Lyman coming and then dropped to the road.

"Lyman, this is Jewel. We were married last June and set up to live in Virginia, but I couldn't seem to settle down, so we picked up and come on back."

"I'm very glad to meet you," Lyman said. He was suddenly abashed himself.

"Yes, sah," Jewel said in syllables that slipped together as softly as a sigh. "I'se right pleased to meet you."

An instant of silence fell on them then, but not an awkward silence.

"Easy, this place has been lonely up here with you gone. You knew —no, you wouldn't. Father was killed."

"Mistah Converse was killed!" Easy repeated after him. "How come?"

"The horse bolted and smashed the carriage against the stone wall just above here. Nobody knows what possessed him."

"I was countin' on seeing Mistah Converse again," Easy said slowly. "I told Jewel he was an awful honest man an' whatever he said he'd do, he'd do. Whether a man was white or colored don't make no difference to him."

"Yes, that's right," Lyman agreed, pride creeping into his voice and into his mind.

Easy shook his head. "Mistah Converse was just about the most righteous man I ever knew," he said, and Lyman was surprised. His own feeling for his father had been affected by Dan's feeling. He had never felt quite at ease with his father after the train ride back from Providence.

"How's Missus Converse?" Easy asked.

"She's—well, she feels pretty badly about Father," Lyman answered.

Easy nodded. "I never known folks that live closer together than Mistah and Missus Converse. I told you so, didn't I, Jewel?"

The small dark head nodded. "Tha's so, Easy," she said softly. And

168

again Lyman was surprised. His father and mother were strangers to him in a way. Easy seemed to know them better than he did.

"What you doin', Lym'n?"

"Oh, I'm running the quarry just now—trying to," he added humbly.

"Mistah Converse would like that!" Easy said, and Lyman was grateful.

"Here, come get in the buggy." Lyman helped Jewel in. She was slight and wiry like Isabel, he noticed, and then was shocked in his mind at likening Isabel to a colored girl. He lifted the reins and they drove up the road in the September dusk.

"This the horse, Lyman?"

"Yes. Say, it's a wonder he stood still while I was talking to you!"

"You can't tell about horses. Something must have skairt him that time."

"I guess this was where it happened. Right about here. The buggy was smashed up against the wall there." Three pairs of eyes looked at the road, the wall, the darkness of the woods growing to the road. It looked innocent enough tonight. Wonder stirred them all that in this place Orville Converse should have died so violently.

"Wonder if the horse know what he done?" Jewel said softly, and Lyman was startled at her imagining it so vividly. They all looked at the horse's head. One big pointed ear flicked back toward them, but his feet moved evenly up the road.

"That there's the turn-in for the quarry, Jewel, like I told you." Jewel's head turned.

"Here we are," Lyman announced as they drove in through the gap in the stone wall that enclosed the Converse Place. There was a light in the kitchen.

"It's got big trees," Jewel said softly.

"Elms in front and maples 'long the side," Easy said. "An' there's a butternut tree up by our house, Jewel, remember?"

"I got it remembered, Easy," Jewel answered.

2

THE sides of the soapstone stove glowed with a red incandescent light, as though blood suffused the cold gray substance with life. Lyman turned his chair nearer to the heat.

"You know, Oliver, I think I'll take this stove out and have a fireplace built over there between the windows, with a soapstone mantel. You could use long slabs that would really show the quality of the stone."

Oliver Weatherbee switched around on his high stool. "I wouldn't do that if I was you, Lyman. I don't think Mr. Converse would ever of stood for the expense."

"I think I will. It would make a good display." Lyman ignored Oliver's remark.

Oliver pulled on his overshoes, put on his scarf, overcoat, and cap, and started for the door. "Morning stage is in, Lyman. I'll drop over and get the mail."

Lyman grunted and turned back to his desk. But as soon as Oliver was gone he allowed himself an intermission. He lit his pipe and stood with his back to the stove. Now in December the little office was cold along the floor and in the corners. The snow came down steadily outside and the low picket fence across the street was almost covered.

Easy said Jewel had never seen so much snow, that she wanted to be out in it and turning up her face to let it come down on her eyes and in her mouth and laughing at it. Easy ought to be along soon now. He was back at his old job of driving the ox sled between the mill and the quarry and the railroad and he and Jewel were living in the smokehouse with a leanto kitchen built on.

It seemed queer to Lyman and a little embarrassing when their own house stood there with empty rooms in it. Not that he had actually invited Easy to share the house, nor had Abbie. The idea had just lain uncomfortably in their minds. The smokehouse stood across the dooryard and under the shelter of the hill with the butternut tree to shade it in summer. Abbie said the light in the new windows was a lot of company, even if it was colored company.

Warmed through now, Lyman went back to his chair in front of the desk and was busily at work when Oliver brought in the mail.

"Letter from your aunt, Lyman, and two that looks like orders, and a bill's all."

It was irritating to have Oliver tell over the mail as he came in. Eagerness trembled in Lyman's hands as he took the letter, but he opened the orders and the bill first. Then his eye raced along Aunt Matilda's black spidery handwriting.

I am relieved that Judge Whitcomb will be there to advise and direct you and I suppose the foremen of the quarry and mill will continue. Perhaps your father's shocking death brought you to your senses and you are really taking responsibility. I can't understand Dan's having so little sense of responsibility that he would stay away. . . .

The name Isabel was in the last sentence.

Isabel is to be married to Chauncey Westcott III on Christmas Eve. We realize that it is too long a journey for you and Abigail, and Abigail is not out of mourning yet, of course. . . ."

He must have uttered some exclamation, for Oliver turned from hanging up his wraps. "Is your Aunt Matilda pleased with the way things are going, Lyman?"

"Yes, very pleased," Lyman answered bitterly.

Lyman pretended to be hard at work, but his mind was far removed from the affairs of the quarry. Why hadn't Isabel written herself? Why had she never answered the letter he had sent her through Sam? Sam had written that she had seemed glad to get it and excused herself and went upstairs to read it soon after he came. Her mother was "formidable," Sam wrote. Perhaps Isabel no longer cared, but his mind refused such a heresy. He went back over the time he had held her in his arms in the library. You could tell about a person. She was doing this only because they were cousins. He jabbed the point of his pen into the paper in front of him and when a splinter of steel broke off and flew across the room he swore heartily as he hadn't since the vacation at Newport.

"Your father, Lyman, discharged a man for blasphemy, a good worker he was, too," Oliver said sententiously. "I always admired him for it."

Lyman was intent on replacing the broken pen point.

"Oliver, I'm going to have to take a trip to Boston to see some people who . . . uh . . . are interested in the quarry."

"In buying it, you mean, Lyman?"

"I don't know yet. It isn't an affair that I want to risk on paper," he answered. "You take care of everything here as you know my father

171

would like it. I'll have to go up home and back before the stage leaves." He was laying papers in the drawers, fastening the new orders together on the spindle, in a fever of eagerness to be off.

"How long will you be gone, Lyman?"

"I don't know. I'll send you a telegram." Lyman slammed the door behind him and hurried up the street to get his horse and cutter. The cutter made him think of Isabel, Isabel's hand underneath the robe, Isabel's face stung with the cold, her freckles powdering the skin and her eyes deep-set and dark.

The trip up the hill was endless. The horse's head bobbed up and down as he pulled. He had to walk the whole way. Through Lyman's mind, like the whir of the runners on the snow, ran a question: What good will it do to see Isabel? She's going to be married, going to marry Chauncey Westcott, on Christmas Eve. What if she won't even see you?

But he had to see her and talk to her. He had to be sure she wanted to do this thing. He had to tell her . . . tell her again how he loved her.

"Lyman, it's only midmorning!" Abbie looked up from the stocking she was knitting. By the other window in the grandmother's rocker was Jewel. He was grateful that she was there so his mother wouldn't ask so many questions.

"I have to go to Boston on business, Mother." He spoke importantly, his eyes not quite meeting his mother's.

"What happened, Lyman? I don't believe your father ever went to Boston in the winter."

"Nothing serious, Mother. Just some gentlemen who are interested in a large order that they want to talk to me personally about." He ran up the stairs to his room and threw things into the bag he had taken to college last year. Hurriedly he changed into the suit he had had made by a tailor in Providence, his gloves, his best hat, the cravat with the little flowers, and the overcoat with the velvet collar.

His heels pounded joyously on the stairs. He was going to see Isabel. He patted his mother's shoulder. "Jewel, you and Easy look in night and morning, won't you? I won't be gone long. I've decided to go to Malden to catch the train without waiting for the stage. I believe I can get an earlier train. Good-bye." And he was on his way back down the hill.

As the train pulled into the Providence station the next evening Lyman sat on the edge of the plush seat looking eagerly out of the window. Sam wouldn't fail him. Sam would see that she got there. He had sent Sam a telegram from Malden.

The engine made such a noise that the voices of the porters could hardly be heard. People rushed back and forth, met each other, picked up bags and valises and hurried off again. The gas lamps burned dismally behind dirty globes. Lyman hoped for a minute that Isabel might be there on the platform waiting for him. He stepped off the train and searched the faces he met. Sam should be here. His telegram had been long and carefully worded. He placed his hat carefully on his head and pulled on his other glove.

"Lyman!" Sam Andrews came up to him and took hold of his arm. "Your train was late. Miss Holbrook is waiting for you in the station." Sam seemed hurried and embarrassed. "If you have any time . . ."

"I don't believe I will," Lyman said uncertainly. Now that he was actually here doubts assailed him.

"Well, I'm in Hope, remember. Come around tonight if you can."

"Yes, thanks, Sam. You don't know how much . . ."

"Sure, that's all right. See you then, Lyman. I've got to go."

Lyman hardly heard him. He picked up his bag and walked across the platform to the waiting-room. He lifted the latch of the heavy door. There were only a handful of people now; his eyes moved eagerly over the room. A slight figure in gray rose from the bench in the corner. She wore a veil. He would have known her anywhere by the quickness of her movement.

"Isabel!" He said her name under his breath and crossed the room like a man almost home. He held both her hands in his.

"Oh, Lyman, your train was late." She sat down quickly and he sat beside her.

"I'm sorry, Isabel, to ask you to meet me here like this."

"That doesn't matter. Mr. Andrews brought me. Mother thinks I'm at Mr. Emerson's lecture. I've heard him before, so I can tell her all about him."

He found it wonderful that she hadn't changed in any way. Her face was just as he remembered it. The freckles were a golden powder under the skin; her mouth, her eyes, were just the same.

"Lyman, you've grown-up so! And you're running the quarry yourself. I was so glad when the dividend came as usual so Mother had to admit you were doing well. Don't, Lyman, someone will see us." She disengaged her hands from his.

"Let's get out of here," he said.

She hesitated, then stood up. He took her arm and felt her trembling. It was sleeting outside the station and he called a cab.

"Will you be too cold, Isabel?" He tucked the robe around her knees and got in beside her. "I have to wait between trains. Drive slowly for about an hour," he told the cabby, and closed the slit in back of the driver's seat. The cabman, knowing the last train in or out of Providence that night had come and gone, drove off grinning.

"Lyman, I . . . Why did you come like this?"

"I came because I love you. And you love me, you can't say you don't, Isabel." The horses' hoofs clopped down the street. The sleet scratched against the windows and the street lamps shone transiently in on their privacy.

"I do love you, Lyman," Isabel confessed in a small troubled voice. "But we can't ever marry, don't you see? Mother and Chauncey want . . ."

"What do *you* want? That's all that matters," he rushed on. "Why do you have to marry him now? Why can't you wait a little? Things will work out. I'll be able to satisfy Aunt Matilda. Isabel, don't you see that it's wicked to marry Chauncey when we love each other? If I were Chauncey . . . Answer me, Isabel!"

She didn't answer. Her gloved fingers played with the cord on her muff. Lyman slipped his arm around her. She was still trembling so that he took off his coat and wrapped it around her shoulders.

"Lyman, this is the best thing to do. I've thought and thought about it," she said finally.

"But why is it? Why can't you wait? You'll be sorry all your life."

There were no more street lamps now and the cab was dark, but the darkness held them close together. Lyman felt her quick strong hands tighten. Out of the stillness she said softly:

"Because it won't do any good to wait and you won't give up while I'm not married."

"That's not fair to Chauncey," Lyman said finally, as though it were nothing to him.

"I think Chauncey guesses, Lyman, but he's sure I'll forget you. We're going to Paris in the spring. I . . . I'm crazy to see Paris."

Lyman had a sick sense of hopelessness and a dull anger. She could talk of wanting to go to Paris in the face of their love. "Well, I might not be able to take you to Paris right away, but I could someday, I know."

She felt the hurt in his voice and put her hand on his cheek, turning his face toward her in the dark. "Don't be angry, Lyman. We can't help being cousins. You know I would love more than anything being with you just in Vermont."

"Isabel," Lyman said sharply, "how much is there in this business of being cousins? Maybe it's just a superstition! Why don't we talk to someone about it? If your doctor said it was all right, Aunt Matilda would let us, she'd have to! Where does he live? We'll go and talk to him right now." It was a relief to do something.

"Oh, Lyman." Isabel's voice was hopeful.

Lyman flipped open the little shutter in front and gave the driver the address. He held her close for the few blocks it took to reach the place. Neither of them spoke.

"I'll stay here, Lyman," Isabel said, pulling his coat around her.

Lyman worked the bell pull at the doctor's office door strongly.

"The doctor's office hours are over, sir," a maid told him. "Can you come back . . ."

"This is terribly important, it's a matter of life and death." Lyman stepped boldly across the threshold and the maid gave way. He followed the hall to the rear, where a light streamed out of a room, and burst upon the amazed doctor in his slippers, reading. The doctor's cheeks puffed out under his white mutton-chop whiskers and he took his glasses off, frowning.

"Doctor, I'm sorry to disturb you, but this is a matter of the greatest importance. Do you forbid the marriage of first cousins?"

The doctor's feet came down from the hassock. "I didn't catch the name, young man," he said, closing one eye and opening the other wider to look at the young intruder. He noticed his rumpled hair and heightened color.

"It's Converse, but that doesn't matter. I'm a stranger here in Providence. I just came to ask you about this. It matters terribly." Lyman's face twisted in his earnestness. "Everything depends on it, sir."

"Now what is this? You want to marry a girl who is your first cousin . . . Or have you married her already?" the doctor asked, laying aside his journal, that was the record of lives lived, in the face of the anguished living in front of him.

"We want to marry each other," Lyman said.

"Sit down, young man." Lyman sat on the chair opposite the doctor. His fingers tightened on his knees.

"I wouldn't advise it. I must warn you against it."

"But there's no law against it, is there?"

The doctor had seen desperate faces like this before in his office. He went on patiently.

"I don't know of any law on the statute books, but there's a law of nature. I don't advise you to go against Nature. She's stronger than the law or than you are by a long sight."

"But . . ."

"All you have to do to get an insane person is to double the worst peculiarities in a sane person. We all have them, you know. You seem to me to be a little unbalanced at the moment. Now you double your peculiarities, and you'd have some children that would be fine ones, or so experience tells us."

"We wouldn't have children, sir. All we care about is each other."

"You can't count on that. Carrying on your kind is a pretty strong impulse. The salmon swim upstream to spawn if it kills 'em."

"But, sir . . ."

The old doctor wagged his finger solemnly at Lyman. "It's simply an extension of this same rule that forbids sisters and brothers from marrying. Inbreeding isn't practiced with animals."

Lyman heard him through impatiently. "But it wouldn't be a . . . a criminal offense if we wanted to take the responsibility on ourselves." Lyman's eyes had a strangely intense look.

"Young man, you are arguing with Nature, not me. You're nothing but an atom in this universe. The ways of the Lord cannot be safely defied without bringing punishment down on both your heads." The doctor was standing now, his voice raised against the defiant look on Lyman's face. He must get to him. The boy—he couldn't be more than nineteen—looked as though he weren't listening.

Suddenly the doctor had one of those flashes of intuition that had sometimes helped him to a diagnosis. Not two weeks ago young Chauncey Westcott had been to see him about a possible bit of infection he had picked up in the army from some camp follower. Young Westcott seemed cured, but he had urged him to wait a year before marrying the Holbrook girl and Chauncey had told him with a laugh:

"You don't understand, Doctor. There's a young cousin she thinks she's in love with, but her mother wants her to marry me, so if there's no great danger I think I had better marry her now."

So this was the cousin. He looked more closely at the young man, contrasting him with Chauncey Westcott. He must be five years younger, a different type altogether, a more serious, introspective sort. He'd never take life easily.

"Does the young lady feel as strongly as you do?" he asked more gently.

The face in front of him grew more despairing. "She's waiting now to hear what you say. That's why I hoped you could . . . could support me a little." Lyman realized suddenly how long he had been here, that Isabel was waiting in the cold cab.

The doctor had that uncomfortable feeling of holding the fates of three people in his hands. For a moment he wished he could give the girl to this young man, then he put his glasses back on his nose.

"Tell her what I said. You must be wise for her sake. You'll both find happiness with someone else if you'll let yourselves." He went with him to the door and saw the cab waiting by the horseblock. The young man looked too lightly clad without any overcoat.

"Thank you, sir," Lyman turned to say halfway down the walk.

The whole episode upset the doctor so much that he tossed the journal over on the table and poured himself a good two fingers of brandy.

"Lyman, you were so long!" Isabel said.

"Are you cold, sweetheart?" Lyman had never called her that before. His lips formed the unaccustomed endearment tenderly.

"Just a little."

He put his arms around her and held her close to him as the horse clopped, clopped down the street. Her lips under his were cold.

"I shouldn't have left you out here, darling," he murmured.

"Lyman," she whispered. "Lyman, I made up my mind while you were gone. I don't care what Dr. Higgins said, I'll marry you. You were right and I was wrong and timid and cowardly." Her words came swiftly. As they passed a street lamp he saw her eyes and the expression of her face. "Lyman, we can go away, can't we? We'll be married and go right away."

He sat silent, holding his arm tightly around her, her hands in his.

"Lyman! What did Dr. Higgins say?"

"I . . . Isabel, the doctor said . . ."

Isabel pulled away from his arm so she was facing him in the half-dark of the cab. "Lyman Converse, do you mean you're scared by anything Mother or Dr. Higgins says? I'm not any more!"

He couldn't make himself repeat the words that kept sounding in his mind: "It's idle to argue with Nature. . . . You must be wise for her. . . . The ways of the Lord cannot be safely defied." His face was white in the dark. He could only press her hand so tightly it hurt her and say:

"Isabel . . . we can't. There are laws of nature . . ."

"Oh, Lyman!" Disbelief and reproach were in Isabel's voice. He must make Isabel see.

"Isabel, the world runs according to certain laws. If you break them, I guess everything goes wrong—you know, children and . . . things like that," he faltered. "Don't you see, Isabel, I want to so terribly but . . ." Dr. Higgins's words were better than his. "The laws of nature are . . . are bigger than we are."

Isabel sat up very straight on the edge of the seat. "No laws of man or nature are bigger than we are if we don't let them be!" she said. She lifted her head defiantly and then, suddenly, her head was against his shoulder and she was crying. He stared wretchedly over her head out the window. Then he slipped back her little fur hat and pressed his lips against her smooth head.

"I wish you hadn't come, Lyman," Isabel whispered.

"But I had to, Isabel. I love you so."

Isabel straightened her hat. "Tell the driver to take me home, Lyman. The lecture would have been over long ago. Please, Lyman," she said quietly.

Lyman lifted the little flap again and gave Isabel's address. The horse turned and the cab swung around. They had come so far and no farther. There was no use now.

"Lyman, I'll love you always," Isabel whispered.

He choked as he tried to answer. Clumsily, he kissed the side of her head. The driver was stopping.

"Don't get out, please, Lyman. Mother might be waiting. Oh, Lyman!" She kissed him quickly and held his head in both her hands. "There'll never be anyone like you." Then the cab-driver was holding open the door and she was gone. He rubbed a bare place on the window and watched her going up the walk.

There was no train out till seven in the morning. His feet turned naturally toward the campus. It was hard to believe that last winter he had been living here. He had known Isabel only three months at this time last year.

There were lights on in Hope. He waited until someone finished drinking at the well and went on. Then he went up to drink himself. When the icy water touched his stomach he remembered that he hadn't eaten since morning. He'd get Sam to go with him. Pete's oyster house would still be open. He walked across the middle campus and counted the windows until he found Sam's. There was still a light. Sam was waiting up for him, it must be nearly eleven. He walked close to one of the lighted windows and looked at his watch. It was ten after twelve. He wondered what Isabel had told her mother.

Now that he was here he didn't want to go in. He couldn't talk to Sam tonight. He would write and thank him.

He felt like a ghost walking across the campus looking at the outside of the buildings. He tried to remember things, unpleasant things, so he wouldn't want to be back here.

From inside the building there came a sudden howl, a book shot out of an open window onto the snow-covered ground. There were shouts and another yell. Someone was getting it! The light in an upper window went out. Someone was singing now, a raucous refrain he remembered, then a window banged down.

Lyman realized he was cold. He buttoned up his collar and turned his back on the campus. It was too late now to go back. He went the long way round past Isabel's house once more. The house was dark and even the polished door pull was lost in the shadow of the door-frame. The walk in front of the iron fence was shoveled clean of snow and his footsteps sounded loud in the night. It seemed as though Isabel must know they were his. He stood still looking at the face of the house wondering which windows were Isabel's. But no face appeared at any window. The cold chilled him and he walked on.

He stopped in at the oyster house where he had eaten his first oysters last fall and where he had been chaffed by some sophomores. Tonight it smelled too strongly of fish, but it was warm. The only customers were two old men and a student who was drunk. He looked familiar but Lyman couldn't remember his name.

"A dozen fried oysters and a bottle of beer. Give me a cup of coffee too, and some fried potatoes," he ordered. He sat up at the counter and watched the old fellow opening oysters. He wondered what he had meant to do as a young man—not open oysters, probably. Well, no one did what he wanted to do, so he needn't kick.

Then there was nothing to do but turn up his coat collar and walk back down to the station and wait for the morning train back to Malden Junction.

The trip back seemed twice as long as the trip down. He tried to sleep, but he kept seeing Isabel's face in the cab, illumined by the flashes of street lamps. He closed his eyes and tried to remember her saying she loved him. He felt her hands pressing his head, but his head ached now. Now she would marry Chauncey. She would go to Paris and be lost to him forever. She hadn't said so, but why shouldn't she? He couldn't marry her.

Why didn't he make a clean sweep and go West? There was his mother . . . and the business . . . but they hadn't held Dan. What was the matter with him that he stayed here? Why did he listen to an old fogy of a doctor?

One of the passengers got up and stoked the stove at the end of the car. A cloud of smoke belched out into the air. Lyman went over to stand by the stove.

"Aren't you Orville Converse's boy from over Painesville way? You look enough like him!" a man in the seat nearest the stove called out.

"Yes, yes, I am," Lyman said wearily, like a man confessing to a fault. Now he was in for it, he'd have to talk the rest of the way to Malden.

It was snowing when the train pulled in that evening. He stood on the narrow platform wishing he didn't have to get off. It was dark as pitch. The engine, wheezing and snorting, seemed the only warm place. Lyman took his bag and started for the livery stable.

"Lyman, you did come! Your mother told me you had to go to Boston on business and I was visiting in Malden, so I came down to see if you might be on this train. Can I beg a ride home with you?" Louisa Tucker stood beside him, smiling up in his face.

"Why, of course. If you'll wait in the station I'll drive right back for you," Lyman said.

"Oh, it's just a little walk. I'll go with you." She laid her hand on his arm and together they walked through the snow to the livery stable.

"Wouldn't you like to stop at Mrs. Hardin's and have a bite to eat first? You haven't had any supper, have you?"

"No, I haven't," Lyman admitted. He slowed his pace to match Louisa's.

3

"LYMAN, what you want for that smokehouse?"

"I don't want anything, Easy. You can have it, just as you always have, but now that you're married don't you want something bigger?"

"I want to pay for it, Lyman, an' have a deed of sale. Not that you'd ever do it, but when I was back down South there was folks there, colored folks, that'd been given places before even they was free and if they couldn't show a bill of sale them carpetbaggers'd get a paper that'd put them right out. I want it all down clear."

"Sure you can have it, but with Jewel going to have a child I should think you'd need more room."

"I aim to build us on another room on the south side, an' then one on the north, maybe. It's a real good start of a house, Lyman, an' there's nothing to hinder me from building on. Jewel, she wants a doorstep of soapstone like yours, an' I figger'd I'd haul one over some-day if it's all right with you."

It was duly recorded that Abigail Converse sold the smokehouse to Ezekiel Williams for the sum of five dollars. Easy had his soapstone doorstep in front of the little door and Jewel swept it every morning through the long snowy winter. Abigail liked looking up there every night to see their light, and in the daytime found the smoke from their chimney good to forecast the weather by.

Lyman still wondered why Easy had come back to Vermont. Easy had said things were different, and then that about the carpetbaggers, and now and then he would stroke his head and say the war had changed things down there, certain sure. His old master and his son were both killed in the war and Mrs. Pennicook looked like an old lady. "She didn't remember me!" Easy's face was mournful.

"But how did you find Jewel so quick, Easy?" Lyman asked one day when he rode over to the mill with him on the oxload of soapstone.

"I see her trying out cracklin's on a outdoor fire on the Ashwood place an' she was laughin' at somethin' an' that was the first laugh I'd heard since I got to Virginia. I was scairt she'd be married already, but she was living with her mammy and pappy and her brothers 'n' sisters on a place they'd rented off the plantation."

Lyman tried to see how it had been, but it was hard to fill in the little things. His eyes were Vermont eyes and he couldn't piece out what a plantation would be like.

"I asked her what her name was," Easy went on. "An' she said 'Jewel. Don't I look like somethin' precious?' An' I could see she was quick-minded like Miss Willie. An' she was pretty an' I couldn't never marry a homely woman an' live with her all my days."

That bothered Lyman as much as anything. He kept studying Jewel to see wherein her beauty lay. He never could look at her without wondering about it, and wondering what beauty was to Easy. He remembered him talking about Willie's hair, but Jewel's was black and kinky and she wore it in two little braids fastened down with pins so her head was almost the shape of her skull. Her eyes were dark-brown and shining. Her nose was as carefully shaped as any white nose and her lips were not so thick as Easy's.

They could hear Jewel laugh often from the woodshed or the kitchen when the windows were open. Once Lyman stepped out the front door in the morning and saw Jewel run up the hill as fast as a rabbit and Easy after her. He caught up with her where the fringe of firs came down to meet the pasture edge, and Jewel's little shriek came down off the hill like a stone they had set rolling. Easy picked her up and brought her back down to his little house, carrying her in his arms, her head against his shoulder. Lyman stepped back inside the house with a strangely desolate feeling.

When Lyman stopped in at the smokehouse, which they spoke of now as "Easy's house," Jewel plumped the pillow in the big chair Easy had bought at an auction and then busied herself in the leanto kitchen. It was a warm, cozy place to Lyman. Pictures from magazines were tacked up on the walls and Abigail's old quilts were on the bed. Abbie was teaching Jewel to piece one herself, a woolen one made from Orville Converse's clothes. Jewel was a neat housekeeper, but always her house was a little warmer than the rooms in Lyman's house, and the faint smell of cooking and wood smoke and a fainter more penetrating scent of bodies mingled in the air. Lyman felt it was a married household and didn't drop over often, confining his talks with Easy to the times he rode with him on the oxload or saw him at the quarry. Of a snowy day Easy sometimes came over and sat in the woodshed talking with Lyman as they used to do as boys.

"I saw Miss Isabel, Easy," Lyman told him the week after he got back from Providence. He stood outside the quarry office with one foot on the runner. Easy sat on the sled. "She's going to marry Chauncey Westcott Christmas Eve." It was a relief to tell someone.

Easy's eyes were sympathetic. "I was afraid of that. That's what that Burwell say he's goin' to do las' spring." He flicked the snow with the long lash of his bull whip. "I know how you feel, Lyman. I'm sure sorry." The voice was very soft, softer than any voice on the street of Painesville.

"Of course she was my first cousin." A shadow of a question lurked in his voice.

"Powerful lot of that down South. It don't allus work out so good," Easy observed. Simon Peterboro passed by and spoke to Lyman, including Easy with his eyes. Oliver Weatherbee came back from the post office. Mrs. Blanchard passed and nodded. To them all Lyman seemed to be giving directions to the colored man, Easy, who freighted soapstone for him. They would have been amazed if they had known that Easy was the only one in Painesville he confided in.

"Well, I better be goin'," Easy said.

"Looks like more snow," Lyman answered. Their eyes met briefly but with full knowledge of the other's thought. "Stop and tell Mother I'm staying in town for supper tonight at Louisa's, Easy?"

"I'll do that, Lyman." He drove off sitting high on the stone blocks, a bag of burlap for a seat.

He was going here too often, Lyman told himself as he walked up the street to Louisa's. She was beginning to count on him every Wednesday night. She wanted him to come on Thursday night, but that would mean going to prayer meeting. He wouldn't do that. That would be as good as saying to the town that he was "serious." Oliver Weatherbee had tried to josh him once about Louisa. He had spoken to him sharply for it, too, but it was pleasant going up here. It broke the monotony of the winter evenings at home.

He liked the lights of the house streaming out through the small panes on either side of the door and through the fanlight above. The lamps were lighted in the parlor and there was always a fire in the parlor stove the way there used to be at home when Willie was with them. Tonight Louisa was playing the organ when he went up the walk. He watched her a minute through the window, and when he raised the knocker he could see her leave the organ to come to the door. He remembered the day during the war when she hadn't had any mail and her eyes were red from crying, but she was always smiling when she came to the door now. They seldom mentioned John at all. It made Lyman feel a little guilty.

"Come in, Lyman. It turned so cold I was afraid you'd think you had to go straight up home, but Easy's there and he'll look in at your mother, won't he?"

"Yes. I told Easy I'd be staying in town a little longer than usual."

"A *little* longer—Lyman Converse, don't tell me you have to rush away tonight!"

"Well, not too early," he admitted. He hung his hat and coat on the hooks that grew out of the corners of the hall mirror and set his overshoes carefully on the bottom of the umbrella stand.

"Go right on in, Lyman. Father's in his office. You bring him out while I dish up." Louisa's voice floated back to him from the kitchen. It seemed to beckon to him and the kitchen looked inviting. Always before he had talked with the Doctor or looked at some book in the parlor. Tonight on an impulse he followed Louisa to the kitchen.

"Let me help," he said. "I often help Mother now."

"Then you'll have to wear an apron!" Louisa took one from the bottom drawer of the kitchen dresser and tied it around his waist. "It just suits you, Lyman."

He carried in the tureen of soup and fussed about how hot the handles were and Louisa laughed at him. He had an odd sense of saying what he was supposed to say, like lines in a play. "Chicken pie, Louisa!" he exclaimed as she took it out of the oven.

"I remembered that you liked it." Louisa seemed to lay more significance on the simple fact than was called for. He felt a little uneasy. "Now you call Father and we're ready. Here, I'll take your apron."

"Well, Lyman, I hear you're doing a firstrate job at the quarry! Oliver Weatherbee says you have a mind of your own, and since Oliver has none of his own, I imagine he values that a good deal in you."

"Oliver isn't doing anything to develop my mind, though. He's always telling me what my father would do."

"Yes, I can believe that." Dr. Tucker chuckled.

It was pleasant eating dinner in the dining-room on the long table after the corner of the kitchen table at home. The lamp on its suspension bracket was brought down low and enclosed them in its warm circle of light. The silver shone on the best white cloth and when Lyman touched his lips with the white fringed napkin he noticed how soft it was. After urging, he passed his plate for another serving of the chicken pie and wild-strawberry jam. Glancing up, he met Louisa's eyes. Something in the way this meal seemed planned and served for him, the way Dr. Tucker talked to him as though he were a contemporary, made him feel older and at ease. His eyes held Louisa's a second and they both smiled. He noticed the way her dark hair swept down on either side of the part, like the sides of a gable. How calm and good she looked! Her eyes and mouth weren't always changing and the pink color stayed in her cheeks, but there was no shimmer of gold flecks beneath the skin.

Someone came to get Dr. Tucker while they were eating their sauce and fresh sponge cake, and Lyman and Louisa were left to finish alone.

"This is certainly delicious cake, Louisa," Lyman said.

"It's a pleasure to cook for someone who enjoys things. Father doesn't know what he's eating half the time."

He wondered if it were a sign of inferiority that he did like food so much. Perhaps a man should have his mind so occupied that he ate merely for nourishment.

"Did you ever think, Lyman, if your mother hadn't suggested that I might get a ride back to Painesville with you we might not have come to know each other so well?"

Lyman frowned, trying to remember what they had talked about that night. He hadn't thought of that as beginning anything, exactly.

"You seemed so blue and lonely and discouraged it hurt me to see you. And here in town, when I'd see you go by, you looked so solemn and old for your years."

"I guess I've just been busy with the quarry." The picture Louisa drew pleased him.

"Of course all that responsibility has made you more mature. Goodness, you seem older than John was when he went to war."

A subtle satisfaction crept along Lyman's mind.

"You've been working too hard, that's what I think. You must stay downtown more often. You're always welcome here, you know."

"Thank you, Louisa," Lyman said, and put a period to the conversation more quickly than he had meant.

"They're getting up a singing school again. Why don't you join it? You have such a true voice."

He was surprised that she had noticed his voice.

"You must have sung last year in college."

"Yes, I did a little. Easy ought to join the singing school. He loves to sing. We could go back and forth together."

Louisa hesitated. "But now that he's married I don't imagine he'd want to come back down in the evening."

"Oh, I don't know. He sings in the choir and he used to be in that singing class the year the war ended. I guess they were all younger than you. You weren't in it." Lyman realized how his words sounded. "Or you were wrapped up in John and didn't have time," he appended hastily.

Louisa sat quietly at the table turning the thin silver spoon between her fingers. "Do I seem old to you, Lyman?"

He was uncomfortable. "Why, no, Louisa, of course not—what an idea!"

"I am five years older than you."

"Are you really? I never thought about it," Lyman said uncomfortably, and yet Louisa had always seemed John's age to him.

Louisa smiled and rose to take out the dishes. Lyman followed her out to the kitchen, wondering now how soon he could leave without offending her. The front door banged and Dr. Tucker stamped in carrying his worn old doctor's bag with him.

"Just saw a hopeless case of sugar diabetes. Let's have something to buck up our spirits, Lyman, before our own constitutions betray us."

"Oh, Father, Lyman doesn't . . ."

"Thank you, sir," Lyman said quickly, following the Doctor into his strange-smelling office.

When Lyman drove into the yard at home it was after midnight. He had sat talking to the Doctor all that time. Louisa had finished up the dishes and come in to sit with them, but the office only had two comfortable chairs, and it smelled so strongly of carbolic she left it and sat in the parlor instead, urging them to join her there as soon as they finished their discussion. But one subject led to another and Lyman had forgotten about her when they came across the hall from the office a couple of hours later.

"I'm sorry, Louisa. It was so good to talk to your father about some of my problems."

"Of course, Lyman, I know. Come again soon, won't you?" And he had left feeling that Louisa was an understanding woman.

The house was warm and a lamp burned in the kitchen, but his mother didn't seem to be there. He called as he went through the house. Then he went outside again. Under the brow of the hill light streamed out of the windows of Easy's house.

At his knock Easy stepped out in the snow bareheaded, his sleeves rolled up above his elbows.

"Hurrah to Gideon, Lyman!" he said, holding out his hand. "I got a son! Jewel's had her baby an' she did fine. Your mother's in there now."

The light from the little house struck full on Easy's face and Lyman could see how jubilant he was.

"Congratulations, Easy! That's wonderful! What are you going to name him?"

"Jewel an' I talked about it some. If you wouldn't mind an' Missus

Converse wouldn't, we thought we'd like to name him Orville after your father 'cause he was the man that took me in."

"Why, no, of course I wouldn't. That's pretty fine," Lyman said heartily, ashamed of the sudden possessive way he felt about his father's name.

"I feel like I got to let off steam, Lyman. There's a jug over at the quarry. Let's you an' me have a little somethin'."

They walked together through the snow. Now that they were out on the road they were silent. Then Easy began to whistle. Lyman was taken up with the strangeness of this thing that had happened to Easy. Easy had a son. Easy was only two years older than he, only twenty.

"Lyman, you 'member that night we was at the spelling match an' Miss Willie had her baby down at Tuckers'?"

"Yes, I do," Lyman said.

Easy laughed, a low sound in his throat. "I thought how it would feel to get you a baby, but I didn't know you'd feel this good!"

"You feel pretty good, Easy?"

"Man alive, I feel wonderful!" Easy let loose a queer, hilarious yell that echoed through the dark trees as exultantly as the bugling of a bull elk.

Lyman wondered if he would ever feel that way.

4

LYMAN sat at his desk after Oliver had left. He took out again the note on thin bluish paper and reread it before transferring it to the file marked Personal Correspondence. There was a small pack of these notes now, all on the same kind of foreign-looking paper, all postmarked "Paris, France." They all began "Dear Cousin Lyman" and ended "Faithfully, your cousin, Isabel." This one read:

Thank you for the check from the quarry of 10/4/69. It speaks well for your efficient management. It was gratifying to know that the output has been so much increased.

Autumn has been more beautiful than ever in Paris. I feel as though we woke and walked and breathed within a great amber glass, so yellow is the light and the leaves of the trees on the boulevard are so golden. Chauncey has been in England for the last month, but is returning next week. Mother is quite frail and preferred staying in Paris, so I remained with her.

Faithfully, your cousin,
Isabel

The note always followed the same pattern: acknowledgment of the dividend check, a word of commendation couched in the most formal tone, and a brief paragraph that mentioned both her mother and Chauncey and usually the weather, or some concert or lecture. One Thanksgiving there had been a card from Chauncey saying "Remember the Thanksgiving day at our house in '65? You should taste the wines here! Chauncey."

Lyman sometimes wondered what Chauncey did. Isabel never said, though he seemed to travel about a good deal. Last year he had asked if they would be back in the States in the spring and Isabel had written: "I believe we shall make our home in France, at least for the present. Chauncey likes it best and Mother is not anxious to try the trip home." She did not say whether she herself liked it best there.

Whatever brief word Isabel wrote stayed with him oddly. This noon as Lyman walked down the street from lunch at Mrs. Belknap's he had thought about the yellow light in Paris. Here there were more scarlet leaves on the maples than yellow. If there had been any excuse for writing Isabel so soon, he would have added "Ours is a ruby-colored glass." No, "ruby" wasn't the color of the maples, they were more the color of blood, some bright arterial blood and others the darker blood of the veins—Converse blood that was linked to Holbrook blood and ran in a deep mysterious way forever uniting them and separating them.

He returned the letter to its envelope and placed it in the Personal file, locking the padlock afterward. He wondered whether Isabel was happy. Did she still love him? That was what she meant by signing herself "Faithfully," he told himself again.

Once Oliver Weatherbee had written a letter for him and signed it "Faithfully yours" and Lyman had flashed out at him irascibly,

"For heaven's sake, Oliver, sign 'Yours truly' in a business letter." Oliver had opened his mouth and then thought better of it and copied his letter over.

It was unfortunate that tonight with Isabel's note warm in his mind his mother should talk to him about Louisa.

"That dear girl was up today, Lyman," Abbie said at supper.

"Was she? Did she drive up?"

"No, she walked all the way. She said she loved the fall so. She went by the quarry office and wanted to go in and get you to walk with her, but you looked so busy she didn't dare."

"Oh," Lyman said, gratified that he had looked so busy, wondering if that was when he had been reading Isabel's letter.

"She played the piano for me. Lyman, I do think you mean a good deal to her. I can tell from little things, like her being so interested in that tintype of you as a baby."

"Oh, I don't think so, Mother. It's just because I'm John's brother."

Abbie shook her head. "That's not it." She sipped her tea as though making up her mind while doing it. "It would make me very happy, Lyman, if you and Louisa should marry. She's like a daughter to me already."

"I'm afraid not, Mother." In his embarrassment Lyman passed his plate for another serving of beans and brown bread that he didn't want. He noticed how sad her face was in repose.

"Do you remember how your father liked my baked beans, Lyman?" Abbie asked irrelevantly.

"That's right, he did," Lyman said, feeling his mother's loneliness press against him. For an instant he wondered what she did all day—the housework, the cooking, some sewing. Her hair under her cap was graying, but she wasn't old. It wasn't comfortable seeing life through his mother's eyes.

"I asked Louisa up for supper tomorrow night, Lyman. I said you would go by for her," Abbie said quite cheerfully.

"I wish you wouldn't do that!" Irritation bristled in his voice and he was sorry for it. Why was it so easy to hurt his mother? He saw himself through the years like Judge Whitcomb, whose mother was eighty-three, taking her to church, driving with her, eating interminable meals like this, growing older with her until there wasn't very much difference between them.

"Why, Lyman, why not?"

"Of course, Mother, it's all right if you want to ask her, only . . . I don't know that she wants to come."

"Louisa looked very pleased when I asked her. You know she's teaching all day till four o'clock. Louisa must be fine with children."

He pushed back his chair. "Thank you, Mother, that was a good supper," he said to make up for his annoyance.

"I don't know. I thought the brown bread was a little heavy." Abbie's tone was tremulous, apologetic. When he was little, Abbie's words had always seemed so sure. How had this change come about in so few years?

There was no place in the living part of the house where he could be alone, Lyman felt. His mother's anxious loving eyes were on him, bothering him. He went out to milk, glad of something to do. In his father's day the milking was done at five, but he didn't get home early enough for that and they milked only one cow now. They had given the other cow to Easy as a wedding present and he kept her on the Spring place. Lyman wondered if he hoped to build a house there sometime.

Lyman knelt on the ground to light the lantern. In the barn he felt more comfortable and free. Sitting there milking, his eyes searched out the things hanging from the rafters, some lost in the darkness, others standing out. The lantern caught the light on a buckle or a shining nailhead. An old ox yoke hung from the pegs on the beam at one side. That belonged to a team of oxen his father had sold to a former owner of the quarry. He remembered when his father bought the quarry and came home and told Abbie, she had smiled and said: "Well, you got back the ox team, didn't you, Orville? But you went a long way round to do it, seems to me." That was what he missed, those flashings of fun his mother used to have with his father.

He himself owned the ox team now, he supposed, and the yoke. The quarry itself was a yoke in a way, keeping his head bent, bowing him under its weight. He looked away, wishing he hadn't thought that.

His eyes moved past the wheel with the spoke out to a long scythe that hadn't been touched since his father's hand had swung it. Now in the fall it made him think of the long green grass of summer as though summer were a long time gone. Dan and John used to compete with each other with that scythe on the slope at the south of the house, and he had run along beside them, wanting John to win and then wanting Dan to win. John was always telling him to get out of the way for fear he'd be cut, like little Hattie Spring, but Dan would let him take the little sickle and cut around the bushes.

He finished milking, but he sat there leaning against the side of the stall. Beyond the scythe hung an old toy boat with a piece of a rag for a sail and nails to mark off a deck. Dan had made that for him to sail in the creek. It was too heavy and always falling over, but he had never told Dan for fear he would feel badly. John had made one for Easy, he remembered, that took longer to make but sailed better than his. He wondered where that one was. A tin candle dip was strung up beside the toy boat. By the door, where it was a wonder it hadn't hit someone on the head, was an old chair with a rung gone. He went over to it now, walking in his own light, and took it down. A person could fix that if he could find the right kind of wood. He carried the lantern into the woodshed and hunted around till he found a piece of pine. It wouldn't match the chair exactly, as the chair was maple, but whittled down and sanded and oiled it would do. When he went back in the kitchen with the milk he carried the chair along.

"Forevermore, Lyman, what did you bring that old chair in for?"

"Oh, I thought I might fix it," Lyman said, feeling a little foolish. While his mother was straining the milk he lighted another lamp and got out the tools from the cupboard that had once been the brick baking oven by the old fireplace.

"If you're going to sit here, Lyman, I'll put in another stick," Abbie said. She brought out the rags she was cutting for a rug and sat on the other side of the table humming a monotonously happy little tune he remembered from his childhood. This was the way his mother had used to sit in the evenings when he was a boy, only his father filled the chair where he sat now.

"Jonathan used to be such a good hand to fix things," Abbie said. "Daniel would rather buy a new one. Your father used to get angry at things he tried to mend."

Lyman tapped the whittled ends of the new rung in place. "This jacket bother you, Mother?" he stopped to ask.

"Mercy, no, the house is so quiet most of the time I nearly go crazy some days."

He sanded the rung, stopping now and then to feel the wood with his fingers, feeling at the same time a sort of contentment in his fingers. He felt comfortable here with his mother, smoothed out, like the pine wood.

"There!" he said with satisfaction. "That's not bad."

Abbie came over and inspected it. "That's a real good fit, Lyman. Seems as though with a rung gone a chair gets to wobbling before you know it."

"Of course it needs to have some oil rubbed on it," he said deprecatingly.

"I'll do it tomorrow. Hot oil and spirits of turpentine's the best."

Lyman put away his tools, liking, for the first time in his life, the feeling of seeing them back in place. When he took up the paper he felt oddly like his father. In conscious imitation he aped his father's way of hunching his chair back until the light fell right on the print.

"The wind's sprung up. I'm afraid it'll take all the leaves down if it blows like that," Abbie said.

"Did you notice how red they are this fall?" Lyman asked.

"I pressed a couple from the big maple out front and sent them to Dan's wife," Abbie admitted, not raising her eyes from her cutting. "I don't know as they have maples out West there. I thought Juliet would like them, maybe."

"Of course she would. That was nice," Lyman answered, but feeling his mother's loneliness again. He would send a leaf to Isabel tomorrow, just put it in an envelope and send it to Paris. They couldn't have maples there if most of their leaves were yellow.

"Read the editorial, Lyman. Your father always used to read it aloud to me."

Lyman turned the page. "It's called 'A Warning.' *Our farms are becoming tenantless. The lung tissues of society supplying fresh blood to the throbbing heart-centers, the cities, are becoming fewer. Almost whole hamlets slough away and leave bad cavities, in which the life-blood is not eliminated.*

We seek the homes of our ancestors; their roof-trees fell long ago; a few straggling rosebushes still blush beside the old garden wall; an aged pear or plum, sprung from a seed in the old Colonial times, still yields to the blandishments of the Blossom Week, but desolation reigns around and kine quietly crop the herbage around the old hearthstone. Many of the wind-swept hills were inhabited of old. Is the race less hardy now? Old cellar places meet one at every turn, places where the

roots of civilization had fastened themselves and died out. Their top-
pling chimneys are monuments which bear sad evidence of the scat-
tering of home circles![1]

"Like the Spring place and the Dombey place. Just think of all the
farms there used to be up past us when you were a child. Now we're
the farthest farm up the hill," Abbie said. "And that about the scattering of home circles . . ." She didn't finish her thought.

The comfortable content of the evening was gone. Lyman rattled
the paper as he turned it over to read the ads. *Dubuque, Iowa. Will attend to purchase of real estate at Western rates for Eastern clients.* It
was signed by Thad Davis, Dubuque. Thad had lived right here; he
had sat with Jeb and Easy and Lyman in the graveyard the night they
heard about Lincoln's assassination.

Woolen factory and machinery at auction. That must be the Blaine
mill at Malden. Emory Blaine was going West.

"There's a blind blowing somewhere, Lyman. Listen to it!" Abbie
said.

"I'll get it," Lyman murmured, and went on reading. His eye had
caught something else, an account of the new quarry at Wallingford,
Vt.

*About 800 tons of stone were raised from this quarry last summer.
. . . Couldn't but observe the marked difference between this quarry
and the valuable Converse Quarry at Painesville. In this one no over-
lying rock—good soapstone is found by merely removing soil and
gravel that rests upon it, while in Painesville there is a great quantity
of hornblende, in some places ten feet thick, which must be blasted before soapstone can be reached.*

"Lyman, you just sit there! Go fix the blind before the wind breaks
it all up." Abbie spoke sharply, as though he were a small boy again.

"I'm going right now," Lyman answered. He must find some excuse
to visit the quarry at Wallingford. If it was as good as the fellow
claimed, he could use it. His orders were increasing every month and
it would be better to own it than to compete with it.

The wind met him full in the face at the corner of the house, blowing down from the darkness of the quarry and the wilderness beyond.
He shielded his face with his arm to get his breath.

[1]Actual editorial in 1866.

5

LYMAN looked down at Willie's smooth yellow head with the same cascade of curls that had seemed so beautiful to him as a boy. "Like maple syrup," Easy had said. Lyman remembered that now—of all things to remember!

"Dan was different after the war." His voice wandered uncertainly, trying to find something to comfort Willie with, to comfort himself with.

Willie's face was buried in her arms on the table. It was the first time since he had come yesterday that she had cried. Maybe it was good for her. He walked over to the window and rubbed a clear space on the pane so he could look out at the miserable crooked street that was the main street of Helena, Montana. The snow had mixed with the mud and frozen into deep ruts. A few people walked by wrapped up to the ears. He felt the cold through the glass and turned back to the heat of the stove.

If he had seen Dan buried, he could believe it more easily. But there was only a wooden marker above frozen snow to show him. Dan had been buried eight days before he got here and he had come as soon as Willie's telegram reached him. He had it still in his vest pocket. It read:

DAN DIED SUDDENLY TONIGHT. CAN YOU COME? WILLIE.

"Sounds like double pneumonia," Abbie said through her sobbing. "Out there where it's so cold, and Dan was always the one to catch cold easy." She had sat in the kitchen and rocked back and forth, her arms folded close to her, looking without seeing at the road down the hill. "John and Orville and then Dan," she said over and over in a sort of plaintive monotone. Lyman had asked Jewel to stay with his mother, and Easy had driven him over to Malden to catch the train West ten days ago.

But it wasn't pneumonia. "Dan was hanged, Lyman," Willie said as soon as they were by themselves in this hotel room.

He hadn't taken it in at first. Willie had said it so quietly and she looked so dressed-up and pretty, just like she used to except that she had paint on her cheeks.

"He shot a man, Si Dolan, at the Lucky Spot saloon, for jumping his claim. Dolan didn't happen to be armed at the time, so Dolan's friends hurried Dan out and hung him." Willie hadn't cried then. She had been as calm as a late afternoon with all the light gone out of it. She told the story as though it might have happened to anyone.

"Does Juliet know?" Lyman had asked right away. Juliet was six, with black curls like Dan's. She had called him Uncle Lyman and put her arms around his neck. He hadn't expected to find her so . . . so grown-up.

"I'm not sure. The hotel proprietor told her he was killed in an accident, though it was in the paper." Willie went over to the bureau and took out a clipping. "I won't lie to her if she finds out. She adored Dan; it wouldn't make any difference to her any more than it does to me."

Lyman read the clipping:

Dan Converse, driver for Gilmer and Salisbury Stage Co., shot and killed Si Dolan in an altercation over a disputed claim. Dolan was unarmed. Justice was summarily administered by hanging in Dry Gulch two miles west of town. Persons involved in the necktie party are unknown.

To gain time before he lifted his eyes to Willie's face Lyman had read and reread the printed words.

"But you can't hang a man without a trial. There must be a way to find these men and . . ."

Willie shrugged. "Oh, we know who they were, Dolan's friends, but what's the use? Dan's dead." She had been so cool then and so collected. She mentioned Dan easily and talked about her plans.

"Why don't you let me take you back to Vermont, Willie? You and Juliet. Mother's so lonely."

"Oh, Lyman, you know I don't belong there. I could stand it for Dan's sake, but not any more. I've thought about it and I've decided to go on to the West coast. I know I can get a place with a good stock company out there."

"But what about Juliet?"

"I'll have her right with me. She'll be all right, Lyman; don't look so shocked. I've been acting right along in Virginia City, and here too. Sometimes my earnings and the dividends from the quarry were all we had. I could have earned more if I hadn't stayed with Dan. I've lost Dan, I can't give up Juliet. I'll write you when I play in Boston and you can come and see me." She smiled at him with a flash of her old gaiety.

They had a terrible dinner in the room that served as dining-room. Lyman felt that people stared at them, but Willie seemed not to notice and Juliet chattered all through the meal.

"Tell me about when Papa was in the war," Juliet commanded. And he told her. He had Dan leading his company in charges against the rebels. He remembered what Chauncey had said about him and repeated it now for Dan's child and for Willie.

"Every man in his company would have followed him to death gladly," he said, leaving out the word "hell."

But now Juliet was in bed in the next room and Willie sat here at the table with her head on her arms.

"Lyman, I can't think yet about living without Dan." Her words were muffled and he had to bend near to hear what she said. Then she sat back and he saw her face. It was as deserted of life as the old Spring place. "It's going to be hard to care about living even for Juliet," she said almost in a whisper.

"I know," he told her, though he didn't quite. She didn't seem to blame Dan. He wanted to ask so many questions, but he held his tongue. Then he couldn't help it. "But, Willie, I don't understand. Why didn't he try to settle his difficulty about this claim by law? Why did he kill the man? I mean . . ."

"Oh, you can't understand, Lyman, unless you've lived in this country and seen other men strike gold and had your claims prove to be worthless and then heard of a new strike and tried it there and been too late. And Dan wasn't like any prospector just waiting for his luck, he worked hard at other things. He drove the stage and carried gold to Benton. He could have worked with the road agents, but he never did."

Willie made Dan's honesty sound like a rare virtue. Lyman felt the queerness of it. Of course Dan would be honest. . . .

"And then last summer he tried his luck again. Juliet and I went with him and camped up in the mountains. It was beautiful, Lyman. I didn't care whether we found gold or not. We were so happy." Willie's mouth worked pitifully and he looked away across the room at the cracked mirror. That was how he noticed the dried red maple leaf stuck in the frame. It must be the one his mother had sent her.

"Dan came back one day wildly excited. You know how excited he could get. He'd found a good show of color and some good nuggets in the dirt. I held them in my hand and I was excited too. He staked out a claim and posted his name on a piece of paper on one of the stakes the way they do."

"That's the way a man stakes out a claim to a bee tree back home," Lyman said. Willie went on as though she hadn't heard him.

"Oh, Lyman, we were frantic to get back to Helena to register the claim, and I started packing up while Dan went for the horses. They'd been driven off and it took Dan until night to find them. When we got to Helena the next day, Dan's claim had been registered in Si Dolan's name. You can't imagine what it was like!" Willie's eyes burned and her mouth was tight with hate. She looked as though she could have killed Dolan herself.

"Dan went all over town to find Dolan, but he'd skipped out again. He nearly went wild. He kept saying it was our one chance and we'd never have another. I told him it wasn't and that it didn't matter, I'd rather have him forget the gold and build up a freighting business here, but you know how Dan was!"

Lyman nodded.

"Dan went back in the mountains. I was afraid to have him go, but I couldn't keep him from going. He was away a week. When he came back he looked terrible, Lyman. He hadn't eaten or slept hardly at all. He had been drinking, but he was sober when he got home. I was acting that night, and when I came back late he was up here sitting in that chair you're sitting in. He was so quiet and hopeless it scared me more than his being angry could have."

As Willie told it Lyman could see Dan here. He could feel Willie's nights of waiting and worrying.

"And then Dan told me he'd been right. It was a real strike and Dolan was rich. I asked him if he'd showed Dolan his stakes and he said the stakes were gone and Dolan just laughed and told him not to hang around that claim if he didn't want to get hurt. 'He's smart, Willie,' Dan said, 'and I'm just a poor damn fool.' And he cried, Lyman," Willie whispered.

Lyman looked away from Willie. He tried to think of Dan crying.

"He couldn't get over it, Lyman. He began drinking hard and the stage company let him go. When he was drinking he'd talk and talk about how rich a strike he'd made. He made enemies out of people who'd been his friends before. And all fall he just brooded. He'd go where he knew Dolan was and just sit and look at him. 'I'm his conscience,' he told me once when he was half-drunk. 'I just sit and trouble him.'

"I knew he'd kill Dolan if I couldn't get him away from here. I thought I could in the spring. When he didn't come home that night, I was almost sure he'd done it, but I hoped he had got away and would send for me from some safe place across the mountains. I'd have gone to him and we could have started all over again."

"Where did he kill him?" Lyman asked, almost ashamed of his curiosity.

"In the Lucky Spot. He used to go there every night and sit across the room watching Dolan." Willie's tone was lifeless, almost disinterested.

The room had grown cold. Downstairs someone walked heavily and the flimsy walls shook. Lyman couldn't look at Willie. He was trying to find the right thing to say. He wished she would cry again.

"Dan must have been out of his mind or he'd never have killed the man," Lyman said slowly. He didn't want Willie to feel that Dan was a . . . had murdered the man in cold blood.

Willie turned around in her chair and leaned forward.

"You don't understand Dan any better than your father did. It would have been kinder if I'd written you a letter saying he died of a fever. I don't want your mother to know ever, or anybody in Painesville, but I thought you were different, and you adored Dan when you were a boy. I sent for you to come way out here so I could tell you. Listen, Lyman, Dan wasn't out of his mind and he wasn't drunk. He knew exactly what he was doing. I don't suppose you've ever wanted something hard enough to kill the man who took it from you. You look like Father Converse when he realized I was an actress."

Lyman sat quietly under Willie's scorn, feeling that it helped her but feeling its sting at the same time.

"Well, Dan was lucky to have you, Willie," he said after a long time.

"Do you really think so, Lyman?" Willie asked almost eagerly. "Maybe I wasn't good for him because I was so ready to go any place he wanted to go."

"Dan would have gone anyway."

"Oh, yes, once he made up his mind to a thing, he'd do it," Willie said almost proudly. "He never looked at any other woman, Lyman. I don't believe he loved anyone but Juliet and me. That's a great deal for a man like Dan."

Again Lyman wondered. Willie made a virtue out of something you expected. If you loved a woman, of course you would be faithful to her.

"I thought if you came out here I could make you understand about him. The West isn't like Vermont. You mustn't blame him!"

Lyman studied the crack in the marble-topped table and even speculated as to where the marble came from. He didn't blame Dan—blame wasn't the word, but he wasn't sure that he could understand.

"I want you to have this ring of Dan's. He bought it in St. Louis before we took the boat up the Missouri. Dan was so excited that day. He bought me these gold earrings and a new dress for Juliet. He was so sure we were going to make our fortune out West. I never saw the ring off his hand."

Lyman took the ring and turned it in his fingers. The only man's ring he ever remembered noticing was his father's wide gold wedding ring. This was a massive-looking ring with a man's head cut into black onyx.

"The head makes you think of Easy, doesn't it?" Lyman said.

"I never thought of that. How is Easy?"

"He's fine. He felt badly about Dan's death." Lyman wondered with a sudden pang whether if Easy had come out here with Dan things might have turned out differently.

When he left Willie that night, Lyman went out into the strange Western town curiously. Dan had known these streets and buildings as well as he himself knew the main street of Painesville. The street was so dark he stumbled over a chunk of snow, but lights shone mistily behind the frozen windowpanes. Two horses were tied to a hitching post in front of a saloon. Their hot breaths showed white in the dark. Lyman looked close at the sign on the window. That wasn't it.

Just under a lantern that hung in front of a doorway he met a Chinese wearing a long queue down his back and turned to watch him until he disappeared down the dark street. A real live Chinaman! He couldn't get over it.

This mining camp was bigger than the town of Painesville. It was still alive at midnight. Music came from another saloon. He went across the street to read the name over the door. Occidental Saloon—that wasn't it. He'd have to go in somewhere pretty soon to get warm. "The Lucky Spot," Willie had said. There it was!

The door pushed open easily. There was too much to see all at once. The bar ran down one side of the crowded room. A couple of girls were dancing on a kind of stage at the back and a man was playing a fiddle. Nobody paid much attention to them. Along the other side of the room men were playing cards. As Lyman stood by the door he saw a man throw his cards on the sawdust-covered floor and get up from the table. Another man took his place and a new deck of cards was produced. Nobody bothered to pick up the ones on the floor. There was a bigger table toward the back, just under a hanging lantern. The light striking on the green-covered top made the men's faces greenish. How could Dan dare to shoot a man here in such a crowd?

As he went over to the bar he caught the eyes of a woman in a shiny blue dress cut lower in the neck than any woman's dress he had ever seen. His glance followed the line of her bosom and moved away quickly. There was a big mirror back of the bar. The room looked even more crowded in the mirror. The men lining the bar drinking were different from the men he knew back home. One of them made him think of Jeb Holmes, or the way Jeb would look when he was ten years older and had drunk a little more. But there was a look about some of the others that he liked, a kind of quick, tight, ready look. It made them different from the men around the livery stable or Peterboro's store. He was thinking about it when the bartender stood in front of him, blocking his view of the mirror. The man was fat and red-faced, the size and build of the blacksmith at home. His eyes fixed Lyman coldly.

"Whisky," Lyman ordered, wishing he didn't feel self-conscious when he ordered a drink. With the thumb of his left hand he rubbed the wide band of Dan's ring. It felt clumsy on his hand. Dan had worn the ring the night he was here. He turned his hand over and the black polished surface reflected the lights.

Lyman took his drink slowly. Once he thought the bartender stared at him a little long. Perhaps he saw a resemblance to Dan. He studied the men lined up at the bar wondering which of them were Dolan's friends and if they felt uneasy seeing him. But no one seemed interested in him except the woman with the shiny blue dress, who leaned against the bar beside him and smiled at him. He looked at her face and thought it large and cheap and painted. Her hair was too yellow.

"Aren't you lonesome all by yourself?" she asked. Her voice was softer than her face.

"I'm all right, thank you," Lyman answered.

The woman raised one eyebrow and moved away from him. He wished now that he had talked to her a little. He should have bought her a drink. As a matter of fact, he did feel lonely. He tried to listen to the talk around him, hoping, almost fearing he would hear some comment about Dolan or Dan.

"It's goin' to chinook tonight," the man next to him announced to the world at large.

"No sign of it yet. It's cold enough to freeze hell over," the bartender said. Lyman listened. He wondered at what table Dolan had sat playing when Dan shot him. What if he should lean on the bar and say to the bartender:

"I'm trying to understand how Dan Converse felt. He was my

brother. I'm trying to feel what he felt sitting in this place." But he was glad no one could read his thoughts as he stood there drinking the sharp-edged drink.

He watched the man on his other side pay for his drink with some gold dust and the bartender pour it onto a scale and weigh it. Dan had killed a man because of gold like that! Something between pity and wonder touched his mind.

"You like the looks of gold, mister?" The fat man behind the bar was talking to him, Lyman realized with a start, and he looked up with a half-smile as the big hand tilted the dust into a larger pouch and put it down under the bar. The man did not smile and his eyes continued to size Lyman up coldly. Lyman ordered another drink, more to explain his presence at the bar than because he wanted it. He thought of getting into the game of poker back there, but he hesitated. He had no money to lose here. Dan couldn't have left Willie much of anything, Willie and Juliet. If he had thought of Juliet that night Dan might have kept his head. How could a man with . . . "Don't blame him," Willie had said. Well, she'd have an income from the quarry all her life, he'd see to that.

A hand touched his. Lyman looked quickly in the mirror. The woman in the shiny blue dress was back. He moved his hand, slipping it in his pocket.

"I thought you looked familiar! You're Dan Converse's brother, ain't you? I saw his ring."

"Yes, I am," Lyman answered. Why should she know Dan's ring?

"Buy me a drink and we'll go over here and talk," the woman said.

When they sat at the table against the wall the woman clasped both hands around her glass. "Your brother had something to say to everybody, and when he had any luck at cards he always bought drinks all around."

Lyman could almost see him. He tried to catch the sound of Dan's voice calling out to someone in here—this frowsy woman in blue or the fat man behind the bar. . . .

"And he could drive that stage like nobody else, he had an air! I went to Benton once with him an' he let me sit up between him and the messenger. We rode all night and we sang everything you ever heard tell of." She pushed her empty glass toward him. "We had plenty to drink that night, too."

Lyman looked around uncertainly, then he got up and went over to the bar. This time he fixed the bartender with a stern eye. "Another whisky."

"You know, when I study a little I can see you look like him. You're younger, though, aren't you?" the woman said when he came back to the table.

"A couple of years," Lyman admitted. He felt this third glass too strongly. Across the room a dark-haired girl in a buckskin jacket laughed. She was leaning over the shoulder of one of the players watching the game.

"That's Lucy. She cried all the next day after they hung Dan," the woman told Lyman.

"Why should she cry for Dan?" Lyman asked slowly, watching the dark-haired girl. "She looks Indian."

"She's a half-breed. He was a friend of hers same as he was of mine, that's why. She'd go wild if she saw that ring. She wanted it and he'd never give it to her. I guess his wife must have gave it to him. He'd play with all us girls and buy us a drink any old time, but he was stuck on his wife. I sure feel sorry for his wife. She never comes in here, but I've seen her. I've seen her act, too, an' she's a regular tear-jerker. I cried myself the time I seen her."

"Did you know this man Dolan?" Lyman asked.

The woman made a face. "I knew him enough. He ought to been shot before Dan got around to it."

"Then why . . . why did they . . . hang Dan for it?"

"Well, you can't go killin' a man that ain't got a gun on him and get away with it, not in a civilized town. You could over in Virginia City a few years back or in Benton down along the river before the Vigilantes cleaned them up, but it ain't safe no more. Dolan had plenty of friends, of course, an' he'd tipped them off to hang around with him when Dan was around."

"What about Dan's friends?" Something in Lyman made him hesitate to ask questions and something urged him on.

"He'd been actin' pretty ugly since fall an' drinkin' too much. People get tired of you if you just sit and curse all day. I don't know who his friends were, come to think about it. He lost his job with the stage company, you know, an' he'd come in here sometimes in the morning and stay most o' the day. It was awful to see him get that way. Joe— he's the big one back o' the bar—he'd put him out sometimes. I heard his wife used to take the kid with her to the theater when she was actin'. I see he was bad that night. He was sittin' right over there— see, back o' the faro table, all alone."

Lyman saw the table and the heavy chair. A spindle was gone from the back. It stood outside the circle of light.

"Dolan was over there toward the bar, playin' poker an' actin' a little high. I was up at the bar myself when I see Dan start. He said somethin' to Dolan an' Dolan said somethin' back, but Dan kept walkin' toward him. I jumped behind the man next to me when I see his gun. He was a good shot an' it was all over like that." The woman's mouth and a movement of her hands showed how quickly it was done.

Lyman swallowed. "Then what did Dan do?" he asked in a low voice.

"He went on outside an' one of Dolan's friends went to the door to see which way he went an' everybody crowded around Dolan. He was dead all right. I didn't hear what they said, but I seen the bunch of 'em start out the door an' Joe said to me, 'They'll hang him, they won't wait for no law.' Honest, you wouldn't guess how fast this whole place was empty! Lucy an' Flo an' me sat over there an' waited an' Joe had a chance to clean up the bar. This place was like a funeral parlor, believe it or not."

Lyman nodded. He glanced around the room. It looked gloomy enough to him right now.

"Jim came back first an' drank down his drink 's though he was froze to the bone. 'They strung him up,' he says, an' Lucy, of all people, that always wanted Dan herself an' never could get him, speaks up and says, 'Did they tell his wife?' An' Jim nods an' says, 'Stevens an' Black went over together to tell her.' Lucy's not a bad sort."

Lyman stood up. "I have to go," he said, wondering how you left a woman like this. "Thank you for telling me about Dan." He didn't want to hear any more. He had come here with some idea of feeling closer to Dan, but the place didn't help. It was too strange. Even this woman with her smell of perfume and sweat and her low-cut dress bothered him. He laid a dollar on the table a little awkwardly and went quickly across to the door. He worried a little lest he had offended her, going so quickly. Dan would have known what to say to her and how much money to give her.

He had passed two cross streets—paths they were, really—before he realized that the night had changed. It was warm! The snow was melting underfoot. This sudden change must be the chinook they were talking about. You could breathe without the icy-cold striking your lungs. But such a change was too quick. At home, in January the cold was constant. This was as unnatural and incomprehensible as the changes in Dan, something that belonged to this strange wild country where Dan had . . . died.

Lyman asked a man in the street the way to Dry Gulch. The stranger told him without seeming to think it queer that he should ask. People out here were so much more indifferent than they were back home. A man asking a direction at three o'clock in the morning would be a subject for speculation and comment back home. Here nobody seemed to care anything about you.

His eyes grew accustomed to the dark and his ears to the dripping sound of melting snow. The soft, irrational breath of this softened temperature touched his face too gently. He stiffened against it. His best trousers were soaked and mud-spattered up to the knees. The skirts of his overcoat were spattered too, and the lining was soaked with perspiration under the arms. He unbuttoned it and let it flop open as he walked, he was so hot.

He had to guess at the place until he found a rope hanging down from one of the trees. It was a rocky sort of place, and the warm chinook wind sighed through the bare branches and made it more lonely. Why had he come here? By standing here he couldn't know what Dan had thought, nor why he had done this thing. He turned the heavy ring around on his finger.

6

THE cold held fast back in Vermont. The deep snow that covered the stone wall had a frozen crust so hard you could walk on it. The branches of the trees were hard-cased in ice. You couldn't look for a thaw for another month. "Seasonable weather," the *Malden Times* called it, and it seemed right to Lyman. Riding up the hill in the evening with a fur cap pulled down around his ears and a buffalo robe over his knees, he often thought with revulsion of that queer, irrational thaw out West, that "chinook."

Life in Painesville seemed to freeze, too, into more rigid form. Folks were thankful their woodsheds and barns and carriage houses were all joined to each other, and they didn't go far from their own stoves till the cold spell was broken. That too suited Lyman since his return from Montana. He put in longer hours in the quarry office and went directly home when he was through, not even lingering around the stove in Peterboro's store or trying his luck at a game in the livery stable.

Abbie had closed off the rest of the house and she and Lyman lived in the big kitchen and the two bedrooms. Abbie had brought out daguerreotypes of Dan and John and Orville and set them on the shelf above the sink. Lyman looked at them each time he washed. The one of Dan showed him in uniform, his jaunty kepi on one side of his head. He was smiling.

"I can't help but feel, Lyman, if I'd been there to care for Daniel I could have pulled him through his pneumonia. Dr. Tucker always said your father would have died of cholera that time if it hadn't been for me."

"Willie did everything for him, Mother, that could have been done," Lyman said again, as he had said ever since he had come back. He sat down at the table and ate the supper Abbie had ready. He dreaded these meals. All the thoughts his mother had had all day alone trickled out into plaintive comments.

"Juliet favors Daniel more than Willie in looks, you say, Lyman? I was just trying to think how she must look."

"I said she was dark like Dan, but she has Willie's eyes and Willie's ways. She'll be a beauty some day," he said again, and thought of Juliet calling him "Uncle Lyman."

Abbie didn't eat a heavy meal at night. Orville always said the stomach needed a hot meal at noon and something light to sleep on, and Orville's least idea had now become a law for Abbie. She brought her cup of tea from the stove and sat across from Lyman stirring it. He went on eating, dreading what she would say next.

"You would think Willie would want to come back to Daniel's folks instead of going farther out West. She knows we've got the room and everything to do with," Abbie complained. She had said this before and Lyman had answered gently, but tonight he said sharply:

"I don't know that we made her so happy when she was here that she would want to come again."

"Lyman, if you mean to criticize your father . . ." Abbie's usually pale face flushed.

Lyman passed his cup over for more tea and ignored his mother's agitation. "She'll come and visit us sometime," he said mildly.

"I do wish you had been there for the funeral," Abbie said again. "They didn't have it at the church, you said?"

"No," Lyman answered patiently. "The town's so new they just have a little church."

That satisfied Abbie. "And Daniel would have so many friends, everybody would want to come," she added.

Lyman set his cup down sharply on the saucer and moved over to the rocker under the lamp bracket. Behind the cover of the *Malden Times* he could think his own thoughts. Since he had returned he was the town's authority on the West. When he went into the store today for tobacco, Mr. Peterboro asked him about the Indian troubles out there and the winters, and Obadiah Hall said, "I suppose you'll be getting the fever and moving out West like the other young fellows."

"Not I!" he had answered, more vehemently than he needed to. But it was the truth. He had no desire any more to go West. Sometimes he thought of those log buildings along that crooked street, and the frozen ruts that showed how deep the mud must be, and saloons everywhere you looked, and then he thought with an odd satisfaction of the main street of Painesville covered with clean white snow, bordered by trees and neat white clapboard and brick buildings. He liked some order to things, he told himself, though last year he would never have thought of order.

But it was not the rough look of the town, he admitted, as he stared unseeingly at the news sheet in front of him; it was what had happened to Dan there that made him glad to get away from it and made him want to forget it now. Here Dan's name was on the roll of honor of those who had fought in the War of the Rebellion, proud as anything: "Captain Daniel Peabody Converse." Dan was the only captain on the roster. Lyman had stopped to read Dan's name and John's there just yesterday when he crossed the common.

He went up to bed early these nights, but he didn't sleep. He thought about John and Dan: the time John had stayed in bed in the morning and said he didn't ever want to get up; Dan shaving the first time, and showing John how to tie his cravat in front of the mirror above the dresser over there. "Participants in the necktie party are unknown," that clipping had read. Lyman had it now in the file marked Personal under lock and key. He didn't want to leave it with Willie and now he couldn't bring himself to destroy it.

He remembered how John would throw his arm over his head when he slept and Dan was always kicking the covers out with his feet. He remembered how John would get to giggling when Dan tickled him and the bed would rock with his squirmings. He had hardly known them since he had grown up, and he had things to say to them, to ask them, before they died. He thought of the three of them growing up here—and for what? For John to be killed in the Wilderness and Dan to be hanged out West, and for him to go along living his life in this valley, running the quarry.

A great sadness rose in him. His father and mother might better never have met and raised them, or his father prayed till all his sonorous phrases must still be caught between the lath and plaster of the walls. They came back to him now, cold, hollow phrases learned from a page as thin and brittle as a pressed fern leaf: "Oh, Thou Lord in Heaven! Jehovah, God of Life . . ." God of Death, it should be. "Thou knowest the innermost secrets of the human heart . . ." Then He should have known Dan's heart. "Forgive us, we pray . . ." For being born and growing up only to die again? The phrases he hadn't heard since his father's death seemed to echo from the cold floor boards.

Downstairs his mother slept lightly and wept into her pillow for John or Dan or his father. He had heard her sometimes as he crossed the kitchen late at night, but he hadn't gone in to comfort her. What was there to say? Did she think of the nights she had spent putting hot oil on Dan's chest for croup? And John had been a sickly baby, they said, and his mother had carried him on a pillow on her arm all the first month of his life. Did she wonder what good it was now?

Suddenly it came to Lyman lying in the cold dark of the winter's night that John must have thought these same thoughts as he lay dying in the army hospital. He had wondered what Dan had thought when they took him up that rutted street to Dry Gulch. Now he felt he knew; he had had to come all the way back home here to find out.

It was like death itself to look at your life and feel it useless. This was their fate, the Converse fate, to die violently: his father killed by his own horse, John, who had never wanted to fight, killed in battle, and Dan hanged. Lyman . . . was he to die in bed in Painesville? He shivered and pulled the feather bed closer around him.

Then deliberately, like a child, he shut these thoughts out of his mind and opened the door to the old dream: If Isabel were here in this empty bed and he could hide his head on her shoulder until this dark loneliness was gone! "Isabel," he whispered in his mind, forming the word soundlessly on his lips like a charm to say over and over, but tonight it didn't help. Tonight Isabel was Chauncey Westcott's wife and lived in Paris.

He got out of bed and walked softly across his room to the washstand for a drink of water. The old floor creaked and his mother called out from below.

"Lyman, Lyman, are you all right?"

Like a coward he crept back to bed and lay pretending sleep until his mother gave up calling.

In the morning he woke unrested and looking into his mother's face across the breakfast table saw her weariness and loneliness and grief. But all he could do was to praise the salt pork that tasted like the brine of tears and ask for another cup of the weak hot tea.

"Stay close to the fire, Mother," he warned affectionately as he left, and went out quickly so he wouldn't feel too clearly the sad empty day that lay on her hands. He was thankful to leave the house and go down to the village and busy himself in the quarry office. There the substantial things of the day mocked at the anguish of the night.

He worked so steadily that Oliver was always at least two letters behind in his work of making copies. He was going to acquire the Wallingford quarry, and he spent a great deal of time setting down figures and talking to Hiram Goodspeed at the bank. The acquisition would make more money for Willie and Isabel.

People in the village said that Lyman Converse kept to himself, you couldn't seem to get next to him. "Not much like Dan. Yes, sir, Lyman's more for business, Dan was always the lively one." Lyman walked through the village street unknowing that people commented on him. His quick glance that moved away from anyone he met did not invite conversation. But his mind was less often on the affairs of the quarry than on Dan. Suppose he had been the one to go West, to kill a man and be hanged, and Dan lived here and ran the quarry?

He tried to think how it would be as he walked back down the street at noon and the bare elms threw sharp shadows on the snow like the shadow of a gallows tree.

He avoided Louisa. She asked too many questions about Dan and Willie. Lyman had grown skillful at parrying questions, but they tormented him nevertheless. Dr. Tucker was interested in the West and asked questions, too. Sometimes he felt as though the Doctor's eyes held unasked questions.

He reminded himself that he hadn't heard from Dan even when he was living, and John had been dead since '64. Why should he miss them so now? But he missed them both, and his father, deep in his bones and nerves and blood. Going and coming, getting up and lying down, the refrain ran through his thoughts: John killed, Father killed, Dan hanged . . . John killed . . .

"Lyman, you're looking poorly this winter," Mrs. Davis said when she stopped in to sell him a ticket to the Congregational ladies' church supper. "Come to think of it, I remember there was consumption in your father's family. You ought to go West. Thad says it's awful healthy country out in Ioway. Maybe you need a wife to feed you up and put some flesh on your bones!" She went off simpering and shaking her finger at him. Mrs. Davis had a daughter, Anabelle.

Maudie Ingram, who was Mrs. Peterboro now, met him on the street and asked if he'd been sick. He looked at himself in the wavy mirror on the office wall when Oliver was out, but he looked for a resemblance to Dan and lost sight of his own image.

One day he wrote Isabel before the dividend from the quarry was due and departed from the regular pattern of their correspondence.

March 10, 1870

Dear Isabel:

I realize now how very young I was in Providence. I have changed since that time in every way except one, my feeling for you. Chauncey cannot mind my writing this. It does not matter if he does, he can do nothing about it but forbid my writing you.

In January I was called out West by the sudden death of my brother Dan. I wish Chauncey would write me all he remembers of him in the army. Any least reminiscence would be greatly valued by his wife and daughter as well as by myself. I remember how brave Chauncey said he was and how much loved by his men.

I am thinking of engaging a man in New Haven, Connecticut, to secure orders for soapstone products. A three months' trial would not cost the quarry an irreparable amount and would show whether or not he could profit the company sufficiently. The quarry must be made to show a greater profit with Willie and her daughter largely dependent on it.

And then the pattern again:

There is no color here now, all is black and white, and cold (he held his pen poised an instant over the black-velvet top and then added), *as cold as a sentence written in black ink on the white page of a letter.*
I regret to hear of Aunt Matilda's continued ill-health.

Faithfully,

Your cousin,

Lyman

Tonight when he reached home he found Louisa there visiting with his mother. They ate supper together and Louisa had brought a fresh crumb cake he had to praise. He supposed she had come to spend the whole evening visiting, but Jewel came over after supper and he found the women had planned a quilting bee. Abbie had a fire in the unused dining-room and her quilting frames were spread resting on four chairs. Jewel's quilt was ready to tie.

Lyman sat down with his paper under the lamp as usual, relieved that his mother had someone to talk to, liking the light streaming across the threshold from the other room, and Jewel's high shrill laugh when she did something wrong, and Louisa's voice, contralto after his mother's high soprano tones. He and his mother had been shut in too closely. The extra room gave him space to relax a little. Then he began to hear their woman talk.

"Orville bought this piece of goods for a suit in Bennington the year after we were married. I made the most of it, but he took it to a tailor to finish up and put the padding in. He saved it for best for four or five years and then when he couldn't wear it any more I made a little suit for John out of it, Louisa, and put bright buttons on it to make it young-looking."

"That gray would have matched his eyes," Louisa said. "A light-haired man looks good in gray, I always think," she added.

Lyman remembered he had worn gray last time to Louisa's for supper.

"This salt-and-pepper worsted is from Orville's old mackintosh. It was my brother Nate's to begin with and Matilda sent it to Orville. It was imported from Scotland and wore like iron. I made Daniel a coat out of it and his first long pants. He wore them with such an air! I can see him now plainer than that daguerreotype out in the kitchen. Daniel did love anything new!"

Lyman threw his paper on the woodbox and took his cap from the peg behind the door. Women went on and on keeping the dead alive by all the things the dead had worn and touched and even liked to eat. "He wore his suit with such an air!" The woman in the Lucky Spot had said Dan drove with an air!

There was a light in Easy's house and Lyman walked across the snow keeping in the path Easy's feet had packed down. He hadn't been over to see Easy since his trip West, but he always listened for the sound of the ox team passing the quarry office and Easy's footsteps and whistle when he came past the house at night. Sometimes he heard four-year-old Orville shouting at his father from the door of their house, or the crying of the new baby girl. They had named her Ruby because, as Easy had told Abbie, Ruby was a jewel too.

"Come in," Easy called out in answer to his knock.

When Lyman opened the door, heat and cheer rushed at him and a faint, good smell of sausage and fried mush. The many magazine pictures on the wall and the lace curtains at the small windows, tied back with bows of red calico, gave the impression of a bright clutter.

Easy sat in the big chair he had bought at auction, his stockinged feet on the bed that had neither head nor foot but was a feather tick on a bedframe. Jewel was never through singing the virtues of the feather bed over those of a cornhusk tick. On the bed little Orville played with the cat, and in the low trundle bed, close beside the big bed, he could see the dark head of the baby.

"Well, Lyman, the womenfolks musta smoked you out! Sit here!"

"Don't move, Easy." Lyman sat down a bit gingerly on the edge of the bed.

"Say, Lyman, just heft that boy an' see how he's grown. Jus' pull him over by his feet an' pick him up!"

Orville looked back at him with bright button eyes as Lyman picked him up carefully. Orville was as dark as Easy, and in the overheated little room his face was shiny with perspiration.

"My!" Lyman said. "How much does he weigh, Easy?" He held him under the arms, his fingers stretched around the proud little body. He could feel the expansion of the lungs and the strong breath of a living animal.

"Take 'bout a half-dozen soapstone registers to weigh as much as that boy!" Easy boasted. "He's a husky one!"

Orville began to laugh as Lyman lifted him higher and higher until the dark little face was above his own. He looked at the shining eyes,

the small white teeth, the round head so like Easy's, and laughed himself, for the first time since he had come back from the West.

"Hello, Orville Converse Williams!" Lyman said. "You've got my
father's name, you'd better be a good boy!"

"That's right. You hear that, Orville?" Easy shook a long brown
finger at him.

"Good! Me good!" the child cried.

"Then you get in that trundle bed fast's a rabbit hoppin' over a
stone wall!" Easy commanded, and when Lyman dropped him on the
big bed the child grinned at Easy and crawled into the low bed with
his sister.

There were no chairs in Lyman's house as comfortable as this; they
were all spindle-backed wooden or haircloth ones. Jewel had laid two
thicknesses of quilt over the original seat to cover the worn places and
added two pillows at the back. Lyman settled down into it.

"Put your feet up, Lyman. There ain't no other way to balance yourself." Easy was right, and Lyman rested his feet on the quilt-covered
bed.

"You want somethin' to warm you, Lyman?" Easy asked. "I got some
real good applejack a man over on the Riceville turnpike give me."

"I don't mind, Easy," Lyman said. "I guess I'll take my coat off. It's
warm in here."

The whisky was smoother than the last he had had at the bar in the
Lucky Spot.

"I had some whisky out West that peeled the lining off your throat,"
Lyman said slowly. "You ought to see all the saloons they have in
those towns, Easy. And they stay open all night, I guess."

Easy made an appreciative sound in his throat. "How was Miss
Willie?" he asked.

"It's been awfully hard on her, Easy, but she's just about the same.
You know what I thought when I first saw her with her hat off?"

"What's that, Lyman?"

"I thought how you used to say her hair was like maple syrup."

Easy smiled. "Jus' the same as."

"It still is," Lyman said. The habit of taciturnity he had adopted
toward all questions about Dan or Willie gave way. A long pause
spread between them. Lyman set his glass down on the floor beside
his chair and took out his pipe.

"Daniel take good care of Miss Willie?" Easy asked.

"I guess he did. Anyway, she was happy with him." He wondered
why he had said so much, still it was natural with Easy. "I didn't tell
Mother, of course, but she's going back on the stage."

"She liked her actin'." Easy reached over to the woodbox and selected a stick to whittle. He took aim and one of the white pine chips landed on Orville's wide-awake little face, bringing forth a giggle. "Now you shut your eyes an' go sleep, Orville Williams, or I'll push your bed right under the big bed!" Easy said sternly. "Miss Willie'd like that, all right," he went on. "Remember those playbooks of hers? I read the whole bunch of 'em."

"Remember when we took different parts and read them aloud?" Lyman asked.

"Yessir. An' we both liked *Julius Caesar* best." Easy chuckled. "Miss Willie said there wasn't no part good enough for a lady in it. You gather Dan'l done well by himself out there, Lyman?" Easy asked.

When others in the village had asked that question Lyman had called it prying and had managed to tell them nothing, but this was different. Easy was—he had grown up with Dan.

"He just missed out on a gold claim that might have made him rich."

"Jus' when he died?"

"Just the summer before—a real good one."

"Dan would of took that hard," Easy said sympathetically. "Mighty hard!" In the warm stillness of the room they could hear the even breathing of the two sleeping children.

"I guess it drove him almost crazy," Lyman said.

"Sure it would. What happen, Lyman? How come he missed out? That ain't like Dan."

"A man stole it, jumped his claim, they call it. He went in and registered it before Dan and Willie could get to town."

Easy bent forward. His face listened, his eyes, bright and soft in the beginning, hardened, narrowed. His full lips folded tight together. His big hands knotted around his corncob pipe.

". . . so there was nothing he could do but watch Dolan get rich."

"Did Dan'l get him a lawyer?"

"No, it was no use. He just brooded and took to drinking. He lost his job driving the stage. All the winter before he . . . died, he'd go where Dolan was and just sit watching him."

Easy nodded understandingly. "Puttin' a hant on him," he murmured. "But, Lyman, they musta come to a fight!" Little drops of sweat glistened on Easy's forehead.

Lyman nodded. "Dan shot him, Easy, and Dolan's friends . . . they hanged Dan."

Easy let his breath out slowly, but in that small room it was like the sound of a rushing wind. "There, Lyman." He laid his big hand gently on Lyman's shoulder. Sudden sobs that had been there a long time racked Lyman's chest. He couldn't stop, but it didn't seem to matter with Easy. "Nobody else must ever know, Easy," he said when he could manage the words.

"Nobody goin' to know ever, 'cept us," Easy answered.

When Lyman lifted his face from his hands Easy sat staring straight ahead of him, his dark forehead furrowed.

"He done right, Lyman, Dan done right."

"No, Easy. You can see how he came to do it, but it wasn't right."

"Sometimes a man gotta kill."

Lyman listened, not believing Easy, but somehow comforted a little.

"My pappy killed a man. I found that out when I went back," Easy said in a low monotone. "He killed the overseer on the place where he was sold to, 'fore I ran away."

"What happened to him?"

"I guess the dogs almost killed him first an' then they hung him up and then they burned him. He was a good man, my pappy was. I don't know what that overseer done, but I believe it was somethin' so bad my pappy had to kill him." When Easy looked at Lyman belief stood out in his face.

To kill was wrong. Dan was wrong and Easy's father was wrong, but the way Easy looked at it eased the weight on Lyman's mind. He took out his pipe and Easy passed him his tin of tobacco that was stronger than Lyman's.

"When Jewel an' me was first married I bought us some land to live on down there. After I got the crop in an' the place fixed up, a piece of poor white trash come along with a sheriff an' a paper that showed I didn't own it. First I went to town to get me a lawyer and then I can see I was licked before I started. I figured, Lyman, it might end by me killin' somebody, an' I waked Jewel up and we packed our stuff and left right then in the middle of the night and started back up to Vermont. That's why we come back, I didn't never tell you before.

"You see, Lym'n? Here in Vermont folks can seem to remember what the Bible say about killin', but out West and back down South even you an' I might come to kill somebody!"

"I guess that's about what Willie tried to tell me, Easy," Lyman said. They sat a long time without talking. Easy filled the stove again without breaking into their silence. Then they heard Jewel running across the snow. She came in holding the tied comforter in her arms.

"Jus' look at this, Easy, an', Mistah Converse, you too." She spread it out on the big bed. "Ain't that jus' beautiful!"

Lyman looked at the bright yarn tying the sober pieces of his father's clothes. The quilt was faced and bound in turkey-red calico.

Then he looked back at Jewel's glowing face. He saw now how Easy thought she was pretty.

"I'm goin' to have that spread over my bed when this nex' chile is born, Easy, you remember that." She and Easy laughed together and Lyman noticed that Jewel was expecting again.

"Good night, Easy." Lyman wanted to say more but there was too much to put into words.

Easy stood in the open doorway. "You come again, Lyman."

When Lyman came in his mother and Louisa were both in the kitchen.

"Oh, Louisa, I'll harness up Scout and drive you down."

Abbie started to say something, but Louisa's fingers touched her arm. "Thank you, Lyman. Are you sure it won't keep you up too late?"

"I couldn't sleep this early anyway," Lyman said, feeling as though he had been let out of some dark lonely room.

As Louisa tucked the night clothes she had brought back into her sewing basket, her eyes met Abbie's. Both women smiled.

7

Quarries at Painesville and Wallingford   Mill at Goddard

June 4, 1872

Dear Isabel:

I am writing you on one of the new letterheads so you may see how well it looks now that we own two quarries. Of course the one at Wallingford is a much less valuable deposit, but its excavation is comparatively cheap and its nearness to the railroad makes the product easier to ship, so I do not believe we are incurring too great a risk in acquiring same.

You will note that your dividend check is larger than the preceding one. I hope and trust that it will continue to grow. I see no reason why such should not be the case. You should see the yard at the mill piled high with soapstone conduits which are so much superior to wooden pipes and drains that I feel they must soon take their place entirely.

Lyman placed a period deliberately at the end of the sentence.

I am taking a step which may seem strange to you in view of my protestations of devotion. That devotion has not changed, but I have come to the conclusion that it is right and fitting for me to marry Miss Louisa Tucker who was once engaged to marry John. I have examined my feelings most carefully and realize that I am not offering her a heart which has never known any other love, but she has known love before too, and loneliness such as I have known. Respect, sympathy, and affection may perhaps be sufficient.

His pen rested. Then he wrote again.

May I hope to have a word from you before June 26, when we shall be united in marriage?

Remember me to Aunt Matilda and Chauncey.

Faithfully,
Lyman

He sat in his chair a long time after he had folded the letter and slipped it into its envelope. He was right in doing this, wasn't he? All men, unless they were of a headstrong and precipitate nature, felt a few misgivings. Perhaps even Dan, but he doubted it. John was growing more shadowy in his mind. At John's funeral he remembered Mrs. Bragg and Thad Davis's mother talking about Louisa. Their words had stayed with him all these years. "I wouldn't wonder a mite to see her die an old maid. Anyone can see her heart's broken." He hadn't wanted her heart to be broken then. And now that Dr. Tucker was gone he didn't want her to be lonely. That was love too, a fine, tender kind that made you feel good and a little noble.

The time he had gone off to Providence on that wild-goose chase to try to persuade Isabel not to marry Chauncey Westcott he hadn't really thought about Isabel. He had only felt passionately that he couldn't let her go. He was eighteen then. Now he was twenty-four, and he put the thought of Isabel and his youth from him and thought instead of Louisa as she had been the night her father had died suddenly of a heart attack. Mrs. Davis and Maudie Peterboro were there, and the Reverend Mr. Dwight, the new minister, but she had sent for him, and when he came across the yard she was in the woodshed waiting for him. He remembered how she had cried a little against his shoulder and said, "Send them all away, Lyman. Just you and your mother stay with me."

It had seemed natural then for him to take care of all the funeral arrangements and afterward he had pretended an errand at the mill and asked Louisa to ride with him because his mother whispered that she should get away from the house for a little.

They had talked on the way. "It's the loneliness I dread," she had said, but without any tears. "You know what that's like, Lyman, losing your father and both your brothers."

He had wanted to tell her how he had felt out West after he put Willie and Juliet on the train and about those first weeks back home here, but she spoke just then and he let it go.

And then, suddenly, marrying Louisa had seemed the thing that John would want him to do. He had mentioned it to Easy, not about Louisa at first, but about marrying.

"I suppose you're a lot happier married, aren't you, Easy?" he asked casually when they were fixing up a wall the winter had tumbled down.

"Yes, I am, Lyman. Jewel was the right one for me," Easy answered.

Lyman continued awkwardly, "A man's not so lonely if he's married."

Easy moved a big boulder back in place before he answered. It was so heavy it had made him grunt doing it. "I don't know about that, Lyman. Some folks are born lonely, can't ever get away from it marrying. It's like a hant. An' then another thing, Lyman, a woman's different from a man. She don't think 'bout the same things, seems like. She thinks 'bout havin' things like quilts and china an' children, an' about religion. A man thinks about . . ." Easy's glance followed the strong line of the mountain before it came back to Lyman . . . "other things," he finished.

Then Lyman told him, "I'm thinking of marrying Louisa Tucker, Easy. She's a fine woman."

Easy was working on the wall again by then. "Yes, she is, Lyman," was all he said.

It would all work out well. His mother would come to live with them after a few weeks. Louisa wanted her. They would move down to Louisa's brick house on the main street that had seemed the finest house in town to Lyman when he was a boy. Leaving their own house up on the hill hurt him, but Louisa thought it too inconvenient and harked back to the danger of the hill road, where, she reminded him, his father had been killed. But that road and going up and down, on foot and on the ox wagon and driving, were part of him, he would miss it. The house on the hill had never stood empty since the day it was built. Of course Easy lived right in back. He could keep an eye on it. And then in summer they would live up there, he thought comfortingly. Thinking of living there in the summer made it easier to think of moving down this month.

A sharp tapping on the window startled him. Louisa was looking in at him, smiling. She came around to the door.

"I declare, Lyman, supper's been ready and waiting for half an hour. I told your mother I knew you had forgotten the time and were still working."

He looked up almost stupidly, too deep in his own thinking to come out of it at once. "Oh, Louisa, I was just finishing a letter. You were good to come over for me." He stood looking at her, making no move to get his hat or coat, only taking pleasure in the clear oval of her face and the white V of forehead between the softly waving darkbrown hair. He always felt the tranquillity of her face and of her nature, the order of it. Life with her would be ordered, he told himself, and serene and good. When he let himself remember the face of that woman in the Lucky Spot he was thankful for Louisa.

"What are you looking at, Lyman? Silly! Get your hat and we'll go."

He put his arm gently around her shoulders and kissed her on the temple. Ever since John's death he had felt that he should be gentle with Louisa. She turned her face to his and put her arms around his neck; the swift almost fierce demonstrativeness surprised him.

"Lyman, I do love you," Louisa whispered. "I thought you'd never see."

"Why, Louisa, thank you," he said a little huskily.

When they stood apart Louisa laughed. "Now I'm the one that's forgetting supper is ready. Hurry, Lyman."

"Maybe we don't need anything to eat," Lyman joked. He took his hat from the peg. She couldn't have loved John any more than this, he thought.

"Do you want to drop this letter in the box as we go by?" Louisa asked, holding the envelope in her hand.

"Yes, I may as well. A letter takes so long to get to Europe."

"37 bis Avenue Victor Hugo, Paris, France," Louisa read slowly. "Doesn't it sound foreign?"

"It's to my cousin Isabel Holbrook . . . Westcott. She owns a share in the quarry, you know." Lyman took the big brass key from its nail by the window and locked the door behind them. "Twenty-two more days, Louisa," he said as they walked up the street in the early June twilight. He felt lighthearted as he dropped the letter into the slit in the door of the post office. Yes, this was the right thing to do.

"Twenty-one tomorrow," Louisa said, a smile erasing her pensive expression.

"Beats all, the way it stays so cold," Mr. Gray declared, hitching up his horse in the dark of the shed back of the Congregational Church.

"Yep. Don't seem like June's the month for weddings any more, does it? Or gardens either. It's been so wet I haven't got my garden in yet," Jake Green grumbled.

Asa Pettingill cramped his buggy carefully so he could come as close to the church step as possible to save his wife's wedding attire. Sitting in the buggy, he could look way up the aisle and see the people still lingering, and the lamps lit and flowers and ferns on every window sill. It was a pretty sight. And this was one of the most satisfactory weddings, both parties from old families here and going to stay here. That's what he liked about it.

"Wasn't it a pretty wedding, Jake?" Martha Green asked, covering her lap carefully with the robe.

"Yes, 'twas. Too bad it had to rain, though."

"I never saw a sweeter bride. There was something saintly about her. But seeing Mrs. Converse sitting there all alone in their pew made me want to cry. She's been through plenty since the war."

"Yep, I guess she has. I missed old Orville Converse there. Lyman looks quite a bit like him, don't he?"

"Jake, you better hitch the horse in the hotel shed. Louisa's awful partial of her lawn," Martha warned as she got out in front of the Tucker house.

Neighbors had come in to do for Louisa, and Abbie Converse treated her like her own daughter already. Jewel was helping in the kitchen and Mrs. Peterboro said she was surprised how quick and handy she was around. The house stood wide-open in spite of the rain, and a person could have worn his overshoes right in on the parlor carpet and never been spoken to that night. Louisa and Lyman stood in the parlor before a mass of ferns Louisa had brought in from the woods. She looked serene and smiling and often she glanced up at her husband.

Lyman stood taller than Louisa, smiling and shaking hands with his neighbors. Across his new waistcoat was draped John's watch chain that Louisa had given him for a wedding gift. "It seems as though John would want it this way," she had said, snapping the chain back on John's watch that Lyman had carried ever since John's death.

"Well, Lyman, you're a lucky young man," Asa Pettingill told him.

"Yes, sir, I know I am," Lyman answered. He was, he felt. Louisa was one girl in a hundred. He thought now of the night he had asked her to marry him. It was right in this room, over there on that sofa where Mrs. Gray and Mrs. Peabody were sitting. Louisa had been talking of what she was going to do.

"Maybe I should go to a larger place to teach," she said. He had thought of Painesville with Louisa gone.

"Don't go, Louisa. We need you here," he said.

"Do you really, Lyman? Then I'll never go," and the way she had said it . . .

"Thank you, Judge, I know we will be." He shook hands with Judge Whitcomb and the Judge's mother, who used to pay him ten cents a pail for blackberries when he was a boy.

"I thought you were going to be a bachelor there for a while, Lyman, but I see you was just bidin' your time," Nathan Osborn joshed him.

"You can see why, right here," Lyman answered. Funny how you knew the right answers almost as though you had done all this before.

"I'm glad you're going to live down in the village, Lyman. We can count on you more regularly for choir practice," Mrs. Osborn said, squeezing his hand and leaning toward him.

"I remember the time when your father declared he'd never come down to the village to live as long as there was a hill left. He never was reconciled to the church being moved down to the valley."

"That's right." Again Lyman had an unhappy feeling of deserting the house on the hill, the Converse place. But in the summer . . . maybe not this summer, with their just being married, but his mother would be there till fall. They'd go up and stay overnight. He wondered if they would sleep in the parlor bedroom Willie had had.

"They're waiting for us in the dining-room, Lyman." Louisa touched his arm. "The table's lovely, wait till you see it."

He had that same disconcerting sense of being somebody else as he sat down beside Louisa at the head of the table. Mock orange and white lilacs from the Peabodys' bushes decorated the table, and white candles, and a three-tiered wedding cake with "Lyman and Louisa" written on it in frosting. This was his wedding. The Reverend Mr. Dwight rose to ask the blessing. Lyman opened his eyes and looked across the bowed heads through the pantry door and saw Jewel standing there and Easy back of her. Easy hadn't come to the reception by the front door. Nobody had thought to ask him. Lyman started to push back his chair, but Louisa's hand reached over on his knee under the best white cloth. He covered her hand with his and noticed how cold it was.

"A-men," pronounced the Reverend Mr. Dwight.

"What is it, dear?" Louisa asked under the talk and rustle around them.

"I don't believe anyone invited Easy. He's out in the kitchen with Jewel."

"But I don't think he'd feel right in here. He's so much happier out there with Jewel, don't you think?"

"He's . . . my best friend," Lyman started to say and then he didn't, but the creamed chicken and Jewel's beaten biscuits were tasteless.

Louisa threw her bouquet of white lilacs and syringa from the stairs after the wedding supper. Lyman stood below watching her. He remembered the night he had stopped in to borrow a book and Louisa had thought he was John for a minute. "I wish I could be John," he had said, he had felt so badly for her. Louisa's dark eyes shone. There was a white blossom tucked in her dark hair. She lifted the bouquet and threw it and ran up the stairs. No, he wasn't playing John. He was himself and Louisa loved him for himself.

Mr. Peterboro shook him by the hand. "You've got a lovely bride, Lyman."

"Yes, isn't she?" Lyman agreed. He was surprised to see that Mr.

Peterboro's eyes were red. He was blowing his nose. "God bless you both." Mr. Peterboro had chased him out of his orchard when he was a little boy. He had always thought of him as a crabbed old man.

"Lyman, is your valise all packed?" his mother asked. Her eyes were wet, too. Weddings affected people strangely.

"Yes, everything's ready, Mother. We'll be back Saturday. I want to see Easy before I go." He made his way through the congratulations to the kitchen.

When he got to the pantry he could hear Jewel and Easy laughing. Jewel was washing dishes and Easy was drying. It seemed as though the gaiety of the wedding was out here.

"Lyman, I surely meant to bring you down that arrowhead you give me way back in the quarry shed, remember? For luck, didn't I, Jewel?"

"He don't need no arrowheads," Jewel answered, white teeth flashing.

"Lyman, there's just one thing I want to advise you—don't ever start out like this wiping dishes for a woman!"

"How's he going to know he's married if he don't do that?" Jewel asked, laughing. Marriage was a natural thing, out here he felt more comfortable about it.

Easy tossed the towel at Jewel. "Woman, you can have your dishrag. I'm goin' to get the horse an' buggy for Lyman. It's a sorrowful shame you got to go way over there in the rain, Lyman."

"Oh, that won't be bad. It'll give us a chance to get acquainted."

Their burst of laughter made him feel how witty he was.

"Well, I must go and get my things. You take care of Mother, Jewel, won't you?" He felt as though he were going a long distance, and they were only going to Malden tonight and take the train for Boston in the morning. Still, it seemed that way.

"You know, Lyman, I'm glad it's raining. I like being closed in together," Louisa said when they were driving up the Malden road with the boot snapped in place in front of them and the reins slipped through the little slot in the boot.

Lyman closed his hand over hers. "It's snug all right, kind of the way a coat pocket must feel to a mouse." He felt smoothed out and easy in his mind, able to tell her the funny little things he thought of.

"It's as dark as a pocket all right." Louisa laughed delightedly. "But I guess Scout knows his way. Lyman, I've always admired the way you went right on driving Scout after your father's death. You're very brave."

"Oh, no, Louisa, I don't think I am. You know Mother wanted me to shoot him and I took him out to do it, but I felt as though if I could drive him I ought to be able to run the quarry. It sounds childish, I guess . . ." His voice ended apologetically, but he wanted Louisa to know. He had never tried to tell anybody how he felt except Easy . . . and Isabel.

"Still I would have been afraid of him. I am yet, a little," Louisa said.

"Scout's as gentle as any horse you'd want to see now. He's nine years old."

The rain came against the oilcloth boot and splashed under the horse's hoofs. The only light on the road came from the lantern that swung beneath the buggy.

"I'd almost like to ride all night," Louisa said contentedly, and the darkness gave her voice a strange nearness.

"I did out West, going from Utah up to Helena that time."

"When Daniel died?"

"Yes," Lyman answered, thinking of the swaying, bumping motion of the coach and the rough bleak look of the places where they had changed horses in the night, and the violent mountain peaks, bare and snow-capped, always above them in the daytime. "That was a wild ride," Lyman said tentatively, wanting unaccountably to tell her about Dan, but he said no more. No one must know, never anyone in Painesville, no one but Easy. But the feeling of that night walk out to Dry Gulch crept into his mind again, like a cold fog, pressing too close on his brain. It came back like this, any time. He was never done with it once and for all; that sense of dread and heaviness and a loneliness too deep to endure, the loneliness of a woman in a blue dress with hair too yellow, of Willie taking the train for the coast, and his own loneliness knowing he had lost Dan long before. Why did he think of this now, on his wedding night? If he told Louisa just a little . . .

"I do feel so sorry for Willie. She was Southern, of course, and Mother Converse told me she had been an actress, but I liked her just the same."

Anger swept across Lyman's mind for an instant like fire over grass, and then was gone, leaving the dead grass of hopelessness behind.

"She was a wonderful wife to Dan," he said flatly.

"I hope I can be a wonderful wife to you, Lyman," Louisa said, laying her head against his shoulder.

For answer Lyman put his arm around her. They were going faster now, rushing through the dark without seeing where they were going. Scout knew the way. Lyman liked sitting back feeling them drawn along like this.

"I think we were always meant for each other, after all, don't you, Lyman?"

"I guess we must have been," he murmured. This winter he had seen more of her and noticed things: the wild-rose color in her cheeks and the serenity that he didn't have and how like a daughter she was to his mother. . . .

"Don't let's hurry, Lyman. We're almost there," Louisa whispered.

Lyman bent his head suddenly in the dark, his lips pressed full on hers, drowning all loneliness, all sense of loss and sadness, all thinking.

He hardly heard her smothered "Oh, Lyman, my bonnet!"

8

"I ALWAYS lock the door, Lyman. I forgot to tell you there's always an extra key under the shell there on the whatnot," Louisa called down from the stairs. "Oh, it's nice to be home, dear, even though Boston was wonderful, isn't it?"

Lyman turned the key in the lock. But like a child he had to lift the big conch shell to his ear first and listen to the sound of the sea caught in those pink whorls, like a man's soul caught in the rounds of his daily living. Then he took the lamp and followed Louisa up to the room that would be theirs from now on till the end of their lives, perhaps, the big east room at the head of the stairs. It would be different if this had been his home and he had brought Louisa here, but it was Louisa's and he had moved in. As he went along the hall his hand brushed the backs of the books he had looked at when he came to borrow one so long ago.

Louisa was putting away clothes in the drawers of the dresser when he came up. Her dark hair hung down her back over her soft red dressing-gown. Then he noticed they were his things she was laying in the drawer, his shirts and drawers and undershirts.

"Look, Lyman, I'm giving you Father's dresser. It's nearer to the door and easier to get at."

"Yes, thank you." The ceiling sloped at the sides. He walked across the room until the angled wall stopped him, just as it did in his own room at home. He selected the tall-backed rocker as his own and laid his coat over the back. It was strange to be here in Louisa's room. He would get used to it in time, he told himself.

"There! I never can settle down till I have things put away." Louisa pushed the drawers closed with her body. "I don't believe we've been here more than a couple of hours either. Isn't it good to be back, Lyman?"

Lyman was glad they had come home at night. He needed to get a little used to living here before he went out through the gate and met people in the village. The Peterboros lived next door—Maudie Ingram and her husband, not the old people—and on the other side lived Mrs. Mat Osgood with her daughter Esther. Esther was a spinster. No

225

chance now of her marrying. She worked in the bank sometimes. Her mother always hinted about her being promised to Reuben Hall, who was the first boy from Painesville killed in the war, but Lyman remembered them at singing school and he'd never seen any signs. Well, Louisa wouldn't be a spinster, he thought with an oddly impersonal satisfaction.

Louisa was folding back the quilted spread now, opening the bed.

"I hope these sheets won't be damp. Maybe I shouldn't have made the bed before I left, but I couldn't help it. I wanted everything ready." She brushed powdered specks off the sheets. "That's lavender. I scattered some in the sheets. Oh, Lyman. It's just the way I planned it all!" She knelt at the side of the bed to say her prayers and Lyman finished undressing. This was the way it would be, a kind of nightly routine. He stood by the window in his tucked white nightshirt, waiting until she was through to open it. Louisa's smooth dark head bowed against the plump edge of the bed touched him, it was so rounded and defenseless. He must never hurt her or make her unhappy. Her hands folded in front of her on the bed curved in meekness and supplication. Her slender body leaned against the bed without losing its straightness. Without words or salutations he prayed too—let it be a good living. There were so many years ahead, it seemed to him tonight. Let him love her as she loved him. He was still awed at her sudden little possessively affectionate gestures. "I've loved you so long," she had whispered one day, and he wondered when she had begun to think of him instead of John, but it wasn't a thing he could ask.

She slipped into bed while he opened the window and blew out the lamp.

"Esther Osgood will hear the window and know we're home. She sleeps on this side of the house," Louisa said. "Poor Esther."

There were no close neighbors on the hill. It made Lyman uncomfortable to think of Esther Osgood aware of their comings and goings.

"We're so late we better go right to sleep tonight," Louisa said.

"Yes," he agreed, thinking that Louisa made everything orderly, even love. "I'll go up to see Mother the first thing in the morning."

"Of course, dear. She'll understand if I don't go up with you this first time, don't you think? I have so much to do before church."

"I'm sure she will." He wondered what she had to do that couldn't wait, but he was glad to go alone.

"Lyman, remember, you can bring down anything you want to from the hill, a chair or books, anything you want. This is your home now, you know."

"Yes. Thank you, Louisa." He had tried to find a shorter name for her. There was Lou, but it hardly fitted her. He tried "dear" and "sweet," but they didn't seem quite right. There was an aloof dignity about Louisa that couldn't be ignored. It was part of her sweetness and serenity, and he respected it. No, to the end of their lives he would call her Louisa and she would call him Lyman, as it was on the wedding cake.

He lay after Louisa was asleep trying to feel at home in this strange room and thinking what he would bring down from the hill. He really hadn't many possessions. Relics of his boyhood, like the sailboat Dan had made, were stored in the barn, but they were toys he was through with. He had a few books from that part of a year at Brown, the volume of Wordsworth, Plato's *Dialogues,* just texts. He might bring those down, but they would be lost at the end of Dr. Tucker's bookshelves. He thought he would take them over to the office and keep them on the top of the desk. That whetstone in the woodshed would be handy to have here, he liked a sharp knife. There were a few tools, but maybe Louisa had as good ones. Besides the whetstone, there really wasn't anything.

The air of the June night was sweet but very still. It smelled of garden flowers down here instead of fir and yarrow and clover from the pasture. A dog barked and he didn't know whose dog it was, there were so many dogs down here in town. In the daytime you could see the store from these windows and the horses out in front of the blacksmith shop. If he put his head out far enough, he could see whether Oliver had opened the quarry office in the morning. He turned restlessly and then lay very still so as not to wake Louisa. She never seemed to move in her sleep, one hand under her cheek and the other on the pillow. Now, lying awake while she slept, he felt older than she, but often in the daytime he remembered he was younger.

He watched the tree by the window. He couldn't make out any leaves, just the dark mass of it. It was a maple. He had played with the little winged seeds when he used to bring Louisa John's letters. At home, he looked out on the biggest elm on the farm. His father had said it must have been there when the Indians hunted on the hill. He knew now what he wanted to bring down here to make him feel at home—he wanted the bare freedom of his own room above the kitchen, with the woodshed roof outside and the space and the view of the elm and the Green Mountains beyond, the round one and the sawtoothed one. He wanted the whole blamed hill. He wanted . . . more than this. He hadn't let himself admit that before. Louisa was sweet and fine and loving, but they would always be separate in their ways of thinking. He remembered with dismay that he had thought of trying to tell her the way he felt about Dan and John. He had thought once that he might even tell her about Isabel sometime, but he realized now that it would have worried her and she wouldn't have understood. He pulled the covers carefully up around her shoulder, as though to make up in tenderness for their lack of understanding.

"I'm going to walk up the hill this morning. It'll feel good after all that train-riding and going around in cabs in Boston," he told Louisa.

"But then you can't be back in time for church, Lyman. It's our first Sunday, you know. I've been thinking about it and I've decided to give up our pew and go to yours. With your mother living and your name on the pew it seems the right thing to do."

"Louisa, if you'd be any happier . . ." he began.

It was very early. The village street lay under a Sunday-morning calm and the store and the bank and the post office were securely closed. Louisa had come with him to the gate. She stood there in her pink morning dress looking up at him. The wild rose was in her cheeks.

"No, Lyman, I want to do that." Her tone of voice said, "I want to give you this gift."

"Thank you, Louisa." He went around the house to harness Scout.

When he had crossed the covered bridge and started up the quarry road he felt better. After all, he told himself, he had never been with anyone so steadily before. It was natural to be glad to be alone for a little. He'd get used to living in town. If he had married Isabel and were living in Providence . . . but that would have been so different. Isabel was older now, and changed, probably, he reminded himself, and brought his mind away from her by watching for wild strawberries along the road.

Scout drooled over the watering trough and flicked his long ears at the brown-and-gold butterflies that always flew around his head here in the summer. Then he trotted briskly up the road, only asking with his ears whether they should turn in at the quarry.

The tall brick house stood there waiting for Lyman as he came over the last thank-you-ma'am on the road. No, a few months in the winter were all he wanted to live in town. Louisa would have to live here the rest of the year. He had never seen his house so clearly: the bricks a faded red on the east side where the morning sun warmed them, darker on the north, the smooth gray sills and doorstep of soapstone, the three broad chimneys rising under the elm trees. It was a good place, and he belonged here.

Orville Williams sat astride the stone wall, and when he saw Lyman he let out a yell and ran to tell Jewel and Easy, his quick heels almost white against the dark skin of his legs. Abbie heard him and came to the door. Now, after only a week's absence, she looked grayer and older to him.

"Oh, Lyman, I've missed you—and where's Louisa?"

"She thought you'd understand, Mother. She had some unpacking to do or something." He tied Scout to the iron ring in the gatepost, since they would be going back down to church so soon, and went into the house.

"You weren't too lonesome while we were gone?"

"Oh, you don't know, I forgot. Isabel came the next day."

"Isabel!" The name said aloud caught him like a sudden stitch in the side. "Here?"

"Yes, she came back from Paris because Matilda's been so poorly and she said she'd always wanted to come up here again and see this house and the place where her grandfather lived, even if it was only a cellar hole now, and the quarry. Her husband stayed in England. Just think of it, Lyman, she and Matilda came all the way across the ocean alone!"

Lyman leaned against the doorframe. "Is she still here?"

"Yes, she said she didn't want to go without seeing you. She wrote you she was coming but I guess the letter didn't reach you. She hadn't heard anything about your marriage. Didn't you write her?"

"Where is she now?"

"She was up early and said she was going to walk over to the quarry to see it when the men weren't working. She seems so interested. I suppose she takes after Nate. He was always interested in the quarry."

Lyman looked around the familiar kitchen. Isabel had been here, in this room. She was here now.

"I guess I'll walk over and meet her." He made himself walk slowly. Abbie followed him to the door. "Lyman, don't be late for church."

Easy and Jewel, coming over to see him, caught a glimpse of him walking swiftly down the road.

"Where's he going so fast?" Jewel asked in amazement.

"He's gone to find Miss Isabel, I guess," Easy said, scowling a little at the bright June morning.

Lyman cut across the road and came out at the foreman's shed as he had that other morning when Easy was hidden there. He was half afraid, half eager. In spite of his hurry his face was pale.

When he saw her he stood still watching her. She was sitting with her back to him on a big block of soapstone. Her hat was on the stone beside her and the sun burnished her head to copper. She was all in black, and her hands looked small and white below her black sleeves.

He wondered what she could be looking at. The levels of the soap-stone reached far down below her, their white cut edges looking like old scars. All the machinery of quarrying littered the place: the derricks, the chains and saws and block and tackle, and the long iron crowbars the men used. The new summer's green came down to the quarry's edge, but the great cavity of the quarry itself scarred the place. Why did she sit looking into the quarry when the beauty of the virgin timber lay just beyond? She straightened her shoulders and dropped her head back as though to feel the sun on her throat, and Lyman felt in his own taut muscles her yearning for sun and rest more than for beauty. Seeing her here was so like one of his own daydreams that he hardly dared breathe.

He mustn't startle her. In a voice as casual as though they had been talking together he spoke her name. She stood up quickly and turned toward him, the same slight willowy figure he remembered.

"Oh, Lyman! I said I wanted to come back here, and you see I came."

"I couldn't believe it when Mother said you were here. And you've been here all week!" It was necessary to talk, not to be still. The place was too close.

"I didn't intend to stay so long, but I couldn't go away before I had seen you."

Her hands were just the same, quick and strong and so alive. He held onto them as long as he could. She laughed as she drew them away. "You look as though you don't believe me yet, Lyman. Have I changed so much?"

"Yes, you have changed." He saw that her hair that had been smooth around her head was curled above her forehead. Her brown eyes were as bright and quizzical as a squirrel's watching him. The freckles didn't show under her clear skin. He missed them. Somehow she looked older . . . maybe it was the queer tight black dress. She seemed less simple.

"Oh, no, I haven't really. But you, Lyman, I hear you're married. I came in on the stage the day after your wedding. I was standing in front of the post office looking around when I saw Easy. He knew me, too. He brought me up to your mother and on the way he told me about the wedding. Isn't it a pity that I didn't get here on the day?" She spoke too lightly, smiling at him.

"No," Lyman said in a tight voice. "I couldn't have stood it if I had looked up and seen you in church. I'd have come straight down the aisle to you." His face was stern in its intensity. His voice was thickened and his last word was almost inaudible.

Isabel's eyes clouded. Her face was as pale as the white scars on the soapstone. She shook her head. "Lyman, I'm sorry. Whatever I do turns out to be wrong. I knew I shouldn't come. If I'd known you were married I never would have, but as soon as I knew we were coming back to the States I thought of seeing you."

"You didn't get my letter, then?"

"No. We sailed from Cherbourg in May. But I have one here, the one you wrote me two years ago telling me that Dan had died and say-ing . . . you hadn't changed." She took a folded piece of paper out of the bag that hung from her wrist. "No one should keep a letter two years!" Her voice had an odd sound suddenly, a bitter sound.

"Why not? I have all yours."

Isabel sank down on the block of soapstone and Lyman sat on the other side of it. He laid his hand flat against the smooth surface as though he was measuring his fingers on it. A silence in the morning is deeper than a silence at night. In the sun it can take the shape of a wall that is hard to penetrate.

"You married the girl your brother loved. I remember your telling me about her," Isabel said finally, looking away from him. "I remem-ber you said, 'If you could see her you'd know what a terrible thing it is not to be able to love someone.' So you let her love you, Lyman, since she couldn't have your brother. Aunt Abigail is very happy about it."

"Yes," Lyman said.

"Are you happy?"

She had no right to ask a question like that. He got up from the stone and stood looking at her. The blood rushed into his face. She looked back at him defiantly, face tilted, eyes bright and burning.

"I couldn't have you," he said.

"No, and I couldn't have you, so I married Chauncey. It's like a game, isn't it?" She burst out laughing. "We must be crazy, Lyman!"

Lyman watched her, uncertain of her meaning, testing the brittle sound of her laughter that stopped so suddenly. "How is Chauncey?"

"Oh, Chauncey! He's fine. He's in London, living with an English-woman he thinks he's in love with. He wants me to get a divorce. There isn't much point now, though."

Divorce was a thing Lyman had never thought of. He only knew the meaning of the word as he knew the meaning of certain words in the Bible. Her way of speaking of it was so light it angered him. She was too worldly. She made him feel stupidly simple and countrified. He didn't want her touched by a word like "divorce."

"Do I shock you, Lyman?" she asked, smiling.

"I don't like it," he said.

"I'm sorry." She was all contrition now. Her voice was gentle. "But, Lyman, you can be hurt only so much and then you decide you won't be hurt any more, don't you see? I've had a very good time in Paris. I love it. I shall go back there. Don't feel too badly about me. I'm not shocking. I lead a model life. I go to art galleries, I hear music, I drive in the park and ride horseback. I've made many friends, interesting people. Some of them are Americans, and you would like them." She dropped her head and played with the steel fringes of her bag. "I had even dared to hope that you might go back with me and see Paris," she said in a low voice. She lifted her face and her eyes swam in tears, but she was smiling at him. "I told you I was crazy."

"That I could go back with you?" he repeated incredulously.

"Oh, I know you can't. It was crazy to dream of. You probably wouldn't look at a divorced woman."

"You mean . . . If you were divorced you thought of marrying me? What about . . . ?"

"Was it children we were worrying about, Lyman, so long ago?" She laughed again, that thin little laugh. "And you went to my family doctor to ask if it would be right for cousins to have children!"

Lyman watched her without speaking.

"That's the funniest part of all. Chauncey was being treated by that same family doctor for an infection that I contracted. I had never been sick a day in my life, but I was very ill then. I made the doctor in Paris tell me exactly what was wrong. He explained it to me and told me I would be all right but that I could never have a child. Even I could see what a joke it was on me. I almost wrote you at the time."

"Don't, Isabel," Lyman said. The horror he felt showed clearly on his face. Pity stung his eyes and caught in his throat, and then anger seared the edges of his mind. "Chauncey ought . . ." he began.

"No, poor Chauncey! He thought he was cured, the doctor thought so too. It wasn't pleasant for him. He was badly worried when I was so ill—almost as worried as he is now over his own health. I don't bear him any malice now. I did for a while," she added, looking away at the side of the quarry.

Lyman watched her face that changed with every thought. She looked so slight, almost fragile, in the bright sun. Now he could see the shimmer of freckles under her eyes. She looked as young as she had when he first met her. How could she face such a thing? She could talk about it plainly, an ugliness that was only whispered among the boys at Brown. But the ugliness hadn't touched her spirit. Why had he ever thought he could love anyone else? Why had he ever let himself marry Louisa?

She turned around, twirling the bag on her wrist, and smiled at him. "Well, that's all!" The tears were still in her eyes. "If I'd been strong and noble I would never have told you any of this. Don't be sorry for me. I don't like pity." Her voice sharpened to too thin a point, as though it might break. "Come, we must go back, Lyman. I promised Aunt Abigail I'd go to church this morning. I didn't tell her I've been going to a Catholic church in Paris."

"Don't go, Isabel. There must be some way . . ."

"There isn't any way, Lyman. But I still love you. There, I had to say it just once," she said in a very low voice.

He stood there stupidly in the sunshine staring at her. His mouth worked suddenly so that he couldn't speak. He thought with a shudder of Louisa's possessive little outbursts of affection, her long-suffering compliance—and then he forgot Louisa.

The sun warmed the trunks of the trees way into the woods, picking out the slender birch trees and the gray boles of the beeches and hard maples. It lay bright on the soapstone and on Isabel's head against Lyman's shoulder.

"I don't feel this is wrong, Lyman, here in the sun."

"It isn't," Lyman said, kissing her again.

They heard Easy calling from the road.

"Don't let's go," Lyman said.

Isabel shook her head slowly. "You've been married a week, Lyman. From Aunt Abigail I gather that your wife loves you with all the love she had for your brother."

"She loves me in her way, but, Isabel . . ."

Isabel laid her fingers gently on his lips. She began tucking her hair into place, tightening the strings of her bag. "I have so much more than I had when I came. The letter is true, you haven't changed. I think I couldn't have stood it if you had changed. That's my only excuse for not being noble and going away quickly before you came back."

"I'd never have forgiven you if you had," Lyman said. He couldn't manage her light mood, even to make it easier. She couldn't make him into Louisa's husband so swiftly.

When he wouldn't come, she went ahead of him toward the road. There was nothing to do but follow. Easy was waiting with the carriage. Abigail sat in back ready for church.

"I was afraid you had missed each other. Isabel, will you want to go back to the house before church? We're late now."

"No, thank you. I'll just put my hat on and pretend I've forgotten my gloves," Isabel said, pinning her hat on her head. "My, the quarry was interesting, Aunt Abigail. Lyman explained it all to me."

Lyman didn't attempt to do more than answer the questions Abbie put to him about the wedding trip. "We heard a lecture by Professor Agassiz and went to a concert. We stayed at the Parker House . . . yes, very expensive." He was glad that he sat up in front with Easy and he did not even turn his head, because he could not bear to look at Isabel.

"The late bell is tolling," Abbie worried. "Orville always liked to be in his pew by the last bell. Louisa will be waiting."

Louisa stood at the gate when they drove up. She wore her "going-away" dress and the hat with pink roses, Lyman noted. Her tranquil face had a worried frown. Lyman came around to help her into the carriage, but he hardly looked at her.

"Lyman, we're so late! It seems too bad to go in so late when everyone will be craning their necks to see us."

"Then it will serve them right," he said. "Louisa, this is my cousin Isabel Holbrook. She came while we were away."

"How do you do. It's too bad you didn't get here in time for the wedding."

"Yes, I was so sorry," Isabel said. "Aunt Abigail told me what a lovely wedding it was."

They rode up the street to the church. Isabel was between Louisa and Abbie, sitting forward to make enough room on the seat.

At the door of the church Louisa touched Lyman's arm. "Just this first Sunday, you could be excused from the choir so we can sit together, don't you think?"

Lyman shook his head. "I ought to be in the choir." He was grateful that he could follow Easy into the seats at the rear of the church. Mrs. Whipple passed them hymnbooks open at the right page. Mr. Kellogg poked Lyman in the back. Lyman turned to see his lively wink.

"Hard to get out of bed these mornings, eh?" he whispered.

Lyman sang more loudly: "How firm a foundation, ye saints of the Lord."

For the hymn before the sermon the congregation turned to face the choir. Lyman sang the first verse without looking up from the page. Behind him Easy's deep voice sang the bass. Lyman lifted his eyes and looked over at his father's pew. Isabel was farthest in, by the window. She was looking at him. When his eyes met hers she smiled almost gaily, unaware of the eyes of the choir on her. Everything about her was different, from the wide-brimmed hat she had put on so carelessly in the carriage to the cut and draping of the black dress. Abbie beside her seemed quaint in the Paisley shawl she had worn to church for the last twenty years. Lyman's eyes came at last to Louisa. The pink flowers on her hat moved as she sang. Her color was high, as though she felt everyone looking at her. She sang to the end of each line and then glanced up. Now she met his eyes and smiled happily and proudly back.

Lyman ceased to sing. He stood there holding the book. Mad ideas raced through his brain. What if he told Louisa frankly . . .

The Reverend Mr. Dwight preached interminably. He had married them a week ago tomorrow. Lyman remembered the words of the ceremony, said in this place before these same people. He remembered the minister's deep voice asking: "Wilt thou, Lyman, have this woman to be thy wedded wife, to live together . . . in the holy estate of matrimony: Wilt thou love her, comfort her . . . and forsaking all others . . ." That meant Isabel. . . . "keep thee only unto her, so long as ye both shall live?" He could still hear his own voice, so much lighter and weaker it had sounded after the minister's, saying "I will."

"So long as ye both shall live." Time ran past the windows of the church on and on, like the road that wound back up into the hills and met the Boston Post Road and crossed the mountains and came to the plains and finally out West to Dry Gulch. Time was made up of mornings saying good-bye to Louisa at the gate, looking over at Peterboro's store, and unlocking the office of the quarry . . . and nights of coming home again and praising Louisa's cooking and locking the door and going up the stairs to the room at the end of the hall, of opening the window so Esther Osgood would hear it—mornings and nights, nights and mornings!

But he had taken a vow, and Isabel might be divorced in Paris, but Louisa would die sooner than utter the word "divorce." Louisa loved him and trusted him and this marriage was his doing. He had asked her to marry him.

He tried to bring back the way he had felt driving in to Malden in the rain with his bride. Sitting soberly in the choir, his eyes on the minister, he tried to summon up that sudden sweeping desire, but his mind veered off and he thought instead of Louisa saying condescendingly "Poor Esther." If she ever said "Poor Isabel . . ."

He thought of Paris with Isabel, of any place with Isabel, talking to her, telling her all that was in mind. He shifted on the hard choir chair. His eyes sought his father's pew again. Louisa's sloping shoulders in the new brown cashmere, her bonnet with the pink flowers covering her hair . . . Louisa, his wife. On the other side of his mother,

Isabel was looking at the minister with her head tipped ever so little to one side. She rested her elbow on the window sill. Below the brim of her black hat her copper-colored hair was coiled in a knot that hung in a kind of black woven bag. Lyman clasped his hands together until the knuckles stretched the skin white.

"Let us pray!" the Reverend Mr. Dwight exhorted. Lyman bowed his head in his hands gratefully, but the words of the prayer rolled over him unheard.

It seemed to Lyman after church that the entire congregation had gathered around the Converse pew to greet the bride and groom and meet the elegant stranger in black who sat with them.

"Nate Holbrook's girl, well, well! Guess Vermont wasn't good enough for him, eh?"

"I thought for a minute there that you'd brought home two wives and was aiming to have one of these harems," Mr. Holmes said brightly. "I'm sure relieved now to know this is just your cousin!" Lyman joined in the laughter and moved slowly up the aisle, propelling Abbie gently along ahead of him, one hand touching Isabel's elbow, and walking beside Louisa.

"That would take a braver man than I, Mr. Holmes," he managed.

"You and Lyman will come up on the hill for dinner, Louisa, won't you? I've planned on it," Abbie said.

"Oh, thank you, Mother Converse. If you don't mind, this first Sunday is sort of special—in our own home, you know."

"There'll be other Sundays, Louisa. After all, Isabel's only here for a short time. I think we better . . ." Lyman began.

"Well, of course, Lyman, it's just whatever you want. I only thought . . ." Her voice hung reproachfully in the air, reasonable and kind the way it was when he was too importunate.

"Oh, Easy's going to drive me over to Malden this afternoon and it would make too hurried a meal anyway. I am just glad you got back before I left," Isabel said.

Panic rose in Lyman's mind. "Isabel, you can't go so soon. You've hardly seen Painesville, and there are some business matters I need to talk over with you at the office while you're here." She must see she couldn't go like that.

"I'll leave them to you to handle, Lyman. Really, I don't dare stay any longer. Mother is very poorly, you know. Good-bye, Louisa." Isabel kissed her lightly on the cheek. "Good-bye, Lyman." She held out her hand, swift and alive as life itself.

"I'll bring Scout down to you in the morning, Lyman," Easy was saying. Lyman felt Louisa's hand on his arm. He followed her into the house and stood there making hard work of fastening the screen.

"I hated to be firm, but our first Sabbath is too precious to us to give up. I'll just run upstairs and take off my best clothes before I get dinner." Louisa's voice beat against his ears.

What had he said? Nothing but "Good-bye, Isabel." "I don't dare stay any longer," she had said. Now she was gone. Easy would drive her over. Why couldn't he have driven her over himself, and had that chance to talk? Why had she hurried away so fast? He had all his life long for Louisa.

"Oh, Lyman, hadn't you better take off your wedding suit? Why don't you put on that gray one and be comfortable?" Louisa came by him on her way to the kitchen.

"Perhaps that would be a good idea." Lyman went on up the stairs. His hand touched the white balusters as he went, breaking for a moment the pattern of bars that their shadow cast on the rug below.

PART FOUR

I

Dear Cousin Lyman:

Mother died last Wednesday and was buried Saturday. I am glad
that she did not have to be an invalid any longer, for you know she was
energetic by nature and liked to have an active part in all that was
done in the house.

I wanted you to know at once but I didn't want you to come down
for the funeral, which I feared you would be tempted to do out of
kindness. It was better for us both that you shouldn't come. I have
many friends who were glad to help me in every way, and Mina is
here with me.

As soon as I can sell the house and get my affairs in order I am going
back to Paris, though I dread the trip across the water. I do not want
to keep this house. It seems too quiet without Mother springing out
of her chair and rushing downstairs to attend to Mina. I used to dis-
like the turmoil, but today I have sat the entire time in the parlor
acknowledging flowers, and the quiet depresses me. The avenue outside seems much farther away than the two thicknesses of lace curtains and the glass pane. Even the sun has a quietness about it. I sat
thinking of us, separated in the same way, and yet, I thought, the sun
warms me through the windowpane and the net curtains. I can see the
strong arching branches of the trees and all the life going up and down
the street. It is not shut away from me completely. Dear Lyman, do
you think I am easily satisfied that I draw pleasure and comfort from
such thoughts? I am not, but they are something.

I saw Professor Gilmore the other afternoon. He asked about you
and said, "That young man has a very interesting mind. I wish he had
stayed with us longer, for he seemed in search of something. I believe
the college could have helped him find it." I told him you were running
soapstone quarries in Vermont with great success. You remember how
he is, Lyman? He thought a few seconds, and then he smiled and said,
"Well, you know, my dear, the word 'quarry' means the thing hunted

or sought." Did you ever think of that? I never did, but now I find the idea keeps coming back to me.

Please remember me most kindly to Aunt Abigail and Louisa,

Faithfully,

Your cousin, Isabel

Lyman read the letter on his way up the street to the livery stable. He carried it with him on his trip to Dunlap, where he hoped to persuade the president to choose soapstone blocks for the new bank building. Before Isabel's letter came, securing the order had seemed so important; now he talked to the president and explained the advantages of soapstone as a building material, but he did not care personally. When he received the order he was not elated.

Isabel was going back to Paris.

While she had been in Providence she had seemed within reach. He had known that someday he would go to Boston on business and from Boston over to Providence. All fall and winter he had held such a trip out to himself as a reward . . . for what? For going so quietly in the house after Louisa that day last June. He had listened all through dinner and all through the bright aching June afternoon for the sound of Easy calling from the door on his way over to Malden. Isabel had told him to drive right by, Easy told him. "They'll be at dinner," she said. He hadn't seen her again.

He had planned his trip to Providence over and over again. He wouldn't write her beforehand. He would just go up those white steps and pull the shining door pull. Mina would come to the door and he would go into that long parlor until he heard Isabel running down the stairs. Always when he thought of it they were sitting in the library talking, with a fire in the fireplace lighting up the carving on the mantel and Isabel's hair. He would perhaps kiss her before he left, perhaps not. Looking at Isabel, talking to her, would be enough.

But now he must go at once. "It was better for us both that you should not come," Isabel had written. That wasn't so. Isabel didn't really believe that.

He would tell Louisa tonight as soon as he got home of Aunt Matilda's death, that he needed to straighten out certain of Aunt Matilda's affairs. Louisa would see that he must go. She would wonder that Isabel hadn't written at once so they could both attend the funeral. Louisa considered attendance at a funeral as an obligation to the Lord. But of course now that she was expecting a child, she could not consider going herself.

239

It would be very easy for him to go. He would leave tomorrow on the stage. He might need to stay several days, a week even. He would mention that to Louisa. This time he would get over to the college. He might even drop in and see old Gillyflower. A terrible eagerness to get away for a little possessed him. He hadn't been out of Vermont since his trip West. He hadn't seen Isabel since last June.

At Malden he found Scout waiting in the livery stable. It would be one o'clock in the morning before they reached home. There were patches of snow in the gulch. They stood out white and sudden enough in the moonlight. The road was icy and Scout stepped cautiously. Lyman was unaware of the change of pace, he was so lost in his own thoughts.

He wondered if Isabel had secured her divorce, if she still thought about it. "There isn't much point now," she had said. He looked coldly down the black-and-white road. If he should just drive away from Painesville someday, from Louisa and the brick house. Who could really stop him? His mother would grieve and pray about him, Louisa would go on just as she was. She would grieve and pray and continue in good works. She could still feel superior to Esther as she opened the window on the east side. And the quarry? Perhaps Louisa would run the quarry office. He would burn those letters in the Personal file before he went.

When they came to the curve at the top of the street Lyman saw his house all lighted up. Louisa only left one lamp in the hall if he was out late. He pulled the reins through the ring of the hitching post and hurried into the house. Abbie was coming through the hall with her apron on.

"Oh, Lyman, I'm glad you're back. Louisa had her baby tonight about suppertime. It's a boy. But she's an awful sick girl. The doctor's only just gone."

Lyman hung his hat and coat on the hatrack. In the mirror he saw his mother's face behind him over the stair rail, tired and anxious.

"She's been through everything!" Abbie whispered.

Lyman tiptoed up behind her to the room at the head of the stairs. There was only one light in the room and the sloping eaves made a shrine of the big walnut bed. Shadows stretched over it like drapery. Louisa's face was white against the white pillow slip, her hair lay in a dark braid on either shoulder. She looked as though she were dead.

Then her eyes opened, but no light was in them. They were still glazed with pain. They rested on him almost as though she didn't know him.

"Louisa, I'm sorry," he said softly. Then he knelt by the bed to bring his face nearer to hers.

Her pale lips softened a little and then folded against each other again. Her eyes closed, and kneeling so close he saw the tiny veins in her lids. He knelt there a minute longer, seeing the weariness in her face that couldn't quite cover the pain.

This was his wife, Louisa, his mind cried at him. He heard his mother coming up the stairs again and got to his feet, but he didn't take his eyes from Louisa's face, trying to block out Isabel's from his mind once and for all.

"She's sleeping now. You better go downstairs for a piece. There's some coffee on the stove, and a doughnut."

He went down the stairs as softly as he could, but the stairs creaked under his tread. The kitchen door was closed, and as he opened it the heat from the stove came at him. Close by the stove was the cradle that had been in Louisa's family. He crossed the room and bent over it. He had to pull the blankets down to find the small pink head. This was his son. Upstairs by Louisa's bed he had not even thought of the baby. He poured himself a cup of coffee and found the doughnut in the crock in the pantry.

Abbie opened the door. Her face was frightened.

"Lyman, go get the doctor again. Louisa's having convulsions. I thought she was all quiet and then she started drawing up. Mary Holmes was took like this and she never got over it, but with Mary it was before the baby was born. It's good the baby's born. He looks healthy enough."

Lyman hurried down the street to the doctor's house. The moon was gone now and the street was dark as a pit. He felt the path dip down at the Ingrams' fence. There at the gate the lilac bush leaned out over the fence, then the store, the post office. . . . The doctor's house was dark. But when Lyman knocked a window raised on the second floor.

"Yes?" Dr. Gaines called out.

"It's Converse, Doctor. Mrs. Converse is worse again. My mother says she has convulsions."

Dr. Gaines had taken Louisa's father's place. He had bought his instruments and some of the calfskin-bound books. He had had a new soapstone sink put in his kitchen when he came, but Lyman didn't really know him. He wondered whether he was really good, and tried to think of people in the village he had cured. He stood waiting in front of the dark house. With his foot he felt the roots of the tree growing across the path and remembered stumbling over them as a boy with bare feet. He could almost feel the sharp pain in his stubbed toe,

Louisa's pain. . . . "She's been through everything," his mother had said.

The door banged sharply. Lyman was grateful for the presence of the doctor beside him walking back up the street.

"I'm sorry I had to be away tonight," Lyman said.

"Nothing you could do," the doctor's voice answered. "She's a little old for her first baby. You can't tell a thing about it; some women don't have a mite of trouble and others, seems to tear 'em apart. She had a bad time, but I thought she was all right when I left." They were walking as fast as they could up the street, but it seemed long to Lyman.

"She kept calling out for you, though," the doctor said in a kindly tone. "She kept saying, 'John, I want John!'"

They came to the house and Lyman held the door open for Dr. Gaines and then went out to sit in the kitchen by his new son, listening to the sounds upstairs. Now and then he stood in the doorway to the bedroom, but Louisa knew nobody. Once Dr. Gaines called him to help hold her still in bed, she writhed so in her convulsions. Her hair had come loose from its braids and hung around her face. She had bitten her tongue and it had swelled and protruded from her mouth, distorting her whole face. Lyman, looking at the blotches of color on her face and her eyes that stared without seeing around the room, felt a deep pity for her and for himself. A sense of guilt rested on his mind. He looked over at the doctor. The doctor shook his head. Lyman heard his mother catch her breath.

"She's took bad," she whispered, and the doctor sent her on some errand to the kitchen.

For an instant the convulsion ceased. Louisa lay still, her eyes closed, her poor tongue protruding from her mouth that the doctor had kept open with a padded stick. Lyman relaxed his hold on her arm. If she came through, if she lived, Lyman told himself, he would never let himself think of Isabel again. While Louisa had been suffering he had been planning to go to Isabel.

Louisa lunged violently as though to spring out of bed. Lyman's arms ached from holding her so tightly. Louisa gurgled, her head fell back sharply. Lyman moved so he could support her head with his other arm. It was heavy against him.

"The morphine's taking effect," the doctor murmured. Louisa's breath became stertorous, her taut body relaxed. Together they moved her head more comfortably against the pillow. The doctor's hand was on her pulse. Lyman moved his fingers on the other wrist, fearfully. He felt the beat of blood against his finger. It seemed to hold him there, bringing him almost too close to Louisa, making them one as no other physical union had.

He felt the doctor's eyes on him. "Her pulse seems strong," Lyman murmured.

"You're feeling the pulse in your own finger there." He moved Lyman's fingers to the right place. Now Lyman felt a different beat, much softer and faster, more terrifying. "Feel it?" the doctor asked.

Lyman nodded, trying to make that frightened beat stronger by holding his fingers more tightly on her slender wrist. That was true enough, he thought, the beat of his own desires was so strong it blocked out Louisa's. If she lived, if that pulse only held . . . A feeling of great tenderness filled him. He took his fingers from her wrist and smoothed back the tangled mass of brown hair from her face. The morning light came in through the windows and laid a false glow of health on her cheeks. Lyman drew the shade of the window toward Esther's.

"If she doesn't have another convulsion she may pull through," the doctor said. Abbie took their place and they went out together.

Lyman stood on the doorstep and watched the doctor go down the street the few doors to his house. The street was just the same as it had been when he and Easy were boys, yet he felt its strangeness: the yearning of Esther's windows, the smugness of Maudie Peterboro's door, the sorrowing droop of the elms that arched above the street, the straightness of the path to his own door. He went back up to Louisa.

Louisa lived, but three weeks of days lightened and darkened down the main street before her lips lost their swelling and closed in their old serene line again and her face lost its blotched and swollen look. Lyman spent much of each day in her room sitting beside her, touching her hand when she woke. One day he sat there lost in his own thoughts, his eyes out the window, when Louisa spoke suddenly for the first time.

"What shall we name the baby, Lyman?" She spoke distinctly, like herself. He didn't let his voice show the relief and surprise he felt.

"What would you like to name him?" he asked gently.

"Well, we can't name him Orville, Easy's spoiled that," Louisa said. "Father's name was Nathaniel, but I never liked that."

There was a pause that seemed long to Lyman.

"How about naming him Jonathan? Would you like that?" he asked.

Louisa turned her face away and closed her eyes wearily. "Yes, that would be nice."

"We'll call him Jonathan Tucker Converse, then," Lyman said. "I'll go down and tell Mother and have the town clerk put it in the town records."

June 18, 1873
Painesville, Vt.

Dear Isabel,

I was relieved to hear that you had arrived safely in Paris and that it seemed good to be back. I was greatly saddened by word of Aunt Matilda's death. I had hoped to get down to Providence before you left, but Louisa gave birth to a boy on April 8 and was so ill for several weeks that I never went farther away than the quarry office. Both she and Jonathan are doing well now.

It seems sad to me that you sold the house in Providence, but I suppose it was the only thing to do in view of your decision to live in Paris permanently.

I trust that the winter will be a pleasant one.

He hesitated over the "Faithfully," and then wrote as was his custom,

Faithfully,
Lyman

He read the letter over and was dissatisfied with it, but it was all his conscience would let him write. When he told Louisa and his mother of his aunt's death, Louisa said at once, "You should have gone to the funeral, Lyman." And his mother said, "To think of Nate's wife dying and none of his own kin there!"

"I planned to go as soon as I heard from Isabel, but that was the day John was born and you were too sick for me to leave you, Louisa," Lyman said, not looking at her, ashamed of the sharp pang it gave him to realize how simple it would have been to go.

In December he heard from Isabel again.

Dear Coz. Lyman:

You cannot imagine how grateful I was to receive your letter with the draft from the quarry. Chauncey's affairs were in a bad state after Jay Cooke's collapse and my own inheritance has been sadly affected. Thank heaven for the quarry! That and the foreign bonds Father left me have maintained me this winter. Chauncey is in the south of France now and complains bitterly of his altered circumstances and claims that he can send me nothing. I do not mind, I wish to be free from him financially.

I have changed my address, as you will see, and am living in a modest

pension but a very pleasant one with a garden that will be lovely in the spring. It is near the Louvre, which is the place I haunt the most.

A happy Christmas to you and Louisa and Jonathan.

Faithfully, your cousin,
Isabel

In January, owing to the depressed condition of affairs that spread even to Painesville, Lyman was able to purchase the Clark mill four miles from Painesville and so get ready to expand the quarry business in the spring. This impressed Judge Whitcomb, who was president of the bank in Malden, and when the bank at Painesville ceased to function he made Lyman a director and most of the people transferred their accounts to the Malden bank. "My, that would please your father, Lyman," Abbie said proudly. "And surprise him!" Lyman said with a smile. It seemed strange not to have a bank in Painesville.

"It's my idea that Lyman Converse'd make a good town clerk," Sam Peterboro declared one night at a meeting of the town selectmen. "He's young, but he's done real well for himself and he's Orville Converse's son."

"And then there's another thing," Asa Pettingill put in. "We want to keep these young fellers here and not have them all gallivantin' off. Makin' him town clerk'll help to tie him here."

Dr. Gaines was one of the new selectmen. He dropped the legs of his chair to the floor. "What's Converse's first name? I thought it was John."

"Nope, that was his brother that was killed in the Wilderness. This one's name is Lyman."

2

LYMAN wondered if other men dreaded Sunday the way he did. In the morning there was church. He sang in the choir, and he liked that. The sermon was long and dull, but he had a chance to think his own thoughts comfortably. He had a chance in bed in the morning too, but he couldn't think comfortably there. They rose an hour later, but the alarm of his mind went off at six-thirty Sundays as well as weekdays. He lay there, pretending to be still asleep, feeling that Louisa was awake too.

While Louisa prepared the Sunday dinner that was always the best one of the week he walked down to the quarry office with John. The postmistress opened up the office for families who drove in from the country, and the men stood around talking. Newell Applebee, who ran the carriage works now, was usually there and Ben Holmes, who had the cheese factory, and Peterboro and Pettingill, the businessmen of the town. But everyone had dinner about one, and they couldn't any of them linger long. Newell Applebee's wife would send one of the children over for Newell and John would be pulling at Lyman and saying, "Come on, Father," and they would all scatter to their Sunday dinners.

But after dinner there was a piece of time that was a man's own. While Louisa and his mother did the dishes Lyman took John and crossed the street over to Peterboro's or stopped in at the carriage works. A Sunday idleness lay on the new buggies or over the back end of the store. Sometimes Lyman dropped in at Judge Whitcomb's and they talked about what was happening to the country. But the Judge was over seventy now. Talking with him made Lyman feel old too. John found it dull at the Judge's, and Lyman had to keep an eye on him to see that he didn't touch things he shouldn't or escape to the street.

Another uncomfortable thing about Sunday was that he tried to do things with John. He began by trying to remember how he had felt at seven, but he had no memory of doing things with his father in any close intimacy. His world had been a secret world that no one but himself ever really entered until Easy had come along.

He didn't feel he could make his way into some world of John's, nor did he know how to. This afternoon he and John walked up the street together, John kicking a stone ahead of them with his toe. Lyman watched him curiously. John was a slender little boy with dark-brown hair and Louisa's eyes. Sometimes Lyman felt he wasn't boisterous enough for a boy, but there wasn't anything you could do about that. He looked shyly sometimes for signs of himself in John, but he never really found them. Louisa was proud of the way the boy minded. He sat more quietly in church than most boys his age. Lyman could see him from the choir and he never seemed to be fussing with a string or marbles or even turning the pages of the hymnbook.

"Shall we harness Scout and drive up the hill?" Lyman asked.

"To the quarry, Father?"

"Oh, I thought we might stop at Grandfather's place," Lyman said. It was strange that it had come to be that. His mother always called it that now and so did Louisa.

"Let's," John said, and Lyman felt strangely warmed. They harnessed the horse together and rode quietly down the Sunday street, through the covered bridge, and up the thank-you-ma'ams of the hill road.

"I used to go up and down here on foot and never think anything about it," Lyman said.

"Didn't you have a horse then?"

"Oh, yes, Grandfather had a horse. He had this horse, as a matter of fact."

"This same horse!" John looked at him in amazement and Lyman could see that it upset his idea of time. Suddenly he set himself to bridge the gap and bring his boyhood close to John's.

"I had my own horse for a while. His name was Ned. He was brown with a white blaze. I thought the world of that horse."

"What happened to him?"

"Well, I wanted to join the army and I was too young for that, so I gave my horse to the United States Cavalry." Lyman's voice was very quiet at the end. It didn't hurt him to think of giving up Ned the way it always used to, and the discovery shocked him and made him feel older than thirty-two.

"What did your father say?" John asked.

"He was angry, because the horse was worth quite a little money, but I thought he was wrong about that."

"Why?"

"Because I thought the horse was mine. When a thing's yours, you ought to be able to give it away if you want to."

"You should have asked first," the sober little boy beside him said in a reproving tone.

Lyman pursed his lips thoughtfully. He tipped his head to one side so he could look at John. "You know, son, I'm glad I gave my horse away."

John's brown eyes were fixed on him with surprise. "Why?"

"Because it was a good feeling to give something away that I cared about. It was a real sacrifice."

John considered this a moment, then he seemed to give it up and return to his original line of thought.

"What did your father do?"

"He whipped me."

"Did you cry?"

"Yes, but not then, and not because of the whipping—because I missed my horse."

"Oh," John said, and Lyman was ashamed of the sudden irritation he felt. He wished he hadn't bothered to spend this Sunday afternoon with his son.

They rounded the bend and the house stood before them. The branch of the elm tree that hung down to the second-story window was all yellow and the woodbine against the corner was so red it made the bricks look faded. The reins lay slack in Lyman's hands. The wheels turned so slowly in the dust they hardly made a sound.

A long-legged brown-skinned boy came running around the corner of the house. He stood poised as if to run again, staring up at the second-story window.

"That's Orville Williams, isn't it, Father?" John said.

Lyman nodded. Orville was so tall . . . how old was he now? He was born the year Easy came back . . . the year . . . He must be thirteen.

A brown face appeared at the last second-story window in the room that had once been his mother's summer bedroom.

"That's Ruby," John said.

Ruby was grinning down at her brother Orville.

"I saw you go in! I knew you were hidin' in there. We said no fair in the house," the boy called out indignantly. "You know what Pop said! He said he'd beat the tar outa anyone that ran through the house!"

The face in the window lost its grin in a pout. Then a small dark face appeared beside her. That was Sam. He was nine, two years older than John. Easy and Jewel had five now: Orville and Ruby and Sam and Ashwood and Opal. He called the roll, pleased that he could remember their names.

At that instant Sam saw Lyman in the buggy and pointed. Orville looked at Lyman and fled around the corner of the house. Sam disappeared from beside Ruby, but Ruby continued to stare at them through the window without moving. Lyman was sorry they had run away as though they were afraid of him. He waved and called out to them and Ruby smiled back a little uncertainly.

"Why don't you run and play with them, John? It looks as though they were having a good time." But John sat stiffly back against the seat, his hands tucked under the bend of his knees.

"Mother don't want me to play with them," he said.

"That's nonsense! I grew up with Easy. He lived right in our house."

"Mama said she'd never want me to live up here in the summers like you wanted to, not with the darkies running all over," John offered, looking at the front of the brick house.

"You get right out and run and play with Sam and Orville if they'll let you. I'll explain to your mother," Lyman ordered. He watched as John walked slowly across to Easy's house.

Lyman tied the reins through the granite hitching post, but he was looking up at Ruby, still in the upstairs window. She stood so stiffly, almost like a sentinel, her dark face so sober that it showed no expression. He took off his hat and bowed to her. The rigid little figure seemed to relax. This time she smiled broadly and waved, then she disappeared from the front window. Ruby was an attractive-looking girl, she had Jewel's small features and Easy's carriage.

Easy came out of the little house that now reached out another wing, this time toward the apple orchard. One of the children must have told him Lyman was here.

"Hello, Easy!" Lyman called out.

"H'llo, Lyman!" Easy called back, with no reproach that it had been so long since he had come up here, no shade of surprise. Lyman felt comfortable with him. But just as Easy reached the corner of the house Ruby opened the front door and came out as though she belonged there.

"It's a nice day, Mr. Converse, isn't it?" she said in a grown-up tone of voice. Then she saw her father and her smiling poise deserted her. She was a Negro child found guilty.

"Ruby, what you doin' in Mr. Converse's house?" Easy demanded sternly.

"Oh, Easy, that's all right. They were just playing hide-and-seek. It was good to see some life in the old house," Lyman said, but Easy was not mollified.

"You know I told you never to set foot in property that don't belong to you!"

"Yes, sir," Ruby said, one slender hand plucking nervously at her short pigtail, but her eyes moved from her father to Lyman without fear.

"You go help your mother with the baby," Easy commanded.

Standing there together, both men watched the girl walk slowly across the grass, jump over the row of currant bushes, and continue an otherwise dignified retreat toward the low white house. Easy shook his head. "What gets into that girl? Her mother says she's just notional, but she knows as well as her name's Ruby Williams that I give strict orders for none of 'em to hang around that house, let alone goin' inside."

"Why shouldn't she? Any child would go in a house that's left deserted so many years. Easy, I've been thinking about it for a long time. Louisa's never going to live up here, even for a summer. I don't know that I'd want to either. It's been too long ago. Why don't you and Jewel move in? I'd kind of like to go on owning it, but eventually I'll deed it to you. There's never going to be any sale for houses up on this hill."

Easy shook his head. "No, Lyman. Thank you kindly, but I seen enough o' that down South, colored folks movin' into the old plantation houses. It's a sad uncomfortable thing to see. The houses don't fit 'em right. We got plenty o' room, Lyman. There's the whole hill to spread out in. I tell Jewel she's got to look lively if she sets enough souls out here to populate the hill again. Jewel thinks it's pretty lonely up here some days, 'specially in the winter."

And there they left it.

"I wonder how that front door come to be unlocked." Easy fussed. Lyman took a key from his pocket and turned the lock without going inside. It seemed a pity to leave the house standing empty there with all of its furniture in the rooms. His mother came up about twice a year and Jewel came over and helped her clean it.

"I keep the other key on that nail in my front room, you know, Lyman, back o' the picture o' Lincoln."

"It's all right, anyway," Lyman answered mildly. He thought with amusement of the key dangling from the ribbon on Ruby's flat little chest, and he had seen the quick furtive movement of her hand that slipped the key inside her gingham dress.

"Come over to the house, Lyman?"

"No, thanks. Let's sit out here," Lyman said, sitting down on the wide soapstone block in front of the door. Easy brought out his corncob pipe. Lyman had the old brier he had bought so long ago at Brown. He offered his tobacco pouch to Easy, but Easy laughed. "That isn't strong enough for me." He filled his pipe from a paper package he took from his shirt pocket. The tobacco smoke mingled with the haze of the fall air.

"John's growin'," Easy said. "He's a mite taller than my Sam."

"Spindling, though," Lyman said. "I wish he lived up on the hill. I believe it was healthier up here."

"I guess it's healthy," Easy assented.

Conversation trickled slowly, as from a pump that drew from a dry well. Today Lyman hunted for something to say. His being married had made a difference.

"We did real well at the quarry last week, Lyman."

"Yes, we did at that," Lyman said. This week he would be sending out checks to Willie and Isabel. It always gave him pleasure. That made him think of Willie.

"I had a letter from Willie last week, Easy."

"Is she well?" Easy asked.

"Yes. Juliet's sixteen. Willie has her in a boarding school on the Hudson. She says Juliet wants to go on the stage but she won't let her."

Easy nursed his pipe in his large brown hand. "How she goin' to keep her from it?"

"I don't know. Willie has an engagement in London this winter and she's taking Juliet with her. I wrote Isabel to go and see her."

"They ought to take a shine to each other," Easy said. "Willie's gone a long ways."

"Yes," Lyman said, "and I've never seen her act in all these years! She was out West so long, and then she came to New York, but that was when Louisa was sick. Louisa feels as strongly about the stage as Father did."

"We seen her act, Lyman, in that parlor in there. She used to make shivers go down my spine when she'd do Lady Macbeth an' them witches."

"Mine, too, but I remember her best reading *East Lynne.*"

"I do too, Lyman." The two men were quiet, remembering.

"Not it!" John dashed out from behind the lilac bush and raced for the butternut tree that was goal. Sam was after him. It pleased Lyman to see them playing together.

"Mr. Converse, would you desire a glass of lemonade? Ma made some." Ruby stood before them holding a tin tray with two glasses on it and a plate of cookies. She had changed her dress and unbraided her hair so it spread in a thin fuzz in her neck. She wore high laced shoes that were too long for her, and the pointed toes turned up. Lyman noticed that the string was gone from her neck and surmised that she had hung the key again behind the picture of Lincoln.

"Thank you, Ruby," he said, smiling at her. Helping himself to a ginger cooky, he noticed that it matched exactly the brown fingers holding the plate. He watched her walk back around the house. Her shoes gave her an oddly stilted walk and her head on her slender neck made him think of a sunflower. At the corner she looked back at them, and then ran quickly to the little house.

The lemonade was cold in the thick glass with the nicked rim. It had mint leaves in it from the bed by the kitchen door. Lyman wondered as he sat there sipping it why he felt so much better up here.

"Whadya think of this here cement, Lyman?" Easy asked.

"Cement? Oh, why, I don't know much about it. They use it more in England, I guess. Why?"

"I was talkin' to a man in Malden the other day. They're usin' it for the foundations of the new church there 'stead o' granite or soapstone."

"Is that so? I'll have to drop around and see it."

"It's a lot cheaper an' handier than havin' a stonemason, this gentleman was telling me." The way Easy kept on with the subject bothered Lyman. He looked at Easy. His brown face was impassive but the big black-and-white eyes looked mournful.

"You don't think there's such a thing as cement cuttin' in on the soapstone business, Lyman?"

So that was it. "Not seriously I don't, Easy. Cement's a cheap-looking affair compared to stone, and aside from building they can't make cement that will stand what soapstone will. I had an order the other day from a college way out in Michigan for soapstone sinks and counters for their scientific laboratories. There isn't anything that can take the place of soapstone, Easy."

Easy grinned. His eyes shone again. He ran his big hand back over his close-cropped head. "That's good, Lyman."

"Did you have a good time, John?" Lyman asked as they drove back to town. The hill was so steep the horse had to take it slowly, hunching his plump rump against the breeching to hold the carriage back against the steep pitch.

"Yes," John answered slowly. "Only Mama wouldn't like it, neither playing with Easy's kids nor playing on Sunday. Let's not tell her."

"Of course you can tell her." He didn't like John's reasoning. He would talk to Louisa about it.

"Sam asked me why I never asked him down to play at our house in town."

"What did you say?"

"I said there weren't any colored children in town. And then Ruby, she's the big one, she looked mad and she took Sam in the house to make some lemonade and when she came out she wouldn't give me any because she said it was only for colored boys on the hill. But her mother was standing in the door and heard her and she boxed her ears good and brought me a whole big glass."

Lyman thought of Ruby again bowing to him from the front window as proudly as though she owned the house.

"Isn't Ruby bad? I'm glad Jewel boxed her ears," John said with evident relish.

"No, Ruby isn't bad, John. You hurt her feelings." He glanced at John's puzzled little face and had no heart to go on. They crossed the covered bridge that connected the hill with the village, the bridge that connected his old separate life with his life with Louisa. He felt depressed and hopeless as he drove up the street to the brick house where he lived now.

Louisa was playing the organ when they went in. Lyman saw her through the window just as he had seen her that evening when he went to supper, long before he had thought of marrying her. She lifted her hands from the keys when she heard them before she released the pedals and the overtones still filled the room, then came to an abrupt end as she swung around on the stool and came out to the hall.

"Did you go to the quarry, Lyman? I wish you'd tell me when you take John with you. Jonathan Converse, look at your trousers!"

John looked down guiltily. Each knee had a large damp spot. His shirt front was spotted. When he looked up his eyes were full of tears.

"Oh, Louisa, boys have to play. His clothes will wash," Lyman said in exasperation.

"Were you playing with that colored tribe, John?"

"I told him to, Louisa. They're fine clean children. Easy grew up with me. John was afraid you wouldn't like it and I gave him permission."

"You don't seem to care what I think or say, do you, Lyman?"

Lyman was conscious of the anguished, frightened look in John's face. "Run up and change your clothes, John," he said gently, then he leaned against the doorway and faced Louisa. "Don't say things like that that you don't mean. You know I do care about what you think. But if my mother and father couldn't turn Easy away from their home because he trusted them, we might at least treat him and his children as friends and equals."

"Do you like to see your child play with colored children? And that oldest boy is a disgrace to your father's name!"

Lyman watched Louisa's face, but his mind cried out to walk away, not to see her like this, her dark eyes shining out of peepholes between her eyelids, her lovely color heightened by anger, her mouth hard and tight.

"Louisa, Easy named his first child after Father to honor him, to express his gratitude."

"Well, I don't suppose he could know that the boy was going to turn out a peeping Tom, a . . . a dangerous character." Louisa's voice was shrill.

"What are you trying to say about Orville, Louisa? That day he painted the fence for you you said he was a good worker!"

"Oh, he works all right, but when he was doing the east side there by Esther's house, she told me she was in the bedroom on the west— you know she sleeps downstairs in the summer—and she was standing by the dresser in only her dressing-gown, brushing her hair, and she felt someone's eyes. When she looked at the window there were two eyes in a black face staring in at her! She screamed and ran out of the room. She said she'd have been right over to get me except that her heart was palpitating so hard she had to sit down on the sofa."

Where was the look of serenity on Louisa's face that had drawn him to her? He looked at her wondering that her face could change so. It was twisted and sharp. He looked away and picked up the pink conch shell, turning it in his hand so the polished pink lip of it was uppermost.

"What do you think of that, Lyman Converse? Maudie Peterboro says down South they'd hang a Negro if they caught him doing a thing like that."

Lyman lifted the shell to his ear and listened unhappily to the insistent roar.

"Esther says she's heard that colored boys develop faster than white, that at thirteen she wouldn't be a bit surprised if they have . . . you know, ideas!"

"Oh, Louisa, for heaven's sake, Esther made a mountain out of a molehill. The fence is so close there he probably just thought he'd look in to see what the house was like."

"All right, if that's what you think. I'm sure I hope you're right, but I won't have John playing with any of that tribe!"

"Louisa, I won't have you telling him he can't. When I was a boy . . ."

"Oh, I know, you lived up on the hill and did everything with Easy."

"Louisa . . ." he hesitated. He set the shell back on the whatnot so that the delicate pink surface was hidden. "I don't like to have you talk this way or think this way." For a minute his eyes held hers, then she gave a sniff, her mouth tightened.

"Somebody in this family has to think of what's good for Jonathan." She went down the hall to the kitchen and he followed. He sat in the chair by the window and watched her fill the teakettle and light the spirit lamp under it.

"If you had married John and he had come back, you'd be living up on the Spring place now, probably," he said thoughtfully. "You and Jewel would be neighbors. Did you ever think of that, Louisa?"

Louisa was looking out the window. "That was why I didn't want John to hire a substitute and get out of the army that time when he had a furlough. He wanted to buy the Spring place right then, and I never intended to live way off up on the quarry hill."

"Oh," Lyman said. "I thought it was because you didn't think it was right for a man to hire a substitute."

"Well, there was that, too, but . . ."

Lyman got up. He could trust himself no longer. "I'm going on down to the office for an hour or two, Louisa."

"But I just put the water on for tea. I thought we'd have tea and some . . ."

"I don't want any supper, we had such a hearty dinner," Lyman answered. "Where's Mother?"

"She went over to sit a while with Mrs. Pettingill. Lyman, you ought to eat something."

Lyman went down the straight walk to the street. He saw Dr. Gaines and bowed to Judge Whitcomb reading on his porch and met the Asa Greens riding past in their buggy, but he was only dimly aware of them. The trees were bright-colored and all the white clapboard buildings shone in the late October sun, but Lyman did not see them, so blinded was he by his own bitter thoughts. Jonathan had died in the Wilderness, and he himself must live without Isabel in a wilderness because a serene-faced girl could not bear to live beyond the covered bridge!

255

In the office of the quarry he sat down at the cherry desk and pulled paper in front of him. A great yearning for Isabel moved his pen.

October 10, 1880
Painesville, Vt.

Dear Isabel:

I wonder what you are doing on this Sunday afternoon in Paris, what you are thinking. It seems at the other side of the world from Painesville. I wonder if I shall ever see Paris or find my way to your address and pull the bell as I used to do in Providence. And sit in your library and have tea and discuss all polite matters and the affairs of the world, but really hear nothing but the sound of your voice. It seems too impossible ever to happen.

I cannot understand now why I felt I must stay here and run the quarry, yet I did. I have been thinking of trying to sell. If I could get a price that would mean a good return to all of us, I should be tempted to do it. Would it be agreeable to you?

Today I drove up on the hill with John. He is seven now, a fine-looking boy, I think you would say, but he seems a stranger to me. I wonder if I did to my father, though I doubt whether he ever stopped to think that deeply about Dan or John or me. His mind was full of the work of Abolition, then of winning the war, and finally of the quarry. I believe he was a fortunate man to be so made.

Write and tell me what you are doing. It helps to try to picture you.

Faithfully,

Lyman

It was like a love letter, and he read it over feeling it was wrong to write it, wrong to Louisa, and yet how could it hurt her? Since John's birth he had written only of business affairs. And Isabel's letters in return hardly needed to go in the Personal file. Now she would know how he had felt all the time. Some warmth seemed to come from the written page into his fingers and into his mind. He sealed the letter and propped it up against the pigeonholes of his desk while he went over the new booklet advertising Converse & Holbrook Soapstone Products.

When he went back up the street, it was after ten and most of the houses were dark; Louisa had left a lamp in the hall for him. Its light came through the fan and the slender panes at either side of the door and laid geometric patterns of light on the dead October grass and the soapstone walk. As Lyman turned the doorknob, Louisa came down the stairs in her red dressing-gown, her hair loose over her shoulders.

"Oh, Lyman, the Reverend Mr. Dwight was here to call and I had to say you had some letters to write at the office, but I could see he felt you were breaking the Sabbath. I didn't want him to think that, so I said you always wrote your relatives on Sunday."

"Thank you, Louisa. As a matter of fact, that was the truth. I wrote Isabel."

"Well, I'm so relieved. I've felt I'd told a falsehood and it weighed on my mind." She looked so like a child for a minute that he touched her arm gently. He felt good, too, that he had told her about his letter. It made it almost right.

Upstairs in the big front chamber he took off his coat and laid it over the back of the chair. Louisa was already in bed, her face averted modestly from him toward the wall. He turned down the light and opened the window before he undressed.

"Lyman?"

"Yes."

"What did you write Isabel about?"

He smoothed the creases in the Sunday satin tie he had taken off. "I wanted to sound her out on the idea of selling the quarry. Oh, there's nothing definite, I just thought if I should get a good enough offer it might be a good thing to move to a larger place for John. Of course I don't know just what I would do, but with capital to invest . . ."

"Lyman, you mean we could move to the city, Boston or New Haven or Albany?" She was sitting up in bed. He had never heard her voice sound so excited.

"Perhaps, if I could sell the quarry at an advantageous price."

"I would be so glad, Lyman. I always tried to get Father to move to the city."

"Well, we'll see. I just wondered how you'd feel about it. I rather feared you would hate to leave Painesville."

They talked a while in the dark, figures of a contented marriage. But after Louisa had said, "Good night, Lyman" and gone to sleep, he lay awake.

The middle of November he heard from Isabel.

October 21, 1880
Paris, France

Dear Cousin Lyman:
When your letter came I had just come in from a rainy walk along the boulevard. Paris is sometimes beautiful in the rain but not today. I was chilled through. The pension looked depressing and the face of the concierge seemed to sneer at the painting materials under my arm. I have taken up painting, Lyman—don't laugh at me. I am very serious.

257

But the concierge wasn't sneering. Instead she handed me your letter and I was emboldened and asked her to send up some hot chocolate and a croissant to my room to celebrate. I lit my fire and changed my wet clothes before I opened the letter, so you see it was very like having tea with you in the library at home. Nothing seems too impossible. Who knows? You may come here after all.

Sell the quarry by all means. I will not deny that I depend on my income from it, but if you should sell perhaps you would be so good as to invest my share for me. I wonder what you would do and where you would live if you moved from Painesville?

Think of your having a son seven years old! You are very lucky. I should love to see him. Don't worry about him. Perhaps boys know their mothers best when they are young, their fathers when they are a little older. Sometimes I feel that most people are strangers to each other—only you and I have never been strangers, have we?

Thank you for your letter. The rain continues to roll down the windowpane and my fire has burned low, but I feel very gay.

Faithfully,
Isabel

Lyman sat at his desk in the quarry office rereading the letter that had come in the morning mail. Isabel asked for no explanation of the reserved businesslike tone of his other letters, nor of the tone of his last impulsive one. It was as though she understood. One sentence he read again before he put the letter away carefully in the Personal file. "Sometimes I feel that most people are strangers to each other—only you and I have never been strangers, have we?"

3

SUMMER 1885

LOUISA was making blackberry jam. The rich sweet smell filled the house, infusing its prim coolness with a heavy fragrance deeper than attar of roses or balsam. Yesterday Lyman and Easy had gone berrying on the hill back of the quarry. Lyman had taken John along, and Easy's whole brood had gone except Orville, who was working at the quarry now, doing a man's work, and Ruby, who "helped" the Asa Pettingills. On the way back they had stopped at the old Spring place. Where the house and barn had burned down blackberry bushes had grown up. They picked their biggest ones there. The berries that grew down in the old cellar hole and against the half-buried horseblock were as big as your thumb and so plumped out with sweetness you hardly knew they had any seeds at all. John had filled two lard pails and Lyman had filled a milk pail.

This evening Lyman stopped in the kitchen on his way to the meeting of the town council, drawn by the heavy-sweet fragrance of the cooking berries. Louisa was finishing her last batch after supper.

"Want to taste, Lyman? I believe these are better. I got the others a mite too sweet," Louisa said.

"I like jam sweet. That's what you make it for, to put sweetness on your bread," Abbie objected. She was doing the dishes so Louisa could go ahead.

Louisa lifted a spoonful. "It's hot, don't burn yourself." Lyman blew carefully on the spoon and tasted. Both women waited motionless for his verdict.

"I don't know about 'better,' but it's delicious. I want some when I come home, too."

"Lyman, call John in on your way. He's playing ball back of the blacksmith shop. He has to take a bath tonight, it's Saturday."

"I'll tell him, but if he's playing a game don't expect him to stop right away."

"Well," Louisa temporized. Her face gentled as it always did toward John. "Tell him to come in a few minutes."

Lyman felt the pleasantness of the summer evening as he went down the street. The band was practicing in the grange hall. He could pick out the moist notes of Sam Durant's cornet and the militant boom of Bert Hubbard's drum. He missed the old Judge sitting on his front porch. Peterboro had startled him just yesterday saying that now the old Judge was dead he didn't suppose Painesville would ever have another judge, it was too small. But it was pleasant living in a village this size, just the same. Of course if the sale of the quarry had gone through a couple of years ago he would have been glad, but he couldn't get the figure he had asked and there was no sense in giving it away. Too many people were dependent on the quarry for their income. He believed Louisa was more disappointed than he was. Still, his going to the legislature at Montpelier had given her a change from Painesville during the winter. He enjoyed that himself. It gave him a good feeling to think the town wanted him as its representative. There was even talk of running him for Senator, but he didn't take too much stock in that.

The sound of the ball game came to him way down by the Greens' corner. He had missed all that as a boy living up on the hill. It was good for John. He heard the sound of the ball against the mitt, the dull thud as the bat was thrown down on the ground, and boys' yelling. He listened for John's voice. They were cheering someone. He remembered the time at Brown when he had played ball on the middle campus and someone had called out "Yeah, Converse!" Funny to remember that all these years!

The blacksmith was hard at work. His shop was dark inside. but Lyman could see his fire. Someone was in there talking to him.

" 'Lo," Lyman called.

" 'Lo," the aproned figure answered from the shadows.

" 'Lo," someone else called out, and Lyman answered, " 'Lo." It was the standard salutation of the male population of Painesville.

Lyman climbed the wall back of the shop and looked for John among the boys. There was a certain pleasure in seeing your son when he didn't know you were around. John always seemed a little self-conscious in his presence.

Then he saw him—on the cross wall by himself. He looked lonely over there. Why wasn't he playing? For a moment Lyman wanted to go over to him, but he stopped himself. Maybe John wanted to play, maybe the others didn't want him. Maybe he wouldn't want his father to see him just at this minute. Lyman stood quietly half-behind an apple tree. A kind of yearning for the boy ached through him. It was worse than some slight to himself. John looked thin, he thought. His knees were crossed and his hands were clasped around them and he sat quietly in spite of the excitement of the game. Why didn't he call out to them, cheer, or jeer or . . . something!

That was the Peterboro boy up at bat. He hit the ball a good crack. The ball made a clean arc underneath the early evening sky. Lyman's eyes followed it with the others. It was going beyond the outfielder. Lyman saw John jump off the wall. He was running now, head back, hands out. Lyman held his breath, watching, wanting him to catch it. The dirty little sphere was coming down. John caught it and threw it in.

"Yeh for Johnny!" someone yelled out. Lyman stopped the shout that rose to his own throat.

"Hey, John, you wanta play?" the Peterboro boy asked.

John shook his head. "I've gotta go," he said.

Lyman wondered impatiently why he didn't stay and play. He walked rapidly around the blacksmith shop, suddenly uncomfortable at seeming to be there spying, but he waited until John came along.

"Hello, John. I just stopped by to tell you your mother thought you better start home pretty soon."

"I know. She wants me home early to take my bath."

"She's still busy with her jam. If you're in the midst of a game you could finish it all right."

"I wasn't playing. I was just watching."

They walked along together. "I used to play baseball at college," Lyman said, hoping John would say more, but they came to the corner and Lyman turned up toward the Town Hall. "Well, good night, John," he said.

"Good night, Father," John answered.

John seemed always to know just what he wanted to do, Lyman thought as he left him. It made him seem so mature, almost older than he himself sometimes.

Lyman unlocked the door of the Town Hall. The room had a cool cellarlike air that fitted the storage place of the town records. He lit the green-shaded student lamp on the table and opened his minute book. He liked this job of town clerk. When he had first taken office he had read over all the records. The earliest ones were written in homemade ink and were so badly faded he had to guess at some of the words. He liked coming across the names that were still alive in the town. A Converse had been there at the first town meeting. He came across the first time Ezekiel Williams, Negro, was listed as a taxpayer, and he found the mention of his father's death by a runaway horse. His father had been town clerk too, and Lyman, looking at his signature, saw how they formed their C's alike. He noticed the signatures of the other town clerks: an Ephraim Whipple, a Matthew Harget, Timothy Green . . . He wondered if any one of them had sat here at this desk writing the records down with a letter in his pocket that poked fun at this office.

Oh, Lyman, Isabel had written, *I can see you in your office at the Town Hall inscribing all the births and deaths and marriages, like the figure of Fate. Do you draw a solemn face over the problems of the town and give your measured judgment? Only don't be ponderous, Lyman, it seems to be a state that men are prone to. I met Chauncey one week end last spring on business matters and he is so ponderously serious over his health, which, however, is pathetic.* Lyman touched the letter with his fingers as he reached in his pocket for his pipe.

Asa Pettingill came straight from his milking and smelled of the barn. But it was better than the scent of hair oil that Oliver Weatherbee exuded. Dr. Gaines seemed always to have a whiff of ether about his broadcloth coat. John Peterboro smelled properly of bay rum and boot polish; he took his position seriously and dressed up for the meetings. Ezekiel Williams, newest selectman, came in last and took his seat at the long table, his dark bright eyes shining with pride at his place here.

"Read that last motion again, will you?" John Peterboro asked.

Lyman read: "That the selectmen be instructed to dispose of the apples in the graveyard on the hill and appropriate the avails of the same toward re-erecting fallen headstones and improving conditions of graves in said yard."

Asa Pettingill nodded. "Might as well, it won't cost us a penny and I like to see a graveyard kept up. It does credit to a town."

Lyman crossed a *t,* thinking how Isabel would smile at the serious business of the town selectmen of Painesville. Not even an apple should go unaccounted in Vermont. It was growing to be a habit for him to see things both through his own mind and through Isabel's— but not all things. He never looked at Louisa through Isabel's eyes, nor at his own living here with her. He had the feeling that Isabel would be clever and a little cruel. Kindness was natural to him.

Lyman was the last to leave, locking the door behind him as he left. On the porch of the hotel the guests sat rocking in the warm summer dark. Their rockers, teetering on the planks of the porch, and their low voices were coming to be as much sounds of the summer night as the chirp of the frogs below the bridge. The summer boarders in the town were a source of never-failing excitement and interest to Louisa. All she learned about them she passed on to Abbie and Lyman at meals. When she appealed to Lyman now and then after some particular climax—as that Mr. Leicester from New York had taken his invalid wife's nurse out riding twice, and that people thought it certainly looked strange. "Don't you think so, Lyman?"—Lyman would pause before answering and say finally, "I don't know anything about it, Louisa, and care less." But he knew that Louisa and his mother discussed the summer boarders as they did up the supper dishes, and drew their own conclusions without his help.

"Lyman?" Louisa called from the dining-room where she sat mending when Lyman reached home. Abbie had gone to bed. The fragrance of the jam hung in the air.

"John get home all right?" Lyman asked.

"Yes. He came at eight, just as I told him to. He *is* so reliable, Lyman. For a boy his age I do think it's wonderful."

"He's twelve. If he's ever going to be relied on . . ."

"I know, but just the same . . ." Louisa had a way of beginning a sentence and not finishing it.

Lyman sat down in the straight-backed rocker. "I went over past the ball game tonight. John wasn't playing, Louisa. He seemed sort of out of things. It worried me."

Louisa smiled serenely as though from some secret source of wisdom. "John is different from other boys, Lyman. I'm glad you noticed it too. He's more thoughtful and quiet. I think already he feels he has a call."

"A call!" Lyman was disturbed.

"To the ministry. I used to pray as a girl that your brother Jonathan would give up the idea of farming and go into the ministry. I thought maybe the Godlessness of the army would lead him there, but now my son, named for him, will go into the ministry." Her hands were still over her work. Her face had a look of such happiness that he was silent. She was right, of course, John was *her* son, but . . .

"Has John said anything about the ministry? Have you told him what you hope he'll do?" Lyman asked.

"Not in so many words. It's too early yet, but I'm as sure as I am of my own name, Lyman!"

"It doesn't seem fair to John to plan for him that way, Louisa."

Louisa lifted her head as though to meet a challenge. "Do you suppose, Lyman, that half the men who fill important positions in the world would ever have done so without the dreams and prayers of their mothers behind them?"

"I . . . don't know, Louisa," Lyman said. "But promise me you'll let John alone to grow up and choose his own work. You pray and dream, but don't try to influence him too much."

Louisa's dark-brown eyes met his lighter ones that were as stern as Orville Converse's and fell back on her mending. She took up her needle and threaded it through the woolen sock with firm fingers. "You don't know how strong prayer can be," she said, as though to a child. "Oh, Lyman, don't you want some bread and jam? There's a little dish there in the pantry."

"No, thanks, not tonight. My stomach bothers me some."

Louisa lifted her face. "Mother Converse always said the Converses had weak digestions. She gave me her blackberry-cordial recipe she used to make for your father. It's easy to make except that I don't like having to put brandy in it, but I guess if you just use it for illness it's all right. Look at that, Lyman, you've gone right through that sock! Do you think it's any use to try to pull those threads together?" She held up one of his gray woolen socks.

"No, it's too far gone," he said, wondering at the things on which Louisa wanted his decision and the others which she decided for herself.

"I haven't locked up the barn yet," Louisa said.

"I'll tend to it," Lyman answered. On his way to the barn he stepped outside. It was hot for Vermont. The dark was like the fold of a dark blanket pulled too close around him, but the air was fresher than the atmosphere of the house. Inside, the heavy blackberry scent was sweet to suffocation. The sharp pointed roof seemed to bear down too sharply on the house, and the hourglass elm above the roof was an added weight upon it.

Lyman put his hand in his pocket and found Isabel's letter, like secret laughter. He stood there in the dark holding the thin blue paper with Isabel's handwriting on it, feeling a sense of escape. Then he remembered the postscript that he had hardly read and stepped close to the lighted window to read it again.

P.S. I am sending Louisa a box of hats I had early this season, thinking she might enjoy having a Parisian bonnet. The blue one, tell her, was from Worth. I only wore them one season, so they are as good as new. But if you think Louisa would not care to have my old bonnets, say nothing to her and burn them. I just thought a Paris bonnet might be fun to have in Vermont.

Isabel

He must get to the post office himself tomorrow in case the hats were there. Certainly he would never risk giving them to Louisa, but he would not tell Isabel that, she might smile too sharply. Neither would he destroy them. He might perhaps give them to Jewel.

"Lyman!" Louisa called from the woodshed.

"Coming," Lyman answered.

4

LOUISA packed Lyman's valise sorrowfully. As she moved around the bedroom taking out his best linen shirt that she had tucked herself, his black broadcloth suit, his lighter-weight underwear, she almost wished that she were going too. She crossed to John's room and took out his best suit, his shirts, and the tie made from one of her father's cravats. It was bad enough for Lyman to go without dragging John along. But she packed carefully, crumpling old paper patterns to keep things from wrinkling, remembering soda for Lyman and the cough mixture for John.

Abbie came and stood in the doorway of the bedroom. Her eyes were troubled, her lips puckered unsurely over her plate. Her tone of voice was apologetic.

"I'm sure I don't know what's got into Lyman, Louisa. I guess it's because he felt so bad when Daniel went. After he came back from out there he wasn't like himself till nearly spring."

Louisa made no answer, moving more busily at her task.

"I always said Daniel's wife was a good woman in spite of her being an actress and knowing Lincoln's murderer and all," Abbie quavered. Once Louisa and Abbie had been conspirators together, but through the years Abbie's oft-repeated comments had grown monotonous even to Louisa. Now when Louisa spoke of Mother Converse a tried note crept into her voice. People in Painesville said: "Louisa's just like an own daughter to Abbie Converse. Abbie's a lucky woman."

Louisa turned impatiently, her dark eyes snapping. "If he's just doing it for his brother's widow, why does he have to drag John along and give him a taste for play-acting? How does it look, with John intended for the ministry? A pretty thing it'll be when he's in a church if his congregation hears he has an actress for an aunt!" Louisa's tone of voice made Abbie directly responsible.

"They never need to know. I'm sure Daniel's wife never bothers us. In all these years she's never so much as come up here to see me nor brought her child that's my first grandchild, and we took her in without a word when Dan married her." Abbie passed the blame to Willie.

"I imagine Painesville was too small and dull for her!" Louisa said. "I wonder how her girl turned out?"

"I had a nice letter from Juliet when I sent her that bridal-wreath quilt I pieced for a wedding gift. She didn't marry an actor, you know."

John was so excited when he came home from school that Louisa sent him to fill the woodbox. Her tone was sharp, but she had the feeling that it didn't touch him. She watched him through the window and thought how tall he'd grown. At fifteen he was taller than she was.

"I guess I better change my clothes now. I saw Papa and Easy at the office. They'll be home by one o'clock."

"Easy!" Louisa said.

John nodded, but his face wore a guilty look. "I guess Easy's going with us." He fled upstairs. He was sorry he had said it. He didn't see why his father had to ask Easy to go along, either. Mama was provoked enough about their going without Easy's going too.

Louisa stood by the front window and pinched the dead leaves off the geraniums. Two bright spots showed angrily on her high cheekbones. Resentment stiffened her lips. She watched Lyman coming up the street, walking through the fallen leaves at the side of the path like a boy and waving his hand to Mr. Davis driving by. She noticed sharply how young he looked. He was forty and she was only forty-five, but it divided them. Her own hair was streaked with gray, Lyman's was still light. Sometimes she had the feeling that he kept things to himself. He didn't talk as much as he used to, or did she just imagine it? Once his caresses had frightened her a little, but now . . . It was odd that two people lying down to sleep in the same bed every night could be so separate. Then the uncomfortable feeling left her mind. Lyman was the handsomest man in town, she told herself with a satisfaction that she hid deep under her thoughts. Even if he had not sold the quarry and moved to the city, he wasn't countrified. That woman from Boston who stayed at the hotel last summer said her husband thought it was remarkable to find folks like herself and Lyman in a town this size. At the legislature the Montpelier paper had spoken of Lyman as "one of our outstanding Representatives."

"Hello, Louisa. John ready?"

"He's ready and waiting," she answered, more sharply than she meant. "You better change your own clothes."

While he dressed Louisa went out to the kitchen to fuss over the lunch she had packed for the train. Mother Converse was there by the window sewing carpet rags together.

"Louisa, it's just a pity you aren't going along," Mother Converse

266

said, and it was as though she voiced Louisa's own thought. "Lyman wanted you should. It nearly spoils the trip for him, your not going." Louisa was silent so long Abbie spoke again. "Louisa, I said it's a pity . . ."

"I heard you. It's very fine that Lyman feels he can go. I wouldn't feel right spending all that money to go and see someone all painted and powdered and acting on the stage."

"I suppose that's the way Orville would feel," Abbie said thoughtfully, "but it's really Daniel's wife Lyman's going to see."

"But he doesn't need to take John along." Louisa's voice had a hint of tears in it. Abbie tore vigorously at her carpet rags.

When Lyman came downstairs a scent of his Cologne came with him. The sunlight caught the front lock of his hair and gave it a brighter color. He wore the suit he had bought last winter for the legislature.

"I'm sorry you're not going, Louisa. I know Willie would like to see you. Come on, John."

The sound of the door knocker broke in on the uncomfortable tension in the room. "That's Easy," Lyman said. "Good-bye, Louisa." Lyman came up to kiss her, but Louisa stiffened.

"How could you take Easy with you! People will see you in the theater together, Lyman. I shan't let John go one step!" She put out her hand and held John's arm. She hadn't wanted him to go anyway and this gave her a good reason. She felt strong in the righteousness of her position.

Lyman's light-brown eyes looked steadily into hers. "I asked you to go first, Louisa. When you wouldn't, I asked Easy. He thought a great deal of Willie. Now Easy and John and I are going to Boston together."

Louisa looked back at him for a long moment, then her eyes filled. She gave a choked sob and hurried out of the room, past the front door where Easy was knocking again and up the stairway. John stood where he was, looking anxiously at Lyman.

"Come in, Easy!" Lyman called out cheerfully. "We're all ready. John, here's your bag. Good-bye, Mother. Take care of Louisa. We'll be back late Friday night." His voice sounded excited, almost glad. Then they were gone.

Louisa, crouching by the upstairs window, watched them go, wanting with all her soul to be going too—to Boston, to stay at the Tremont House, to see the shops. She could have gone with them and not gone to the theater. Willie could have come to the hotel to see her. She would have been pleasant but cool to Willie. She wondered how

Willie would look after all these years. She had heard that an actress's face aged sooner than anyone else's. She looked at her own in the mirror over her dresser. Of course her eyes were a little red now, but her skin was firm and clear and the color on her cheeks was her own. She would have liked Willie to see her.

Louisa flung herself across the bed without stopping to take off her shoes or fold back the quilted counterpane. Lyman could at least have come up and said good-bye. He could have asked her again. His brother Jonathan would never have acted like this. Lyman got so stubborn. Then her anger moved to Easy. He was always trying to go places and do things with Lyman as though he were just as good as anyone.

About five Abbie tiptoed anxiously up to her door and opened it a crack. "Louisa, I've made some supper for us."

"I don't care for anything, thank you, Mother," she said in a sad, tried voice. Abbie would tell Lyman that she felt so badly she didn't eat a thing for supper.

By the time it was dark she was both hungry and bored with lying on her bed. She wouldn't go down just yet. Mother Converse would go to bed early. Then she thought of Lyman and Easy and John getting into Boston. She lay imagining the city: the hansom cabs and private carriages, the street lamps and people in crowds, the great houses back of iron fences, and churches and city buildings. She had only been to Boston once with her father and once with Lyman. People wore white gloves to the theater. She could have worn her five-button gloves and her striped taffeta . . . and Lyman never could tie his tie so it looked right! John had never been to Boston, she would like to watch him looking at everything. Perhaps people would think that Easy was their servant. Easy did have good manners.

The church bell ringing for midweek prayer meeting was a relief. Louisa slipped off the bed and smoothed the spread. She put on her hat and hurried down the stairs. "I'm going to prayer meeting, Mother," she called out, her voice as clear as the church bell.

"Oh, Louisa, take a cup of tea first," Abbie pleaded.

"No, thank you," Louisa said sweetly. "I don't want to be late."

Louisa was up early the next morning. "This will be a fine chance to go up and clean the house on the hill for winter, Mother. I've been over to the livery stable and they'll let us have a horse and buggy. It'll only be a quarter if we drive ourselves."

Abbie's head ached after the disturbance of the night before. She drank her tea before she answered. Sometimes Louisa wore her out and she almost wished she were living by herself.

"I don't feel very spry, Louisa. The house hasn't been cleaned since spring and it'll be a sight."

"You won't have to do very much, Mother, just help me go through the closets and drawers. I'm going to get Jewel and Sam or one of those children to do the hard work. I'll give them a dollar for the day."

"I don't know as Lyman would like that, Louisa. Jewel never would take any pay. It was more like being neighborly," Abbie objected.

"Oh, well, I guess she'll be glad of the money. It'll be a load off my mind getting that place cleaned up once more." Louisa was already carrying their few breakfast dishes over to the sink, and by eight o'clock they were on their way up the quarry hill.

Abbie sat quiet most of the way. She had been sick last spring when Louisa cleaned the house and she hadn't been up all summer. "I remember when Mary Davis used to live in there," she said, pointing to an old turnoff. "The Pettingill folks lived up this road, and the Springs. Hannah Spring was married three months before I was and my Jonathan was born about the same time her Lionel was born."

Louisa's mind was intent on other things. She hardly listened to Abbie's wandering reminiscences.

Abbie caught her breath. "Right there's where they found Orville." She stared at the tumbled stone wall and the beech tree beyond it. "Sometimes I'm glad Orville didn't have to know 'bout Daniel's death, but he'd take a lot of comfort in Lyman and your John."

"I guess Father Converse wouldn't think much of their going off to the city to see Willie act," Louisa said tartly, and then was sorry.

Louisa drove in past the house and tied the horse in the old shed. When she saw Opal, Easy's youngest child, she sent her to ask her mother to come and help. The little girl shook her head. She stood on one leg and studied Louisa.

"No, ma'am, she can't 'cause she's over the hill birthin' a baby."

"Whose baby?" Louisa asked.

"The Pringles'. They come an' got Ma early this mornin'."

Louisa made a tsk with her teeth. Pringles were shiftless folks who had some eleven children already.

"Are you the only one home?"

Opal shook her head. "No, ma'am, Ruby's home."

"Oh, well, that's fine. You go and tell Ruby I'd like her to help me. Let's see, Ruby has been away, hasn't she?"

"She's been in Boston," Opal answered proudly.

"In Boston! Was she working?"

The little girl nodded. "Some of the time, but I don't think she can help you, 'cause she's been sick."

"I'll go and see her." Louisa was impatient. She walked up the path to the low sprawling white house and noticed the clean doorstep and the curtains in the windows. She knocked briskly.

Ruby opened the door. She wore a faded dressing-gown and her hair was pinned on her head in some semblance of a pompadour, but she was hardly more than a shadow of herself. Her eyes looked coldly at Louisa.

"Oh, Ruby, I wonder if you can't help me clean the house for the winter. Mr. Converse is away and it's such a good chance to do it."

"I'm sorry, Mrs. Converse, I don't feel able to."

"When do you expect your mother back?"

"I don't know, but she doesn't do cleaning for folks any more," Ruby said.

Louisa hesitated a minute. "If she gets here in time, maybe she will for me. Mr. Converse took your father down to Boston, you know."

"That's right, I did hear Mr. Converse was going with him," Ruby answered. "I'm still pretty weak, Mrs. Converse, so if you'll excuse me."

The door closed and Louisa walked back over to the big house. It wasn't so much what the girl said as the way she said it that angered Louisa. It was all Lyman's fault, he gave them ideas. Well, she would pitch in and do it herself, then!

Abbie had unlocked the house and gone in, but the familiar rooms were too much for her. She sat in the chair in the kitchen looking around as though she were waiting for someone. Louisa walked briskly through the house.

"It's not as bad as I expected. Just dust is all, and the windows can stand washing. There, Mother, I'll build a fire here so you'll be cozy and you just sit here till you're rested," Louisa said in a kindly tone. Abbie sat so still, her hands idle in her lap and her face so empty and sad it made Louisa uncomfortable.

It was a relief to Louisa to be doing something. She built the fire and put water on to heat and then started upstairs and worked down. She wiped woodwork and polished windows till they shone, and blacked the little parlor stove so it wouldn't rust. Upstairs, in the chamber above the kitchen the roof had leaked and mice had left tracks over the washstand. She glanced out the window that opened on the woodshed roof remembering Lyman's saying he used to climb out there. The whole house was too big for one woman to do in a day, but it satisfied Louisa to wear herself out while Lyman was off having a good time. She wondered if he would even remember to bring her something from Boston.

"This house ought to be sold," she said aloud in the parlor. "All this good furniture not doing anybody any good!" She tore clean sheets to cover the mirrors so the frost wouldn't turn them green and wavy and wrapped all the lamp chimneys in old newspapers from the stack in the woodshed. One was dated May 1864. A headline spread across two columns telling of the Battle of the Wilderness. She read a sentence or two, remembering the day that paper had come. It was the next day's paper that had listed the Vermont casualties with John's name. For an instant the old desolate grief swept through her, wiping out scruples against theatergoing or real or fancied hurts. But she fell to wiping the oval picture frame above the mantel and the feeling disappeared.

"I declare this house is more of a job than ours in town," she told Abbie.

"It's a big house," Abbie said. "Orville's father built it for a big family. But it's a pleasant house. I'd forgotten how nice a view there is from the kitchen window," she added wistfully.

"Well, I guess we'll go. I do think Lyman ought to sell it."

"I'd hate to see it sold," Abbie said. "All my children were born here and I came here as a bride . . ." But Louisa wasn't listening. She went back to pull the shades halfway on the windows.

Jewel came up the road as they drove out of the yard. She had a bandanna tied over her head and carried a basket. When she saw Abbie her face lighted up. She looked hardly older than the day she had come to Vermont.

"I wish you were staying up on the hill, Missus Converse, I surely do," Jewel said. "I'm sorry I wasn't here to help you."

"What's the matter with Ruby, Jewel?" Louisa asked.

Jewel's face sobered. "I don't rightly know what ails the girl. She just don't feel good. I think travel will sprink her up."

"I thought she just came from Boston!"

"Yes'm, she did, but she didn't have a very good job. This time Mistah Converse goin' to see Miss Willie about takin' Ruby to help her dress an' do her hair an' all. Ruby'd be good at that."

"Oh," Louisa said, irritated that Lyman didn't tell her these things. "How are the boys, Jewel?" Abbie asked.

Again Jewel's face came alive. "Jus' fine, thank you. Orville's goin' to the Bible School in Virginia an' he'll be havin' his own church pretty soon."

"Why, is Orville going to be a minister, Jewel?" Louisa found it difficult to keep annoyance out of her voice.

"Yes'm. He's got a knack for preachin'. An' Sam's down to Boston in a great big hotel. He says he's goin' to get him a job on a train. Sam allus was for travelin'."

"Then you only have Ashwood and Opal here," Abbie said.

"Tha's right, an' Ruby right now. Ash is drivin' for the quarry."

"I expect Easy will have a good time seeing Miss Willie," Abbie said. Jewel beamed. "Seemed like he couldn't hardly wait to get goin'."

The two women drove down the quarry road in the late October afternoon. Abbie looked back and saw Jewel still standing in the driveway of her old home, waving. Halfway down the hill they passed one of the oxloads of soapstone and Ashwood, Easy's youngest boy, walked beside the oxen, flicking his long whip at the red leaves overhead.

The next day of Lyman's absence Louisa cleaned their own house in the village. Abbie felt she was possessed. By suppertime she was looking out the window toward Malden and dressed up in her best brown challis with the gold brooch at her neck.

"They couldn't get here in time for supper, Louisa," Abbie said.

"No, but they may be hungry when they do get here. I thought I'd have something ready for them."

Abbie went to bed at ten, but Louisa waited up. She knit furiously at a sock while she waited. How would Lyman be? He could be so stern and silent. Maybe she had said too much. If she just hadn't come out so firm and said she wouldn't go, she could have changed her mind at the last. Louisa got up restlessly and moved across the room. She took a piece of the candied ginger she saved for teas from the covered dish on the parlor table and ate it hungrily. She would tell Lyman how pretty the house on the hill looked and say maybe they could go up for a week next summer. That would please him.

It was after twelve when she heard them stop. Her hands were cold as she put her knitting away and went to the door, and her voice sounded high and eager as a girl's. "Hello! I was afraid you weren't coming tonight," she called.

John came right in, but Lyman stood talking to Easy a minute by the buggy.

"How was it, John?"

"Oh, Mama, she was wonderful! We had supper with her afterward in her room in the hotel."

"Easy too?"

"Yup. Aunt Willie thinks a lot of Easy."

"How . . . how does she look?"

"She's beautiful," John said solemnly. "Even with the paint. Papa says they have to wear that or they look pale in front of the footlights."

Louisa didn't like his excitement. "Poor Aunt Willie. I don't think it would be much of a life going from place to place acting all the time."

"I think it would be great," John said. "But Aunt Willie says being a minister is kind o' like being an actor."

"Why, Jonathan Converse, it wouldn't be anything like it!" Louisa said indignantly. Then she heard Lyman coming and sudden embarrassment made her disappear into the pantry.

"I thought you both would be hungry after your long ride," she said, bringing out the cold chicken and fresh-baked bread. "Did you have a good trip, Lyman?" She started back for another plate without looking at Lyman coming over to her.

"I'm sorry you weren't there, Louisa." He kissed her on the forehead.

She wanted to say, "I am, too. I wished I had gone," but she couldn't say it.

"I had no idea how good Willie was," Lyman was saying. "I was almost afraid when I went, but she's . . . why, she's a great actress, Louisa!" There was a strange, elated note in Lyman's voice.

"In that red-velvet thing at the end wasn't she beautiful, Father?" John asked.

"Yes, in the court scene. She was Portia, Louisa, in *The Merchant of Venice.*"

Louisa filled Lyman's cup. Her throat felt dry. Lyman and John both seemed different. She felt left out. She didn't mean to say it just then, but she came out with "Well, your mother and I went up on the hill and cleaned your house. It was a job! Your mother couldn't do much and Jewel was away. I thought I could get Ruby to help me, but she said she was 'too sick.'"

Lyman looked anxious. "Easy said she wasn't well."

"Is she really going to work for Willie, Lyman?"

"Yes, Willie is glad to have her. And she will be taking her to London this winter."

"Think of it, Mama, Aunt Willie acted in London last year!" John put in.

Louisa looked from one to the other. They didn't seem to know what they were eating, they hadn't said a word about the currant tarts. She rinsed the dishes and left them on the sink board without washing them.

"You better get up to bed, John," she said shortly. John came back downstairs half-undressed.

"Here, Mama, here's the playbill. I brought it home for you." He handed Louisa the printed sheet. "There's her name, Miss Willie Delaney."

"She doesn't use her married name!"

"She wouldn't, knowing how Father felt about the stage," Lyman said.

Louisa went ahead up the stairs. It was good to have Lyman back, but she wished he'd get through talking about Willie. Lyman opened his valise and took out the clothes Louisa had packed so carefully. He had stuffed them in any which way.

"Here, Louisa, Willie helped me buy this for you. She says it's the latest fashion." He took out a fur collar.

"Oh, Lyman, it's beautiful! There isn't another like it in town!" All the stiffness went out of Louisa's manner. She put the short cape over her brown dress and stood in front of the oval mirror. The black sealskin set off her hair and dark eyes.

"Like it?" Lyman asked.

Louisa dropped her cheek against the fur. "It's lovely, Lyman. Thank you." But afterward in the dark she had the feeling that he was still thinking about Boston. She asked about Willie and Juliet.

"I brought some pictures of them for Mother. I'll show them to you in the morning. Juliet looks even more like Dan than she used to."

Then there was the silence again. She wished she could tell Lyman how she had missed him. Instead she said, "Lyman, you don't think seeing a play and everything gave John ideas, do you?"

"In God's name, Louisa, it wouldn't hurt him to have some ideas about some place besides Painesville. He's fifteen, you know. I think it was a fine experience for him. Next year he'll go to Brown—the seminary, if that's what he wants. He needs to get some ideas."

Louisa lay silent, worrying. Lyman had as good as sworn.

Lyman had his own thoughts. He felt as though he had been contented with too little here. What was his life but a humdrum row between the quarry and the office and his home? Louisa belonged to his brother John, now as surely as the day John went away to war over twenty years ago. He himself had never really taken his place. As for young John, Willie's eyes had twinkled talking about him. "Why, he's like your brother when I first knew him," she had said. "Before he'd been through the war. He changed, you know. He would never have married Louisa when he came back. You were always too kind, Lyman!"

Willie had said so many things that stayed uncomfortably in his mind. He had waited until they were by themselves to ask Willie about Isabel. Isabel had gone from Paris over to London last winter to see Willie act, but all she had written was: "Willie made the best Lydia Languish I have ever seen. She had splendid notices. It was so good to talk to someone who knew you, Lyman."

"Why, Lyman, Isabel's in love with you!" Willie said. "Did you realize it?" The knowledge put into words had been with him all the way home.

"Is she happy in Paris, Willie?" was all he could manage for an answer.

"Happy?" Willie made a little face and spread her hands. "That means so many things, Lyman. She loves living in Paris. She knows interesting people, Daudet and Augustine Brohan—all kinds of people who are doing things. She works hard at her painting and she's an exquisite person, Lyman, not beautiful, almost homely in a way, but different from anyone else!"

Now he lay in the dark and savored each word Willie had spoken about Isabel, picturing her, remembering, until his yearning for her was intolerable. The things he had taken pleasure in all these years seemed nothing: the little notes on foreign paper, like hidden laughter in his pocket, he had told himself, the "Faithfully" at the end of her letters. What were these for a man to live on? He hadn't seen her since '72, sixteen years! He turned restlessly to get away from his own frustrated feeling.

As he turned Louisa reached out her hand and touched his shoulder. "Lyman, perhaps I was . . ."

Without a word he drew her soft body to him, measuring his thigh against hers, feeling her breast against his chest.

Lyman went downstairs in his nightshirt. His bare feet made hardly a sound as he walked through the dark house. He sat down in the kitchen and buried his face in his hands. He would never go back to share that room or that bed.

He was no better than a man who buys a woman for his pleasure, he told himself, he was lower because he was less honest about it. He had filled his mind with Isabel, making himself believe for a little while that he held her in his arms instead of Louisa. Once Louisa had tried to speak but he had stopped her lips with his own so he couldn't hear her. He had been at the quarry as on that Sunday morning so long ago and his lips were on Isabel's.

Now he told himself in excuse that Louisa had called for John when she was in labor, but that was not the same, she was delirious. Perhaps he had been delirious, in a sense, but nevertheless a deep sense of shame filled his mind. If he could tell Louisa, he would feel better, but he couldn't. Louisa could not understand such a thing. It would mean telling her that he didn't truly love her, that he never had; that all these years . . .

A little light came through the window and fell across the kitchen table. He stared at it dully, trying to see it as it moved deeper into the room, but he could only see it after it had spread. Its advance was as imperceptible as the steps by which he had come to marry Louisa. He was cold and cramped from sitting in the straight wooden chair. He went back upstairs and lay on the bed in the spare room across the hall, where Louisa had spread her best challis dress and the new fur cape. After a long time he fell asleep.

5

Dear Isabel:

This is a strange letter to write. I have thought a long time before penning it. A month ago Louisa gave birth to her second child, a son. We have named him Holbrook, Louisa because it was Mother's maiden name, I because it is in a sense your child. I let myself think that it was you I held in my arms when I begot it. It was wrong, a wrong against both of you, but hearing Willie talk about you made me want you so terribly, and it has been so long a time.

Lyman sat back in his chair, drawing idle lines on the black-velvet top. Would Isabel understand? Would she be shocked? Now in the middle of the morning the illusion of that fall night seemed impossible. It might seem so to Isabel. If he could tell her, watching her eyes and her mouth that changed so quickly with her thought . . . but it wasn't a thing to put on paper. Holbrook was Louisa's child, Louisa's and his. He tore the sheet into small pieces and carrying them over to the stove, set fire to them. Then he took a new sheet.

August 12, 1889

Dear Isabel:

I have been a long time answering your last letter, but certain circumstances will explain my delay. A month ago, just three months after Mother's death, Louisa gave birth to a baby boy. We have named him Holbrook because it was Mother's maiden name. I hardly need add that the name is dear to me for other reasons as well.

The baby is strong and healthy, but Louisa has been ailing since. John enters the theological seminary in the fall, which gives his mother great joy and satisfaction.

The check from the quarry is somewhat smaller this time, I am sorry to say. Our salesman in Boston resigned his position and indeed the orders he has turned in of late have been negligible, so he is no great loss. Soapstone is not so much used in building now as formerly, but there are still plenty of fields in which it is indispensable.

It is hard to believe that Ruby is a professional singer. I understand what you mean when you say she has distinction. She deserves her success after nearly starving to death in her first attempt in Boston. It is odd that Paris should be more generous in accepting a colored skin than America. You should see Easy's face when he talks about her. He has need of his pride in her. Ashwood, his youngest boy, got himself a child by a slattern white girl who lived near the mill. He married her, but they are practically ostracized in the community. He is only seventeen. Easy asked me if I wanted Ashwood to give up his job in the quarry and I of course said no, but none of the men will work beside the boy. He drives the ox team alone. I understand that Orville, my father's namesake and Easy's oldest boy, is an eloquent preacher. Easy's firstborn and mine both ministers! As the years go by Easy and I have more and more in common.

I have read with pleasure the new book by Daudet that you sent, and taken pride in the fact that he is a friend of yours. I thought what a difference there is between his Thirty Years of Paris *and my thirty years of Painesville. We have, however, this in common, that we both know you.*

Faithfully,

Lyman

P.S. Thank you for sending the new box of hats to Louisa. She was greatly pleased with them and will enjoy wearing them to Montpelier when I go to the legislature in the fall. I believe she is supplied now for some time to come.

L.

He reread the letter. That was better, safer anyway. He frowned over his postscript. It would have been simpler if he had given Louisa the first box of bonnets Isabel sent, but he hadn't, and now Isabel would keep on sending them.

The stage was in when he came past the post office, so he gave his letter to the driver. Five Negroes had come in on the stage and stood around the post office laughing and talking together. They were all elaborately dressed. The women wore veils and wide-brimmed hats. The two men wore louder suits than was the custom in Painesville. Both of them smoked cigars that left a heavy smoke under the elms.

As Lyman came by one of the men stepped up to him. "Please, can you tell us how to get up to 'Zekiel Williams's place?"

"Yes, it's two miles up that hill," Lyman said, wondering. "Does Mr. Williams know you are coming?"

"Well, no, not rightly, but his son Sam told us we could board up there."

"We want to get out of the dreadful heat in Boston!" one of the women explained in a high, affected voice.

"Tha's right!" another woman said, and they all burst out laughing.

"Well, you can hire a buggy at the livery stable up the street, or if you wait about half an hour, one of Mr. Williams's boys will come by with an empty wagon he carries soapstone on. If you don't mind perching, you could ride up on that."

"Thank you kindly, sah. That sounds all right to me."

"That'll give us time to see this burg," one of the women said, and again came that shrill laugh.

They left their bags on the platform of the post office and sauntered up the main street, a curious spectacle to the prim windows of the watching houses. The village was used to Easy and Jewel, but not to strange Negroes.

Lyman stopped at the store for groceries on his way, so that when he reached home he found Louisa had already seen the newcomers.

"Did you ever in your life see such get-ups!" Louisa had been listless since the baby's birth. He was glad to see her interested.

"They're quite a sight," he agreed.

"Where do you suppose they're going?"

"They're going up to Easy's to board, they said."

"Oh, Lyman, they'll prowl all around your house and probably through it. I wouldn't be surprised to hear they were sleeping there!"

"Not if I know Easy. The town's full of white boarders every summer, a few dark ones will give us some contrast. How are you feeling?"

"All right. The baby slept all forenoon."

"Stay right there and I'll bring you something to eat," Lyman said. He was very gentle with Louisa. Since Abbie's death in the winter he had helped about the house. If the baby cried in the night he took care of it. He had moved his things into the spare room and Louisa had made no protest. The doctor's shaking his head over her having another child made the move seem reasonable. They had never spoken of the night that Lyman came back from Boston.

Lyman took the baby out to Louisa to nurse and she lay there in the cool woodshed with the sun making a lattice pattern across her light dress and the baby's head. Lyman stood a minute remembering the time he had stopped in when Dr. Tucker was alive and he had been just a boy. Louisa had looked so tranquil with the same lattice shadow falling on the sheet she was hemming.

"I'm going up to the quarry this afternoon, Louisa. Would you like Maudie Peterboro or Esther to stay with you?"

"No, I don't need anyone. I'm going to start a shirt for John. Look,

Lyman, Holbrook looks like you, only I believe he's going to have red hair. I had an uncle with red hair, Uncle Rudyard. I suppose he takes after him."

Lyman laughed. "That's just the sun on it," he said, but he looked at the reddish color of the baby's hair and thought of Isabel's hair with a kind of superstitious wonder.

Since spring Easy had been foreman of the quarry. Two men had threatened to quit and Lyman had let them go. They came from somewhere east of Painesville. In Painesville, Easy was a town selectman. People hardly remembered he was colored except when they thought of Ashwood. Ashwood and his white wife lived by themselves well out of town in a little shack below the mill. Lyman felt sorry for the boy living in such a place after the comfort of Jewel's house.

Today Lyman passed Ashwood driving the wagon up the hill with the Boston Negroes chattering on it.

"Man, look at that classy house!" one of the Negroes called out as they caught sight of the Converse place.

Lyman smiled and touched up the new four-year-old that had replaced Scout. He arrived at Easy's house in time to warn Jewel about the boarders. Jewel was upset. "Sam never wrote me, but then he's no good at writin' letters. How long you s'pose these folks'll stay, Mistah Converse?"

"Charge them plenty, Jewel, and they won't stay so long."

Jewel's eyes calculated. "You think four dollars a week's about right?"

"For bed and board? Oh, I'd make it seven, Jewel, a dollar a day. Where will you put them?"

"This weather Easy an' me an' Opal can sleep outdoors. Oh, we got plenty of room, only I don't know's I like havin' strangers in. Let me show you the lace Ruby sent me from Paris!" Jewel brought out several yards of cotton lace wrapped in tissue paper. "From Paris, Mistah Converse. It makes Paris seem as close as Bennington, don't it?"

"Almost, Jewel," Lyman said.

He was thinking of Paris as he drove on over to the quarry. It was dull in the late summer, Isabel wrote. The leaves of the trees on the boulevards were covered with dust.

It was dusty here, too, and the blackberries growing along the stone wall were filmed over, but there was not enough traffic on the hill road to stir the dust into the air. He supposed it was duller here, but he never stopped to think about it any more. His own work filled his days. He wondered if Isabel would find him dull if they were to meet after all these years. Then he heard the sounds of the quarry: the voices of the men, the creak of the derrick, and the clang of a crowbar against stone. The quarry was hidden from the road, and the sounds seemed to come from the heart of the earth beneath the woods.

Easy stood deep in the quarry pit, but even from where Lyman was standing he looked big. He was taller than any of the men who worked with him. With the years his weight had come to match the width of his shoulders until he was the biggest man in Painesville, and the town took pride in his strength.

"Good and cool down here, Lyman!" he yelled up with a broad grin.

"Pretty far from Heaven!" Lyman called back, and the men working near enough to hear joined in the laugh. Lyman knew all the men by name. Some of them were older than he was. There was old Ephraim Davis, and Zadoch Grimes. There was Abe Hopkins, whom John had almost hired as a substitute, and Jim Bartholomew, who had started at the quarry the week after he got back from the army. Lyman loved this quarry best, even though the other one, closer to the railroad, made him more profit.

He stopped to watch the great blocks of soapstone swung out and spun around by the block and tackle to land at the loading point. He never could help touching the smooth greenish-gray stone, it was like nothing else he knew. They were cutting at a lower level, opening a whole new layer. Sometimes he marveled that the vein never ran out. Plenty there yet, the geologist from Montpelier told him, one of the richest veins in the East.

Lyman was on his way down, on a bench about twenty feet above Easy, when one of the men working there said, "I found something in the quarry I thought maybe you'd like to see, Lyman."

"What's that, Gillan?" Lyman asked. Gillan was one of the old-timers.

Gillan reddened. "I don't know if it's anything or not. Maybe it was just hollowed out by the rain, but I kinda got the idea it might have been a dish, some kind of a bowl, once." He took a rounded lump of soapstone from a niche in the wall and handed it to Lyman.

"They say the Indians didn't know of this deposit," Lyman said, "but maybe they did, after all. This does look like a bowl," he added slowly. "Some of the tribes did use soapstone, you know."

"You can have it if you want, Lyman. It's kind of a curiosity," Gillan said.

"Thank you. I'll put it down in the office." Lyman's hands fitted around the curved sides of the bowl. There was a pitted place where the weather had-eroded the surface, but the rest was smooth, and pleasing to the touch.

"We had to dig quite a big hole to find that there treasure!" one of the men joked.

"That's so." Lyman laughed with them.

"The thing hunted" Professor Gilmore had said the word "quarry" could mean. It had turned out to be an empty bowl, after all. He turned it again, feeling its deep hollow. Somehow it slipped from his hands. He moved quickly to catch it and stepped back off the ledge of rock.

A frightened cry went up from below. Gillan was closest to him and tried to grab his arm, but Lyman fell the twenty feet to the floor of the quarry. He landed upright with his full weight on his heels and fell forward unconscious. Easy was the first to reach him.

"For God's sake go get the doctor. Take Lyman's horse, he's the fastest," Easy said hoarsely. He picked Lyman up gently and carried him as though he were a child up the ladder to the next bench.

"Here, Easy, let me give you a hand," Abe Hopkins said.

"Get out of the way," Easy muttered, but he was breathing hard. At the next bench a smooth block of soapstone, longer than a bed, was roped ready for lifting to the loading ground.

"Here." Easy jerked his head. The man running the derrick was quick to see what he intended.

They laid Lyman on coats spread on the stone. Easy crouched protectively over him as the stone was carried out over the open quarry. Easy's lips were moving, but no one could make out what he said. A ghostly silence filled the quarry. The only sound was the creak of the hemp ropes lifting the stone and the anxious chug of the pump that kept the quarry free from water.

Easy carried Lyman to the cot in the little shed where he himself had hidden his first night on the hill. When Lyman opened his eyes, someone brought some rum and Easy poured a little between his pale lips. Easy's own face had paled to a dirty brown, his eyes were bright and troubled.

Lyman stirred, then he groaned.

"Where, boy? Where you hurt?"

"My feet," Lyman said and he groaned with a fresh spasm of pain. Easy cut off his shoes and held the feet in his big hands, warming them.

Long after quitting time the men hung around the quarry, sitting on the big blocks waiting. Ashwood Williams was there, apart from the others but near the little house, chewing a spear of grass, waiting too. The doctor and Easy were with Lyman in the office.

They carried him on the old cot all the way to Easy's. Lyman watched the trees above the road but they jerked and wavered so. The pain at the back of his foot, both feet . . . no, the right one was the worst . . . made him so weak. He closed his eyes and bit his lip to keep from crying out at the blockhead who jerked the end of the cot that way. Then he remembered something. He made a great effort.

"You've got boarders, Easy—my house," he managed to say.

The men set the cot in the kitchen of the brick house and Easy built a fire in the stove for all that it was August.

"You'll be with him?" Dr. Gaines asked outside.

"I won't leave him, Doc," Easy said. "How bad you think it is?"

"Both heels are broken, and the right one is bad. He'll never walk again without a cane. I'll stop and tell Mrs. Converse about the accident and I'll be back up tonight."

From Easy's house came a shriek of laughter and a loud Negro voice. Easy strode across the grass toward the voice.

"Easy, these are summer boarders from Boston Sam sent up here . . ." Jewel began when she saw him.

"I don't care who you are. You keep quiet as the dead!" Easy ordered. To Jewel he said: "Lyman fell in the quarry. He isn't ever going to walk again without he got canes." Then he went back to the brick house.

The first week of September Lyman had a letter from Isabel. He sat in the parlor of the house on Main Street and held the letter in his hand a long time before he opened it. Louisa had brought it up from the post office.

"Why don't you open your letter? You look as though you were afraid of it. It's from your cousin, isn't it?"

"It's just about the quarry," Lyman said. He slit the envelope and glanced over the page quickly. "Yes, that's all. The dividend check was smaller this last time, you know. I was afraid she'd be disappointed." He put the letter back in its envelope and slipped it in his pocket.

"Well, was she?" Louisa asked. "I guess it takes a lot to live in a foreign country like that!"

"She hopes the next quarter will make up for it. She never says a great deal." Then Louisa went on to the kitchen and Lyman took the letter out again and read it.

Dear Lyman:

With the birth of a new son to fill your mind I do not wonder that you hadn't written. My congratulations to you and Louisa. Of course I was delighted with his name. I am sending a little French dress and bonnet I bought for him yesterday and a funny thing that pleased me, perhaps because it made me think of the mantel at home—or was it that block of soapstone in the sun that morning at the quarry? It is a cat carved from soapstone that my friend Amy, the sculptor, found for me. Put him in your office and you will find yourself stroking his back. He looks just like a Maltese cat. On second thought, I shall keep him another week for myself before I send him on to you.

Ruby came in for tea the other afternoon. She has learned how to dress appropriately and she looked very well. I think she may have been a little homesick, for she talked about their house on the hill and each member of her family and you and your mother. She mentioned Ashwood—you see, I know them all now—and said, "That could have happened to me if I had stayed on in Boston without any job." Are colored people always tolerant, do you think, Lyman? If I had some sin to confess I should certainly choose Ruby to tell it to. Ruby was asked to sing the other night at a salon at Augustine Brohan's. She is a popular actress, you know. Ruby was quite a success.

As for me, I am taking painting lessons again and work every minute that there is light, not for the world, surely, because my paintings will never be that good, but for myself. To pay for them I am giving English lessons to a French girl who is an invalid. Her papa pays very well.

I went to the Church of the Madeleine this morning to ask a blessing on little Holbrook and then, suddenly, I found myself asking a blessing on us all, you and Louisa and me.

Faithfully,
Isabel

Lyman did not hear Louisa come back. She stood in the doorway of the dining-room across the hall watching him read the letter. He hitched his chair over to the parlor stove and tearing the letter into pieces, dropped it in. He was moving his chair back when she came into the room.

"Here's your dinner, Lyman," Louisa said.

"Thank you, Louisa. I'm going to try getting around tomorrow," Lyman said.

6

HOLBROOK became Holly the winter he was four. He had a red toboggan cap and red cheeks that were round as berries. The post-mistress called him "Holly" one winter morning when he trudged down the street with his father and the name clung to him. Lyman called him "Holly" in a letter to Isabel and she wrote back: "What a perfect name for a chubby, red-cheeked boy! Holly Converse, he'll carry it always." Louisa came to call him that too.

"Holly, sit up and eat your cereal!" "Holly, is your throat sore?" "Lyman, tell Holly he must not make faces in church!"

Holly followed Lyman everywhere he could. It was easy for Lyman to take him. His cane and the little boy's short legs made their rate of progress about even, and going with Lyman kept him out of Louisa's way when she was cleaning house, or baking, or having the Ladies' Aid. Holly liked best to ride in the buggy with Lyman, his sturdy little legs first sticking out straight, and then dangling down from the seat as he grew a little older. When they went through the covered bridge on the quarry road Holly always laughed aloud and said, "Go fast, Papa, and make it thunder."

Holly was completely at home at Easy's house because he went there so much. Lyman left him there when he went on to the quarry and he played with Opal and tagged after Jewel. Ash let him ride high up on the soapstone blocks and flick the heavy ox lash sometimes. Ash often had a child or two of his own along, lighter-colored with sharper-cut features than Ash's and the dull look of the girl who was their mother. Ashwood never stopped at his own house when he went by, keeping his eyes down the road. So Holly had to catch his rides with Ash by watching for the gray blocks moving slowly along past the trees or listening for the creak of the wagon and the slap of Ash's whip.

Lyman used to wonder sometimes at how easy it was to talk to Holly, remembering some of his uncomfortable attempts to talk to John. It was odd how different children could be. Louisa left Holly more to himself than she ever had John. When Holly was four she had gone to the World's Fair. Lyman hadn't gone because of his crippled foot.

"But you go, Louisa. Holly and I'll be fine."

"I s'pose I could get Esther to come in and get your meals and keep up the house," Louisa said, her eagerness to go in the cadence of her voice.

"Oh, no, that's not necessary. We'll go up and stay in the old house on the hill. Jewel will take care of us."

"Well . . ." Louisa anguished over going or not going all of June, but in July Lyman put her on the train at Malden.

"I do think, Lyman, it's an opportunity of a lifetime!" Louisa said anxiously. "If it weren't for that . . ."

"You're quite right to go, Louisa," he assured her. "There's no reason on earth why you shouldn't." He felt closer to her than he had in a long time because he could see how much she wanted to go, but that she felt she shouldn't. She was usually so sure of the rightness of what she did.

"You look fine in your new suit! You don't look more than twenty-five," he told her when he was seeing her off at the station.

Color flew into Louisa's face, her eyes brightened with pleasure.

How easy it was to do, how much better he felt because he had pleased her. Why weren't they like this to each other all the time?

"See everything, Louisa, so you can tell us about it. You don't do this every day."

Louisa leaned closer to him. "You do think we can afford it, Lyman?"

"Of course we can. The quarry's doing well," he answered heartily, embarrassed by her carefulness.

"You'll be all right?" she asked again.

"We'll be fine, won't we, Holly?" He was suddenly glad he had Holly.

"I don't believe I'd go if it weren't that John ought to see it. It'll be such an experience for him." John was to meet her at Springfield.

"I suppose you'll keep busy, Lyman?"

"Oh, yes. I'm going down to Boston on business while you're gone and . . ."

"I guess your letter-writing'll keep you from being lonesome."

Lyman looked at her quickly. What did she mean by that?

"'Board! All aboard!" the brakeman was shouting. People were crowding on now. Louisa was up on the platform of the train.

"'Bye, Mama!" Holly was calling. Lyman held him up on his shoulder so he could see better. Holly was throwing Louisa a kiss. She had climbed on in such a hurry that Lyman hadn't kissed her. He should step up on the platform now, but with his cane, and the Peterboros there . . . They were going to the Fair, too. Maybe she hadn't missed his kiss.

"Good-bye, Louisa." What had she meant? He imagined things. She had just meant busy with all the correspondence of the quarry, that was all. The train was moving. Louisa was waving, waving and smiling. He waved his hat.

"Well, Holly!" He walked back to the buggy wondering. Louisa couldn't know how he felt about Isabel. He reached in his pocket for her last letter and read it as they drove back to Painesville and Holly slept on the seat beside him.

> *Brittany*
> *July 4, 1893*

Dear Lyman:

I am always a little homesick on the Fourth of July. Bastille Day on July 14 is the Day of Independence here, you know, and the flags wave and the cannon are fired and the Parisians go on picnics, but I think nationalities reveal their differences most clearly in their celebration of their holidays. There is a fine fervor about Bastille Day, but none of that almost religious solemnity of our Fourth of July speeches. And naturally, France looks back to the flaming figures of the Revolution, we look back to Washington, Adams, and Franklin. There! Is that not a good point to make?

I am in Brittany, as you can see, and I love it here close to the sea. It is like Newport but better. It pays me to rent my apartment in Paris to American tourists, of which there are endless hordes, and live here very inexpensively and delightfully. I can make enough in three months to pay for the whole year's rent. Very clever of me, is it not? It is done in Paris all the time.

I live very simply here, even to wearing the wooden shoes and plain black dress of the peasants. I spend all day painting the square white houses and the wharves and the peasants themselves. I have thought some days when I have delighted in the little village, "This is what Lyman likes about Painesville, this tranquillity and simplicity, knowing all his townspeople. Maybe he has been right all these years to live in Painesville."

What you say about the soapstone from South Carolina sounds alarming. I mean that it is quarried so cheaply that they can undersell the New England soapstone. I suppose labor is cheaper there. Maybe you should try again to sell the quarry?

> *Faithfully,*
> *Isabel*

He had never told Isabel about his fall. He didn't want her picturing him with a limp, and somehow as long as she didn't know of his lameness it seemed unreal to him. Until he stood up or started to walk briskly across the office he didn't think of it himself.

It was good to be back in the old house on the hill. Holly's feet clattered back and forth through the rooms and up the stairs one step at a time. Lyman had to take one step at a time, too, on the stairs he had once raced up so carelessly.

Jewel set out their meals in the big old kitchen and they ate them at the long table Orville Converse's father had built. Once they sat there eating at noonday with the door open into the woodshed. The sun came across the woodshed floor and stood waiting just outside the door, one light golden foot on the sill. Lyman had forgotten to eat for thinking. He had a feeling of reaching deep down into the patience of the summer day, losing his own irritations and frustrations. Holly clattered his spoon against his plate and sang in a monotone Louisa would never have allowed at the table. There was no need to hurry through the meal. Lyman wasn't going down to the office this week, there wasn't much to do. They had enough stone quarried for all their orders. The order from Ohio had been canceled, the salesman in New Haven had sent in only a small order. There was no immediate building around Painesville.

Lyman thought of the Representative at the legislature last winter. Stevens had been on a committee with him. He was in the quarry business, he told Lyman. "Soapstone?" Lyman had asked. He remembered now how the man had smiled. "Oh, no, granite," he had said. "Vermont granite!" Lyman had thought of the two stones that rimmed the spring on the hill, one granite, hard and sharp and rough, the other soapstone, smooth and almost soft.

"I guess the soapstone business is dying out in the state," Mr. Stevens remarked.

"I haven't seen any sign of it yet," Lyman had answered. "I'm in the soapstone business myself." The man had avoided him after that, but Lyman had caught his eye on him several times in the meetings.

But there were signs and he saw them. He must make an effort this winter to find some new markets. But the biggest difficulty wasn't the demand as much as the expense of quarrying and transporting from a quarry so remote from the railroads as this. . . .

He looked over at Holly. Holly had fallen asleep over his meal without Lyman's noticing it. His head lay on his arm beside his plate. Lyman helped himself out of his chair and lifting Holly carefully over his shoulder, limped in to lay him on the one bed that Jewel had made up in the room off the parlor that had been Willie's. Now the house was too quiet. He opened the front door and went out to sit on the front step to smoke his after-dinner pipe. Here he was, at forty-five, sitting on his doorstep smoking his pipe in the middle of the day, he mocked at himself. He was no hustler, no organizer or promoter. What had he done with his life but keep a running business going a little longer?

He smoked and looked out across the meadow that stretched beyond the stone wall. Easy cut the hay on the place and sold it for him, keeping out enough for his own needs. The hay hadn't been heavy this year. Then Lyman saw something else. Three small green firs were growing in the west corner of the meadow, seeded from the woodlot beyond. They cast their low pointed shadows into the field. Why hadn't Easy cut them down? What would his father have thought of fir trees growing in the meadow as though the wilderness were creeping back into the fenced land that his own father had cleared?

The word "wilderness" fell into an old groove in his mind. That word with another. "The Battle of the Wilderness" Lyman said aloud wonderingly, remembering the shivers that the words had started down his spine when he was a boy. Jonathan had died in the Battle of the Wilderness. Lyman knocked out his pipe and limped into the shed to see if he could find an ax. The sun beat down on him as he crossed the meadow to the fir trees. His ax blows sounded thinly against the noonday stillness until the little trees were felled.

"Hey, Lyman, what you doin'?" Easy's hearty voice called across from the road.

"I'm cutting down these trees you missed," he called back.

"Oh, them! They don't bother me none. I kinda liked 'em in that corner." Easy laughed.

Lyman stooped to pull the trees over to the wall. Easy was right. He had no fears of the wilderness, only he, Lyman Converse, made something ominous out of three little fir trees. Some of the warmth and content of the summer day seemed to come back with Easy's comfortable laugh.

When Louisa returned from the World's Fair, John was with her. They seemed like strangers to Lyman. He drove them over from the station and listened as Louisa told what they had seen, turning to John for confirmation: "Wasn't it, John?" "I told John I wouldn't believe it if I hadn't seen it." "John thought so too."

Lyman studied John a little shyly. John was good-looking, with

Louisa's clear skin and dark eyes, but he seemed so serious. Next year he would graduate and be a full-fledged minister. Lyman looked for some sign of a God-given call. Perhaps . . . How could you tell? He couldn't ask John if he was sure, but he would have liked to know.

John belonged to a fraternity at Brown, not his, or rather not Chauncey's, but a fraternity. "Do you like the boys in it, John?" he had asked him diffidently.

"Yes, indeed, Father. The men are superior to any of the others, I think, and the scholarship standing is higher than . . ."

"Well, that's fine," Lyman said hurriedly.

"You look splendidly, Louisa. I believe the trip did you good!" Lyman said when they were home again.

Louisa flushed. "I feel fine," she answered.

They brought souvenirs back: the luster pitcher with a picture of the World's Fair on it and the words in gold underneath, the sandalwood fan, the six silver spoons with "World's Fair, 1893" engraved on them. These souvenirs came to seem to Lyman like landmarks.

That summer Louisa told him she had decided to put a porch across the front of the house. "I wouldn't be using your money. I've got a little left from what Papa willed me," she said.

"You keep that, Louisa. If you're sure the porch won't spoil the looks of the house, we can afford it, I guess."

They were standing in the sitting-room. Lyman was ready to go down to the quarry office. Louisa picked up the fan that was spread out on the marble-topped table for decoration. She wasn't looking at Lyman.

"I supposed you would want to save every cent you could from the quarry to send Willie and that precious cousin of yours!" Louisa's fingers closed the fan and evened the edges one against the other. Then she looked up and found Lyman staring at her, his face colorless, his mouth shut tight into a thin, hard line.

"Well, it's the truth," Louisa added, her eyes snapping. "Mother Converse told me one time how when you were in college you had such a case on your dear cousin Isabel that your father had to take you out of college." She was opening the fan now, spreading it out on the table as it had been.

Lyman limped past her out the front door. The door banged so hard the knocker sounded of itself.

"I don't care. I might as well say it as think it," Louisa said aloud to the startled room. And then she put her mind on the size of the new front porch. It would have jigsaw work coming down from the roof, like the house pictures she had seen at the Fair, and painted white against the brick it would add a whole lot to the looks of the plain old front. She could see herself sitting there of a summer afternoon and people, summer people who came from away, asking "Whose is that handsome house?"

She felt a trifle uneasy about Lyman as she went about her housework. But by the time she had finished dusting the room she told herself that if he was mad it just showed he admitted it was true.

"Where are you going, Holly?" she went to the door to ask, seeing the little boy's stocky figure trudging down the walk.

"To see Papa."

"Come right back here," Louisa said sharply. "You play right here in your own yard!" The little boy's face puckered up. "Here, come and get a cooky first," Louisa made amends.

John came out to the kitchen. He looked troubled.

"Mother, I couldn't help but overhear. Did Father, really? I mean, I always wondered why Father left college in the middle of his freshman year. I thought it was his marks."

"No, that was it," Louisa said ambiguously. "I guess you might as well know it. He was so daft about his cousin I guess he didn't study a word and just wasted his father's money. His mother was relieved when he married me and settled down."

John's eyes were still troubled as he went back to his studies, but not over his father's sins. He thought himself in love with a young lady in Providence whose father wanted him to give up the ministry and go into a bank. He would never mention it to his mother, of course, but perhaps his father might understand.

Lyman had not stopped at the office. He saw Oliver Weatherbee's white head bent over the desk by the window as he limped on down through the town as far as the covered bridge on the quarry road. But he was getting tired. His right foot ached and he came slowly back to the old carriage works. The works had been bought by a New Hampshire concern. The big warehouse was empty except for a few old sleighs. Then Lyman saw on the side of the old building an announcement that brought him to a standstill: his campaign poster. It was the first time he had seen it hanging in a public place.

FOR STATE SENATOR
LYMAN WEBSTER CONVERSE

His own picture stared back at him. He looked quite a bit like his father! He stepped closer to read the paragraph in smaller print:

Born in the state, of Vermont pioneer stock, owner of one of the lead-
ing soapstone quarries in the state; loved and respected by his em-
ployees and by his fellow townspeople; a leader in Church and com-
munity life. He has served his community as town clerk and Represent-
ative to the legislature (four terms). Honest, capable, loyal to Vermont
people and industries.

Lyman swallowed. The color had come back in his face. Of course
that wasn't all entirely true. Asa Pettingill and Gillan and Grimes had
done the writing. Asa was the town politician. He had planned places
for him to speak, people to see, he was the one who had persuaded
him to run in the first place. He remembered Asa's words: "Why not,
Lyman? You've got as good a chance as anyone. I don't know of a
mean thing you've ever done to anyone an' you've made the quarry
business grow when most business around here has moved out. Didn't
they get you to be director of the bank at Malden 'cause folks had so
much confidence in you?" And when he had objected that people
wouldn't want a man for Senator who was lame, Thad Davis's father
had called out from his chair by the stove at the back of the store:

"Your brain ain't lame, Lyman. That's what we want you to use for
us."

". . . loved and respected by his employees and fellow townspeople"
he read again slowly. He had seen the bills before, but not to read them
like this, alone. Pride warmed him like the sun, and he forgot about
Louisa for the rest of the day.

Lyman was not elected state Senator.

"It was powerful close, Lyman," Nathan Hall reminded him.

The house was full of people who had dropped around to offer con-
soling remarks. Louisa had been ready for them, ready to receive their
congratulations or consolations, whichever way it turned out, with
fresh-baked bread sliced thin and fruit cake and sweet cider in her
best goblets, or coffee. She wore the dress she had bought for the
World's Fair and was as gay as anyone, but the disappointment rested
like soggy dumplings on her mind. She had been thinking of herself
as a Senator's wife for several months now. The wives of the Senators
were always asked to pour at the big teas at Montpelier. . . .

"Lyman didn't really want it," she said to Maudie Peterboro. "The
quarry keeps him so busy."

"It certainly did look like he was going to get it there for a while,"
someone else was saying. Then Louisa looked up and saw Easy and
Jewel coming right in the front door as big as life. Maudie Peterboro's
eyes followed hers.

"You can be thankful they didn't bring any of those dreadful boarders with them. Do you remember last summer?"

Louisa nodded. Jewel and Easy were dressed quietly enough. Jewel wore a clean blue lawn and a blue-velvet hat with a blue rose caught under the brim. "Now where on earth would Jewel get a hat like that?" she murmured to Maudie.

"Oh, probably her girl, the one that sings, sent it to her. It looks kind o' French," Maudie surmised.

"How do you do, Missus Converse." Jewel came toward the two women.

"Why, good evening, Jewel. Did you walk all the way down the hill?"

"No, ma'am, we rode down," Jewel answered. "Is Holly gone to bed yet?"

"Yes indeed. He's been asleep a long time!" Louisa managed to make her voice sound reproving.

"Can I jus' take a peek at him? I brung somethin' for him." Jewel took a greasy-looking package from her bag. "It's a gingerbread man. My, he do love 'em!"

"How nice of you, Jewel. His room is at the back of the hall, upstairs," Louisa said patronizingly.

Easy's big hand shook Lyman's. "Well, there's one thing, Lyman, I'd get awful tired writin' you letters about the quarry every week if you was to be away all winter!" Standing in this crowded room he seemed bigger than he was. When he laughed the sound gathered up all the laughter in the room and swept it on its deeper wave out into the street and the fall night.

"That was it, Easy, I didn't want to give you writer's cramp, so I thought I better not win," Lyman said.

"We got the ground spaded up, next time we'll grow a real crop on this here election business," Henry Waite said. "Next time we'll see you get it, Lyman!"

"It's just that folks around the state don't know you like we do, Lyman," the Reverend Mr. Dwight declared.

"Some o' the boys from the quarry are outside. They don't want to come in, but they want to give you a hand, Lyman," Easy told him.

Lyman stepped out on the narrow front porch to shake hands with the men.

"Thanks," he said. "Thanks, Jim. Thanks, Abe. It was good of you to come. I feel almost as though I'd won the election instead of lost it. Here, wait till I get you some cider." He limped back in. No one offered to get it for him. The men had seen him around the quarry enough to know he liked to manage by himself. Jeb Fuller knocked Louisa's star-of-Bethlehem plant off the wire plant stand. It rolled off into the syringa bush and nobody saw it.

When everyone had gone but Esther, who was out in the kitchen helping Louisa wash up the cups and glasses, Lyman went out on the porch again. He had a queer elated feeling that was new to him. People in town thinking enough of him to come down when he'd lost the election! He wondered why. He had never given much thought to how people felt about him, he wasn't very sociable. He had tried hard at Brown to make friends. Since then he'd just gone along tending to his own business. He wished he could tell Isabel about this, but it wasn't a thing you could tell very well. He had run for a small office and lost it . . . that wouldn't tell her why he felt so good. He saw someone stopping in the road out in front, somebody in a ramshackle buggy. A man was walking toward the gate. It was Ash, Easy's boy.

" 'Lo, Ash!"

" 'Lo, Mr. Converse. I just thought—Rosy an' I had to come to town an' we was just drivin' by . . ."

"Well, thank you for stopping, Ash." Lyman went out to the buggy. "Good evening, Mrs. Williams," he said.

"Evenin', Mr. Converse," the girl everyone called Rosy answered.

Lyman sat for a long time on the porch step before he went back into the house. His lamp waited for him on the hall table. He locked the door and went upstairs, past Louisa's closed door, to his own room.

7

THE church looked just as it had for the last forty years, and yet it looked different today to Lyman. He had come late purposely, walking slowly up the street as the late bell was tolling. Holly was with him. Louisa had gone ahead with John, she was more nervous than he was. Lyman had marveled at John's coolness all through breakfast. Of course he had been preaching for six years now, in his church over in New York State. Louisa had been to hear him preach, but Lyman never had. That was queer when you stopped to think about it, because he had heard Easy's boy Orville one time in a little colored church in Boston.

Listening to Orville, he had forgotten the preacher was Orville Williams. He had looked like some young prophet out of the Bible burned brown under an Asiatic sun. But it had been the boy's voice that had surprised Lyman; it had such warmth and tenderness that it made his words say more than they did of themselves. The church had been a mean enough place: the window in back of the pulpit had one piece of stained glass, the other panes were painted a blotchy green. It was poorly heated, and smelled so that Lyman had pulled his coat more closely around him. When Orville had led his congregation in the singing, his voice had sounded like Easy's.

At the door of the Painesville church Lyman sent Holly on down the aisle to sit with Louisa and took his place in the choir before he looked up to see John sitting on the carved chair back of the pulpit. John wore the broadcloth Prince Albert coat Lyman and Louisa had given him when he graduated from the seminary. He looked young up there, Lyman was worried for him.

Then he saw Jewel come in with Opal and Orville and file into the last pew on the right. Orville Williams was home for vacation too! Lyman glanced around at Easy. Easy was beaming proudly.

The Reverend Mr. Dwight would never think of asking Orville to preach in this church, he knew, but to pray—a prayer wasn't as important as the sermon, and it would please Easy. Lyman took one of the old blue quarry cards out of his pocket—he used them for memoranda now. He wrote a note, then, leaning over the high rail that separated the choir loft from the pew in front of it, tapped Asa Pettingill on the shoulder.

Asa read the card and looked around at Lyman. His mustache drew down skeptically and he shook his head ever so slightly. Then, apprehension in every wrinkle of his thin alpaca trousers, he walked up the aisle to the pulpit. The Reverend Mr. Dwight came to the pulpit's edge and leaned over so that Asa could whisper in his ear. The action was the essence of secrecy. The minister read Lyman's blue pasteboard and glanced back at the choir and congregation. He crossed the platform to speak to John and Lyman saw John nod. John had always been like Louisa about Easy's children. Lyman relaxed. John had grown up.

The Reverend Mr. Dwight rose to read the notices for the week. "We are fortunate this morning in having in our congregation two sons of Painesville who grew to manhood here, receiving their first glimpse of God in this very room, perhaps. Both young men heard a call to go forth and preach the Word. It will be our pleasure to hear the Reverend Jonathan Converse preach to us this morning and to hear the Reverend Orville Williams lead us in prayer at the conclusion of the service. Will the Reverend Mr. Williams come up and sit with us on the platform?"

There was a stir in the church. Lyman glanced over at Louisa and thought he saw her back stiffen. The heads of the congregation turned to the right as though drawn by a string. It seemed a long moment before Orville rose and walked down the aisle to the pulpit. He was six feet tall and his tread made the boards of the aisle creak under the worn red-and-yellow carpet. Lyman glanced sidewise at Easy, but Easy's face showed nothing, only his big hands were knotted together between his knees more tightly than they needed to be. When they rose to sing the hymn before the sermon Easy's voice swelled joyfully, but Lyman could hardly sing for the nervousness he felt for John. He watched him across the congregation that was so largely made up of summer people now. Their hats contrasted sharply with the hats of the Painesville women, the haircuts of the men who had come from the city with the Painesville haircuts, but they were all a blur to Lyman. John's face was sober and confident. He was holding the hymnbook with Orville and they were both singing.

Nothing he had ever done himself, not even the speeches around the state when he was campaigning for Senator, had made Lyman so cold with nervousness. John walked over to the pulpit and turned the leaves of the big Bible. He wished John would smile or say a friendly word about preaching here where he had been a boy.

"The text for my sermon this morning is found in the First Book of Samuel, the second chapter and the twenty-fifth verse. 'If one man sin against another, the judge shall judge him; but if a man sin against the Lord, who shall entreat for him?'" John closed the Bible so that the heavy cover fell with a thud. He spread out the sheets of his sermon with a crackling sound on top of the Bible. He frowned sternly down on the pews.

"The text I have read to you proclaims a warning that is more greatly needed in our country and in our time than ever before in the world's history, perhaps. We have come to think that if we sin not against our fellow men we are leading upright lives worthy of the reward of a place in Heaven. But this is not so. We may still be utterly condemned for sinning against the Lord God of Israel!"

Lyman sat thinking this over. He doubted that. Sinning against your fellow men was something you knew about. If you didn't sin there, you weren't apt to be sinning against a God you didn't know too much about. How was John so sure? Was it just his youth? Lyman couldn't think of any time in his own youth when he had felt so sure of right and wrong.

John stepped to the other side of the pulpit as though he had been taught to do so. "Let me give you the setting for these burning words of Eli's . . ."

Lyman was surprised at John's grasp of the historical background, he talked about the old Jewish world as though he had lived in it. He spoke of the whores at the door of the tabernacle with righteous anger. Perhaps he looked at his sheets of paper more often than was good, but that didn't detract too much. His choice of words amazed Lyman. He developed his theme carefully and it was logical. He preached a little too long, but now he was coming to the summing-up.

"I tell you that we are so occupied with our sins against our fellow men that we never think of our sins against God, and the Lord our God is a jealous God . . ."

Was He? Lyman wondered. Jealousy was one of the most contemptible of man's sins. God should be above jealousy.

Suddenly Lyman wished his father could be here. His father had had little satisfaction in Jonathan, because he was killed so young, or in Dan, or himself, but this grandson would have made him very proud. Thinking about his father, Lyman lost the track of John's thoughts. He was raising his voice, describing the wrath of a jealous God, and his voice sounded strained and angry.

". . . for I warn you again in the words of the text that if you sin against God there will be no one to entreat for you." John wiped his face with a white handkerchief he extracted from the tail of his Prince

Albert. His face was flushed with his oratory. He lifted his hand and prayed rapidly,

" 'Let the words of our mouths and the meditations of our hearts be acceptable in Thy sight, O Lord, our strength and our Redeemer.' "

Lyman found his own hands cold and damp. He felt physically tired out. The boy had vigor in his preaching, even if what he said did not fall in with his own thinking, but Lyman had never been an orthodox churchman. As he sat in church he had thought his own thoughts mostly. He had thought of Isabel often, here in the quiet. There had hardly been a Sunday in all these years that he hadn't remembered the anguish of the Sunday when Isabel sat with his mother and Louisa over there by the window. He had sinned against God, probably, but he had no feeling of guilt or fear.

After the hymn Orville Williams stood before the pulpit where his father had stood so many years ago as a runaway slave. There were plenty of people in the room to remember that, Lyman thought. He lifted his long dark hand and the sun caught the underside that was lighter. His voice was deep and warm after John's.

"Dear God, we know that we have sinned against You again and again and again, and in the days of Eli an' Samuel there wasn't anyone to talk for us, we were lost. But since those Old Testament days Christ has come. You sent Him, Lord, and made Him a man so He'd understand us. And then He was killed for us, the worst way, the most shameful way, and buried in the dark earth that we're all afraid of. But the grave couldn't hold Him and He rose up and went up the golden stair to Heaven and there He is right now, pleading for us. And we sure thank You, God, that now there *is* someone to entreat for us, to set us free from the slavery of our sins. Listen to Him, God, because He knows how we are and why we do such bad things, and He can explain to You. We thank You for the warning our brother gave us this morning. Help us to remember it and do better. Amen."

The church was very still. Lyman looked around carefully. Some of the summer people were smiling; two women were whispering. He couldn't tell much from the backs of heads, but to him it was as though Orville had answered John. John had left them worried and Orville had given them hope.

Lyman didn't linger after the benediction. He could see Orville sometime up on the hill. He didn't want people to feel they had to praise John to him. He felt as embarrassed as though he had preached himself.

As he came out of the church onto the grassy path that led to the road he felt the same relief he always used to feel as a boy when church was over and he could stretch his legs. Holly shot out of the crowd and came after him and they went slowly down the summer street well ahead of anyone else.

"I fell asleep once," Holly said. "Church always makes me sleepy, church and spelling and . . ."

"And Sunday dinner." Lyman smiled at him. He went on down to the post office to get the Sunday mail. When he found a letter from Isabel he took it into the quarry office to read. He hadn't expected a letter this month.

June 29, 1900
Brittany

Dear Lyman:

Ruby is down here with me. I brought her in the hope that the sea air would do her some good, but I am afraid it won't help. She has tuberculosis and the doctor in Paris tells me there is no hope of her getting well. If we had suspected it sooner, perhaps, though he says that wouldn't have made much difference. She knows it, and takes it with amazing indifference. Do you think it is because colored people have had so much sorrow as a race that individuals do not expect to be free from it? While we do, and are enraged when something happens to us, or at least I am. But the poor child misses her singing and she cannot bear to tell her mother and father. She thinks you can do that best.

She has come to mean very much to me and I cannot reconcile myself to one so alive and proud and full of music dying in her twenties. She has many friends in Paris, all white, both young men and women. She could have married. That she hasn't is not because of her color—that would not make any serious difference here in Paris to the young artist who is madly in love with her—but because she is not in love, unless it it is with her singing.

Chauncey came to see me once last winter when Ruby was there and he asked her to sing some of those songs Easy sang in Newport that time you had him down. Ruby stood against the yellow curtains at the window, as slender as one of my ebony candlesticks, and sang in that warm, throaty contralto of hers. I swear there are tears in it. Chauncey was so completely charmed he lost his pathetic, loggy look and his poor bulgy eyes actually had a sparkle in them.

Chauncey and I are very civil with one another, but anything that was ever between us is so long gone that we seem in effect strangers. I know that he is drinking himself slowly to death. When we see each other it only makes him realize, I suppose, as it does me, how old we both have grown, which is unpleasant. He is finally marrying again and I have my divorce. It seems too late now to take my own name again, so I leave the card as it is on my door, Mme Isabel Westcott.

I am always anxious for some news of the quarry. The last check was better and encouraged me. I now have four little pupils in English, which is a great help financially.

Always faithfully,

Isabel

Lyman locked the letter away in the Personal file and glanced at his watch. He had sat over his letter nearly an hour. Louisa would be waiting for him to congratulate John on his sermon. He wondered if John was anxious to know what he thought. He tried to remember the sermon now, he seemed to have heard it a long time ago.

He looked up and down the street for Holly. Then he saw him coming at a terrific speed down the main street on the Peterboro boy's new bicycle. He waved as he went by but he couldn't stop until he had run up the slope of the old carriage shop.

"Come on, Holly, we better go home for dinner," he called out to him, starting on ahead with his halting gait.

8

"LYMAN, I want you to stop and talk with Professor Colton before you go. Mrs. Colton loves it here and she'd like to stay all summer, but the Professor tells her it's too quiet and he misses men to talk to. They're really unusual boarders."

Louisa followed Lyman out into the hall talking in a low voice. Lyman turned, and the bright morning light fell on Louisa's face. She looked old, he thought. Her iron-gray hair, just released from its nightly confinement to curlers, was ridged as stiffly as the hair of a Rogers figure. He noticed the lines furrowed on her forehead. The wild-rose color was still bright on her cheeks, but now the furrows seemed more a part of her than the color he had known so much longer. He hadn't looked at her so frankly in a long time. When they ate together at meals or driving in the buggy over to Malden, he didn't look quite at her.

"Do stop and visit with him on your way out, Lyman. Talk about President Roosevelt or business. I told him you were a director of the bank in Malden. It wouldn't hurt you to be more sociable." Then Mrs. Colton came down the stairs and Louisa turned quickly. "Good morning, Mrs. Colton. Your breakfast's all ready." Louisa's manner changed from one of anxious secrecy to gay sociability as she went with Mrs. Colton.

Lyman hated this business of boarders. He hated a stranger like Mrs. Colton coming down the stairway. He felt a little unnecessary as Louisa's husband and guilty that she was taking boarders at all. The income from the quarry was less, that was true, but he could support his wife without her resorting to boarders. But when he had objected Louisa had acted abused and said, "If I want to make a little honest money so I can take a trip to see John when I want to, I can't see that you should object, Lyman."

"But I make enough money, Louisa, for you to take a trip when you want, and I don't like taking strangers in." He had known before she spoke what Louisa was going to say. He could see it in the resentful flash of her eyes.

"As long as you give two-thirds of what income there is to Willie, who's married again and has no need of it, and to that cousin of yours who is wealthy enough to live in Paris, I prefer to make some money of my own."

He had walked away that other time, but he didn't this time. He took hold of her shoulders and held her even when she tried to switch away from him. It angered him that he was so aware of the fragile feeling of her shoulders in his hands. He hadn't touched her since that night sixteen years ago, and yet he could remember.

"Listen to me, Louisa," he had said coldly. "It isn't a matter of giving. The money I send Willie and Isabel doesn't belong to me. When Father died I was given the farm on the hill and one-third of the quarry. He had no idea that I was going to run the quarry, and he had made no will since Dan's marriage. Willie and Isabel each happen to own a third of the quarry."

"But you don't take a salary for all the work you do!" That was the thing that rankled in her mind.

"It pleases me not to take a salary. We have not suffered with the third interest that my father left me. John has been educated to suit you and we have enough put by for Holly's schooling. Don't bring up this subject again or I shall walk out that door and never come back." He had taken his hands from her shoulders.

"Then don't say anything to me about taking in boarders," she had retorted, shaken but defiant.

That had been in the spring, three years ago. Each year since they had had "a couple." At least when the boarders were in the house he was free from the long hard silences that spread between them in winter, and Louisa's conversation that had come to be a dribbling out of all the bits of news she had gleaned through the day in Painesville. But he felt annoyance at the presence of the boarders in their house and a deep sense of shame at the meagerness of their own living. He was glad that Isabel couldn't see or hear them.

He could hear Louisa talking animatedly to Mrs. Colton in the woodshed, which was screened in now to make a "summer dining-room." "We think it's a pretty view, a little cold-looking in winter, but . . ." Louisa had a noble air about her staying in Vermont in winter. Lyman's mouth twisted sarcastically as he stood in the hall. He turned the conch shell over on the whatnot.

There wasn't any way he could leave without being seen. Professor Colton was firmly planted for the morning on the front porch and Louisa had the rear covered. He opened the screen door.

"Good morning, Professor Colton."

Professor Colton turned his chair toward Lyman and held his cigar in one hand.

"Oh, good morning, Mr. Converse. Sit down, won't you? I'm just digesting my breakfast over a cigar."

Lyman sat down reluctantly.

"Have a cigar?"

"No, thank you. No, thank you," he repeated. Mr. Colton was hard of hearing, and held his hand cupped around his ear.

"You operate a soapstone quarry, your wife says. I was wondering . . . I'm not familiar with soapstone. Of course I know the granite and marble for which your state is noted, but I don't believe I could identify soapstone. I mean to get up and have a look at that quarry. What is the stone used for principally?"

Lyman resigned himself. "It is indispensable wherever a substance is needed that will withstand chemicals or high temperatures, such as in laboratories or for furnace registers, stoves, things of that sort. It has a great variety of uses. It is used in building. You can see it all around here in the sills of most of these brick houses . . ."

"Well, well, that's interesting," Mr. Colton broke in. "Of course I don't imagine it's used in building now, with cement and bricks available. I imagine soapstone would be a little impractical."

"Some people prefer it for its beauty," Lyman said a little stiffly.

"Hmm, is that so? I don't know that I've ever seen it in buildings. Tell me, Mr. Converse, what do the majority of the natives of Painesville do for a living? I don't include you among the natives, naturally."

"I am a native," Lyman said unsmilingly. "I was born up on that hill and I've lived here ever since. I've hardly been away."

"But you're an exception, of course. Your wife tells me you graduated from Brown."

He could hear Louisa intimating as much. "No, I attended one semester."

"One semester! Well, your college course was quite abbreviated!" Mr. Colton gave a little laugh, such as he must give in his classes, Lyman thought. Lyman offered no explanation.

"But what I mean is, the farms seem small. There are no large dairies that I can see. I suppose the mills do some business . . ."

"There's quite a little maple syrup shipped out of here," Lyman said. "We get out some hard maple that is the finest in the country. John Brigg's fishpoles are known from Canada to the South, I venture to say."

"Is that so?" Professor Colton said, nodding his head. "Well, I was interested. Most of these Vermont towns, you know, that are back

303

from the railroads have declined almost to the vanishing point, though of course that is perhaps the secret of their charm for the urban visitor."

Lyman stood up. "Well, Professor Colton, I have to get on down to the office. I'll see you this evening, no doubt." Lyman was conscious of his limp as he went down the walk and supported his weight on one cane and the ball of his left foot while he swung open the picket gate. He would have liked to go off briskly. He glanced back, but Mr. Colton had opened the new novel of Henry James he had had in his hand.

Lyman wondered whether Professor Gilmore spent all his summers in some Vermont town like this. He felt suddenly uncomfortable at the thought of his coming here, though he might be able to talk to him now. Then he realized with a wry smile that Professor Gilmore had been in his late fifties in '66!

"Hello, Mr. Converse! You see we had to come back again!"

"How do you do. That's fine! We're always glad to see Painesville's friends come back," he found himself saying, switching his cane to his left hand and shaking hands with the Haverstroms. They had been here the last two summers, pleasant young people who tramped all over the hills together. He had come on them one day painting in the old apple orchard of the hill house; that is, Peter Haverstrom was painting while the girl slept on his coat by the stone wall. He had opened the house for them and let them spend a couple of nights there. "I'm glad you haven't run out of subjects here," Lyman said.

"I don't believe I ever will," Peter said. "I thought about the place all winter and tried to paint some of the things from memory, but they didn't turn out right. I guess the Minnesota light was wrong." He laughed.

"Peter's going to paint people this summer, Mr. Converse. He'll be around to paint you, he wants to." Mary had a charming and spontaneous frankness. He could see that Peter was embarrassed.

"I don't think I'd make much of a subject," Lyman said, laughing.

"I'd like to get that colored foreman of yours to let me paint him," Peter said. "Do you think I could, down there in the quarry while he's working?"

"I don't know why not. Easy is very obliging."

"Paint him budging one of those huge blocks of soapstone, Peter, and call it 'Easy does it.'" The girl's laughter was infectious and he laughed with them.

"Ride up with me someday and you can ask him," he suggested. "Where are you staying this summer, at the hotel?"

"No, that's too expensive. We rented the Holmes house, but Jeb's going to keep one room." She laughed again. "Peter's going to do Jeb, too. Jeb's all for it. He's going to get his army uniform out of moth balls!" They went on up the street and Lyman continued on his slow way to the office. The summer people like the Haverstroms did bring new life into the town.

He unlocked the office door with the big brass key that weighted his pocket. After five years he still missed Oliver Weatherbee every morning. But he managed alone, even to pecking out letters on the big typewriter that stood these days on Oliver's old table. Now that most of the soapstone was ground and used for paper filler in the mills on the Connecticut there wasn't the correspondence there used to be. The quarry contracted with a company directly, there were seldom any private orders. It seemed a long time since there had been salesmen in Boston and New Haven sending in orders. And each year the price a ton for the ground stone dropped. He had let the Goddard mill go, and the Holbrook & Converse Quarry Company employed only nine men. His eyes rested on the half-formed stone bowl that had caused his accident and on the gray soapstone cat on the window sill. The children of the village always stopped to look in at it.

There was no use blinking the possibility that it might not pay to run the quarry much longer. He hadn't glossed over the bad signs to Willie or Isabel. He had persuaded them to let him invest part of their earnings the last few years in good railroad stocks. But more than the loss of income, the lessened demand for soapstone hurt him. It was like running hard and finding you had missed the train after all, or feeling the sun darken in an eclipse when it should be still daylight. He stared at the soapstone cat with cold eyes. If things grew worse . . . Well, Caleb Culver had told him last week that the directors of the Malden bank were going to ask him to take the presidency. "You could live in Painesville and get over here three or four times a week. People trust you, Converse, and your judgment." He could live on what he'd make as president if . . . He must write Culver tomorrow that he'd take it. He could handle it easily and the quarry too. His mouth twisted shrewdly and then tightened in a determined line. The quarry wasn't through yet.

The Coltons took all their meals but breakfast at the hotel. Lyman was thankful for that when he went back to the house for dinner at noon. He said so to Louisa.

"But they're the nicest people, Lyman, and they think Painesville is the most beautiful place they've ever been. Mrs. Colton says it's so

unspoiled." Louisa launched animatedly into an account of all she
had gleaned about the Coltons in this short time.

Lyman drank his tea in silence while Louisa took off the plates and
brought the sauce and cake.

"Oh, Lyman, will you speak to Easy today and see if Friday night
will be all right? The Hensleys from the hotel told Mr. Colton about
the hill and they're anxious to go up. Mr. Colton is so interested in
Easy's being a real slave. He thinks it's remarkable his settling up
here. He says it's an interesting social phenomenon."

Lyman felt himself irritated by the way Louisa seized so eagerly
on everything the summer people said as profound. He pushed back
his chair.

"Thank you, Louisa." It helped his self-respect to be punctilious
about the little courtesies with Louisa.

"Don't forget about speaking to Easy. Mrs. Hensley's asked some
others, and there'll be ten all together. They want you to go too."

"I'll ask him."

Chicken dinner at the Williams place on the hill had come to be
an institution among summer visitors to Painesville. A neatly written
sign hung each summer on the post-office bulletin board.

CHICKEN DINNERS $1.00

REAL SOUTHERN COOKING   OLD PLANTATION SINGING
Reservations taken   *P.O. Box 87*

"Do you feel like entertaining a bunch of summer people, Easy, after
you've worked hard all day?" Lyman asked him one time.

Easy had leaned his head back and a slow grin spread over his face.

"Sure, Lyman, it don't bother us none, me and Jewel. Jewel ain't got
so much to do now, an' she likes to cook and see folks eat, an' they
do that. An' you know me, I can sing any time. I guess we kinda like
the company. It gets some life up here on the hill. You know we're
the only folks livin' up here. An' it seems an awful easy way to earn
a dollar. We're puttin' it by for Opal. Pretty soon she's goin' to need
that money to go to school. Opal kinda thought she might go on to
college."

"That's fine, Easy." Lyman had glanced at Opal. She was a little
like Ruby but without any of Ruby's swift, driving pride. Opal's face
in repose was wistful, like Jewel's. But while he was watching her she
laughed at something one of their boarders said to her and her whole
face laughed the way Easy's did.

Jewel set the table outdoors inside a square made by wire strung
from four trees and hung with some lopsided Japanese lanterns. The

comments of the guests were always the same. "Isn't it charming? You should be outside of Boston, Jewel." They learned her first name quickly. "You could certainly do a big business there!"

"Oh, such good food! I always did like Southern cooking."

When he was there, Lyman felt like the interlocutor. They turned to him to interpret this Negro family settled on a Vermont hill. As soon as Jewel and Opal and Easy were out of hearing someone would usually ask questions about them, as they did tonight.

"You mean, Mr. Converse, that this is the only colored family in town?"

"In the county too, except for their summer boarders that come up occasionally from Boston."

"Do they mingle?"

"In Vermont everyone goes about his own business pretty much. I don't know that 'mingle' is the word. Mr. Williams is a selectman, perhaps that explains the situation," he answered.

"He is! I've always heard that if you wanted to find the real New England democracy you only needed to go back to the little backwater towns."

A Miss Tewkesbery from Connecticut leaned across the blue-glass teaspoon holder that was filled with celery. The leafy tops brushed her net yoke. "I heard about the son—I mean the bad one." Interest dilated her pupils.

"Would you pass the giblet gravy, please, Mrs. Colton," Lyman said.

"Mr. Converse, your wife tells me that that beautiful old brick house belongs to you," Mrs. Abbott exclaimed. Louisa had already told him that Mrs. Abbott had diabetes and lived on lettuce and hard-boiled eggs. He had been bored with this tidbit of news, but he found himself noticing that she was eating her chicken and beaten biscuits with relish.

"I was born there," he said, feeling himself a curiosity, too.

"And it just stands there empty! It seems wicked not to have someone living in it and enjoying such a beautiful period piece. When was it built?"

"My grandfather built it about eighteen hundred." He wished Louisa wouldn't discuss the place with total strangers.

"Would you ever consider selling, Mr. Converse? Of course it's awfully inaccessible. A person couldn't use it more than two months of the year, but I mean just for a summer home."

"No," Lyman said, "I've never thought of selling it."

Easy was lighting the big bonfire. It was still light up here on the hill, but the trees of the valley were losing their green color, turning brown, then merely dark. The white spire of the church that was just visible above the clumps of dark trees was no longer a shining needle, but a dull wooden splinter. A bird flying above the table while Miss Tewkesbery shrieked, "Was that a bat?" was neither swallow nor vireo but dark flight. Easy moving from the woodpile against the back of his shed to the fire was part of the dark, and Opal carrying her water pitcher from refilling the glasses was the daughter of darkness. The voices of the summer boarders lost some of their shrillness and were subdued. Professor Colton's cigar gave forth its heavy fragrance.

Lyman remembered this gathering of the dark when he was a boy. He was usually finishing the chores, walking across the open space between the barn and the woodshed carrying the milk buckets that bumped against his legs.

"I don't suppose—I mean, I presume it's asking too much, but I just wondered if you'd ever consent to letting anyone go through your house. I'm crazy about old houses," Miss Tewkesbery said beside him.

"I haven't the key with me," Lyman said, and went to help Opal move the chairs away from the table so they circled the fire.

The crackle of the catching fire was sharp. The flames crept in among the latticed sticks and then, feeling their strength, leaped to the top. Not until the fire flamed out had anyone realized that entire darkness had come, shutting out the valley and the road and the forest beyond from the cleared space around the fire. The bright flames lighted Easy's calm dark face and Lyman's sharper-featured white one as he stood beside him.

"These chairs right for the smoke, Easy?"

"There isn't enough wind tonight to matter anyway," Easy answered.

"I like it over here under this tree. Back to nature, that's the idea," Professor Colton said.

"Isn't the ground damp, Henry?" Mrs. Colton called warningly.

"Dry as a bone," Mr. Colton assured her.

The screen door banged sharply and four figures came toward the fire. One of the women laughed a high laugh and a man's voice answering her was loud and rough. The group around the fire grew silent.

The four didn't take chairs, but sat on the ground near Mr. Colton. They were Jewel's boarders from Boston. "Sam's friends," she always called them. And since they were Sam's friends they were sure to be flashily dressed, good at shooting crap, and apt to leave bottles in the woodlot between the quarry and the road or behind the old house.

The little murmur of conversation began again, the fire crackled and the odor of burning hemlock rose fragrantly on the night air. Miss Watts, the athletic one, slapped noisily at a mosquito.

"What's holdin' you back, Easy? Git along," one of Sam's friends with the rakish straw hat called out, and the other two laughed.

"Yes, Easy, we came all the way up here to hear you sing," Miss Tewkesbery said. Easy dug at the bowl of his pipe with a twig and began to sing as easily as though he were talking.

"Swing low, sweet chariot, comin' for to carry me home."

Always Easy's voice had more volume than people expected, or more warmth. This place between the old Converse home and Easy's house knew it well. The birches far back in the woodlot and the apple trees in the orchard that were dying out knew it, Lyman thought. He remembered driving up the hill with John's body behind and Easy singing this song. As Easy sang the refrain again Sam's friends joined in, whether by prearrangement or not Lyman didn't know.

One of the women sighed when he was through. Professor Colton threw away the stub of his cigar, but Easy was singing again before they could talk.

"Go down, Moses."

Lyman limped across the dark space between the fire and his old home. The fire was too far back to light up the house, only the grass in front was drained of its green. He sat on the soapstone doorstep and leaned against the door. The sadness and disappointment of his life bore down upon him as Easy sang, the sadness of the house behind him and the loneliness of the hill and the slow stealthy steps of the wilderness pushing into the meadow, all the weariness of the years. He was no longer a boy, a young man, he was fifty-seven, older than his father had been when he was killed, too old to make a name for himself or find a way to have Isabel or . . .

Easy's voice swung across the darkness, strong and warm, holding more sadness than any one man could know in his life, making sadness no very great thing after all, only a natural part of man's life like hunger and cold, something that knit one human being to another.

Then across the breath of the night came a terrible thing. The strong volume of Easy's voice broke, lost its impersonal melody, and became personal. Easy gave a hoarse sound like a sob that shocked the summer people listening and that caught Lyman in the throat. There was an instant's stillness that seemed too long to endure. Sam's friends took up the refrain. Then Easy sang out again, the sob gone, strong and full of song. But Lyman knew. Easy had been singing of Ruby, who, like John, had died so young, so far away. Lyman saw her again with the key of his house dangling from her neck, bowing from the upstairs window or walking proudly across the grass in the ill-fitting shoes that turned up at the toes. Strange that Isabel had been at her funeral. She had sent home the picture of Ruby's grave, the one that Jewel had framed now in the crowded little parlor, with flowers in a vase beneath it. Jewel hadn't wanted her ashes sent home and Easy had said, "Leave her rest where she is."

Lyman sat there until he heard the inevitable, "Well, this has certainly been a treat, Easy . . ."

"Yes, I don't know when I've enjoyed . . ." "We ought to be getting back to the hotel." He dreaded the chatter on the way down.

Professor Colton sat beside him.

"You don't suppose the Williamses could be interested in a position for the winter at one of the clubhouses in Cambridge, do you? His wife could cook and he could . . ."

"No. I am sure he wouldn't," Lyman said. "He's foreman at the quarry, you know."

"Well, I just thought I'd ask you first. You seem to know him so well."

Lyman was watching the dark wall of trees that bordered the road on the left hand. It would seem empty when the timber was cut. There was a good deal of birch in there that had always stood out white in the moonlight. He was glad it wasn't moonlight tonight. He hadn't told Easy yet that he had sold the timber standing to the furniture company from New Hampshire. But Easy would agree with him when he knew it was for Holly's college.

Lyman liked to think of Holly at Brown this fall. He would do all the things he himself had meant to do. Holly was working this summer at the quarry under Easy. Just yesterday Lyman had stood watching the sun beat down on Holly's bare shoulders imagining him on the Brown crew. If he himself had stayed that spring of '66 . . .

"What was that?" Professor Colton cupped his hand around his ear and leaned nearer to Lyman, thinking he had spoken.

"Yes, I've known Easy a long time," Lyman said in a louder voice.

9

Dear Lyman:

The Haverstroms came for tea last Thursday. They are charming young people, and they think there is no place on earth like Painesville. A part of me must surely be Vermont, for I was actually homesick listening to them. And she is so young and eager-eyed I felt young again watching her. She is so much in love with her husband she fairly glows, and I warmed myself at their fire.

Yesterday Peter—for they asked me to call them Peter and Mary—took me to the Durand-Ruel Galleries to see three of the canvases he did last summer. I was interested because they knew you, and of course I am always interested in painting, but I'm afraid I expected the usual, although I should have guessed, I suppose, that they were better than ordinary to be hung there.

And then, oh, Lyman, I walked along the gallery and met you looking out of the canvas! I cannot tell you how I felt. I sat down on the seat around the center pillar and looked and looked. I forgot all about Peter and Mary but they did not mind. At first, I didn't seem to see Louisa with you. I seldom think of her as being married to you, but it was good of her too. Someone stood beside me as I looked at it and said to his companion, "There you have the very essence of New England." Peter had called it "Vermont Portrait," you know. When I told Peter the man's comment he said, "Mary and I have a different name for it. We call it 'Soapstone and Granite.'" I see what he means about you, Lyman, and I like it. He has caught the light in your eyes so well and the little fine-drawn lines at the corners of your dear mouth that is as mobile as the river. I could feel my hands on your head and the long, lean line of your face. But do you know, I have never thought of you as growing older! I have seen the changes in myself. I have a streak of gray running up from my part now—red hair does not look well mixed with gray, and I have a brown spot on my temple, like a warning of age. (I suppose if you were here I would hope you would not see these signs, but since you are not I tell them to you.)

But I have thought of you always the way you looked at the quarry that Sunday morning.

Your hair is steel-gray in the painting, like the Seine this gray afternoon, and your color that used to be so high is paler. I felt so sharply all that the years had done to you and to me, and to Louisa too. I went back to the gallery again today alone and sat looking at your portrait. Is it not strange that I have never had a picture of you, nor you of me?

I hear that Picasso, who is one of the leading younger voices, spoke well of Peter's work. Peter's painting of Easy working in the quarry has attracted a great deal of comment. I wish Ruby were living so she could see her father's portrait. The sun on his great dark head and on the gray soapstone blocks is so warm, and you feel the strength of his muscles and the patience of his mind. I am glad he is there with you, Lyman. Ruby told me how much he cared about you.

The one of the covered bridge is very well done. I liked best the torn circus poster on the side and the glimpse of the brook between the loose planks, but by the time I came to it I had spent all feeling and could hardly do justice to it.

We talked about you on the way home. Peter said it was so amazing that you had lived in that tiny place all your life and not become a "character." He mentioned your fall in the quarry, thinking I knew of it. You never told me, Lyman! Mary said: "He's a very distinguished-looking person. When we saw him walking down the street that first morning we were there we wondered who he was." I found myself murmuring, "But of course."

I must stop now. I have so much to think about. The paintings will be in the gallery all month and I shall go to see them—you—often.

Good-bye, my dear.

Faithfully, Isabel

"Mr. Converse, you come in on this cue!" Mrs. Beckett called from the stage of the Town Hall.

Lyman put his letter hurriedly in his pocket. He donned the borrowed mortarboard and gathered the academic robe about him, resplendent with Professor Colton's Doctor's bands, and walked up on the stage where in the fall, when the foolishness of the summer season was past, he would stand to read the minutes of the town meeting.

"You sit over here at this side and seem to be seeing a vision a great way off, and then you turn the pages of the book and start your lines. You're just right for the part, isn't he, Bruce?" Mrs. Beckett appealed to the young man in tweeds who was helping her put on the tableaux.

"Perfect!" Bruce assured her.

Lyman obediently turned the page, feeling a little foolish as he did it, trying not to see the people in the seats in front of him.

" 'Time turneth back,' Lyman began, 'and I seem to peer into the heart of the past, when all this peaceful valley was but a wilderness. These green rolling hills that were the same yesterday as today had seen no white face. Only the redskin followed the trickling rivulet to its source and slipped, quiet as a shadow, through the wooded fast-nesses . . .' "

"Just a moment, Mr. Converse! Indians, that's your cue. You'll have to be ready to come in the minute the seer says 'wooded fast-nesses.' Please, everybody!"

Mrs. Beckett had coached plays at Vassar. They were so lucky to have her. She had even been on the stage herself, somebody said, in a Shakespearian play, probably. She was a forceful sort of woman with gray bobbed hair and a young face and glasses on a black ribbon. She was the one who had asked Lyman to take the part. "We want some-one who fits the role of wise observer, someone who looks like a philosopher." She made it sound like a compliment.

"I should think you'd feel silly," Louisa said at first but after the Coltons said it wasn't as though it were a cheap, silly sort of play, she urged him to take the part.

"Holly will be home in July," Lyman had said reluctantly. "I don't believe I want to be busy then." Then he remembered that Holly had been in a play at Brown. "Yes, I believe I'll do it," he said, thinking of it as a common interest between them. Now Holly had written that he was going West with a classmate if the family didn't mind. He was going to work on a cattle ranch in North Dakota and it wouldn't cost him a cent. Lyman knew then how much he had been looking forward to having Holly home again.

As a matter of fact, Lyman rather enjoyed going to practice every evening. The cast was made up almost entirely of summer people. The Haverstroms were in Europe this summer, but there were others that he knew. He was invited to the hotel for a musical one evening and had a speaking acquaintance with all the summer visitors. They were a change from the people of Malden and Painesville.

"All right, Mr. Converse, now if you'll take it again," Mrs. Beckett said.

" 'Time turneth back,' Lyman began, 'and I seem to peer into the heart of the past, when this peaceful valley was but a wilderness.' "

How had it happened, Lyman wondered as he said his part and then sat in the wings watching the tableaux of the Indians, how had it

313

come about that he had become merely an observer of life? Except for his brief adventure at college and his trip out West, it seemed to him that he had been looking on at life, observing. He had married and had two sons but aside from that . . . and time had gone so swiftly while he was watching.

"I have never thought of you as growing older," Isabel had written. He had never thought of her as older. He tried to picture her with a gray streak in her hair, but he couldn't do it. "I felt so sharply all the years had done to you and me . . ."

"All right, Mr. Converse!" Mrs. Beckett called from her perch out in front.

Lyman came out of the wings holding Dr. Colton's gown closed over his well-worn pepper-and-salt suit. " 'The wilderness retreated before the exhilarating sound of the ax wielded by the Green Mountain Boys, home from the Indian wars. Rocks were piled in walls to mark off the newly plowed fields, and the seed corn of civilization was buried in the virgin soil of Vermont.' "

Maudie Peterboro's boy walked across the sagging boards of the stage sowing seed from the white sack over his shoulder. After whispered directions at the other side of the stage one of the hotel children ran after him, calling "Father!" in an uncertain voice. And young Mrs. Gilbert, whose husband came up from Boston on the week ends, appeared on the stage with a shawl over her head and stood waving to her husband across the vast distance of the imagined field.

Mrs. Beckett nodded at Bruce. "Yes, I think that's good. We want to keep it very simple, but there *is* danger in a thing of this kind of reducing it to too simple a pattern."

Lyman thought how simple the pattern of his life here had become. There was danger, Mrs. Beckett said, in reducing it to too simple a pattern. Why? What was the danger? The danger was that some day it shouldn't seem worth following out. It led nowhere, it merely worked back on itself until the pattern was done.

"Oh, that's too bad! Did you ask his wife when he'd be back, Bruce?" Mrs. Beckett asked. "You see we haven't rehearsed the tableau of the runaway slave yet, but we don't want to get someone else, because he's a real Negro and he ought to be so realistic. His really being a runaway slave adds so much poignance!"

Bruce laughed. "Well, it seems that the old codger had to go down to Boston to get his boy Sam out of jail. He seemed pretty upset. His boy had got into a little trouble over a crap game and it ended in a fight and the police took him in. The old lady didn't know when he'd be back."

Lyman came out of his own thoughts. "Are you talking about Mr. Williams?" he asked.

"Yes, Mr. Converse, you see he should be here," Mrs. Beckett began.

"He'll be back late tomorrow," he said shortly. "I'm bringing him with me when I come back from the directors' meeting at the bank tomorrow." Easy's troubled face when he had stopped in at the office to tell him was still on Lyman's mind.

"Sam didn't mean anythin' bad, Lyman, but he just hasn't the strongness to keep out of trouble. Orville talked to him an' had him down on his knees promisin' the Lord he'd never get into another fight, but he don't do any different," Easy said in a resigned tone.

"I'm goin' to bring him back here this time, Lyman, an' he can either go to work at the quarry or I'll let him farm the Spring place. I'm through givin' him any more chances in the city. All he care about is dressin' up an' shootin' crap an' playin' the piano. Why can't he be like Orville or Ruby? He was brought up the same way. What makes him different, Lyman?"

Easy scowled in his effort to gain his composure. His mouth was twisted to keep from trembling. For a minute Lyman thought he might actually cry. He had never seen Easy like that, even when he told him that Ruby couldn't get well. Then his face had been tragic in its sadness, but now it looked broken and pitiful.

"I'd give him another chance, Easy," Lyman had said. "I think if Father had given me another chance at college that time, instead of yanking me back home, it might have made a big difference."

"You'd have come anyway when your father was killed," Easy said.

"Probably, but I'd have felt different, and I might have found a way to go back long enough to finish college. Sam wouldn't be happy on the hill. He likes it on the trains, he told me so."

Easy had stood there by the window in his office a long time. He picked up Isabel's soapstone cat and fell to stroking it with his dark knobby forefinger. His face straightened out and was impassive again. Lyman had turned back to his desk.

"Well, maybe you're right," Easy said, and then after a pause he added, "You aren't like your father, Lyman."

"No," he had answered, "I guess I'm not."

"We might as well stop here for tonight," Mrs. Beckett announced, "but everyone must be here on time Wednesday night!"

Lyman walked home alone down the dark summer street. Thinking about Easy's boy turned his thoughts to Holly. He missed him this summer, but he liked thinking of him out West. When Holly was little, his favorite story had always been Lyman's trip to Montana on the stagecoach. Holly had sent back a post card saying, "I haven't found a real stagecoach yet but it's still wild and woolly! Having a great old time." Holly always had a good time. Lyman didn't worry about him, the boy got into scrapes enough, but they were due to high spirits. He was no mere observer, he liked doing things. It seemed childish now to be pleased over such a thing, but Holly was elected his freshman year to Chauncey Westcott's fraternity.

When Lyman opened the screen door Louisa called his name sharply the way she always did when she left the door unlatched.

"Lyman?"

"Yes," he answered. He followed the light back to the kitchen, where Louisa sat crocheting.

"Lyman, there's an artist friend of the Haverstroms at the hotel and he came to call tonight. He looks dissipated, but he was polite enough. He'd had a letter from Paris from Mr. Haverstrom." She paused impressively. "Well, the painting Mr. Haverstrom made of you and me last summer is hung in one of the best galleries in Paris, Lyman! And people come to see it and they think it's wonderful! When you write that cousin of yours you better tell her to go and see it! She'll be surprised!"

"Yes, I'll do that. There isn't any check to send this quarter," he said quietly, hurting himself by saying it aloud.

"I thought that was a pretty good likeness of me," Louisa went on, "but it didn't look so much like you. I wonder what he'd sell it for, Lyman? It'd be nice for the boys to have for their children."

"I haven't any idea," Lyman said. "I don't believe we'd want it here, there wouldn't be any place for it."

Louisa did look tonight just as she did in the painting, he thought. Her face showed no discontent. It was a strong, clear face, an easy face to paint, Peter Haverstrom had said. He had had trouble with Lyman's mouth. "Your dear mouth that is as mobile as the river," Isabel had written.

Louisa looked up with a pleased smile. "Mrs. Colton wants me to come down and spend a week with her next fall as her guest. She said it would be doing her a favor."

"Why don't you? That would be fine," Lyman urged.

"I might. I thought I could stop off in Springfield and see John and the new baby. That girl John married never has really invited me to come and visit, but I guess she could stand it a couple of days, her husband's own mother."

"She'll be glad to have you. Cynthia's a nice girl." He wondered how Louisa had come to be so sharp in all she said and thought.

"Oh, I don't say she's not a nice girl, and she makes a good minister's wife, I guess, but she's not John's equal by a long ways."

"John seems happy with her," Lyman said mildly, and went over to wind the steeple clock he had brought down from the house on the hill. Louisa didn't mean anything by her way of speaking, he told himself, it was just her way.

"Goodness, it's almost eleven!" Louisa exclaimed, folding her work away. "Do you want a glass of buttermilk, Lyman? I set it in the pantry for you."

"No, thank you," Lyman said. "You go on up, I'll turn out the lights." He wondered why he felt so tired tonight.

10

YOU can close a shop or an office, Lyman thought as he walked down the street of the village to the quarry office. You can just turn the key and draw down the shades, but with the quarry all you could do was to walk away and leave a gaping hole and feel the same gaping hole in your mind. This morning none of the men would turn in from the hill road and leave their lunch pails in the shed or down by the spring. There would be no clanging sound of sledge hammers pounding the wedges, no creak of the derrick, no put-put sound of the pump keeping the quarry dry. The day would go by without the satisfying boom of blasting. It would be as still as on a Sunday. Water would slowly fill the quarry. In time it would rise to cover the benches of rock, the white scars, the torn and ragged earth, and show only a placid water mirror to the sky.

"Mornin', Lyman," Jeb Holmes called out across the street.

"Morning, Jeb." Jeb with his crutches, he with his cane. Jeb at least had got his in a good cause, he only through his own careless foolishness.

"Got so used to goin' down to the quarry office in the mornin' you can't stop, eh? You goin' to sell the office, Lyman?"

"Not right away. I have a good deal of business to clean up," Lyman answered evenly, glad that the way he felt couldn't show in his face.

"Oh! Some of us in the store tother day was speculatin' as to whether you'd be moving to Malden to live, seein' as you're president of the bank over there an' there ain't anythin' here to hold you."

"No, Painesville's my home," Lyman said quickly. He was glad to come to the post office and end the conversation.

There were three letters in his box: one from Holly, one from Isabel, and one from New York State. He limped on down to the quarry office before he opened them. The letters almost kept him from feeling how different coming to the office was this morning from any other morning. He just glanced at the window with the name in gold leaf on the outside of the glass, hardly seeing the small letters in the lower right hand corner—"Est. 1814." But his mind, which was never an easy mind, wrote other letters on the other side of the window,

"Abandoned 1909." Then it let him go and he sat down at the black-velvet-topped desk and slit the letter from New York across the top. It was from Peter Haverstrom. He had bought an old farmhouse now and wanted a soapstone mantel for his studio, with a wide facing and a broad ledge for the top. "If you can furnish this, please send it on to us and let us know whatever it is. I am enclosing dimensions. Your painting brought us luck and I have actually been selling pictures! A gallery in New York City bought the painting of you and Mrs. Converse. We hope you will be as pleased as we are. You are in very good company!"

Their wanting the soapstone pleased him. There weren't any dimensional blocks that size, but Easy would like quarrying them out up there by himself and he would only charge the Haverstroms enough to pay for Easy's work.

Then Lyman took up Holly's letter. Something about the plans for Commencement, probably. He and Louisa were going to Brown for it.

> *Brown University*
> *Providence, R.I.*
> *May 15, 1909*

Dear Dad:

I hope you won't mind too much, but I have a chance that seems too good to miss. You know I've been editor of the paper here all year and an alumnus who's on the New York Herald *wrote the other day offering me a chance to report for the paper in Paris. It won't pay much, but it will mean my expenses and a chance to see Europe and a chance to get on a paper. I've about decided that I haven't a good enough mathematical mind for engineering, anyway. I'm pretty excited, as you can imagine.*

The only thing bad about it is that I'll have to leave here the thirtieth of May and I'll be able to spend only one night in Vermont before I go on to New York the next day. I'm sorry about missing Commencement. I know you were planning on coming down for it, but this does seem a wonderful chance. I don't know how Mother will feel about my going to Paris, but you will make it all right with her, won't you?

I can hardly keep my mind on my work enough to finish up. And I'm trying to brush up on what French I know.

> *Yours for European travel!*
> *Holly*

Well, Lyman told himself slowly, thoughtlessness was part of youth. He couldn't expect Holly to know how much Commencement meant to him. And a chance to go to Paris was something. "Go it!" he would write Holly slangily. "Go it, and don't let anything stop you!" He worded the letter carefully in his mind, wanting to make it speak the language he imagined Holly and his friends spoke. He must give Holly Isabel's address and write Isabel about him. His thoughts careened idiotically back over the years. He thought of the letter he had written to Isabel and torn up, telling Isabel that Holly was part hers. He wished he had sent that letter. What harm could it have done, after all?

Then he opened Isabel's letter.

Dear Lyman:

I can see from your letter that you are preparing me for the closing out of the Converse & Holbrook Quarry Company. You are turning every stone to effect a sale, you write. "The simple truth of the matter, Isabel, is this." I can almost hear you saying it. "That it has become too expensive to quarry the soapstone so far from transportation. That there is a limited demand for soapstone now." I see, Lyman, I see. You don't need to go on. I was protesting before I was through reading your careful letter, but isn't it sad?

Oh, I don't mean because of the loss of income, though heaven knows that is of importance to me. I shall manage in one way or another. I have my pupils, I shall rent my apartment the end of this month to more of the everlasting tourists and go to Brittany. I shall do very well and I don't want you to worry about me, but wouldn't it be pleasant as one grows older not to have to manage well!

But I mean the thought of the quarry on the hill being no longer worked is sad because it has been worked almost a century, and has been such a link between us. I must be growing old, for I dread having things come to an end.

And I am fearful for you, Lyman. The quarry must be part of you by now. What will you do? I have seen these retired American businessmen traveling in Europe. Their eyes are listless, not like those of their wives or daughters darting brightly from sight to sight. But you are not like other men. Then, too, I forgot that you have the bank interests. You must be a figure in Painesville and the county and even the state, and you have your boys. Perhaps you will "manage well" too. I tell myself not to worry about people, they work out their own salvation, and we, of all people, should know that the human heart does not break, but endures.

But still it is sad and depresses me. And Easy? What will he do? Ruby told me how he loves the quarry. I could see that in the painting of him.

Don't dread writing me the final news. I have lived in France long enough to have no patience with sentimentalists. Send me a statement of the status of the quarry as usual, and the date of its closing.

Only tell me too, Lyman, if there is still a great block of soapstone lying there for the sun to warm. I hope so. I have dreamed of that block of stone when I have been cold. Do you think me a little touched? Perhaps I am. No, you understand me better than that.

Faithfully,
Isabel

Lyman sat so long he was stiff when he moved back his chair. He had not built a fire this morning and the office was cold in the deceitful warmth of May. He had felt when he came in that everything about the quarry had come to an end. There was no use to blow the dust off the desk as he usually did, or to light a fire in the stove. But now he opened the iron door of the soapstone stove and laid a fire with careful attention. He stood beside it holding his cold hands above it waiting to feel the heat. So he had stood many times to think over a letter of Isabel's.

There was a good deal of work to be done before he sent out his statement. Quite a little could be realized from the sale of some of the machinery. If the sale of the mill property went through to the sash-and-door people, that would give Isabel . . . His mind seemed suddenly stripped of the foolish sentiment that had swollen it all week. He could think clearly and shrewdly. And the abandonment of the quarry was due to no fault of his. Time had brought changes, it was only the part of wisdom to recognize them.

The office was warm when he went up to the livery stable to get his horse and buggy for the drive to Malden. He was due there at two. The clean face of John's watch registered noon.

In June Lyman had another letter from Isabel, from Brittany.

Dear Lyman:

I had your note and one from Holly just after I came down here and I wrote him that I should hope to see him in September when I returned to Paris. Imagine my delight this morning when Mme Charette told me a young man had called to see me who said his name was Holly Converse.

Oh, Lyman, he is like you were that fall in Providence so long ago, only he is not so serious. His eyes have a twinkle all the time and he has a great laugh that filled the little garden and an appetite that made Mme Charette beam. I am used to young French art students,

but they are a different race altogether from Holly's. How big he is!
He made me uncomfortably aware that I am old and shrunken. His
French is horrible, and he uses it proudly and without any embarrass-
ment at all! By the end of next winter it will be immeasurably im-
proved, I promise you. His cousin Isabel will see to that!

I see you have brought him up like a child and that he knows nothing
of the quarry affairs. "I'm afraid I have been away most of the time
lately," he said rather ruefully, and when I asked what you were doing
he rubbed his hand back over his stubbly golden hair and said, "Why,
he . . . he's president of a little country bank and people are always
coming to him for advice down at his office. I really don't know ex-
actly." He confessed that his mother was worried about the effect of
Paris on his morals and asked me to help him select something to
send her.

But best of all is his enthusiasm for French letters. I have promised
to introduce him to Daudet when I return. My art teacher, M. Pierre
Boileau, is here in Brittany for a rest and some painting of his own,
and he was delighted with Holly. He wants to paint his head.

It seems uncanny that he can be yours and already in his twenties.
Do you realize that you were only seventeen when we met, and I was
sixteen?

Holly bicycled down here and shocked Mme Charette by starting
on his journey back at midnight by moonlight as though it were the
usual way to do. I am so glad he will be in Paris this winter, and I love
him already. If I had a son, I should like him to be like Holly.

Faithfully,

Isabel

P.S. I was amazed to receive the check and hear that there will be at
least another thousand from the sale of the mill. Thank you.

I. H. W.

Holly scrawled him a note, too, but it did not come until two weeks
later.

Dear Dad:

I rented a bicycle, which I am going to buy as soon as I have enough
money, and rode down to Brittany to see Cousin Isabel. Since we had
a bona fide cousin in France, I thought I should look her up. But I
had no idea she would be as she is.

She is very small and slender, and when I first saw her I would have
sworn she was a Frenchwoman. She was out in the garden sitting on

the low wall shelling peas when I arrived. She had a big hat and bare ankles and her feet were in wooden shoes. I thought she was a girl at first. But when she talked I could see that she was American, these French women gabble at you so fast. And her brown eyes and the freckles across her nose look American. Why did I never really hear about her before?

We had the best meal I've ever had in my life. I don't know what half the things were, but truffles and snails were part of it and Burgundy wine that really was something! I had the time of my life. Cousin Isabel—though I am going to drop the "cousin" one of these days—paints every morning and wouldn't let me even talk to her, so I slept late and had lunch with her in the garden around noon.

She is the most interesting person, and knows all sorts of people. I had forgotten that Easy's daughter was over here with her. She has a painting of Ruby that makes her look like an African princess—not the kind with a ring in her nose! I wish I could remember Ruby better.

I took some pictures of Cousin Isabel to send you, but she raised an awful row and wants you to remember her as you knew her. I don't see why. She's still very good-looking. At night she wore a long green-silk dress and her hair was done up high with a comb in it. I tried to tell her how beautiful she looked in the green dress and she laughed and tapped the green wine bottle with her finger tips and said, "Like this wine bottle, only not so empty." She asked all about you. I found I didn't know nearly enough to answer her questions.

I am back in Paris now, working like a dog, really, and trying to read some of the French things Cousin Isabel talks about. I'm trying my hand at verse, but it's not very good. Cousin Isabel said you were so fond of poetry and used to write it. I never knew that. She seems to know you better than I do.

I wish you could come over to Paris while I'm here. It was Cousin Isabel's idea. We could have a great time, the three of us together.

Love,

Holly

P.S. I'm not sure Mother would understand Cousin Isabel and the wine. Maybe you better keep this letter to yourself. I have written her a letter about other things.

P.S. No. 2. I didn't know until Isabel told me that the quarry wasn't running. I got through college just in time, didn't I? Anyway, I won't be any more expense.

H.

The idea of going to Paris became Lyman's daydream. He played with the idea on the trips to Malden and back. It would be expensive, but he could manage it. It might not be too impossible, after all.

He didn't close the quarry office on the main street. He continued to go there each morning. There were tag ends connected with the quarry. People in Painesville who banked in Malden found it more convenient to drop in at the office to talk to him about loans and investments. It touched him that so many people came to him for advice. He managed to fill his days. There was no hurry or urgency about them, but they were not empty. He had plenty of time to write long letters to Isabel, but he waited to hear from her.

It was fall before she wrote again, just a short note telling him how fond of Holly she was and how well he was doing with French. She concluded:

He has found an American girl who is over here studying painting whom he likes very much indeed, I gather. I had hoped to keep him to myself a little longer! I hope he will not fall in love, but I am not sure that he hasn't already. Yet why not? Youth is the time for that.

Isabel didn't mention anything about herself in the note and he wondered why. He missed it.

Easy stopped in at the office whenever he came down to the village. Lyman had hated telling Easy about abandoning the quarry, he had dreaded putting it into words. But there was no need to dread it.

"Don't you worry about me, Lyman," Easy said with a quick smile. "I seen it coming. I seen it way back there when I first heard about cement an' them South Carolina quarries. Don't you worry, I got plenty o' farmin' to do."

Easy was farming both the Spring and Converse places, as well as the old Davis place nearer town—land was cheap on the hill. He put in a big garden and Jewel and Opal brought greengroceries down to town to sell all through July and August. Easy couldn't do it alone, he got Ash to help him. Ash had a couple of children whose fingers were quick at weeding. Jewel wasn't so lonesome with children around again. One day Louisa told Lyman with disgust that "that no-good son of Easy's has taken his white wife and those children of theirs to live in the old Davis house. Part of it's tumbled down, but they're probably all living in one room. Pretty soon, Lyman, people'll be calling it Nigger Hill."

"Don't ever call it that again, Louisa!" Lyman had answered in a voice that was as hard as Orville Converse's when he laid down a law.

Willie had written from St. Louis:

I'm sorry about the quarry, but it supported Juliet and me all those years we needed it, and Dan too, that last winter when he hardly worked at all, and I am grateful to it and you. My husband has a successful wholesale leather business and I have no financial worries after all these years. But I still love those years with Dan best, and still miss him. I wish you could come to St. Louis. It would be so good to see you. Juliet has three fine children now and is very happy. Think of me a grandmother!

No, he needn't have worried about the three of them. And the quarry really owed them nothing, it had served them well, but he himself had the feeling of owing the quarry something. The stone was still there waiting to be quarried. Soon it would be lost under the slowly deepening water. He should have managed some way, perhaps he could have got a spur railway built into Painesville . . . but the quarry didn't employ enough men, even in its busiest years, to make a rail line pay, and the population of Painesville had declined each census since the war. There was no way, but still he felt a sense of guilt that under his management the quarry had been abandoned, and he stayed away from the hill all summer and through September. Louisa's roomers had to arrange their own parties to go up on the hill for "Old Plantation Cooking" and Easy's songs.

And then one day in October Lyman drove through the covered bridge and up the hill, seeing each thank-you-ma'am of the road as an old landmark, fastening a boyhood memory on each turn. Here he had played he was a Yankee soldier shooting the rebs over that stone wall, he couldn't remember how many years ago.

The leaves were turning and there was color even in the cutover land where his father's finest stand of hardwood once walled the road. Some of the stumps were covered with woodbine. He let the horse rest at the spring and sat sidewise looking back down over the valley. The air was clear, no single edge was blurred. He could see the blue line of the mountains beyond the foothills, the road to Woodstock, that was hidden in summer, was visible for half a mile.

Lyman drew a long breath and felt his spirit lift. He had lived down there on the main street in Louisa's well-kept house too long. He belonged on the hill. He wondered suddenly if his mother had felt smothered when they took her down there to live. He could have brought her up here more often if he had only thought about it.

He remembered looking down over the valley from this point, years ago, thinking that Dr. Tucker was wrong when he said a little Northern town like Painesville would suffer in a different way as much as the South. Dr. Tucker had been right enough, Painesville had declined steadily since the war. Too many of the young men had gone: some, like John, hadn't come back from the war, and others, like Dan, had gone West. He could number on two hands the ones who had stayed, like himself. One by one the town's industries had moved away closer to the railroads: the cheese factory and the cashmere mill and the carriage works, and now the quarry. Most of the hill farms were deserted.

And yet the valley had never looked more beautiful to him. The maples flamed deep-red and bright-scarlet and the elms were yellow, but the spruce and hemlock that grew in the cemetery and on the stony pastures burned green. The sumach hung its heavy festoons of Burgundy velvet over the tumbled-down wall, and late asters and goldenrod along the narrowing road held out stoutly against the frost. Lyman gathered up the reins and drove on up the hill. Surely, there was no place in the world quite like it!

When he came to the quarry road he heard a sound so familiar and right to his ear that he held his breath: a steady thin clang of metal on metal embedded in rock. When he came to the edge of the quarry he saw Easy working away on the first bench. Lyman stood a moment watching him. He was cutting out a block of soapstone, looking exactly like the painting Peter Haverstrom had made of him. Lyman limped around to him. "You look as though you need some help!" he called out. Easy's dark face lighted up and Lyman was ashamed that he had stayed away so long.

When Lyman tossed his cane ahead of him and began cautiously to climb down the wooden ladder, Easy made a movement as though to stop him, then instead he came over and stood waiting for him. It was hard for Lyman. Putting his weight on his right foot sent a sharp pain through his heel and up the calf of his leg. He had to wait on each rung.

"Well," he said when he reached the bottom, "well, Easy, how are you?"

"Jus' fine, Lyman. I never did finish getting out that piece for the mantel that painter fellow wanted." Easy's voice was soft after the twanging voices of the village. Lyman's leg trembled from the exertion and he was glad to sit down. "I remembered that some o' the best stone we ever took out come from this vein on this top bench here," Easy went on. "And I jus' thought I'd get a piece of it for him." Easy moved over to the piece he was cutting and laid his hand against it. "Pretty, ain't it?"

Lyman nodded almost solemnly. "Nothing quite like it."

"I was thinkin' while I was workin' here 'bout those orders for bathtubs we got out years ago, Lyman. Why don't you have me get you out a block for a real big tub down to your house? You could take a lot of comfort in it. It might jus' do your foot a powerful lot of good."

"Too much work, Easy. With the mill and so many tools sold, we couldn't work it out right. But I remember one order that was a pretty one, it had claw feet on it, remember?"

"Jus' like a eagle's claw," Easy remembered.

"You were just ready to stretch your line on this side," Lyman commented.

"I got my first hole drilled there."

Lyman leaned heavily on his cane as he crossed to where Easy had been working. "Here, I'll pound a few. You get another hammer."

The two hammers clanging against the iron wedges made a lively racket. Easy whistled. Lyman joined in. Above them the woods flamed with color, but down in the quarry the gray rock matched the gray of their heads.

"We can't finish it today, Lyman."

"Let's break her loose before we stop," Lyman answered, striking his sledge hammer against the wide end of the wedge—plenty of strength in his arms anyway, but his blows were lighter than Easy's and he had to stop and rest. Easy glanced at him anxiously.

A crack began, no wider than a raveling thread, as Easy came down with all his strength on the wedge.

"She's giving!" Easy shouted.

"Yes, sir!" Lyman exulted. Now he could stop. He sat a few minutes gathering up his strength for the climb. He looked down at the floor of the quarry. The grass was bright-green down there, the tall brake fern thrust up boldly in the center. The reedy horsetail and milkweed had taken root where only a few months ago men's feet had tramped the floor bare. Over against the rock side the ebony-stemmed maidenhair fern that loves the damp grew luxuriantly. The ground already had a damp look. In a bare space he saw the shine of still water puddled between the grass. For a long moment he stared at it. Then he helped himself up with his cane.

"You never oughta climb down here, Lyman," Easy worried.

"Why not?" Lyman answered stoutly, and closed his teeth tight for the pain as he set his bad foot on the bottom rung. Neither man spoke until he had reached the top.

"It was a fool thing to do, Lyman, but you made it fine," Easy said with a grin, and Lyman felt a warmth that eased his pain.

"I'm sure glad you didn't give this horse away to the Union Army,

Lyman!" Easy joked when they came to the horse and buggy. "If I remember right, you done quite a lot of walkin' that year!"

Lyman shook his head. "Father was mad, wasn't he?" he said, laughing. "He made me pay for that piece of extravagance!" They laughed together out of the same boyhood memory.

"Why don't you stay an' have supper with Jewel an' me, Lyman?"

"Thanks, Easy, I guess I will." They turned in the driveway of the Converse place and crossed the grass to the old smokehouse.

II

IT was a dry summer. Even the blackberries on the hills were dried up. Many of the wells in Painesville failed. The summer people at the hotel didn't stay as long as they had planned; they said they could be more comfortable at home a summer like this. The farmers were in a bad way. Some of the hay dried at the roots and wasn't worth cutting.

The bank at Malden gave all the credit it could, and a little more. Some of the directors grumbled about the bank president. He was too lenient, they said, especially if a man came from around Painesville. He would sit in the old quarry office and listen without interruption until a body was through telling his troubles, and folks said he would do 'most anything to keep a man from losing his farm or giving up his business. "We need you here to fight the wilderness," he used to say to a man who was thinking of moving out. Lyman Converse was a kind old man—not so old, really, but his limp made him seem older.

Mrs. Beckett was back at the hotel this summer. She said the heat was worse in Boston. She tried to get Lyman to be in the play they were putting on at the Town Hall. He had done it other summers and was good at it, but he wouldn't. He said he was too tired. Mrs. Beckett called on his wife and asked her to try to persuade him to be in the play. "We really do need him, Mrs. Converse—unless you feel too that he's tired out," Mrs. Beckett added.

"I don't know why he should be," Mrs. Converse answered. "He doesn't have much to do any more, just go to the bank meetings at Malden and keep up his correspondence. He's been moody like that all winter. Even when our son John was home he was kind of quiet and mopy. I've half a notion to write Holly, our other boy, that he ought to come home and see him. Five years in Europe is enough for anyone. Holly's not much like John. He got married six months after he went to Paris and then wrote us about it afterward. Oh, no, Susan's an American girl, thank goodness for that! An orphan with some money, I guess, an art student from Ohio. They had a baby boy right off, named him Lyman after Mr. Converse."

Louisa Converse liked to visit with the summer people. She liked to see their eyes rest enviously on her pine highboy or her walnut parlor chairs.

Lyman jogged slowly back from Malden. He was still thinking about the meeting. Several of the directors were for merging with a larger bank, making the Malden bank just a branch. He had held out against it. Couldn't they see that it would take away all their independence and make them less useful to folks? They would be nothing but clerks. He had persuaded them to his way of thinking this time, but it had tired him. The change would come someday. Why hadn't he let it come now? It didn't really matter to him . . . oh, for a few minutes, perhaps, but the feeling didn't last after the meeting. He had felt suddenly that at sixty-six nothing mattered too much.

Lyman flicked the leaves that met overhead with the tasseled end of his whip. A powder of dust sifted down through the air. He wondered foolishly whether it was dusty in Paris this summer with Holly and Susan and Isabel. Then he checked himself. Isabel would be in Dijon in August. Her husband would be painting there. He watched the road above the horse's head, noticing how gray the goldenrod was and seeing the grasshoppers shoot out of the dusty rut.

Isabel had been married over two years now and he still forgot it. It still hurt him. Her letter had come in May—May 12, 1912. He always remembered that the date of the day and the year matched exactly. He remembered every word of the letter, he had read it often enough.

Dear Lyman:

I have made a decision which will be hard for you to understand, but I am asking you to understand just the same.

Next Wednesday I am going to marry Pierre Boileau. You will remember, perhaps, that he has been my teacher for several years. He asked me to marry him five years ago. I could not think of it then, but now . . . I am very tired of insecurity and growing old alone. I have a deep affection and admiration for him and I can look down the years with him with equanimity. He is, which is rare for an artist, financially independent, with pleasant apartments here in Paris and a lovely old home near Dijon.

Pierre knows about you and that I love you. The painting of you and Louisa helped him to understand, I think. "I see," he said, "I see."

He was married before, too. His wife died years ago and he has been very lonely since. We do not either of us expect the impossible at our ages. The marriage is in fact a pleasant way of life. Holly likes him, and he and Susan will be at our little wedding.

Please believe me, Lyman, more than ever,

Faithfully yours,

Isabel

It had taken him a month to write her. Then he had written simply:

Dear Isabel:
I understand. May it be a "pleasant way of life."
                                        Faithfully yours,
                                                    Lyman

It was the most that he could manage.

Susan had written him about the "quiet little wedding of your cousin and M. Boileau. Afterward we had a delicious wedding supper at M. Boileau's favorite restaurant and toasted them in champagne." And Holly had scrawled at the end of Susan's letter:

Cousin Isabel was lovely. She makes all pretty young girls except Susan look quite infantile and ordinary beside her. M. Boileau affects a Fedora hat with a sweeping brim and an imperial. You'd pick him for an artist anywhere, but he's a nice old gent.

Every detail that Susan and Holly had written cut deeply into Ly man's memory. Now and then Susan wrote that they had spent the evening at "Isabel and Pierre's," and once:

We attended an exhibit of Pierre's paintings at one of the galleries and then went back to his studio and celebrated. He loves to give a dinner, and Isabel is a picture sitting at the end of the table. One of the paintings was of Isabel with a branched candlestick behind her. It was stunning, though Isabel protested that she didn't like it.

And just last winter Susan had written,

Holly was home early, so we went for a walk as far as the Luxem bourg Gardens and dropped in at Isabel and Pierre's. Pierre was out, but Isabel was there and gave us brandy and black coffee. All of a sudden, she lifted her brandy and said, "To your father, Holly!" and we all drank to you, Father Converse.

"I am asking you to understand, Lyman," Isabel had written. He did understand, she still loved him. Her marriage was a marriage of convenience. Hadn't he married Louisa? He had been over this so many times since Isabel's letter, but always the reasoning left him with a feeling of weariness. He had no right to feel hurt, it was just that some vital warmth he had depended on seemed to have moved farther from him and he felt cold and more lonely than he had been in his whole life. He remembered the loneliness and the black depression he had felt that winter after Dan's death, but he had been young then and now he was old.

One week followed another while his life seemed to stand still. Monday and Thursday were different from Tuesday, Wednesday, and Saturday only because on those days he went to Malden unless the roads were too bad. He stayed overnight Thursday if there were enough matters needing his attention. Sunday he went to church and still sang in the choir with Easy and looked at the back of Louisa's head and thought over the things that had been in his life and that could have been. He didn't listen to the sermon very carefully, but at least once under the shelter of the Reverend Mr. Dwight's ponderous exhortation he tried to put aside his own desires and thoughts and lift his spirit wordlessly toward a greater strength and wisdom than his own. But he wasn't sure that it could lift so high. Then he walked home with Louisa and ate his Sunday dinner.

Isabel wrote him short notes at Christmas and Easter, but they seemed different. They were filled mostly with accounts of seeing Holly and Susan. When Susan's child was born Isabel had written: *You have a grandson, Lyman, who bears your name. Think of it! I am so glad they are naming him for you.*

Yesterday his grandson was two, Holly had written. Lyman thought about him as he drove along. A new individual bearing his name, "Lyman Converse." He had lived with that name a long time. When he was young it had seemed to him to have a very special meaning, a special look written, something a little remarkable about the way the *L* joined the *y*, but the years had proved there was nothing remarkable about it after all.

He didn't believe he liked saddling another human being with his name. It was kind of Holly and his wife to want to name their son for him. They had done it to please him, but he didn't know that he was pleased. He was tired of the name. His mouth twisted to one side in a contemptuous line and then settled sadly back in place. He was tired of the man who belonged to the name.

Lyman drove into town knowing every building he passed, every person on the street—except the summer people—so well he hardly had to look at them.

" 'Lo, Lyman."

" 'Lo, Nate."

He lifted his hat to Esther Osgood.

"Good trip, Lyman?" Bill Bates ran the livery stable now.

"Pretty good. The country needs rain," Lyman answered automatically.

"Need the horse again today?" Bill asked politely, though he knew well enough that Lyman wouldn't.

"I don't know, I may need to use him this afternoon," Lyman answered.

"Well, I'll keep him in then. If you wasn't going to use him again I'd turn him into the pasture."

"If I'm not here by four, you turn him out."

Bill Bates nodded. Lyman walked down the street toward his house. Bill knew he had no pressing business. Did anyone in Painesville have any urgent business, unless it was the farmers getting in their hay before it rained? But there wasn't any rain, and haying was done.

A gabble of female voices came at him through the screen door of his home. Louisa had three women roomers this summer. The Coltons hadn't been back for two summers. Louisa had moved down to her father's old office so she could rent an extra room. Lyman didn't offer his.

He hardly glanced into the parlor as he passed the open door, but Louisa came out. "Oh, Lyman!" she whispered in vexation. "I thought you were going to stay in Malden overnight. There isn't a thing in the house but some cold beans. You can help yourself, can't you?"

"I have eaten. Don't bother about me," Lyman answered. "I just came in to change to my alpaca suit. This is too hot." He went upstairs purposefully, like a man with business.

"Lyman . . ." Louisa came up the stairs a few steps. "Lyman, could you drive Miss Estes and her friends up on the hill? They've been on all the other rides around here. Miss Estes's sister is younger. She feels there isn't enough to do here."

"I . . ." Don't hesitate, answer quickly, his mind flailed at him. "I have to see Easy about some soapstone."

"Then I should think you could take them up there with you."

"I don't know how long I'll be gone. I wouldn't want to keep them waiting past their dinnertime. We may have to go over to the quarry."

Louisa was disappointed and cross about it. "Well, don't fall in and drown yourself, then, climbing around the quarry with that foot of yours!"

Lyman stood in his small peaceful bedroom with the sprigged wallpaper on the sloping walls, trembling with a sudden bitter anger. He changed his coat because he had said he was going to. He hadn't eaten, but he wasn't hungry.

"Don't fall in and drown yourself, then."

The water was up within ten feet of the top of the quarry. The quarry was drowning, why shouldn't he? Captains went down with their ships. "Lyman Converse, sixty-six, was found drowned late this afternoon in his own quarry." It sounded right, as though it had always been planned that way.

All the Converse men had died violently—his father killed by his own horse, John in the Battle of the Wilderness. The hill was fast becoming a wilderness again. He would die in the wilderness too. He had suffered over Dan's hanging. Dan was better off dead. Why should the youngest Converse boy drag on year after year? He might live to be eighty, ninety, with nothing to do. The bank would overrule him another year and where would he be? The boys didn't need him. Louisa could have this room then.

Almost before he had made up his mind he was getting into his buggy.

"You're back long before four, Mr. Converse, or we'd have got him brushed up a little for you."

"Oh, that's all right. Never mind about that." He drove down the main street and pulled up shortly in front of the quarry office.

His affairs were in good enough order. John would go over his papers carefully and preach his funeral sermon. It wouldn't be easy for him, he didn't know his father very well, but he would think of kindly, sonorous phrases to cover any doubts about him. Holly would want the gray soapstone cat. He was sorry about Holly. His father's drowning would worry Holly the way Dan's death had worried him, but perhaps Isabel could help him. Isabel might blame herself a little, but she would understand. And Easy . . . he'd forgive him. Louisa had wanted to sell his old desk for an antique, now she could do it.

The office was hot and dusty. He lit a fire in the soapstone stove and the room quickly became an oven, but he wouldn't be long here. He opened the file box marked Personal Correspondence and took out the letters and the clipping about Dan. He burned that first. The thin blue paper caught fire quickly. He left the lid off and watched it burn. Words leaped out at him: "Dear Lyman," "Faithfully yours, Isabel." "Thank you for the check from the quarry," "Paris more beautiful . . ." He was watching for the one that said "More than ever, Faithfully yours," then he remembered he had torn that to bits the day it came. There weren't many of them, after all, for all the years. The early ones were worn and much folded from carrying in his pocket, like hidden laughter, he had used to think. Now they were all burned. They lay in the stove in black flaky ashes like the thin black stuff of old ladies' summer dresses. Isabel was old, too.

He locked the door of the quarry office with the big brass key. He would take the key with him. They could break into the office, and it would make considerable noise on this quiet summer street that was drowning in dusty silence under the low-hanging maples and elms. That would be all right. The noise would spread rings of sound in the silence as a body falling into the water of the quarry would do.

He made the horse trot through the covered bridge. He had liked the noise when he was little . . . or was it Holly who had liked the noise? He couldn't remember now.

There was the turn-in to the spring. "You can think it over and let me know by the time we get to the spring"—whether he wanted to go into the quarry or not—his father had told him that time he had come home from college. He remembered he had felt bold and a little shaken when they came to the spring and he had answered no. He had looked up this very road and thought of himself starting out with a hundred dollars to make his way in the world. He hadn't doubted that he could. He didn't know. But he was still here forty-eight years later—almost half a century. A kind of wonder filled him at the way things worked out. Such a little part of your life you spent making decisions and doing things, and the rest of your life you spent remembering that first part. Well, he had made up his mind today to a thing he had not dreamed of then. His hand reached for the whip and he flourished it in the air so that it made a rubbery sound. The horse jumped forward past the spring.

Lyman tied the horse to a tree below the quarry where Easy would find him. He would like Easy to have the horse and buggy, but he didn't like the idea of leaving a note tied to the whip stock. That was too much like the sort of thing a character in one of Willie's old paperbound playbooks might do.

The old shed that used to house the foreman's office was gone now. He had had Easy take it down and use the boards to strengthen the fence around the edge of the quarry.

Not a breeze stirred, and the place had the ghostly stillness of a deserted farm. It was only five years ago that it had hummed with noise and activity, wasn't it? Always when he came up here now he tried to bring back the sounds that used to be here, the way it used to look, but it was growing harder to do.

Four or five great blocks of soapstone lay piled on the ground. "We may want them for some order from someone who doesn't know the quarry's closed," he had told Easy, and he would always keep one there for Isabel. He limped over to them and laid the palm of his hand along the flat surface of the largest. The stone was warm, but not burning, as another stone would be. He moved his hand across it. In all these years he had never quite found the right word to describe just that smooth, soft feeling, not a word that suited him, but today it came to him without trouble, though it wasn't a word used for stone. It seemed to him that the stone was "kind" to his touch. He would like one of these for a stone to mark his grave, but it didn't matter.

Lyman dropped two of the guard rails and stood on the open edge of the quarry looking down at the deep brown-green water that came within a few feet of the top. He could never get used to the water there. He leaned forward a little, as he used to do over the pool made by the spring, and caught sight of his own reflection. His image held no mystery for him now. He knew who Lyman Converse was, what he had done in life and what he hadn't done.

He leaned a little nearer. It would be a sure way, he couldn't swim. There had been no place to learn up here on the hill when he was a boy. He might have learned in Brown that spring, he might have done so many things he never did.

This would be better than growing older and feebler until he stared out at the street with the dull eyes of second childhood. There were enough old men sitting on the store steps waiting for death. He might grow dependent on Louisa, and he couldn't stand that. He had put up with his painful foot long enough.

But for a moment it was hard to throw himself into the water. He dreaded the splash in this quiet place. His body held back. Better to kneel and lean so far over that he lost his balance and slipped in quietly. Then if anyone saw him . . .

He had a queer sense now of someone watching him, and he glanced uneasily around, but the place was empty. He knelt stiffly and leaned forward, watching the vague white reflection of his face in the green-brown water, letting it draw him to it. A shadow darker than the water moved beside his own. It was just above his head. Lyman held himself rigid, watching the shadow. He drew back cautiously, the shadow took form and became another head, split by a line of white teeth.

"Easy!" Lyman swung around. His voice came out queerly hoarse.

Easy laughed. "You an' me had the same idea o' gettin' away from this old heat." Easy's voice was slow and natural. "That water makes it cool, an' if there's any breeze at all, it's bound to be around the quarry. Set back an' have a taste of berries."

Lyman sat back on the ground. He felt shaky. His face was greenish-white as though it had taken some tinge from the water. Easy looked away.

"It's the worst berryin' I ever seen on this hill," Easy grumbled, lying back on the ground to reach the five-quart lard pail of berries he had set down by the guard rail.

"I thought the blackberries were all dried up this year," Lyman managed to say, his voice still unnatural.

Easy laughed. "I got special places on this hill only the bears an' me knows about. Oh, I guess maybe Ruby an' Orville an' Holly knew 'em, too. Here!" He set the pail between them on the ground.

Lyman reached down in the pail and carried a couple to his mouth. It was easier than saying anything. The berries were warm from the sun, plumped-out and juicy. All the sweetness of summer ran over his tongue and down his dry throat. Easy was picking out the red ones, tossing them over into the quarry pool. They made tiny sounds in the water.

"What there is of 'em is tastier than some years, that's a funny thing."

"They're sweet," Lyman agreed, reaching for another handful. He felt hungry, then he remembered he hadn't eaten since his light breakfast in Malden.

Their hands alternated in the pail, Easy's big dark one, his long and white with the heavy black ring that had been Dan's on the third finger.

"Was Jewel planning to make jam of these, Easy?"

"Uh-uh. I was diggin' up carrots down in the garden an' suddenly I got me a notion to see if there was any berries in that old cellar hole on the Spring place, 'member? Sure enough. I guess what's left of the cellar wall kep' 'em from dryin' up." Easy filled his mouth again. "You know, Lyman, ever since we first used to go berryin', you an' me, I've tried an experiment. I'd take a whole handful like this an' pop it in my mouth all at once an' close my eyes. You try it! That's right!"

The two men ate their berries solemnly.

"Good?" Easy asked.

"Mmm," Lyman murmured.

"Now take jus' one or two an' put 'em in your mouth. It's a funny thing, you get jus' as much or more sweetness outa them two as the whole handful."

Lyman was eating his two berries with great concentration.

"I guess you're right at that," he said slowly. "I'll try the handful again."

Easy grinned. He lay back on the ground. "It's going to rain, you know that, Lyman? I heard some thunder when I was pickin' berries."

"I hope it does," Lyman answered. He was eating just two berries now. His lips and fingers were stained purple.

"I'm going to lie right here an' let it splash right down on me," Easy added.

"It would feel good all right," Lyman answered. He moved the pail toward Easy. "If I eat any more I'll be sick."

Easy had his pipe out now. He filled it from his old pouch, then he passed the pouch to Lyman.

"Thanks. It's that same strong stuff," he said, filling his pipe.

Easy grinned. "Too strong for a growing boy!" he said.

"Don't you wonder sometimes, Easy, what good our lives have been?" Lyman asked after a long pause.

Easy took a long time about answering. Then he said: "No, Lyman, that don't worry me. Our lives got a sweet taste in the mouth most o' the time, two-berry-worth anyway. There she comes!"

They could hear the rain in the woods beyond the quarry. It moved across the clear ground and now it was falling on the deep water of the quarry. The warm drops on Lyman's face and arms felt good. The dry, hot air freshened and a little breeze sprang up. Lyman got to his feet. "Come on, Easy, we better be going." With only a glance at the quarry pool he started toward the road. Then he turned back.

"What's the matter?" Easy asked, turning quickly with him.

"In the dark some animal might fall into the quarry," Lyman said. He started to put the guard rails back in place.

"That's right," Easy answered, helping him.

The rain was slackening already. The sky was lighter.

" 'Tisn't goin' to amount to a cent," Easy said. "You feel better after even a little rain like that, though!" Easy glanced at Lyman, he still looked pale.

"Yes, for a while there it was so close I couldn't breathe," Lyman answered.

"Here, Lyman, put your hat on the seat so I can fill it up with berries. You'll have enough for your supper." Easy stood in the road watching Lyman until he was out of sight.

As Lyman drove down the hill into town his hand kept straying over to the berries. They had a sweet taste in his mouth, all right. He hadn't let himself drop into his own mind since Easy had appeared. He didn't now.

He was driving past the store when Jeb Holmes hailed him.

"Hey, Lyman, they been lookin' for you all over creation. War's broke out in Europe an' you got a cable from Paris, France!" Jeb was visibly excited. "Your wife said you was gone up to the quarry."

"A cable!" Lyman repeated.

"Yup. John Peterboro's got it in the store for you."

As Lyman went up the store steps he saw the word WAR written big in white chalk across the bulletin board. There was a crowd in the store. He noticed that they stopped talking as he came in.

"They phoned the cable over from Malden, Lyman, and I copied it down," Peterboro told him, handing him a piece of paper. "It's from Holly. Say, you'd think he was writing a letter, but I guess those newswriters use cables just like penny post cards. It must have cost him plenty."

Everyone in the store was watching him. Most of them knew the message by this time and had already discussed it.

John Peterboro's scrawled writing read:

POWDER KEG EXPLODED AT LAST, ENLISTING IN FRENCH ARMY, SENDING SUSAN AND LYMAN TO YOU FOR DURATION. SUSAN WANTS TO LIVE IN HOUSE ON HILL, PLEASE LET HER. KNOW YOU AND EASY WILL TAKE GOOD CARE OF YOUNG LYMAN. LOVE TO YOU ALL. HOLLY.

Lyman folded the paper and put it in his pocket. He looked at John Peterboro standing back of the counter waiting for him to say something.

"When was war declared?" he asked stupidly.

"Today. We got it in the Boston papers."

Lyman stood reading the black headlines.

"Why do you suppose Holly figgers he's got any call to fight for France, Lyman?" John Peterboro asked him. The store was still, listening.

"I don't know," Lyman said slowly. "But he's twenty-five, he's not a boy any more. I guess he knows more than we do about what's going on over there."

"Brings it kinda close to home, don't it?"

"Yes, it does," Lyman answered. He bought a paper and went outside. He left the horse at Bill Bates's and limped back up the street.

Susan wanted to be in the house on the hill, did she? This must be what he had kept it for all these years. Holly and Isabel must have told Susan about it over there in Paris. It wouldn't take much to fix it up.

He must drive up the first thing in the morning and tell Easy. Easy would take the boy every place with him, all over the hill. Lyman smiled to himself, thinking how it would be. Of course, the boy was only two yet.

He realized suddenly that he was still carrying the hat full of blackberries that Easy had given him this afternoon. This afternoon . . . What if Easy hadn't come just when he did this afternoon? What if Susan and the boy who was named for him had come all this way and found him gone? If it hadn't been for Easy . . . A deep sense of thankfulness lightened his halting step.